YOU CAN'T GET THERE FROM HERE

The Past as Present in Small-Town Ontario Fiction

You Can't Get There from Here

The Past as Present in Small-Town Ontario Fiction

RYAN PORTER

UNIVERSITY OF TORONTO PRESS
Toronto Buffalo London

ISBN 978-1-4875-0424-3

Library and Archives Canada Cataloguing in Publication

Porter, Ryan, 1978–, author
You can't get there from here : the past as present in small-town
Ontario fiction / Ryan Porter.

Includes bibliographical references and index.
ISBN 978-1-4875-0424-3 (hardcover)

1. Canadian fiction (English) – 20th century – History and criticism.
2. Canadian fiction (English) – 21st century – History and criticism.
3. Small cities – In literature. 4. Ontario – In literature.   I. Title.
II. Title: You cannot get there from here.

PS8191.O58P67 2019   C813'.5409   C2018-906243-6

University of Toronto Press acknowledges the financial assistance to its
publishing program of the Canada Council for the Arts and the Ontario Arts
Council, an agency of the Government of Ontario.

For Kareen, Georgia, and Rosie

Contents

Acknowledgments   ix

Introduction: Projecting Difference – The Heritage of
Small-Town and Rural Ontario   3

1 Rural Past and Urban Present: Landscape as Time   27

2 Saying Goodbye to Mariposa: Rebutting the
  Small-Town Convention   59

3 Memory and Departure   97
    Part One: Synthesizing Memory – The Artist as Community   97
    Part Two: Departure, Return, Departure   124

4 Past Dependencies and Consolatory Histories   143

Conclusion: Reflecting on Nostalgia's Restoration   179

Works Cited and Consulted   195

Index   211

Acknowledgments

This book has been a long time in the making, far longer than I would have imagined at the beginning of the process. It is difficult to summarize and acknowledge all of the people who, over the years, have influenced the project directly or indirectly. If I've left someone out, it is an oversight, one that I hope to correct in person at some point in the future.

I would like to thank the incredibly helpful, supportive, kind, and professional people at the University of Toronto Press. Thanks, first, to Mark Thompson for guiding the manuscript through the many rounds of reviews and approvals. Mark offered encouragement and exceptionally helpful advice when it mattered most, and I am very grateful to him. Barbara Tessman provided insightful and incisive edits, which resulted in a much improved manuscript. Thanks to Frances Mundy for shepherding the manuscript through the latter stages of the process, and also to Breanna Muir for her expert advice and suggestions.

I would also like to thank Siobhan McMenemy whose comments early in this process had a lasting impact on the book. Thank you, Siobhan.

Tracy Ware at Queen's University supervised an earlier version of this project. At many points while writing this book I would question my judgement. At those moments, I would simply ask myself: "what might Tracy suggest?" The answers to that question helped guide the rhetorical and analytical aspects of the book. Thank you, Tracy. You are a personal and professional exemplar to people in this field. Thanks to Leslie Monkman who offered his insight and expertise during an earlier version of this project. And while I haven't been a student at Queen's for nearly a decade now, I do want to thank all of the faculty members who helped, taught, or employed me during my time as a student there. Thank you, also, to Gerald Lynch at the University of Ottawa for his kind interest and generous advice over the years.

My sincere thanks go to the people at *Studies in Canadian Literature*. A version of chapter 2 appeared in that journal in 2011, and they have graciously allowed publication of that material in this book.

Thank you to the anonymous peer reviewers of the book manuscript. Your critical insight and expertise improved this project significantly.

Thank you to Paul Barrett for his astute suggestions at many stages of this project. Thank you, also, to my many other friends who listened politely as I rambled on about this topic through the years, but more importantly, for all of the laughs that we've shared.

Thank you to my colleagues and friends at Algonquin College. I am fortunate to get to work with such kind, professional, generous people every day.

Special thanks to my mother, Kathryn, for sharing her love of Canadian literature with me many years ago. My entire family - Rob, Emily, Reg, Genie, Salim, Louise, and Aneessa - thank you everyone for your words of support through the years.

Most of all, I would like to thank Kareen, Georgia, and Rosie. Georgia and Rosie, you have been the source of so much joy and happiness during the years that you have influenced this book in ways that I can't even begin to realize. Kareen, your encouragement, advice, love, and support have influenced this book more than anything else. For all of this, and for our many years together, I humbly dedicate it to you and our daughters.

YOU CAN'T GET THERE FROM HERE

The Past as Present in Small-Town Ontario Fiction

Projecting Difference – The Heritage of Small-Town and Rural Ontario

The small-town setting is an undeniably common feature in Canadian and specifically Ontarian literature. It has also become emblematic of a tired, outdated literary canon. For some Canadian literary critics, the mention of the small town evokes a national experience rooted in the past, while for others it symptomizes a national atavism, a blinkered anti-cosmopolitanism. The small town has also been read as representative of an amiable cultural identity, a window into a past that fuels misguided notions of national benevolence and goodwill. However, none of these interpretive pathways provides much understanding about what these fictional towns really offer. Furthermore, the proliferation, variety, and regional distinction of small-town narratives demand that they not be dismissed as indicators of colonial anxiety, parochialism, or a fixation on the past. Far from simply offering nostalgic visions of a better bygone era or outmoded representations of archaic national experience, small-town narratives offer complex depictions of the imagined divide separating rural and urban experience, and of how the past is shaped to respond to the needs of the present.

Nostalgia is a complex and ambivalent yearning, and, in small-town Ontario literature at least, rarely does it produce portraits that revel in the idyll; if it did, the literature would be easy to categorize, and perhaps discount, as part of a simple pastoral tradition. This book argues that Ontario's small-town literature rarely reflects the simple pastoral or unreflectively imagines the rural and small-town past as a place of peace and simplicity. Rather, Ontario's literary small towns are reflections, and even sublimated explorations, of contemporary life. Over the past century, the emergence of Ontario's small-town literature has paralleled the transition of Ontario from a province largely characterized

by its rural and small-town settlements to an urban province dominated by its industrial, cultural, and administrative centres. Yet the literary towns that have emerged during this time certainly reveal a past
that offers a contrast to the present in which they are written, and also
indirectly comment on the evolving, unfamiliar present. The literature
of small-town Ontario functions not as documents of a receding past or
lost golden age, but as sophisticated statements on the effects of modernity and on the vexed position of the rural and local in an increasingly
cosmopolitan world.

This study examines some of the province's, and Canada's, most
widely read and studied works, those by Stephen Leacock, Robertson Davies, and Alice Munro. It also includes the work of an author
whose major focus includes the history of rural Ontario: Jane Urquhart.
These four key authors have all created works in which is embedded a
recognizable structure of rural past–urban present: a temporal-spatial
distance distinguishes the texts' presents from their pasts. What the
authors do with this structure is reveal the processes by which the past
is imagined as qualitatively different from the present, thus revealing
the mechanisms of memory and projection that result in what Raymond
Williams calls a "problem of perspective," or the enduring tendency to
locate the disintegration of ageless rural traditions in the immediately
preceding epoch. In these literary works, the authors not only examine
how an idealization of the small-town past can be established, but are
themselves in conversation with the notion that the rural Ontario past
was a place of simpler virtue and natural benevolence. These works do
not simply question the validity of this mythos, but rather go further to
explore how a mix of memory, projection, and desire can guide a historical consciousness to reimagine the rural past as safe harbour offering shelter from the tumult and dissatisfaction of the present; in effect,
they question the very discursive categories of "country" and "city,"
and the associations through which these spaces are imagined. If, as
Robert Thacker states, Ontario's "small town ethos is a legacy, an inheritance which helps to explain the present by assessing and redefining
the past" ("Connection" 213), this study sets out to examine exactly
what types of pasts are rendered in this small-town literature, and what
those pasts reveal about the presents in which they were written.

Foregrounded in many small-town texts is the notion of rural difference; the rural past is the blank slate upon which the desire for something other, sometimes something better, is projected. In some cases,
the desire for difference manifests itself in a simple nostalgic idyll; in

other cases, the rural past is what the remembering subjects need in order to justify their own idiosyncratic or artistic pursuits; in still other cases, the rural past becomes the repository for all that has been lost in an inauthentic, technological present. In all cases, the rural past is not simply remembered but is shaped by a shifting melange of reminiscence, longing, and rejection. What we read as literary small-town Ontario is most often a projection of difference – difference that can remain intact only across a temporal, spatial, and/or cultural distance. How we remember the past is a shadow of how we understand the present; with that in mind, this study explores various versions of literary small-town Ontario not as the products of reliable, stable memories, or as sociological documents about a provincial past, but as fluid, shifting responses to the ever-fluctuating conditions of modernity that help us to understand or accept the sometimes bewildering present in which we find ourselves.

The idea of the past as a reflection of the present is something long discussed by heritage scholars. Writers in this discipline view the pasts popularly understood by societies not as the results of an uncovering or illumination of historical detail, but rather as constructions of those societies, which shape the pasts to align with shifts in sensibilities and desires. Perhaps the most useful explanation of the function of heritage is provided by Laurajane Smith in her book *Uses of Heritage*. While heritage might be popularly understood as a repository of cultural items and practices bequeathed to us by the past, Smith states that its real function should be understood as "a cultural and social process, which engages with acts of remembering that work to create ways to understand and engage with the present" (2). The past we remember is influenced by the present we inhabit. The past is not stable but rather depends on the contemporary forces determining its narrativization, its construction and reconstruction. In that sense, heritage studies can help illuminate the significance of the reminiscing processes as they are represented in these literary texts. In addition, the temporal binary of past and present that concerns heritage scholars contains a further dimension in many small-town literary texts: a geographic element. To look out to the small towns beyond the city is also to look back into the past, or so the thinking goes; to travel into the country is to travel into an earlier time. This book explores, interrogates, and challenges that association.

While the texts in question are all canonical works of Canadian literature, their renderings of the small-town Ontario past, particularly

Leacock's and Davies's, have, historically, been read as documents of a Canadian cultural past. In terms of whose heritage is at stake here, it must be stated that the days in which Leacock's Mariposa or Davies's Deptford were discussed as a hallmark of a Canadian or Ontarian identity, representative of some sort of broader or common cultural experience, are long gone. *Sunshine Sketches of a Little Town*, like nearly all the works studied here, has an exclusive focus on the concerns of white narrators and characters who recall a specific time and place. Black people, Indigenous people, and other people of colour are present in these stories, but they are marginal, and their unique cultural questions and issues are not addressed at any length or with any great concern. This study is aware that any claims emanating from the past-based interrogations within these works cannot be inflated to speak to a common national or provincial cultural experience. Rather, this study remains fixed on the mechanisms of memory at work within these stories of small-town Ontario: that is, how the small-town past is shaped by the present, and how the authors of these works reveal, engage with, and depict these various processes.

Notions of small-town heritage and the small-town past are, of course, active outside the literary realm and within the actual towns and villages the literature ostensibly depicts; similar processes of aesthetic shaping occur in the townscapes themselves. For example, the contemporary commercial and residential developments in Baden, Ontario, a small town roughly fifteen minutes west of Kitchener by car, are influenced by a generic small-town ideal or a rural myth. Founded in the mid-nineteenth century, Baden grew slowly; its two feed mills made it something of an agricultural resource centre for area farms, a role it shared with its larger, nearby counterpart, New Hamburg. But beyond that, industry was limited, and Baden, devoid of any large-scale employer of its own, functioned, and functions still, principally as a bedroom community for Kitchener, Waterloo, and Stratford.

However, in the last fifteen years or so, Baden has virtually doubled in size as a result of massive housing developments. This growth is not the result of the community luring an expanding high-tech company or any similar endeavour promising hundreds of new jobs. In fact, the number of large-scale employers in Baden today is little more than it was prior to the town's recent expansion. Baden's function as a bedroom community has only grown along with the size and extent of its subdivisions. The commuters who have filled these huge housing tracts have been offered the promise of a better way of life among these quiet, small-town streets. During construction, billboards at the entrance to these developments advertised "large country lots and small country living" and a "variety of family parks, ponds and walking trails," recreational amenities that align with popular notions of small-town life. These ads allude to an idyllic myth as old as pastoral literature: that outside the urban centre exist ease and escape, and yet, in Baden's case, it is up to the developers to graft these comforts onto the subdivisions. The website of the developer, Activa Group, claims that Baden Country Estates "offers the calm escape of country living that's only a short drive away from area workplaces and amenities." The small town or rural area serves as a secluded sanctuary or "escape" from the business of the real world; when a resident pulls into the driveway in the evening, the vagaries and disappointments of the urban present can be left behind, or so the marketing implies. Ironically, the growth of this small town has more to do with the economic fortunes of its nearby urban centres than with the autonomous health of the town itself.

The myth of the idyllic small town appeals to those whose departure from such towns many years earlier has matured into a quiet longing for childhood, or to those urbanites whose sense of alienation within a city's confines cries out for an antidote to their modern anomie. The small-town myth, a variant of the pastoral idyll, claims that the knowable limits, familiarity, and slower, more "natural" pace of life in the small town are the answer to the malaise attendant to the ceaseless pace of urban modernity. Because the very survival of many of these small communities now depends on displaced urbanites, the appeal of the small town needs to be heightened, highlighted, and distilled in order to better live up to those expectations of rural charm. The physicality of rural settlements, or at least those towns and villages proximate to an urban centre, is shaped to conform to the expectations of those urban exiles as well as day-trippers. While many small towns now function as bedroom communities, others have become aesthetically "traditional" heritage shopping destinations, and Baden's recent growth reflects this trend. For many people, small towns are living emblems of the past or, more accurately, are shaped by an idea of pastness. And many individuals and organizations in small towns – for instance, their Chambers of Commerce – are often happy to both embrace and exude this aura of timelessness and tradition because their communities' economic health and thus, ironically, their futures depend on it.

The idea of the small town is malleable, and the marketers of these subdivisions as well as the owners of businesses in them understand

that. The phrase "small-town Ontario" perhaps most commonly conjures idyllic notions of rusticity, tradition, heritage, community, a
charming parochialism, an unsophisticated wisdom, the natural, and
the authentic. The developers of Baden's housing developments recognize, respond to, and, perhaps, perpetuate this desire, a shared yearning for a corrective to the imagined alienation, malaise, and pace of
an urban lifestyle, a desire that frequently locates fulfilment in vague
notions of rural simplicity and small-town living. For others, the idea of
the small town conjures notions of conformity, constraint, wilful ignorance, a deadening parochialism, and a lack of ambition. The perspective can depend on one's proximity to the small town: for urbanites,
those billboards at the entrance to Baden's subdivisions may proffer the
promise of a real alternative, while Baden's residents may receive the
same promise with a knowing smirk. Hidden within this urban-rural
tension is the possibility that Baden's new dense housing tracts, which
are physically distant from the urban office, may simply duplicate the
conditions that they are ostensibly designed to correct: lack of space,
anonymity, and a hustling daily grind to get to work in the city. The
small town is a pliable cultural trope, and the nature of its manifestations depends on what is required from it: the disaffected urban dweller
may be attracted to the aura of authenticity and heritage that seems
to accompany outlying towns and villages; yet many living in a small
town may see its quiet streets only as inimical to larger aspirations.

Small towns in Ontario's literature are often portrayed as repositories
of time-honoured values, as natural or organic communities, as anti-
quated counterpoints to a degraded, urban modernity, and as places
infused with traditional wisdom that stretch back into the mists of time:
places that harbour a qualitative difference from life in the modern city.
Yet these representations are the products of those who feel displaced,
both in time and space, in the present, and subsequently project onto an
idea of the past the comforting values for which they ostensibly yearn.
However, in other works small-town Ontario appears as a limiting
place in which reverence for the past ensures a type of anachronistic,
restrictive behavioural code: tradition is charming only when you are
not hamstrung by it. Yet these more negative portraits are often the
products of those whose memories shape the past to justify their own
Promethean achievements in the urban centre. The past is malleable,
and our perception of it depends largely on our attitude towards the
present.

A correlative association exists between the small town and the past, but also between the urban centre and the present, and it is from here, this urban temporal-spatial vantage point, that most narrators of the small-town Ontario past speak. In that sense, many small-town Ontario texts align with the theory that pastoral writing is an urban mode about rural subjects. If a literary mythos of the small-town Ontario past exists, it is most often created by urban voices who speak at a remove from their subjects, across a distance that can be spatial, temporal, or even cultural. This distance allows urban narrators to shape these communities into something they need them to be, to see what they want to see, and to remember those past places not as they were, but in a way determined by the present. Because small towns are rarely the here and now of the text, but rather the there and then, the nature of their depiction is reactive or compensatory, influenced far more by events occurring in the text's present than by a concern with memorial accuracy or historical verisimilitude. Beyond any detail of small-town life depicted in this literature, the most important aspect of the small-town myth is that it takes place in a time that is not now and a place that is not here. This urban projection of rural difference manufactures the qualities associated with rural life; the notion of the rural idyll is a product of urban perception, and the aesthetic and experiential contrast that small-town Ontario appears to offer to its urban counterpart is a product of the gulf resting between the dominant city of the present and the imagined differences of the rural past.

The situation in Baden reveals how a place can be refigured and repurposed for a new selection of people based on a popular, conventional, and easily used urban-rural binary: Baden is a place whose associations are provided not just by its residents, but by those outside interests, commercial and otherwise, who shape the townscape and perceptions of it to conform to expectations of a rural type. Similarly, literary small-town Ontario has long been dominated by an urban perspective. The predominant association of small-town Ontario is with the past, whether it is a past of a personal childhood or of an imagined, bucolic social ideal that has been lost in the intervening years. Yet the perspective that consigns the rural to this role can only be one that self-identifies with the centre. This is an inherent paradox in pastoral writing. The urban escapee may depart from the social centre into the pastoral idyll, but she never abandons her identification with the city; the idyll can remain intact only because the escapee never inhabits it and always retains her outside perspective. In Ontario literature, the preponderance of small towns indirectly reveals the degree to which the province has become urbanized over the past century, as well as the process of how the small town becomes an image or idea through which the province's urban reality is expressed, even understood. The majority of Ontario's population has long inhabited the cities; the province is largely urban and industrial, yet its most identifiable literary trope is the small town. While ostensibly the gaze of these small-town texts may appear turned to an imagined yesteryear, subtly their gaze remains fixed on the present in which they are written. This book sees those small towns of the past not simply as a sign of unease with this present reality, but as an imaginative way of understanding the present in which literary figures find themselves. To remember the past is also to shape it, and by examining the nature of literary small-town Ontario, we can understand how the past that is invoked is also a reflection of the present that invokes it.

The small town is an integral part of both social and literary history, and its role in continental expansion in the nineteenth century helps explain its presence in Canadian and American literature. Its relation to an "earlier social condition" leads critic Northrop Frye to read the small-town literary setting as a feature of the pastoral myth (Frye "Conclusion" 238–9). Small-town and rural Ontario have retained this association with an earlier way of life, yet it has also often been associated with a better way of life, a place in which a sense of community and a sense of belonging can thrive. If it is difficult to locate that sense of cultural, temporal, and spatial belonging in the present, it is easily projected onto a past that we regard as an earlier stage in social development; that past must be distant enough to retain its malleability, and is sometimes located in an author's childhood, or sometimes just beyond the scope of living memory. For some Ontarians, the place onto which this projection can conceivably occur is the small town, and subsequently that imagined small-town past is used as an idealized template into which the present could never fit. In a more problematic application, this imagined past becomes associated with a sense of exclusive heritage or tradition, terms that are sometimes deployed to lament the notion of cultural disparateness in the present. The thinking goes that the past was unified and whole, and if we could only emulate that sense of unity and common value, or rather use that past as a scaffold with which to build a revived sense of community, the feeling of displacement in the modern world would dissolve.

Herb Wyile has stated that stories of small-town life are "so ubiquitous in Canadian literature as to be practically consonant with it." Yet
this notion does a disservice to small-town narratives, he states, since
to apply a national label to small-town narratives fails to acknowledge
"regional differences that complicate the unity that such shared concerns suggest" ("As for Me" 85). In a comment that begins to distinguish
Ontario's small-town narratives, Robert Thacker states that "Ontario,
urban Ontario, persists in seeing itself – through its literature, the
stuff of myths – as a place of small towns formed and informed by the
sway of Elgin, Mariposa, Deptford and their like" ("Connection" 213).
Thacker's comment highlights the value people place on this mythos,
that an influential, imagined past shapes the present, and that a "myth
of innocence" (Davies *One Half* 275) inhabits processes of provincial
self-fashioning. This study, however, sees a different relationship: the
present is not explained by the past, but rather the past is a product of
the present that creates it. It is this binary of past and present, country
and city, which Thacker identifies, that rests at the heart of Ontario's
small-town narratives.

The landscape of rural Ontario is densely settled, dotted with numerous established small towns, towns that are really satellites of the cities in this largely urban province. This settlement pattern manifests in
the literature of small-town Ontario as a productive tension and interplay between the small town and the city, represented sometimes by
an actual metropolis, at others as a diffuse modernity that erodes rural
traditions; however false the binary may be, the city and country are
portrayed as oppositional again and again in both the literature and as
part of a cultural zeitgeist. Furthermore, that binary takes on a temporal dimension, between the place that one inhabits and the place that
one remembers: the small town is that place of memory. Even when
depicted in the present, the small town is generally the site of childhood to which a literary protagonist returns to gauge the results of, as
Charles G.D. Roberts might say, the "hands of chance and change."

Because settlement patterns influence the formation and effect of this
rural-urban binary, it must be stated that what is really under inves-
tigation here is the southern Ontario small town. Such towns are not
frontier or resource communities. They are not isolated by distance or
surrounded by rocks and forests. Rather, they are generally part of a
fabric of communities and surrounded by a long-developed agricultural landscape. They exist within close proximity to an urban centre,
close enough to be within a sphere of economic and cultural influence,

yet are held by their residents to be distinct from the city. This propinquity to the urban centre, combined with its association with, as Frye says, an "earlier social condition," allows for the formation of the small-town mythos: as a place of past rural values, as a place kinder and gentler than the nearby, contrasting urban centre, and as a place one can escape to in a sort of pastoral retreat.[1] It is also this relationship that allows for the development of a type of geographic temporality: city as present, small town as past. While this dichotomy exists in the literature of Ontario, specifically southern Ontario, rarely do writers leave it unexplored; rather, they use this dichotomy as a method of examining the imagined relationship between past and present, city and country.

Small-town Ontario was not always a representative of the past. At one point in the nineteenth century, the small Ontario community was a place of future promise, of expanding social and economic opportunity, a status best represented in Susanna Moodie's *Life in the Clearings*, which documents life in Belleville in mid-nineteenth-century Upper Canada. Moodie presents Belleville in its full flourishing, as a place of opportunity and wealth. The descendants of the town's earliest settlers "have become rich, and the village of log-huts and frame buildings has grown into a populous, busy, thriving town" (7). Moodie's Belleville was burgeoning, its commercial and political significance on the rise, and its success at the time only held promise for even greater achievement in the future. Moodie writes: "The day of our commercial and national prosperity has dawned, and the rays of the sun already brighten the hill-tops" (38). Yet with the urbanization of the province, perspectives on the small town would change.

In the late nineteenth century, D.C. Scott published *In the Village of Viger* (1896), a story cycle in which a small community is at risk of passing into obscurity. The most distinct threat to the community, which sits placidly on the Blanche River, is the encroaching boundaries and social influence of the city. The short-story collection opens with these lines: "It was too true that the city was growing rapidly. As yet its arms

---

1 Small towns capitalize on this association. Places like Picton and Collingwood have marketed themselves as weekend escapes, where urbanites can "reconnect and unwind" within an area of "rural calmness and authentic sophistication." ("Welcome to the County" 2016). As Lucy Lippard states, urban escapees want a cultivated rural retreat, where they can enjoy "solitude, authenticity, a good cappuccino, and a nearby health club" (152). This is a type of curated rural retreat, one that caters to expectations of what a small town should be all the while providing the amenities associated with the urban centre.

were not long enough to embrace the little village of Viger, but before long they would be, and it was not a time that the inhabitants looked forward to with any pleasure ... But while the beechgroves lasted, and the Blanche continued to run, it seemed impossible that any change could come" (9). Viger, a francophone village, symbolizes a shift in small-town representation; no longer are these settlements the budding communities of promise, but they and their representative values are threatened by the rise of the cities, which, literally and figuratively, exist just over the horizon.[2] The town of Viger is fading and is described in shades of melancholic regret: "The houses ... were old, and the village was sleepy, almost dozing, since the mill, behind the rise of land, on the Blanche had shut down. The miller had died; and who would trouble to grind what little grist came to the mill, when flour was so cheap?" (9). The time of this town has now passed, as its day-to-day life becomes increasingly dominated by the commercial and cultural life of the outside world. This work emblemizes a conception of the small town as a place left behind, a place dozing on the margins of currency, a place only gently nudged by the forces of progress, while the city bustles along to the staccato rhythm of modernity.

Gerald Lynch has argued that Scott's story collection contains an anti-modern viewpoint and that it expresses Scott's hope that a "humane modern world" could emerge along with the urbanization of the country, a world in which "such concepts as family, community, place, and identity could be redefined without losing their traditional functions" (*The One* 35). The city in this collection threatens the long-standing traditions cradled by the outlying towns and villages, and Lynch suggests that Scott's story cycle seeks alternative methods by which the modern, urban world can be linked to the values of a traditional, rural past. Within a modern, urban nation, what the small town offers is not economic prosperity and social advancement, but rather a vision of traditional values that descend from the distant fog of the past. The small town offers that link: to step into the village is to step out of the degraded present and into a kinder, or at least knowable past. This portrait is the product of a perspective that is distinctly uneasy with the values, direction, and significance of modern urban life.

---

2 Viger is either a francophone Ontario village or a village in Quebec just north of Ottawa. It would be foolhardy to suggest that the themes identified here abide by provincial borders.

The rural community is cast in such a recuperative role in Adeline Teskey's *Where the Sugar Maple Grows* (1901), a collection of sketches focused on characters in the community of Mapleton. Time stands still in Mapleton, as the narrator states: "I returned summer after summer to find little change – the village life was not subject to many variations" (10). What the community has become is an easily used trope that becomes shorthand for all of the things the city has lost: simple innocence, natural benevolence, charity, and kindness. These virtues have a temporal dimension, as they are rooted in a place that itself has changed little over time. The rapidly industrializing city has lost its way, and the residents of Mapleton who do venture into the metropolis are corrupted through ambition and greed. A trip back to Mapleton becomes a trip back in time in order to reconnect with the age-old values of the rural past, a notion regarding a rural retreat that remains strikingly potent to this day.

In 1912, Stephen Leacock published *Sunshine Sketches of a Little Town*, a book similar to Teskey's in form, but remarkably different in its assumptions regarding the small-town past and the big-city present. While the small town is still representative of a past – a collective past, as Leacock makes explicit at times – the narrator plays with the distance in time and space separating the small town and the city. No longer is the small town unreflexively relegated to a happier time and place, but rather that status is ironically questioned, and Leacock draws the reader's attention not only to the urge to locate a better past in the outlying rural towns, but also to the process by which the rural towns and countryside become the site of memory and nostalgia. In so doing, he highlights the degree to which the province had become urbanized, and how the notion of rural virtues rooted in a past is, partly, the product of figments and phantoms projected onto that past. If small-town Ontario is the known past, it is manufactured partly by the urban present. Small-town Ontario, after Leacock, becomes a conscious legacy that incorporates the urban present into its representations of the rural past, and a legacy with which subsequent writers are in conversation.

Ontario small towns maintain a sense of the familiar in part because of their common physical characteristics. For instance, in his autobiography, Leacock suggests there are usually four churches, three taverns, a post office, and many competing stores in Ontario's small towns (*Boy* 70). Margaret Atwood, in her discussion of Alice Munro's works, concurs with Leacock's catalogue of physical features: "Each has its red-brick town hall (usually with a tower), its post-office building and handful of churches of various denominations, its main street and residential section of gracious homes" ("Alice Munro"). This typicality is something James Reaney plays with in his poem "Instructions: How to Make a Model of the Town," in which two speakers catalogue the buildings and streets of a town, and construct a model of it using fallen sticks, leaves, berries, and vegetables. The courthouse and churches become potatoes in the model, the houses are berries, the trees simply represented by their leaves, and the streets sticks.

A small town comprises recognizable physical features, and yet it isn't necessarily these features that are its most important distinction; rather, it is the lack of anonymity afforded to its residents. The ideal of the small town nurtures an associated sense of belonging and comfort because of the human scale of towns themselves. In the anti-ideal, that lack of anonymity becomes a bane to its residents, a restriction and constriction all at once. Thus, a small town is not defined strictly by the number of its inhabitants, but rather by how that community's physical scale allows people to interact with each other and identify with a sense of place. W.J. Keith provides a similar definition in his discussion of literary small-town Ontario, one that acknowledges how the tangibility of the town's physical boundaries affects the relationships of those living within: "'small town' means any cohesive, distinctive, yet relatively compact human community" (148). The term "cohesive" might suggest a community in which relationships are communal and fraternal. Many Ontario authors, such as Alice Munro and James Reaney, make a distinction between a rural space and the small town, between farmers and townsfolk, through their intimate knowledge of differences in behaviour, manners, and education. This study sees the small town and its surrounding countryside as intimately linked, as two regions that compose a community's sense of place, which, in many literary works, exists in opposition to a nearby urban centre's imagined ethos. This study appreciates Keith's definition because it allows the conceptual boundaries of the small town to encompass both townsfolk and farmer, not only because the small town is generally a service centre for these farmers, but also because farmers are a distinct, though often patronized, part of that human community. My usage of "rural," therefore, refers to the town proper, the surrounding countryside, and to its spatially and socially marginal residents.

The city is a place in which familiarity is much harder to cultivate: while the cityscape itself may become familiar, the majority of people one encounters within it will forever be strangers. A town's scale, in terms of its space and population, is comprehensible; it is an intimate place within which one can feel kinship with one's neighbours and be aware of the whole life of the community. These limitations are exactly what contribute to the small town's reputation as a kinder antithesis to the urban sphere. Raymond Williams claims that a small community still maintains an association with an ideal, more natural way of life: "a country community ... is an epitome of direct relationships: of face-to-face contacts within which we can find and value the real substance of personal relationships" (165). The "real substance" suggests something elemental, something absent from the cities, something that has been lost in the headlong rush towards urban modernity: the small town offers a ready-made "sense of community." Within this perspective, the small town is seen as possessing the stable value of a past that, in larger places, has been lost to unrelenting change. Although the British village concerns Williams, his characterization nicely encapsulates the larger myth of the small town as the organic or natural community, as a place dominated by inherent virtue and familiarity, and, most importantly, as part of a kinder rural sphere that provides a stark contrast to anonymous urban life.

The literary small town is part of a critical binary involving the imagined contrast of country and city, which are separated not only by space but also by a belief in their vastly different experiences – social, cultural, and environmental – that appear as inherent conditions of each polarized site. This structure of city and country is nowhere more explicit than in Matt Cohen's 1974 novel, *The Disinherited*. Here, city and country life are fractured by irreconcilable differences, which are embodied by Erik and Richard Thomas: the former the errant son who runs away to the city, the latter the farming father displeased with his son's choice. Here are Richard's thoughts about his urbanite son: "every year in the city seemed to remove him further from his body, every motion and action preceded by that slight hesitation, the time it took to send the signal from wherever he had decided to locate the control centre" (138). While both urbanite and rural dweller can cross into the space of the other, neither can wholly or successfully integrate, since they themselves are marked by this divide: the urbanite, Erik, will never acquire the physical vigour to thrive in the country, while the rural dweller, Richard, will never be able to resign himself to the physical constraints of city life, as he recalls in past experience of the city: "I felt out of place ... sitting in a metal machine running down a piece of pavement. We were being shuttled along like cardboard boxes" (41). This rural-urban split is, in some works, essential and irreconcilable. But why?

As literary tropes, neither country nor city can exist without the other, and each has a part in the conceptual formation of its alternative. W.H. New argues that the ambivalent "'representative' characteristics" of a city/non-city binary in Canadian literature are the product of "a mutual aspiration for and dismissal of the condition of the other" (*Land Sliding* 157). When the urban centre overwhelms or frightens because of its noise, violence, pace, or immorality, the small town only appears to offer a respite, an antithesis to the hustle and grind of the city. Alternatively, when the small town offers merely ignorance, intolerance, or sluggishness, the city becomes the exciting, vibrant, but often illusory goal towards which small-towners strive. This imaginative interplay between the rural and urban spheres rests at the heart of Ontario's small-town literature.

In the late 1970s, Eli Mandel offered a concise statement on how the rural-urban binary operates in literature. He argues that small-town life is hardly the sole focus of small-town literature. He uses Stephen Leacock's Mariposa from *Sunshine Sketches of a Little Town*, the most influential of Ontario's literary small towns, as an example. Mariposa, he suggests, "exists only as a version of a town that we in the cities *think* we remember. Mariposa is not a place; it is a state of mind. It is the dream of innocence that we attach to some place other than here and now" (114). Mandel asserts that this town has nothing to do with representing an actual past, but that Mariposa is formed from a mixture of memory and desire: "[Leacock] plays on this dream of town and city: the city as an image of the small-town mind; the small-town as an image of the city mind. And in so playing, he gives us a clue as to how in poem and story, town and city are metaphors" (115). Mandel's comments allude to how, in *Sunshine Sketches* at least, the dominant images of the country and the city are the products of reciprocal longing;[3] Mariposa as small-town archetype does not simply emerge from depictions of small-town life, Mandel suggests, but is sculpted from across the spatial and conceptual distance between country and city. A "process of perception" has as significant a role in Mariposa's representation as does Leacock's representation of "place" (115).

---

3 In *The Disinherited*, it might be mutual ambivalence

By overemphasizing the "what" that small-town narrators construct, critics largely pass over "how" these narrators construct it – that is, the "process of perception" that Mandel claims is responsible for Mariposa's characteristic ethos. For that reason, this study remains sceptical of the types of broad statements made on behalf of the small town's culturally representative or non-representative status; the small-town past has just as much to do with remembering the past as it does with the individualized circumstances in which the remembering or imagining subject finds herself in the here and now. The small town may be a common setting in Canadian and specifically Ontarian literature, but the nature of its representation depends on the distance – temporal, spatial, or cultural – that separates the narrator from his small-town subject. This is demonstrated in subsequent treatments of the central image of the maple-shaded small-town streets offered by Teskey: "Tall sugar-maples stood here and there on either side of the street, and during the short fervid Canadian summer threw their grateful shade" (10). In Leacock's consideration of that image in his autobiography, temporal-spatial distance allows him to state that small-town Ontario has fallen asleep under its somnolent maples: "the little Ontario town grew till the maples planted in its streets overtopped it and it fell asleep and grew no more" (*Boy* 109). Proximity to her subject, on the other hand, causes an Alice Munro narrator to infiltrate and destabilize Teskey's and Leacock's small-town image: "The street is shaded, in some places, by maple trees whose roots have cracked and heaved the sidewalk and spread out like crocodiles into the bare yards" ("Walker Brothers Cowboy" 3). Leacock's distanced perspective allows him to cast the small town as part of the past, a quiescent thing enclosed by the shroud of its own entropy. Munro's narrator stands under that canopy of leaves and shatters the integrity of Leacock's static image. Where Leacock sees stagnation and repose, an enclosed, somewhat mournful image of finality, Munro sees continued, possibly malignant, growth.

Leacock's and Munro's narrators utilize two very different processes of perception. Leacock's persona is separated from the small town by a distance that is central to nostalgia. Distance in time and space allows the nostalgic subject to see the remembered object more comprehensively, as a whole rather than its parts. Subsequently, this nostalgic perspective provides the past with an aura of comprehensibility, even comfort, as nostalgics conflate *how* they remember the past with that past's reality. It would be a mistake, however, to suggest that *Sunshine Sketches* is simply a nostalgic text, as Leacock consistently and ironically plays with the distance that separates his narrator from Mariposa. The temporal, spatial, and cultural gap separating his narrator from the small town is very much a part of the narrative structure of other small-town texts. Of course, this distance is only rhetorical, built into the narrative structure itself, but it, in turn, effects a certain type of small-town past, one that ostensibly offers an imagined alternative or innocent precursor to modern urban existence; yet even the idyll represented by Mariposa is far more a comment on the need for memory's consolation than it is a product of a sincere belief in a kinder, gentler rural past. The obverse, represented by Munro's narrative technique, transcends the softening effects of memory to question the values commonly associated with the small town. Because rural and urban represent an imaginary binary in small-town Ontario texts, really a product of memory's process, the nature of experience in a small town, Munro's texts reveal, can be as complex and sophisticated as anything gained through urban life.

The contrast between rural and urban life in small-town Ontario literature is the product of urban narrators who reconstruct small-town Ontario from an urban space and time. This is not to suggest, however, that these narrators are simply nostalgic for a rural past, as this line of interpretation would not acknowledge that very rarely do these voices posit an uncomplicated social ideal within their versions of the small town. Mariposa, for instance, a town consistently contrasted by its narrator with its nameless urban counterpart and cited by numerous critics as an image of the Canadian past par excellence, neither functions nor fails to function as an ideal, but circumnavigates one through the narrator's unrelenting irony. Mariposa can be read in the light of Leo Marx's "complex pastoral," a subgenre of the pastoral that "manage[s] to qualify, or call into question, or bring irony to bear against the illusion of peace and harmony to a green pasture" (25). Identifying Mariposa as an example of a "complex pastoral" thus raises questions about why and how it is constructed as such: what symptom of modernity does Mariposa soothe for those wealthy club men deep in the heart of the city for whom the town is manifested, and what are the ramifications of the town's eventual dissolution in the final chapter, leaving these men bereft of further succour? This present book is not so much concerned with discussing the type of idyll or anti-idyll represented in individual small-town texts as it is in examining something Marx identifies as the "pastoral design," which he defines as the "larger structure of thought and feeling of which the *ideal* is a part" (24). What does the narrator "feel" about his or her present condition, and how does his or her reconstruction of small-town and rural Ontario address or reflect it?

At first glance, Mariposa constitutes a small-town ideal that provides a direct contrast to its urban counterpart. The image of the town, however, dissolves and is revealed to be a projection of those in the corresponding city; it exists only across an impassable temporal-spatial gap from the urban centre, and the text ends with the melancholic club men's unresolved longing for a now absent small-town past. The "memories" ostensibly responsible for Mariposa are, in fact, projections from an urban sphere onto a time and place distant enough to maintain the desired fantasy. The degree of distance – spatial, temporal, and cultural – between the narrator and the subject plays a crucial role in establishing the particular nature of small-town Ontario, not only in its most influential manifestation, Mariposa, but also in Deptford, Jubilee, Shoneval, and numerous other communities rendered in the literature of Ontario authors. Narrative distance accommodates the aestheticization of a small-town Ontario experience as something oppositional to urban life, but this difference, often an idealization, can remain intact only when it is constructed across a temporal or spatial divide. A rural idyll is the product not simply of a narrator's rural memories, but also of the dominance of an urban modernity that entices that narrator to construct its conceptual alternative beyond the here and now, as something other than the temporal-spatial present.

Throughout small-town Ontario literature there appears a concern with change, loss, and even decay, a reaction that emerged from actual changes to the status, role, and importance of the small town in Ontario during the early part of the twentieth century. Leacock noticed a trend in the settlement patterns of Ontario's smaller communities: quick growth followed by a slow, melancholic stagnation or decline. Leacock himself was the product of a small, rural community, and, much like the situation that precipitated his move to the city for academic opportunities, small towns increasingly held little promise for their ambitious young around the turn of the twentieth century. His comment on the somnolence of the little Ontario towns, that "they fell asleep and grew no more," is a melancholic description of those towns that did not continue to grow. Leacock's sentiment is echoed in lines from a book by another small-town writer, Alice Munro, in *Lives of Girls and Women*. Munro's narrator portrays Wawanash County, Huron County's fictional representative, as a place that has seen better days, and while it may have had a vibrant past, it does not have much hope for a vibrant future: "It was the same with the history of the county, which had been opened up, settled, and had grown, and entered its present slow decline" (31). The town's name, Jubilee, is a perpetual reminder of the locale's more prosperous days, which would have corresponded to the time of Queen Victoria's golden and diamond jubliees, days that were left behind as the energy of the province relocated to the cities.

Raymond Williams explains the impulse to locate in the rural land-scape a picture of the lost past, an impulse he labels a "problem of per-spective." The problem manifests in the tendency to see the end of rural traditions in the age just before the present one, a tendency that is as old as English literature:

> If we take a long enough period, it is easy to see a fundamental transformation of ... country life. But the change is so extended and so complicated ... that there seems no point at which we can sharply distinguish what it would be convenient to call separate epochs ... [O]ld practices and old ways of feeling survived into periods in which the general direction of new development was clear and decisive. And then what seems an old order, a "traditional" society, keeps appearing, reappearing, at bewilderingly various dates: in practice as an idea, to some extent based in experience, against which contemporary change can be measured ... What is really significant is this particular kind of reaction to the fact of change. (35)

In Ontario, it is these "traditional" towns on the fringes of the cities that appear to harbour this old order, to be a holdover from a different, ear-lier epoch, and against which life in the cities is measured; side-by-side exist the urban present and the rural past, as either end of this temporal relationship exists at opposite ends of the highway. To drive out to the country is to drive out to the past, allowing one to measure the tempo-ral change that such spatial distance implies. This temporal-spatial rela-tionship is made explicit in Jane Urquhart's *Changing Heaven*, in which her narrator states, "The highway connects everything: the countryside and the city, the known and the unknown ... An hour and a half of grey speed and you are able to enter the nineteenth century; its general stores, its woodstoves, its large high-ceilinged rooms, its dusty roads" (44). The rural past is the known, while the urban present is unknown, and the valorization of a "traditional" space in Ontario's small towns is a method of understanding, even contextualizing within a broader tem-poral sweep, the pace and effects of change.

The rise and dominance of the small town in Ontario lasted but a few brief generations and was over by the early decades of the twentieth century, yet its influence reverberates through the memory of these times and their physical remnants. In reflecting the shift towards the primacy of the cities, literary small-town Ontario became a place outside the centre, but one preserved, or in some cases mouldering, on the social and economic fringes; it is a place of childhood, a place of tradition, a place to leave behind and return to. While this notion can only be urban-centric, it also dominates how small-town Ontario has been written for the past century.

Keith states that "[f]or most Ontario writers, the small town about which they write is a version – sometimes idealized, sometimes satirized – of the community in which they grew up" (163). Leacock (b. 1869) was raised in the vicinity of Orillia, the model for Mariposa; more importantly, he returned to Orillia every summer throughout his career, and eventually retired to his home on Old Brewery Bay in Lake Couchiching. Today, Leacock's connection to Orillia is celebrated, as the town holds an annual folk festival named after Mariposa, and his former residence is now a popular tourist attraction. Robertson Davies (b. 1913) spent the first few years of his life in Thamesville, shortly thereafter moved to Renfrew, and later to Kingston. These places find their way into his fiction: Thamesville as Deptford, Renfrew as Blairlogie, and Kingston as Salterton. This study is concerned with Davies's best-known small-town depiction, Deptford, as it appears in the Deptford trilogy. Recently, the town of Thamesville installed a plaque on the house in which Davies spent the early part of his childhood to recognize its connection to his fiction. Munro (b. 1931) grew up in Wingham and, after a long period spent on the west coast, moved back to rural Ontario, where she currently resides for much of the year. She has famously discussed Wingham as her model for a number of her small towns, including Jubilee from *Lives of Girls and Women* and Hanratty from *Who Do You Think You Are?*, the former text constituting Munro's most extended examination of a small Ontario town. While much has been made in the past of Wingham residents' displeasure at being the focus of Munro's stories, the town now closely identifies with Munro's achievements: it has a walking tour of prominent locations that appear in Munro's stories, and it has a literary garden that celebrates Munro's works. In the case of these three authors, the places that have influenced their writings have chosen to celebrate their connections to the literature, to see it as part of the communities' pasts, part of their identities. The final chapter of this study examines two texts by Jane Urquhart (b. 1949): *The Stone Carvers* and *A Map of Glass*. Shoneval from *The Stone Carvers* is modelled on Formosa, a small agricultural community in western Ontario that possesses a distinctive German-Catholic history in an area that is largely British Protestant. *A Map of Glass* takes as its setting a small community in Prince Edward County on the north shore of Lake Ontario. This study is structured on the work of these four authors. However, they are discussed with a number of references to the works of many of their contemporaries, such as Adeline Teskey, Mazo de la Roche, Sara Jeannette Duncan, Raymond Knister, George Elliott, James Reaney, John Bemrose, Matt Cohen, Elizabeth Hay, and Richard Wright, whose works are both contemporaneous and similar in theme to those authors more central to this book.

This book begins with a look at how landscape, rural and urban, acquires a temporal association, specifically within Stephen Leacock's *Sunshine Sketches of a Little Town*. It first situates the book within the context of Leacock's literary contemporaries and then suggests that, while Leacock was working within an established genre of regional idylls, he was also drawing attention to the patterns and conventions within this genre. Leacock's town, Mariposa, is a "middle landscape" located between city and wilderness, yet Leacock's final chapter suggests that the town is, and has always been, a product of reminiscence and longing. Where my argument differs from those of others is in its suggestion that the struggle for control over Mariposa's characteristic ethos is reflected in the tension between the city and hinterland, which I also read as a tension with temporal dimensions between urban present and distant hinterland past. Only through the actions of Josiah Smith, the rough, semi-literate hotel owner who emerged from the distant hinterland past, can Mariposa maintain its status as an idyll of the recent past for the reminiscing urbanites who dominate the last chapter of the book. In *Sunshine Sketches*, Mariposa, while on one hand a product of memory, is also perpetually at risk from the same men for whom it functions as an idyll. However, Mariposa as an idyll is only temporary: it cannot and could never be located geographically; it can only, and only ever did, exist in imagined memories.

Throughout *Sunshine Sketches*, Leacock draws attention to the processes of memory, particularly in his extended description in the final chapter of the train journey that moves from urban present to small-town past. Here, the journey functions as an allegory for how memory sculpts a past from contemporary desires, longings, and regret, and projects into the temporal distance a mirage of the past as it never was. And yet it is this mirage of the small-town past that becomes emblematic of a small-town convention that later writers must contend with in their own stories of small-town Ontario life. Chapter 2 explores Robertson Davies's negotiation of Leacock's influence in his Deptford Trilogy from the 1970s. I argue that this trilogy, but primarily the first novel, *Fifth Business*, grapples with the influence of Mariposa in its narrators' depictions of small-town childhoods. Davies's protagonist from the first novel, Dunstan Ramsay, contends with the small-town idyll and anti-idyll, and struggles to represent his memories uninfluenced by conventions or patterns. The trilogy offers three different versions of Deptford, versions largely dependent on the role the village plays in the protagonists' adult, cosmopolitan lives. The trilogy, in effect, further draws attention to and transcends the small-town conventions by exploring how those conventions are formed and maintained in memory. *Fifth Business* also suggests that the notion of a small-town past–urban present binary is impossible to maintain in an increasingly cosmopolitan world: both urban centre and small-town fringe are influenced by and respond to the same homogenizing effects of a globalizing modernity.

Chapter 3 looks at two works by Alice Munro: *Lives of Girls and Women* and *Who Do You Think You Are?* While ostensibly similar to the works of Davies and Leacock, in that it contains a reminiscing narrator recalling a small-town childhood, Munro's *Lives* is remarkably different from those earlier novels. Del Jordan, Munro's narrator, neither recounts her small-town childhood from a temporal distance nor narrates it in the present first person, but through a shifting hybrid of both. Del does not maintain a narrative division between past and present, between remembering subject and remembered object. By forging the child and adult experience into a unified voice, Del's narration contains little recognizable division between an urban present and rural past, a division that has a recognizable consequence for the depictions of Mariposa and Deptford. Instead, the very same forces that have moulded her community's landscape are Del's primary artistic influences. Her narrative technique approaches organic continuity between the artist and the landscape upon which members of her community have sketched their lives, and is used by Del as an authentic method of depicting her small-town past: this is a far cry from the unfailing affection the former Mariposans have for a place that they see as both remote and irretrievable. Munro's work destabilizes the projected divide between rural past and urban present upon which previous small-town texts are structured.

In some measure, *Lives* is the exception to this book's thesis, and its perspective on the past is revised in Munro's later collection of short stories *Who Do You Think You Are*. This collection questions the past manufactured by memory and stories, particularly when recollections determine action in the present; the past, it is suggested, may offer stories, certainly, but forgetting that those stories are filtered through and shaped by the present places her characters in peril.

Chapter 4 looks at the small-town past dynamic in a more contemporary context; it argues that, as the rendered rural past recedes further in time and is unconnected to personal memory, its representation becomes more malleable, and yet its cultural importance to the present intensifies. To make this argument, that chapter examines two works by Jane Urquhart: *The Stone Carvers* and *A Map of Glass*. Urquhart has been accused of a conservative "nostalgia for pre-modern times" (Branach-Kallas *Whirlpool* 173), and while these two works ostensibly do little to counter that criticism, they are not mired in irresolvable longing for a lost past: they, in fact, contain complex and ambivalent nostalgic yearning. Klara Becker, the Depression-era protagonist of *The Stone Carvers* (2001), endlessly recounts her idealizations of the distant past of her community, Shoneval, to alleviate feelings of loss, which are caused by the disrupting effects of technology on the town's cultural traditions and her personal life. Klara overcomes her melancholy by externally solidifying her memories in a memorial, a structure that comes to symbolize a new national affective community. A modern nation has been forged by collective loss, and this community has replaced prior heterogeneous cultural traditions. Urquhart's modern urban reality is defined by what it is not, which is the cradle of continuous cultural practices; those, Urquhart suggests, experienced their final manifestation in the small towns prior to the First World War. *A Map of Glass* (2005), on the other hand, re-examines the source of that rural-urban binary. Like Klara, Sylvia Bradley longs for the traditional stability she recognizes within a rural past, yet, unlike Klara, Sylvia has no first-person experience with the object of her longing. The histories she constructs through the material remnants of the rural past are, ultimately, self-projections. Even though she imagines herself to be in touch with local history, her story of the local past is unfettered by any past reality. Like Leacock, Urquhart makes a rather subtle, shrewd observation that the notion of rural difference is the product of melancholic, alienated figures whose search for something comprehensible or secure in the past will reveal only echoes of their own voices.

This book examines how small-town Ontario pasts are not only framed in and by memory, but also how these memories are shaped in the present. If Robert Kroetsch has called the small town the "ruling paradigm" of Canadian literature, but remarks that "[t]here seems to be little literature in Canada that tells of the small-town person going to the city" (51), this study suggests that small-town Ontario literature is often already situated in the city, but that memory projects outwards onto the surrounding towns and villages. This memory, though, is more a search than a recollection; it is not simply a search for a fictionalized or embellished past, but a search for a method of understanding the often dislocating present in which characters find themselves.

Chapter One

Rural Past and Urban Present: Landscape as Time

In the winter and spring of 1912, the *Montreal Star* published the original versions of the twelve sketches that constitute Stephen Leacock's *Sunshine Sketches of a Little Town*. The British, American, and Canadian editions of the book appeared within the year. Twenty-first- century readers may view these sketches as humorous portrayals of an insular small town as it really was, an amusing but nonetheless accurate depiction of a bygone way of life in the early twentieth century. Although this collection of interweaving stories is ostensibly set early in the second decade of the twentieth century, Leacock creates a sense of ambiguity around the temporal placement of events. The shifts in setting and narrative voice in its final chapter further add to this ambiguity, since they imply that the previous eleven sketches are retrospectives. The appeal of Mariposa rests largely on its placement into a vague temporal-spatial distance, a non-specific past that is seen through the hazy lens of memory. This chapter argues that Mariposa is not a chronicle of a specific or generalized community contemporaneous to the time Leacock was writing. Rather, these small-town stories are wish images formed partly through memory, partly through projection, to provide the urbanites of the final chapter with an antidote to their dissatisfying urban present. *Sunshine Sketches* is not just a book about a small-town Ontario past but is also, and perhaps more crucially, a book about how notions of an appealing past take shape in the present.[1]

---

1 *Sunshine Sketches* is not the only work in which Mariposa appears. Leacock wrote of the town in a chapter of a later work, *Happy Stories*, from 1943. This chapter, called "Mariposa Moves On," focuses largely on, and in support of, the Victory Loan campaign to back the war effort, as Leacock makes clear in his introduction

Leacock wrote *Sunshine Sketches* during a period of mass emigration from Ontario's rural to urban areas, and, therefore, the book can
be read as a response to social change. While, at that time, a majority
of Ontario's population had been born and raised in rural communities (Baskerville 157), an ever-expanding industrialized and urbanized
Ontario replaced the agricultural community's social and economic
centrality during the early part of the twentieth century. The market
for a nostalgic rendition of a rural Ontario past would have been quite
large in 1912, as is evidenced by the popularity of the rural idylls of the
time. In writing about the small town, Leacock may have been capital-
izing on the shared yearning of transplanted rural dwellers, yet his text
also adapts the model of those idylls for his own satiric purposes.[2]

Leacock's work resembles the rural idylls of the era, a genre of writing
with which Leacock's audience would have been familiar. Eleven years
prior to Leacock's work appeared Adeline Teskey's rural idyll *Where the
Sugar Maples Grow* (1901), a popular book similar to Leacock's in both
form and subject. It comprises sketches set in the town of Mapleton, a
community modelled on Teskey's own hometown of Welland, Ontario,
located on the Welland Canal on the Niagara Peninsula. Each chapter
focuses on an individual and a dilemma he or she resolves by the end of
the chapter, a pattern not dissimilar to Leacock's. In both texts, it is the
characters' virtues that generally resolve the dilemma, yet the difference
between the two works is that, in Leacock's, it is often the appearance
of virtue that is more effectual than its authentic application. Not only
is Leacock's text a satire of the small town, it is a self-conscious satire
of the literary conventions with which Leacock's reading public would
have been familiar. *Sugar Maples* is written in the "kailyard mode," a

---

to the story. Set largely in the barbershop of Jefferson Thorpe, the stories concern
the townsfolk's various reasons for supporting the effort, from the patriotic to the
selfish. These characters and their discussions occupy slim chapters in which the
humour is less forgiving in its ironic ambiguity than in the earlier book. The style
of, and motivation behind, the work has produced a far less complex exploration of
the town, since the stories' civic function is consistently at the surface: Mariposa and
its inhabitants are now merely vehicles to discuss the ongoing fund-raising efforts
for the war, as well as the means for thin jokes. For these reasons, I will not look at
"Mariposa Moves On" in any depth.

2 Ramsay Cook has suggested that "rural depopulation" and rural nostalgia are main
currents running through *Sunshine Sketches*. These become explicit in the book's final
chapter: "The change from rural to urban living has seldom been more nostalgically
described than in the concluding chapter of *Sunshine Sketches of a Little Town*" (164).

Scottish genre of literature known for its sentimental idealization of life in small villages. Teskey's book adapts this genre in order to offer a nostalgic celebration of rural Ontario's specifically Protestant past (Gerson 1096). Self-sacrifice, prudence, hard work, and modesty invariably lead a character to spiritual and/or material gain; in Leacock's work, however, the gain is more often strictly secular (i.e., monetary). Furthermore, the self-interest, whether conscious or unconscious, of Leacock's characters effectively mocks the self-sacrificing purity of their literary models.

In terms of style, Leacock's and Teskey's works share many similarities; both are narrated by figures who possess an insider/outsider relationship with the town. Teskey's narrator spends each winter away among "strangers and foreigners" (9) only to return to the village each summer "to find little change – the village life was not subject to many variations" (10). Leacock's narrator, similarly, knows both the city and the small town; he has resided in and has intimate knowledge of both spheres, a status that allows him to alternate between a rural and urban perspective. Yet this insider/outsider status affects each narrator's attitude towards his or her subjects; while Teskey's is that of gentle condescension (her worldly experience allows her to know these people better than they know themselves), Leacock's ironically undercuts any appearance of idyllic gentleness in Mariposa that his narrator has been careful to craft. Perhaps most significant, at least to this study, is the texts' vastly different understandings of the value of the past. Teskey's book displays a sentimental understanding of the past and the simpler values that ostensibly reside there; Leacock's, however celebratory of the small-town past it may be, ultimately displays scepticism about knowledge of the past, an epistemological vacuum that is filled by nostalgic projection. This scepticism is based on his awareness of the effects of time and distance on memory, as he suggests in a letter from 1942: "I find ... that the world looks very different in looking back on it from what it seemed at the time" (Staines *Letters* 468). Despite his awareness of the effects of memory, he was also aware of the appeal of this type of retrospect, particularly as he aged: "I have dropped into that pleasant retrospect of the past, that is the mark either of great minds or of small ones, I forget which ... [b]ut I take a great and increasing pleasure in looking back to the old days," he writes in a letter from 1937 (Staines *Letters* 320). Leacock's book is, certainly, a gentle parody of idylls like Teskey's, and Leacock's other works highlight his talent as a parodist of literary conventions and styles. Yet *Sunshine Sketches* goes further than mere parody to explore the very nature of memory when it is used as

a soothing balm to console the anomie of the present; this exploration
of memory, a type of meta-critique of nostalgia, further distinguishes
Sunshine Sketches from the idylls popular at the time.

It also distinguishes Leacock's books from others similar in theme
and setting during this era. Mazo de la Roche's *Jalna* (1927), for instance,
carried on the tradition of the regional Ontario idyll with its version of
a British country manor set on the shores of Lake Ontario in the 1920s.
Jalna is, in a sense, the heir of Teskey's project; what both works share
with one another, and what neither shares with Leacock's, is their denial
of the passage of time. De la Roche's book describes a place of picturesque cottages surrounded by neat picket fences and villages where
the blacksmith still plays a central role in local commerce, even though
the book is set in the era of the automobile. *Sugar Maples* is set within
an organic community, an ideal of human relations, that has little contact with the outside world, even though it is on the path of a busy
trade route (the Welland Canal). Both works simply deny the changes
of modernity, which is really a tactical reaction to them. In the early
twentieth century, the areas where both *Sugar Maples* and *Jalna* are set –
the Niagara Peninsula and the Golden Horseshoe, respectively – were
industrializing, and it is precisely these types of communities that wit-
nessed a great emigration to the cities to staff the urban factories. The
modern city in both of these works, though, is not a place offering refuge from the diminishing prospects of farm and small-town life, but a
threatening place in which characters must keep their wits about them
or else be swindled, become lost, or experience defeat. These works
deny the urban industrial reality of the province, as they were written for people who, most likely, found themselves within its midst; the
small town in these books is the place of both economic and community
sanctuary. As I discuss in greater detail below, Leacock's book does not
deny the passage of time, as these other idylls do, but rather contains a
self-conscious exploration of the desire for solace in the past, desire that
"remembers" a wish image that has been set in an earlier, better place,
a place distant in time and space from the here and now.

Leacock's, de la Roche's, and Teskey's books are products of their
time, indirectly exploring contemporary social transitions through the
lens of the imagined past. During the early twentieth century, while
the farms and small towns in Ontario stagnated, a corresponding rural
revival occurred in the province, a revival focused on ostensibly rural
values. Apart from influencing the idylls of this era, this rural nostalgia
even resulted in the election to Queen's Park in 1919 of a political party,
the United Farmers of Ontario whose victory rested on the promise

to "uphold the verities of rural life" (Baskerville 157). This election appears to have stemmed from a diffuse nostalgia; the celebration of a way of life follows its decline, and, therefore, the ensuing enthusiasm is a type of self-conscious restoration. When considering these events as part of the social context in which Leacock was writing, we can see Mariposa's communal whole as a fictionalized community idyll set against its faltering or disappearing counterpart in the provincial social life of the time; the apparent vitality of the community and the desire of all residents to remain at "home" in Mariposa make the community an anachronism, as all idylls are, something of which Leacock no doubt was aware. Yet this context might have us read the work as a simple or sentimental pastoral, a reflexive reaction against urban industrialism; to a large extent, this is a label that could be thrown against, and stick to, Teskey's book of sketches. If we were to see *Sunshine Sketches* as a proponent of this view, however, we could not account for the book's complexity, nor for Leacock's own well-known scepticism regarding rural nostalgia, an attitude fully absent from idylls like Teskey's. As he wryly comments in another work, when urban dwellers seek to rebuild the rural childhood home, that reconstruction is done "not with an ax but with an architect" (*Boy* 49); here, the architect becomes a metaphor for the stylization accommodated by temporal distance, the idealization that rounds the hard and sharp edges of past experience. As the following section argues, retrospective stylization invariably leaves its impressions on reminiscence; where Leacock's book differs from others, though, is that it draws attention to this process.

Mariposa: Past and/or Present

Numerous critical responses to *Sunshine Sketches* through the past century portray Mariposa as a town with which all Canadians are familiar, the cultural ideal representative of a "Canadian Experience" par excellence. Accompanying this critical interpretation is the idea that Mariposa is an accurate reflection of life in early twentieth-century Canada and that, since this apogee, small-town Ontario has experienced a decline both in terms of its moral standards and sense of community. Yet Mariposa was always written as a past ideal, never as a present reality, and critics who use the depiction of Mariposa to evaluate the sorry state of the present have missed some important details that indicate that Mariposa was always already a projection into and onto the past.

One of the central artistic methods of the book is the apparent filter of temporal distance between the narrator and Mariposa, which then has a softening effect on the town's descriptions. Gerald Lynch identifies "temporal distance" as one of the fundamentals of Leacock's theory of humour, as it allows "past disappointments [to be] forgivingly perceived" (*Stephen Leacock* 54). *Sunshine Sketches*, Lynch concludes, "enacts all that Leacock hoped for from humour" (56). Temporal distance allays or dispels any harshness associated with remembered events; a self-interested deception in the present becomes, in retrospect, a laughable hoodwinking executed in the most magnanimous of community spirits, and even the dupe is in on the joke – bonhomie prevails. Even though Leacock's narrator is often part of the action and often narrates in the present tense, he has knowledge of future events: his awareness of the community transcends the simple present tense. During the *Mariposa Belle* excursion, for example, Dr. Gallagher decides to give his collection of arrows to the Mariposa Mechanics' Institute: "they afterwards became, as you know, the Gallagher Collection" (44). Another incidence of prolepsis within the third chapter has the narrator discussing the excitement caused by the marine accident, although the "disaster" has not yet occurred in the narrative. This suggests that the narrator feigns his immediacy, and he is, in fact, recounting these events from a temporal distance. The narrator's position in the final chapter certainly supports this view: he is a raconteur who has been reminiscing all along. Lynch has also commented that the "temporal-spatial distance" between the city club and small town results in an "incorrect" vision of Mariposa as "the ideal 'home' or as an untroubled idyllic community" (*Stephen Leacock* 115). This chapter departs from Lynch and argues that temporal-spatial distance is essential, indeed required, in maintaining the portrait of Mariposa provided in the first eleven chapters, as, simply put, Mariposa as it is represented does not exist outside the projected fantasies of the urban club-men.[3]

---

3 There is much in the book that throws the temporal placement of events into question. Just when are the events of the sketches set? While the final chapter may have us read the first eleven sketches as set during the Victorian period, there are too many subtle references in the sketches to contemporary events and technology. In Chapter 10, there is a reference to "King George," who has dissolved Canada's Parliament, in addition to references to telephones and limousine touring cars, technologies not common until the twentieth century. What is more important to this chapter than locating the time in which the sketches are set is in analysing how the tone of Mariposa's depiction is itself possible only through a sense of temporal distance. Whether the sketches are set in the Victorian period or set during the time Leacock was writing is secondary to the haze of memory that affects their portrayal.

Why, then, does Leacock's book possess this status as the embodiment of a popular idea of Ontarian small-town life when it is, in fact, largely unconcerned with the day-to-day reality of a town's life? Leacock remains far more concerned with the method of memory responsible for that past than with the details of reminiscence. There are other Ontario small-town books that do detail an intricate past of place, offering a picture of life "as it was" in small-town Ontario, yet these are eclipsed by Leacock's sunny misdirections. Sara Jeannette Duncan's *The Imperialist* (1904), for instance, is set in the large town of Elgin, and is far more concerned than Leacock's book with the intricacies and details of town life. Yet this work does not possess the same wide recognition and identification as Leacock's, perhaps because it explicitly examines specific political questions of its day (i.e., Canada's cultural and commercial connection to England). Leacock encourages the reader to see his or her own past in Mariposa through the second-person address; this technique is particularly striking at the beginning of the "L'Envoi," when he suggests to the reader that "you come from the little town" (141). Of course, Leacock is not suggesting that all readers have come from Mariposa itself, or from its real-world model, Orillia, or, for that matter, from any place resembling Orillia. What Leacock suggests here is that Mariposa is a model for how we remember our childhood. It is because Mariposa is deliberately constructed through the hazy lens of memory that it can be regarded as a cultural archetype. If one can disregard the cultural specifics of the text, what develops is a rather evocative representation of how an individual, or group of individuals, sees the personal past from the slightly melancholic vantage point of adulthood. While Duncan's work is a snapshot of a specific place at a specific time, populated by characters with distinct political and cultural concerns, Leacock's transcends specific cultural references in its examination of the way memory works. Contemporary readers may not recognize their own social or political concerns in Duncan's novel, but they will certainly recognize in Leacock's work the quiet sadness of a group of people who, in equal parts, remember and invent their past in order to compensate for the deficiencies of their adult life. And in that way, Leacock's may not be a more accurate representation of place, but his text is a more evocative rendering of the way the past and present intertwine within the individual.

Memory and narrativization both enclose and circumscribe a past, rendering it eminently comprehensible, ordered, and safe. Therefore, Mariposa's appeal is defined only through the soft palette of the retrospective. But we should not forget that the town is also a comment on that artistic method, a feature that distinguishes it from other idylls, as its nostalgia is not only self-conscious but self-reflexive. To address the narrative's retrospective quality and issues relating to the urban and rural divide, I would like to begin by discussing the narrator. Locating both his identity and his temporal perspective is key to my sense of the remainder of the book. The dominant urban identity of the narrator, his city voice, suggests that the source for Mariposa's construction rests not within those "broad" streets of Mariposa, but rather within the melancholic club deep in the heart of the city.

The Narrator

Lynch perceives three different narrators within the book: the narrator of the introduction, the narrator of the "sketches proper" (Lynch's phrase for the first eleven chapters), and the narrator of the final chapter. He states that these three different personae emerge as a result of "an interest bordering on obsession with the reader's perspective on and knowledge of 'Mariposa'" (*Stephen Leacock* 57). Lynch describes polyvocality within *Sunshine Sketches*' narration, and I want to adhere to this critical assertion. First of all, to address the "Preface," I agree with Lynch that the voice is Leacock's. He added the "Preface" when the sketches appeared in book form – it did not appear in their newspaper serialization. As the "Preface" refers to concrete details in Leacock's life, we must separate this persona from the "Mariposan" voice of the sketches proper, who claims specific knowledge of the town. Turning to the narrator of the sketches proper, I claim that his is a disunified voice that is wholly conscious of his varying but simultaneous personae. The narrator's treatment of the town suggests he is an outsider, an observer rather than a participant; the narrator's core voice is that of an urban dweller who ironically appropriates and performs the voice of an authentic Mariposan, rather than that of an authentic Mariposan who has knowledge of the cosmopolitan world. The narrator reveals this core voice in the final chapter, "L'Envoi." Like his audience at the club, he is a club-dweller, but, unlike them, nowhere in the final chapter does he reveal any personal connection to Mariposa. Rather, it is the members of his club audience who have their Mariposan roots revealed to them. The narrator, however, controls the nature and the tone of the reminiscences, as he guides his auditor through both remembered scenes and the final imaginary journey.

Although the narrator poses as a Mariposan throughout the book, even referring to his interaction with the townsfolk, particularly with Jefferson Thorpe (33) on at least two occasions, he subtly distances himself from the Mariposans' expressed ignorance or belief in outright falsehoods. During the height of Smith's battle to regain his liquor licence, one of the main arguments the narrator puts forth on Smith's behalf is the celebration of other cultures' relationship with alcohol: "look at the French and the Italians, who drink all day and all night. Aren't they all right? Aren't they a musical people?" (17–18). The next paragraph starts with "I quote these arguments not for their own sake, but merely to indicate the changing temper of public opinion in Mariposa" (18). Should the reader confuse the expressed sentiment with that held by the narrator, the reader is mistaken, since the misguided summation of different cultural nationalities is something in sole possession of those Mariposans arguing on behalf of Smith. The act of "quoting" distances the narrator from the comic ignorance of these fallacious arguments; what remains unstated in this moment of irony is his recognition of the Mariposans' reliance on cultural stereotypes that, although articulated by the narrator, are in no way held by him.

A similar instance of quoting comes in Chapter 6, with Judge Pepperleigh's decision against the insurance company. After Pepperleigh has given his ruling, the narrator comments on the issues surrounding the verdict: "Just what the jurisdiction of Judge Pepperleigh's court is I don't know, but I do know that in upholding the rights of a Christian congregation – I am quoting here the text of the decision – against the intrigues of a set of infernal skunks that make too much money, anyway, the Mariposa court is without an equal" (81). The humour of the sentence rests in the notion that a "Christian congregation" is justified in defrauding an insurance company because the ethical reputation of such urban companies is degraded in the eyes of the Mariposans. The nature of the organization being defrauded legitimates the fraud, the illegality of which does not concern the court. The irony of the sentence distances the narrator from the prevailing opinion of the Mariposans; the implication is that he recognizes the court's decision as contrary to the rule of law, something that the Mariposans can conveniently disregard when the town is threatened by external forces. Although intended for humorous effect, these acts of quoting allow the reader to peer behind the narrator's appropriation of a Mariposan veneer, as the narrator himself adumbrates an alternate but covert personality, one able to recognize Mariposan "small-mindedness" and distance himself from it.

The narrator's comic asides, often based on the contrast of his implied superiority to the inferior knowledge of the Mariposans, suggest that the implied reader, in order to get the full range of comic possibility, also possesses a greater range of reference than the Mariposans. In the discussion of Mariposa's shifting national allegiances during cultural days of celebration, the narrator mentions Mariposans' enthusiasm for the Fourth of July, which is based on their own indirect or tangential American connections: "Then on the Fourth of July there are stars and stripes flying over half the stores in town ... Then you learn for the first time that Jeff Thorpe's people came from Massachusetts and that his uncle fought at Bunker Hill (it must have been Bunker Hill, – anyway Jefferson will swear it was in Dakota all right enough)" (37). Similarly, through free indirect discourse, the narrator appropriates Thorpe's geographic imagination in Chapter 2 during the height of the banana-lands frenzy: "Anyway, they didn't hesitate [to take Thorpe's money], these Cuban people that wrote to Jeff from Cuba – or from a post-office box in New York – it's all the same thing, because Cuba being so near to New York the mail is all distributed from there" (30). These references rely on common geographic knowledge, but they transcend the historical and topographical awareness of the Mariposans, or at the very least of Thorpe, the most loquacious but least informed character in the book.

Who is the narrator and from where and when does he speak? Can we trust him to provide an accurate version of the town? Much of the book's pleasure rests on this parodic tension between the rural and urban (Keith 157) or between appearance and reality (Lynch *Stephen Leacock* 58); the reader must distinguish between what is provided and merely implied by the author. Is the narrator merely performing a voice or character that, at times, falls away to reveal something more genuine? Periodically, the narrator does offer windows through his ironic narration that further reveal the depth and reality of both his and the Mariposans' character and experience; while the bulk of the narrative combines irony and pathos, these brief windows rely more heavily on pathos, momentarily shedding the indeterminacy of the tone's ironic cloud. The windows still reflect the narrator's superior knowledge, but they also introduce a great sensitivity, a sensitivity that is as much a part of his personality as is the winking joviality.

The irony of the narrator's portrayals relies on the reader's knowledge of the well-known rural type: ignorant, good-natured, laughably earnest, and unselfconsciously moral. During these windows, though, the narrator peels back a character's typified description, and the subsequent characterization transcends archetypes. These windows suggest a fleeting and brief realism within the narration. One of the clearest instances comes at the end of the chapter describing the Whirlwind campaign. It is the sad duty of Mullins to inform Dean Drone of the fund-raising campaign that, despite the initial high spirits of optimism, fails miserably:

> I saw Mullins, as I say, go up the street on his way to Dean Drone's. It was middle April and there was ragged snow on the streets, and the nights were dark still, and cold. I saw Mullins grit his teeth as he walked, and I know that he held in his coat pocket his own cheque for the hundred, with the condition taken off it, and he said that there were so many skunks in Mariposa that a man might as well be in the Head Office in the city.
>
> The Dean came out to the little gate in the dark, – you could see the lamplight behind him from the open door of the rectory, – and he shook hands with Mullins and they went in together. (73)

The narrator seldom relates details regarding temperature and light, but in this case these details contribute to both the pathos and immediacy of the scene. What is only implied earlier becomes fully displayed; these windows clarify the narrator's perceptiveness and sensitivity, but they also further reveal the artifice of his Mariposan identity, the ignorant and provincial booster who winks at the readers to let them in on the joke. The Mariposans' characterizations also benefit from these moments of narrative lucidity, as they allow them to transcend character archetypes; what prevails is a sense of realism infused with pathos. While the ironic indeterminacy establishes distance between the Mariposans and the reader, these windows of realism bridge that emotive distance, and the narrative becomes rather evocative. Furthermore, these windows lack any sense of Mariposa's idealization, suggesting that that can occur only in the absence of proximity.

In the subsequent chapter, Smith uses arson to dissolve the financial threat facing the town: he protects the town from real consequence, and the narrative's sense of temporal distance is re-established. Despite the narrative's brief foray into realism, which equates to a conveyed emotional intimacy, the re-establishment of the narrator's irony subsequently thrusts the momentarily individuated characters back into generic convention. The narrator only briefly reveals emotional depth within the Mariposans, but he also only briefly displays his capacity to recognize it, which suggests that the greater part of his persona rests just out of sight, below the surface of his narration; he performs the rural type, but his irony and windows of realism notify the reader that he, indeed, transcends any easy categorization.

The final chapter fully reveals what before was only suggested. The narrator emerges in his full present-tense identity as a perceptive, sensitive urban dweller whose view of the past is both celebratory and melancholic; Mariposa has come to an end, and, as a result, it gains an associative forlorn affect, while its place in the personal trajectories of the club men becomes contextualized, ordered, more meaningful. If the narrator has been looking back all along, the final chapter displays the process whereby he moves from a unified urban to an ironized rural perspective, but, interestingly, that metamorphosis is accompanied by a temporal shift, implying that a rural perspective, whether authentic or appropriated, belongs among images of the past.

The Train Ride Back

The final chapter, "L'Envoi: The Train to Mariposa," is the work's only full departure in setting and narrative tone. In this chapter, Leacock alludes to the importance of certain influences in the literary construction of Mariposa that have, up to this point, gone unacknowledged – those are nostalgia and memory. The final train trip back to Mariposa reveals the extent to which memory influences the construction of the previous eleven sketches. And it is the omniscient narrator who guides and instructs the memory of the auditor, ensuring that Mariposa is remembered correctly. As the final chapter begins, the reader realizes that the preceding eleven chapters have been filtered through memory. Mariposa is the world of the benign past, a place where labour is absent, and relaxation, ease, good humour, and pleasure take precedence: "[i]n Mariposa there aren't any business hours and the excitement goes on all the time" (Leacock *Sunshine* 128).

The tidy conclusion to each chapter indicates that Mariposans are free from the consequences of their own actions; Duncan's Elgin from *The Imperialist*, the other prominent fictional town from early twentieth-century Canadian literature, is not such as place. In addition to the topic of Canada's political and cultural connection to Britain at the time, the book traces the professional and romantic price for political beliefs deemed unorthodox, or at least too enthusiastic, by the town. Mariposa may be, temporarily, a vision of the small-town idyll, but Elgin is never cast as such. Unlike Elgin, Mariposa is the product of a deliberate contrast to the city, which is, as the final chapter displays, the ultimate and inescapable setting of the book. The two authors write about the small town from very different temporal perspectives. Duncan's town (some might say a small city, as Elgin has a population of 11,000) anticipates further growth and is very much at the forefront of the economic present and future of the province. Leacock, who was writing only eight years after Duncan, creates Mariposa in contradistinction to the bustling industrialism taking over in places like Elgin. His town offers an escape not only from the industrialized city, but also from the dominant values of Ontario's industrializing present. While Elgin represents an essentially forward-looking perspective – and the town is situated within a context of economic and cultural growth – Mariposa marks a distinct shift in the perception of the small town as part of a provincial past.

What results from these two divergent perspectives alludes to the vastly different conceptions each author had regarding the small town. Glenn Willmott conceives of *The Imperialist* as, essentially, an allegory of the developing nation, a *bildungsroman* in which the central figure, Lorne Murchison, moves through the stages of development to adulthood, a growth that symbolizes the nation's own movement towards maturity, which remains unfinished at the end of the book (*Unreal* 21–31). The novel's anticipation of future accomplishment, of anticipated individual achievement, stands in stark contradistinction to the reminiscence through which Mariposa is constructed. As Clara Thomas suggests, while "the captains and the kings have departed from Mariposa" ("Canadian Social" 48), they are just getting started in Elgin. The characters of these two books stand at opposite ends of a *bildungsroman* pattern. The implicit view of *The Imperialist* is towards the future, towards an individual and national identity that is only in the process of formation; as Willmott points out, Lorne's losses will make sense only if they are synthesized into a potential future resolution, one that is only hinted at within the book (*Unreal* 25). The perspective of *Sunshine Sketches*, however, is provided by the men at the opposite end of this *bildungsroman* development: their movement towards urban independence and achievement, unlike Lorne's, is complete, but it has left them unfulfilled; their gaze, thus, turns to the past to locate the existential comfort that has been the real goal of their material striving. Unlike in Duncan's book, the fulcrum of identity in *Sunshine Sketches* is not anticipated within the possible culmination of individual and/ or national growth, but rather is located within a nostalgic vision of a common past that may, for a while, alleviate the club men's current melancholy. The city, while the scene of their striving for years, ultimately does not possess what these men desire; alienated, they turn longing gazes to their childhoods to discover, they hope, what they may have missed while there. However, the attainment of this wish image is impossible, and thus the club men are ultimately left in irresolvable melancholy. The train ride back to Mariposa functions like a *bildungsroman* in reverse, as the auditor hopes to unravel those markers of growth and change that characterize his urban success. If viewed in an allegorical light, this trip could allude to Leacock's discomfort with the industrialization and modernization of Canada's economy.

The *bildungsroman* pattern of *Sunshine Sketches* is revealed only in the final chapter, which belatedly introduces a narrative frame for the previous eleven; the reader now learns that the preceding narrative has been a story that may be told to the club men, but is really a conglomerate manifestation of their collective memory. The chapter begins with the voice of the now melancholic narrator, whose emotive state is an appropriation and reflection of that of his auditor. The narrator, auditor, and reader have left Mariposa for good, and, while the town now is part of the narrative's past, its status as the lost home for the auditor becomes more significant; despite his present domicile in the "costlier part of the city" (142), the auditor still yearns for his lost home. Yet he has nearly forgotten this home, and, more importantly, he has forgotten one of the methods of its access: that is, the train to Mariposa. It was at one time, along with Mariposa itself, a very real part of the auditor's self and identity: "Years ago, when you first came to the city as a boy with your way to make, you knew of it well enough, only too well" (141). The narrator introduces the train only when Mariposa proper is no longer the subject of the narrative, and the train becomes the physical and mnemonic vehicle by which the auditor can attempt to revisit his childhood home; indeed, the very sight of the train transports his thoughts back to his past.

Contributing to the melancholic tone is the juxtaposition between the lightness of the preceding eleven chapters, particularly with the final tremendous joke of Smith's election victory – "Mr. Smith, of course, said nothing. He didn't have to, – not for four years, – and he knew it" (140) – and the absence of both the town and the methods of accessing it at the beginning of the twelfth: "Strange that you did not know of it [the train], though you come from the little town – or did, long years ago" (141). These lines mirror the opening of the first chapter, but while the first chapter introduces Mariposa, the final chapter introduces Mariposa's absence; the town has now become lost to spatial and temporal distance. The auditor's relationship with the present, however, is unfulfilling, even though he has achieved most of the aspirations of his younger rural self. The present has not become what he had imagined or had hoped for; the house that he had once planned to build in Mariposa would have been "much finer, in true reality, than that vast palace of sandstone with the porte cochere and the sweeping conservatories that you afterwards built" (141–2). This comparison of a past hypothetical with his present reality paradoxically equates this imagined past to "true reality," implying that the auditor's actual urban life has veered into artifice or something with which he has become uncomfortable.

The cuisine of the club also proves inadequate when compared to the wild game caught and eaten in the auditor's youth: "Ask your neighbour there at the next table whether the partridge that they sometimes serve to you here can be compared for a moment to the birds that he and you, or he and some one else, used to shoot as boys in the spruce thickets along the lake" (142). As the references move further back into the auditor's past, that past becomes grander, since the specifics of the event, such as who attended, become secondary, while its emotive quality, perhaps embellished by memory, takes precedence. The auditor's inability to distinguish who accompanied him on his partridge-hunting expeditions speaks only of the generic nature of his memories; they are memories formed as much by generalized beliefs about idyllic childhood as they are by personal experience. For the auditor, the present has become inadequate when compared to those memories of a distant, inaccessible, and embellished past.

David Lowenthal explains this type of historical consciousness in *The Past Is a Foreign Country*. As the past is, as they say, "history," it therefore gains an appearance of being complete and stable, and thus an associative illusion of safety and security develops: "Nothing more can happen to the past; it is safe from the unexpected and the untoward, from accident or betrayal. Because it is over, the past can be ordered and domesticated, given a coherence foreign to the chaotic and shifting present. Nothing in the past can now go wrong" (62). Nothing in Mariposa can go wrong because all that can happen in Mariposa has already occurred; on the other hand, pitfalls and trials still await Lorne after his departure from Elgin, as his script is, as yet, unwritten. All that occurred and can occur in Mariposa emerges strictly through memory; it is, therefore, free from the unknown and the unexpected.

Our versions of the past can offer refuge, but accessing a personal past relies on memory, a medium that is subject to a high degree of degradation. The past seen through memory is, therefore, malleable; its evocation in abridged versions counteracts contemporary ennui or anomie, as these versions of the past offer comprehensible, consoling images that have been edited for both context and complication. Memory becomes a solace for Leacock's club men, who occupy a sanctuary of comfort in their urban club away from the chaotic vagaries of business. The club is a most auspicious place in which to carry out these types of nostalgic reminiscences against which the present's inadequacies become more apparent. No wonder the narrator pleads with the auditor to refrain from asking his neighbour about his boyhood fishing experiences, as the whopper's magnificence could not be contained in a single "long dull evening in this club" (142). Leacock here establishes the importance of memory for his entire work; the reader comes to understand that the grandeur of the auditor's childhood events corresponds to the aura of retrospective "splendour" that pervades the previous eleven chapters. Memory governs the narrative's tone and technique. The imaginary trip upcountry aboard the Mariposa Express is an attempt to revisit the source of these memories. While the attempt ultimately fails, the trip is particularly interesting, as it unveils the process by which retrospect gains its affect.

The auditor begins both the chapter and his trip aboard the Mariposa Express lacking knowledge of his own past. He no longer remembers the existence of the train to Mariposa, a method of physically gaining access to the town. His childhood memories are similarly degraded, and to access his personal, yet also conventional, memories requires the narrator's mnemonic prodding: "But if you have half forgotten Mariposa, and long since lost the way to it, you are only like the greater part of the men in this Mausoleum Club in the city … Ask him [the neighbour] if he ever tasted duck that could for a moment be compared to the black ducks in the rice marsh along the Ossawippi" (142). The auditor is in a passive position: he is unable to recall scenes from his own past, and it is the narrator who provides them. Similarly, when the narrator and auditor begin their journey aboard the Mariposa Express, it is the narrator who reveals the identity of the Mariposans and explains their idiosyncrasises to the auditor:

That man with the two-dollar panama and the glaring spectacles is one of the greatest judges that ever adorned the bench of Missinaba County. That clerical gentleman with the wide black hat, who is explaining to the man with him the marvelous mechanism of the new air brake ... surely you have seen him before. Mariposa people! (142–3)

The auditor's ostensible personal past becomes a narrative product of which he then becomes a consumer. As the train moves farther from the city, the idealizations of the train and countryside become more intense, and we realize that the auditor is not travelling into his personal history at all, but into the generalized, communal images formed from typified conceptions of the rural past.

The urban present only alluded to in Leacock's book, the world outside the club, is that fallen world against which Mariposa is constructed. Its commuter trains contain people "standing thick in the aisles" (142), while the city itself is full of "roar and clatter" (143). Here again, tactile details position the reader in close proximity to the narrative events. In contradistinction, as the train to Mariposa exits the city and travels through the outlying farmsteads, the narrator basks in the open countryside, and the distance between the auditor/reader and the narrative object is re-established: "The city is far behind now and right and left of you there are trim farms ... There is a dull red light from the windows of the farmstead. It must be comfortable there ... only think of the still quiet of it" (143). "There" is the farmhouse perceived from a distance; the unsaid "here" is ostensibly the train seat, but it is in reality the leather armchair in the club. Spatial distance serves as the equivalent to temporal distance; observing the farmhouse from the seat of the train is parallel to remembering Mariposa, as both function only across an interchangeable spatial and temporal gap. Yet the "there" of Mariposa and the farmhouse, perceived through the distant, longing gaze provides a contrast to the "here," which is within the noise and "rush and strain" of the city. Despite evidence to the contrary, the narrator himself is unable to traverse this distance, as he can never quite shed his urban identity in the present.

The train trip to Mariposa is disguised as an actual trip taken by the auditor and described by the narrator. We first see the train as an object of Mariposa within the city, and the narrator's description here disregards the perspective that he states is necessary to see Mariposa properly – that is, we need to inhabit it for about six months (3). If we have come fresh to Mariposa from a cosmopolitan centre, we "are deceived. [Our] standard of vision is all astray" (3). The narrator's perspective is "all astray" in the early parts of the final chapter, as he sees the train to Mariposa as diminutive, tucked away in its corner of the station "puffing up steam" (141) in order to take its primary commuters home to the suburbs and the golf grounds. As the train pulls away from the city, the narrator provides a running commentary on its metamorphosis from an electric commuter train into the grand Mariposa Express: "But wait a little, and you will see that when the city is well behind you, bit by bit the train changes its character" (143). These lines serve a dual purpose; they anticipate the further transformation of the train, but they also anticipate the transformation of the narrator, from that of omniscient and melancholic guide of the club men who feeds back to them idyllic scenes from their own childhood to the re-adoption of his former Mariposan persona, the performer of the Mariposan type.

The transformation of the narrator's tone mirrors the transformation of the train. The train is in no real way special or even distinctive until it is distanced from the city and begins to shed its electric engine and the "trim little cars" carrying the commuters (143). Similarly, take the narrator outside of the city, and the train becomes "the most comfortable, the most reliable, the most luxurious and the speediest train that ever turned a wheel" (144). Just as the train sheds the markers of its city identity, the narrator sheds his urban perspective, and the train regains the splendour belonging to recalled images of the past; the narrator, in approaching Mariposa, begins to adopt that "standard of vision" necessary to transcend the appreciation of its "mere appearance" (2). Contrary to the narrator's advice to spend six months in Mariposa, to see the town properly one needs to see it from a temporal distance, in retrospect from the armchairs of the urban club. The train journey thus becomes an allegory of how memory gains its affect: the further back in time we remember, the more the past becomes subject to our exaggerations.

With the revelation of the narrative frame in the final chapter, the auditor also becomes the retroactive source of, and consumer for, the prior eleven chapters of narration; however, the object of the narrator's address does not become specific until the eighth paragraph; until then, the second person "you" serves as an address to the generic reader. This same "you" appears in the first sentence of the book and serves as the object of the narrator's address throughout. Before the clarification of the narrator's specific auditor in the club, the small-town experience is discussed as a national phenomenon; the small town becomes the normalized site of the better past. Here Leacock is using one of the common tropes of western literature: the rural idyll as an image of a happier past. On a larger scale, the idyll does not offer simply images associated with a personal childhood, but also images we associate with a social past, a nascent, more innocent social state. Idyllic images of a better past often say more about the present in which they were created than about the past that they create.

When the auditor finally pulls into the town's station, he has almost reached his spatial and temporal destination, his childhood: "How vivid and plain it all is. Just as it used to be thirty years ago" (145). Before the illusion dissolves, the narrator, auditor, and reader are on the cusp of entering the Mariposa of the sketches proper. This scene has produced interpretations of Mariposa as a wellspring of a Canadian cultural identity: a "national past" (Mantz) or Canadian "home place" (Lynch *The One* 182). However, this vision of the past in the final chapter dissolves, because the memory of it cannot be maintained; it is a figment of nostalgic projection, an elaborate exaggeration of the past. Rather than proposing a vision of a provincial or national past, I think Leacock here is offering something more complicated.[4] If Mariposa functions as consolation for the modern industrialized and commercial nation, Leacock also draws attention to the processes that allow it to be conceived of as such. Particularly significant to this reading is the dissolution of the last chapter's fantasy as the train almost arrives at its goal. That goal is ostensibly Mariposa, and, just as the entire train journey is a re-appropriation of a retrospective, nostalgic tone, the destination will also, ostensibly, reacquaint the narrator and auditor with the town's quintessence, its ultimate and final significance in terms of cultural meaning and identity, be it personal, provincial, or national. This goal, however, proves utterly allusive.

This cultural theme, which pops up in so much of Leacock criticism, is the area related most closely to the theme of cultural heritage. "Heritage," says Laurajane Smith, "is a cultural process or performance that is concerned with the production and negotiation of cultural identity, individual and collective memory, and social and cultural values"

---

4 Guy Vanderhaeghe disrupts the Canadian cultural claims made about Mariposa. He states: "Mariposa is a small town of a particular time, place, and people. It is important not to forget that this is a picture of a lost world, an Edwardian town basking in a bright sunshine of confidence, peace, and stability; a town that has no inkling that it will soon send its sons to perish in the bloody mud of Flanders. We also ought not to forget that it is an Ontario town and a British town" (21). Furthermore, any discussions of a past represented by Mariposa must acknowledge that it is a past of white Anglo-Saxon Ontarians rather than a comprehensive myth of Canadian origins.

("Introduction" 2). These processes are most commonly expressed in the activities of community conservation/preservation groups, historical re-enactments, and heritage societies. What these activities share is their desire to understand, stabilize, and even claim a durable version of the past, often as a reaction to the perceived movement away from cultural norms and values. The value of these activities has been hotly debated, as not only is there often a commercial dimension to them but also heritage proponents can be both punctilious and righteous about the value of their specific pasts.[5] The processes of heritage in Leacock's text revolve largely around the negotiation of identity that occurs in the final chapter in the image of the train journey. Here, though, Leacock reveals how a view of the cultural past can be largely the product of nostalgic longing. Leacock suggests that, if the past offers a view of what once was, a view that proves instructive to the present, we must not simply know the content of that past, but rather examine the operations of memory that produce that past. The final train journey is a metaphor for memory itself, an image of memory's selective and aggrandizing processes. Memory gestures towards unified meaning, a platonic form that guides all subsequent manifestations of culture, a form that our reminiscences, working in tandem with cultural expectations, can only sketch in outline, thus providing fodder for latter-day cultural mimesis; in this case, that mimesis is the narrator's appropriation and performance of the Mariposan type.

Memories may gesture towards the suggested unified meaning of a cultural origin, but transcendent meaning can only be deferred, even as memory appears to approach it. The train to Mariposa, as well as the retrospective affect the journey engenders in the narrator's tone, expresses a Derridean signifier for which Mariposa itself is the endlessly deferred signified. The solace the club men ostensibly receive from their memories is thus always inadequate, resulting in the failure of the imagined journey and the work's melancholic ending. W.J. Keith sees the ending as a statement that "You can't go home again; the pastoral ends conventionally in the contemporary city, after all" (160). But it is an ending more in line with what Leo Marx identifies as a complex pastoral because it

---

5　For insightful critiques of the "heritage industry," see Robert Hewison's book *The Heritage Industry* (1987) and David Lowenthal's *The Heritage Crusade* (1996). For thoughtful defences of heritage activities, see Raphael Samuel's *Theatres of Memory* (1994) and Doreen Massey's *Space, Place, and Gender* (1994).

serves as a complication of childhood longing and the inability of such yearning to provide solace, to root identity in what is believed to be immanent: the stability of identity stemming from early experience. Within the shell of a complex pastoral, Leacock writes in the language of the simpler pastoral, but the final chapter reveals that the text is, in fact, a comment on the longing experienced within the "culture at large." The remembered splendour of the small-town past, what is held up as a model for contemporary urban society, is an inextricable aspect of the vehicle of memory. In this case, the processes of heritage fabricate and project a cultural ideal (located at the other end of the temporal train tracks), one that is then lamented because it can never be (re)accessed or even sufficiently emulated. Mariposa is not the past, but simply one version of a past that can be conjured for those in the present.

The apparent main tension in the book, comic as it is, rests between the contrasted attitudes and customs deemed inherent to the rural and the urban, the past and the present – the classic antitheses. The narrator is largely responsible for this surface structure, and as his narration of Mariposa emanates from the urban present, the dichotomy of country and city forms in retrospect from an urban perspective. However, Leacock's narrator seems unwittingly to provide a glimpse of a pre-pastoral landscape, one further north along those temporal train tracks; the image of the far north displaces Mariposa's originary associations, as it suggests that within the book there exists another temporal-spatial relation in addition to the simple past-present dichotomy of the country and the city. It is difficult to determine whether the narrator is aware of the unsettling effect these northern allusions have on the stability of the existing country-city binary. Lynch characterizes Mariposa as the "typical Canadian town between city and hinterland" (*Stephen Leacock* 57), yet the main tension in the book has long been read as that between the small town and the city. However, with Leacock's allusions to the northern hinterlands, which always rest on the margins of the text, the predominance of the country-city dichotomy dissolves and an alternate subtextual tension between the urban and the hinterland develops. The next section of this chapter attempts to gauge the influence on Mariposa of this third region.

Temporal Landscapes, Temporal Values

Leacock's train journey reveals the malleability of memory and retroactively suggests that the first eleven chapters of the book are really phantoms of urban longing. Within those first eleven chapters, though, Leacock also subtly examines the relationship that exists between the urban and rural spheres. Mariposa may be shaped by urban memory, but, even within that memory, the city's financial and imaginative control over the product of its own wishes is only tentative. Critics, however, have paid little attention to the third region in *Sunshine Sketches*, that which exists behind and beyond the rural-urban dichotomy: the northern hinterland. The importance of this area develops in tandem with the character Josh Smith. During Smith's liquor-licensing battle in Chapter 1, we learn that he is from "the lumber country of the Spanish River, where the divide is toward the Hudson Bay, – 'back north' as they called it in Mariposa" (10). "Back north" is not the phrase of the narrator but of the Mariposans. While "back home" is really the Mariposa of the past for the urbanites, the unending forests and lakes of "back north" represent a past preceding that symbolized by Mariposa. Leo Marx might suggest that Mariposa's appeal is that of the pastoral "middle landscape," a term used to describe the area resting between wild nature and tame civilization. The "middle landscape" incorporates the contrasting values of both spaces (71). In *Sunshine Sketches*, we can view the north as an earlier step on the linear developmental scale inherent to the rural past–urban present dichotomy.

Josh Smith comes from that poorly defined geographic region located somewhere "back north." This phrase implies his movement from the north to the south, but it does not refer exclusively to spatial movement; it also refers to the movement through landscapes that contain temporal associations. In this case, "back north" refers to a landscape that speaks of a different, earlier time than Mariposa: the small town may be the city's past, but the hinterland is the small town's past. The allusions to Smith's place of origin, and the final emergence of the city as the theatre of memory in which Mariposa forms, offer an outline of the real dichotomy operating in the book: that of distant past and urban present, pre-civilized hinterland and conceptual forefront of settlement.[6]

While the urbanites in their club nostalgically idealize their imagined rural heritage, Mariposans do not similarly idealize the step prior

---

6   This is how I see this dichotomy operating in the book: I am well aware that the landscape was populated by Indigenous civilizations prior to the arrival of Europeans.

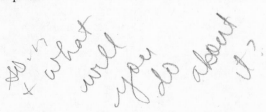

to their golden age. One exception is Judge Pepperleigh's strong suggestion that his daughter Zena read *Pioneers of Tecumseh Township* (93). Mariposa is a construction of the collective memories of those in the club, the consensual "home place" of nostalgic men, and thus there is a corresponding lack of historical interest in the Mariposans, which, as Lowenthal explains, is to be expected: "one thing absent from this [the nostalgic] imagined past is nostalgia – no one then looked back in yearning or for succour" ("Nostalgia" 29). Leacock's subtle inclusion of the northland both undermines the notion that the Mariposa of the past is a static ideal and draws attention to it as a nostalgic reconstruction dependent on a series of negative forces operating within the urban sphere. To the men in the club, Mariposa serves as a fountainhead of individual and cultural identity, yet the hinterland stretching behind and beyond Mariposa, in both a social and historical sense, modifies the club men's veneration of the town, as, in its new context, Mariposa becomes an unacknowledged node on the trajectory of urbanization and industrial development, not its static antithesis or antidote: Mariposa does not exist in opposition to the city but merely as its precursor. The virtual invisibility of this third area accommodates undue attention to the imagined importance of Mariposa-as-origin. The nostalgic reconstruction of Mariposa is a narrative that imagines its own cultural origins as something exceedingly, even fallaciously, innocent; Mariposa might be seen as a pastoral obstruction, as its golden glow conceals its own cultural and social antecedents. Furthermore, while Mariposa constitutes a wish image for the urbanites, Smith reveals the decidedly ambivalent influence they have on Mariposa.

Josh Smith is a character who has received much critical attention. He is one of the few characters who cannot call Mariposa "home," and, consequently, he is viewed as existing somewhat extraneously to life in Mariposa. Some see his influence as inherently selfish and destructive to the ethos of Mariposa (Lynch *Stephen Leacock*), while others come to his defence as a "humane" character (Willmott "Cost" 54) or someone whose influence is, essentially, neutral (MacDonald "Small-Town" 64). Smith does have an impact on the town, but one that does not irrevocably alter or damage the nature of its social makeup. Smith's actions are essentially corrective, as he helps prevent the dissolution of critical social niches by external, harmful influences.

I will venture to call Smith a self-interested humanist, one not above seeking out a dollar, but one not willing to do so to the detriment of others. While his actions disregard the letter of the law – it is unlikely the illiterate Smith could decipher that letter anyway – the system dictating his activities seems improvised, even contradictory, as it incorporates equal parts altruism and self-interest. There are a number of instances in which Smith's actions outline his uncodified system of practice; he seeks to make money, but his other actions counter avarice as his defining feature. For instance, in relation to Thorpe, Smith acts as something of a guardian angel who helps rescue him from financial ruin (34). Lynch suggests that Smith acts as deus ex machina who excises consequence in certain chapters (*Stephen Leacock* 96), but Smith's covert act of charity comes immediately after the description of Thorpe's own planned beneficence (33). Thorpe's plan to use his mining-stock windfall to build a home for "the incurables" germinates from his direct opposition to an urban mode of charity, represented by Carnegie and Rockefeller, who, in Thorpe's words, give to those who "don't want it" (32) – "those" being professors and research institutions as opposed to the poor. Thorpe's conviction about who proper recipients of charity actually are seeks a fiscal balance, a fairer distribution of wealth. His intimations about urban finance may be reflected in his stock-market dabbling, but his naive altruism serves as an example of his inability to thrive in the worldly urban sphere of commerce, an unkind world of experience; Thorpe's ultimate aspiration does not reflect a technologically or economically progressive outlook. Yet his altruism saves Thorpe when Smith seems to reflect back to him his own ethical modus operandi after urban crooks swindle the barber. Smith's subsequent act, masked as a business exchange (34), puts Thorpe's own philanthropic ideals into practice.

Smith also resolves Dean Drone's financial difficulties. In the chapter "The Beacon on the Hill," it is hard to determine what Smith's personal motivations are for setting fire to the Anglican church other than a genuine desire to help a person in desperate financial straits. Smith gains nothing from this act, and rather puts himself and his position in the community at risk, as he becomes an object of interest at the trial investigating the possibility of insurance fraud. He may be the sole benefactor from the failed Whirlwind campaign (Lynch *Stephen Leacock*, 94), but he is also Drone's solution to that failed campaign. Drone's innocence or ignorance of finance positions him as a victim who is completely incapable of independently finding a resolution, something left to the more than capable hands of Smith.

Smith's actions neutralize the detrimental influence of the city by correcting fiscal risks. Urban institutions and characters pose as the real threat, and Smith's interventions restore a financial balance in favour of those townspeople who have been stung by their interaction with the city; many Mariposans receive a type of surreptitious assistance from Smith, whose actions are either out of the public eye or performed at night (in the case of arson, anonymity is essential). These deeds also appear to emanate from Smith's instinctual impulse to assist those who lack the necessary insight or nerve to deal with the offences of modernity, be they actual crimes or bureaucratic disregard. Thorpe is threatened by actual criminals, while Drone is threatened by an unfeeling financial sector whose concern extends only to numerical figures as opposed to individuals.

Smith defuses these urban threats through a value system that appears oppositional to that which extends from the city. The urban influences either disregard individual circumstances through codified and bureaucratic systems or, in the case of Thorpe's defrauding, ignore the individual altogether, since money is the coveted object. Smith's concern for the individual transcends any codified system of response (Smith's hands are never tied by red tape), including the law; the individual, as opposed to a predetermined system, determines his responsive actions. He places capital gain beneath his concern for the individual. An example is that the rooms in his hotel have no set price but go "according to the expression of their [the clients'] faces" (11). Meanwhile, he holds no real allegiances to a particular type or class of clientele: "Anybody was free of the hotel who cared to come in. Anybody who didn't like it could go out" (11). He sees the individual void of trappings of class or status and possesses an instinct for business, but, more importantly, he possesses an instinct for people. This may translate into a sense of the slap-dash within his business practices, not to mention his politics – he goes from being an ardent free-trader to a tariff man in the space of a breath (130). His charitable activities demonstrate that his value system is not always put towards his own self-advancement. Rather than posing as the threat to the organic community of Mariposa, he preserves the organic community by allowing at least two Mariposans to maintain their critical niche within that community, to remain "separate and so different – not a bit like the people in the cities" (28). Smith functions as an improvising saviour who maintains Mariposa as the embodiment of a kinder past.

Smith emerges from the past landscape of the hinterland; he is an anachronism, an illiterate, larger-than-life personality, and a near incarnation of retrospective mythologization. He embodies a distinct contrast to the city within which operates a system that subverts the individual; the city contains the processes of modernity to which Mariposa has not yet been lethally exposed. Smith's actions, conscious or not, maintain the position of individuals within the town while the city eviscerates individuality through prescribed urban niches and production-line employment. Individuals construct Mariposa from the bottom up, while the city subsumes individuals into a top-down social edifice.

For average Mariposans, however, the city is also an attractive, cosmopolitan world they never cease to emulate. The city contains potential, but ultimately ineffectual, solutions for Drone's financial difficulties, as "[u]p from the city" come the costumes for the Girls' Auxilliary bazaar (64), the magic lantern for Drone's lecture on "Italy and her Invaders" (64), as well as the conceptual basis for the failed Whirlwind campaign (Chapter 5). The city possesses various sophisticated necessities, such as the brass beds Smith installs in his hotel (11), as well as the architect who designs the "caff" (15). It also represents for the Mariposans the site of erudition and culture, sometimes valued, as in the case of Smith's "caff," but sometimes scorned, as in the case of Pupkin's suspected poetic rival in love: "It was one of those regular poets with a solemn jackass face, and lank parted hair and eyes like puddles of molasses. I don't know how he came there – up from the city, probably" (104–5). One person's dazzling wordsmith is another's semi-talented, pretentious poseur; Pupkin's scrutiny of the poet reflects the other side of Mariposans' notions of the city as the site of corruption and inauthenticity.

Smith is distinctly aware of Mariposans' ambivalence towards the city, which he exploits to make money. His "caff" is "like what they have in the city – a ladies' and gents' caff" (15). Smith can distil the essence of the city and transfer it into the caff, turning it into a temporary urban or cosmopolitan ideal;[7] the caff is symbiotic, as from it Mariposans receive a great deal of sensual pleasure, while Smith's attachment to it rests on potential material benefit. He displays an equally dexterous ability at distilling the essence of the countryside for those in the city, from which many holiday visitors seek out Mariposa's fresh air and lake. These are the visitors to whom Smith appeals when

---

7 Lynch wittily comments that "Mariposans fall down, figuratively, before this gilded 'caff,'" which Smith has "shaped" from the Mariposans' "golden dreams of city life" (*Stephen Leacock* 70).

he advertises his hotel and caff as a "Summer Pavilion advertised in the city as Smith's Tourists' Emporium, and Smith's Northern Health Resort" (15); the campaign, needless to say, is immensely successful, and the urban tourists soon arrive "with fishing rods and landing nets pouring in on every train, almost too fast to register" (15).

The hotel is a shape-shifter: for those in the country, it typifies what can be found in the city, while for the urbanites it possesses the attributes and benefits of a country lifestyle. Smith is able to abstract urban and rural quintessence to satisfy the expectation of an ideal. As Smith's origins lie outside of this perceived rural-urban dichotomy, he is able to manipulate self-consciously the various affective idealizations at play within what becomes, with the presence of Smith, the surface dichotomy of small town and urban centre. The hotel's remodelling in order to serve rural and urban desires becomes a commentary on the hollowness of that dichotomy, as here a single site serves distinct, even oppositional, purposes. Similarly, the final chapter displays the urban club men's capacity to remodel the town, even if theirs is through retrospect; the first eleven chapters are the sum total of their memories. It is only the Mariposans who lack the voice with which to render their town. Smith's manipulation of the town's affect is thus a temporary intratextual displacement of the urban pole's power of representation over Mariposa within the very text decided by the urbanites. Through its various incarnations, Mariposa becomes a site of contention. This struggle for influence occurs through the contest for the town's sentiment, as both poles of the real dichotomy of hinterland and urban sphere manipulate this malleable space, offering to Smith a material benefit, while offering metaphysical consolation to the urban dreamer.

Judge Pepperleigh's court is another site that highlights Mariposa's liminal position, its status as a place influenced by the contrasting values of both Smith and the city. It is where the forms of the city, jurisprudence, the subversion of the individual to process, and the sequence of objective legal proceedings (or at least the appearance of such) meet the values of Smith, the transcendence of individuals over a system, and instinctual morality restoring financial balance/equilibrium. The mixture of influences comes through in Pepperleigh's decision against the insurance company that, rightfully so, has cried foul over the fire that burns the "Church of England Church" to the ground:

Protest from the insurance people? Legal proceedings to prevent payment? My dear sir! I see you know nothing about the Mariposa court, in spite of the fact that I have already said that it was one of the most precise instruments of British fair play ever established. Why, Judge Pepperleigh disposed of the case and dismissed the protest of the company in less than fifteen minutes! Just what the jurisdiction of Judge Pepperleigh's court is I don't know, but I do know that in upholding the rights of a Christian congregation – I am quoting here the text of the decision – against the intrigues of a set of infernal skunks that make too much money, anyway, the Mariposa court is without an equal. Pepperleigh even threatened the plaintiffs with the penitentiary, or worse. (81)

The goal of Smith's act of arson is to assist the naive Dean Drone in overcoming his financial burden. The ends of Pepperleigh's decision are to protect Smith from legal retribution and to ensure that the abundant insurance funds find their way into the hands of Drone. Smith's influence as financial leveller is legitimated by Pepperleigh's decision, as his court is one of morality, although not necessarily legality. Under the guise of jurisprudence, a formal aspect of Mariposa's intimations towards urbanity, Pepperleigh gives a decision that is explicitly opposed to the tenets of jurisprudence and is based on the affective content of the hinterland influence.

In urban club and in Mariposa, the past – or, more correctly, the imagined past – serves as the corrective balm for present injustice and/or malaise. However, just as the urbanite cannot re-enter the gates of Mariposa in the final chapter of the book, so too is the Mariposan barred from those trains heading north into the mining country at the book's opening:

> It is true that the trains mostly go through at night and don't stop. But in the wakeful silence of the summer night you may hear the long whistle of the through train ... Or, better still, on a winter evening about eight o'clock you will see the long row of the Pullmans and diners of the night express going north to the mining country, the windows flashing with brilliant light, and within them a vista of cut glass and snow-white table linen. (4)

Although these trains head into the north country, they are an object of the cosmopolitan world, and it is not the past that the Mariposan desires, but rather the promise of urban refinement represented by the trains. Yet, in the trains there exists an idealized representation of urban wealth analogous to the idealization of small-town life projected through urban memories of Mariposa. Both representations are from the perspective of an outsider who can perceive that other world only from a distance: a mutual longing maintained only because of distance. This instance of Mariposans' yearning is another narrative window similar to those revealing the emotional depth of the town's inhabitants, and it suggests that the ironic veneer the narrator constructs around Mariposa does not match the reality to which the text only alludes: a type of longing, yearning, or dissatisfaction is indeed present in Mariposa, a town that, by all other accounts, is completely self-satisfied. This is perhaps a rare image of Mariposa that does not emanate from the urban club but is an image of small-town ennui contemporaneous with its urban counterpart.

This image offers a rare occurrence in which the worlds of the club dweller and the Mariposan come into contact. That person staring longingly into the train windows from the railway siding is excluded from the cosmopolitan world, just as the auditor staring out the train window is barred from that final image of Mariposa; each desires but is prohibited from the world of the other, and the space that lies between this visual contact is the distance that allows for both the idealization and the protraction of perceived difference. Yet, as the eyes of the Mariposan and club dweller meet through the transparent barrier of the pane of glass, this image offers a perfect metaphor for the relationship of these two spaces; the train continues north into that ignored third, but no less essential, landscape, as the two players involved in this age-old division long for, but are barred from, the imagined world of the other. Yet the mutual exclusivity of these two spaces presents a false representation of their real interaction, since it disregards the urban pole's control over the nature of rural representation and the suggested growing urban economic influence over the small town and hinterland.

Both city- and country-dweller are prohibited from those landscapes that, to them, embody better ways of life. These prohibitions indicate that these spaces do not and did not exist in time and/or space as they do in either memory or imagination. The train trip taken in the final chapter is illusory, as the train itself serves as a type of fantasy time machine; apart from those previously discussed windows in the narration, Mariposa is seldom represented in the present, as indeed it exists mainly in memory, in a reconstructed pastoral middle landscape. However, the edges of that pastoral reconstruction are frayed by the creeping influence of a distant, urban modernity that Smith temporarily deflects before he makes his own journey to the city as a member of

Parliament. In Mariposa itself, the trains heading north are not entering the past from which Smith emerged but an altered landscape that is now connected to the main sphere of commerce in the city because of its potential for economic development. Smith's hinterland no longer exists as the north-country frontier of the distant past but has become mainly a resource supplier for modern industry and part of the domain of the wealthy urban capitalist. On the very fringes of the text, this exploitative relationship dissolves the real dichotomy of hinterland and urban sphere into a synthesis of vast material gain transferred along that mainline north–south railroad. Those trains, luckily, ignore the Mariposa of the text, but because that Mariposa is a retrospective construction, we might conclude that within the hidden Mariposa of the actual present, its bypass no longer offers safe harbour. Its main contribution now is to offer the wealthy capitalist an image of his idealized origins.

Within Mariposa, Smith offers a humorous parallel to one of the book's main themes: the imagined past as a touchstone against which contemporary errors and crimes are measured. This relationship of the valued past to the degraded present is explicit in the last chapter and incorporates only the recent past of Mariposa and the urban present. Yet the distant past of the hinterland north expresses a largely hidden, but no less corrective, influence through Josh Smith. Unlike Smith's effective efforts at restoring some "equilibrium" to the town, the image of Mariposa dissipates before the very eyes of the auditor, suggesting that the ability of Mariposa's compensatory representation to establish a moral balance in the city has become compromised in the age of increasing wealth disparity and inequality rooted in the city.

Smith actively mitigates the negative influence of the urban sphere and temporarily preserves Mariposa as its moral and experiential counterpart within the very text the urban men have constructed through memory. The duplicity of the urban influence on places like Mariposa is best represented through the character Pupkin Sr, who simultaneously longs for yet despoils the landscape in which he wants to recognize an idyll. The narrator's portrait of Pupkin Sr incorporates biting irony:

His own longing – and his wife shared it – was for the simple, simple life ... Pupkin senior often said that he wanted to have someplace that would remind him of the little old farm up the Aroostook where he was brought up. He often bought little old farms, just to try them, but they always turned out to be so near a city that he cut them into real estate lots, without even having had time to look at them. (102)

Pupkin Sr's experiences suggest that rural nostalgia can both justify and conceal the real impact of the city's influence on the country. Paradoxically, his memory is the impetus for the disintegration of the wish image that stems from his childhood. Urban memory in this case seeks out the comfort believed available in scenes from the rural past, yet his commercial interests always trump his desire for peace and serenity. This short passage encapsulates the marginal theme of urban–small town economic relations in this text; while urban nostalgics pay lip-service to the non-urban values and landscapes located outside of the city, this fondness crumbles in the face of fiscal concerns.

Interestingly, both Smith and Pupkin are outsiders to Mariposa, yet their contrasting influence illuminates the real dichotomy in which hinterland and city grapple over Mariposa's financial control but also – and more importantly for Mariposa's characteristic ethos – its offered peaceful, simple life. Pupkin Sr is a character lifted straight off of Plutoria Avenue from *Arcadian Adventures*. He is the true capitalist whose economic activity drains the small town of its vitality because of the availability of jobs in his, or someone else's, burgeoning factories. He is oblivious to his real impact on places like Mariposa. In spite of its humour, the text hints at the dangers to the town stemming from the dominant urban economy, the more egregious transgressions of which Smith effectively counters. Characters like Pupkin Sr dominate Leacock's subsequent text, yet a countervailing influence equivalent to Smith is absent. If viewed on a continuum with the earlier text, *Arcadian Adventures* contains a much darker, far more cynical summation of an unchecked urban plutocracy, an influence that within the imaginative borders of Mariposa is effectively, if only temporarily, stalled.

Chapter Two

Saying Goodbye to Mariposa: Rebutting the Small-Town Convention

Stephen Leacock's rendering of Mariposa as a typical Canadian small town offers readers an attractive, imaginary, even fantastic ideal of a "home place" whose iconic status and broad recognition is unmatched in Canadian literature. *Sunshine Sketches* has become paradigmatic of a *type* of small-town fiction with which many subsequent texts are in conversation. Specifically, the aspect of the book most resonant in the literature that follows it is the theme of *return*.[1] Many Ontario small-town texts of the past century re-imagine the final chapter of Leacock's work. Yet, where Leacock's imagined return is truncated, these later authors follow through to explore how notions and visions of the small-town childhood home alter when one is allowed access into this past space.

That Ontario authors return to the themes examined in Leacock's work should come as no surprise, yet the ways in which these authors explore these themes in subsequent texts are as diverse as the texts themselves. For instance, the protagonist of Raymond Knister's *White Narcissus* (1929), Richard Milne, revisits his hometown in his temporal present. Knister, himself from a small rural community in southwestern Ontario, had his work published seventeen years after Leacock's, yet Knister's novel literally begins where Leacock's ends. Unlike Leacock's urban travellers, Knister's urban figure is allowed to step off the train into the rural community of his upbringing. Time has changed this community as much as it has left its mark on Milne. He initially finds the village of his birth "foreign" (7) and characterizes it as "torpid" (8);

---

1 For discussions of the role of "return" in Canadian literature, see W.H. New's *Land Sliding* and Gerald Lynch's *The One and the Many*.

this town bears nothing of the exuberance and comfort that ostensibly await the returnee to Mariposa. Milne has come home for a very specific purpose, which is not to relive cheering nostalgic memories, but to convince his childhood love to accompany him back to the city, a type of strategic rescue operation to deliver his loved one from the privations of small-town life to the sanctuary of urban living. The return home is a reluctant but successful one.

Northrop Frye has disparagingly characterized Knister's style as "provincial." The deliberately "heightened" tone of the novel tells Frye that Knister is "a writer who thinks of the highest standards of his craft as being already established outside his community … and as having to be met by very deliberate efforts" ("Culture" 185). That narrative style aligns with the themes of the story as well; a successful urban writer returns to the rural community of his youth and encounters a wicked pettiness among its inhabitants, as if the insularity of the community itself has turned malignant. The successful urban writer stays only long enough to rescue his sweetheart from the clutches of her maddeningly perverse parents, and the book ends just before the two hightail it back to the city to live, it is assumed, with reasonable, erudite sophisticates. The rural area has changed in Milne's absence, and not for the better. The city offers refuge in this instance, which is an inversion of the failed pastoral movement away from the city into the country sketched at the end of Leacock's text.

Knister's novel possesses an ambivalent reputation among Canadian critics. The heightened style is a method of deliberate distancing between the narrator, whose perspective never veers far from Milne's, and the small-town setting, a distance on full display in the juxtaposition between the narrative prose and the dialogue: the one erudite while the other a caricature of rusticity. Implicit in this style is an element, however small, of reflexive, almost immature, condescension to one's unsophisticated rural origins; the same attitude is most likely prevalent in university dorms across the country. The narrator seems infatuated with the urban standard with which he now appraises the rural community. Knister's book is not without its loving descriptions of rural landscape, nor void of a hearty respect for the people who work the soil, but, as Frye suggests, the "deliberateness" of his diction constructs a protracted, artificial distance between the returned small-town boy and the small town itself, a distance that, when examined closely, is perhaps not as great as the boy would like it to be. If Mariposa is the idyll for Leacock's club men, formed in their minds from long years away from home, Knister's rural community approaches the anti-idyll, as it is written by one whose departure occurred only too recently and whose attachment to the place has not yet faded.

Another of the texts in which Leacock's influence can be gauged is George Elliott's *The Kissing Man* (1962), a collection of interrelated stories set in a single small town. Yet, apart from a number of superficial influences (the single setting, the cycle of interrelated stories), the way both texts portray the past, specifically how the past and the present interdepend, is vastly different from each other. Leacock explores how memory shapes notions of origin and identity as seen in the symbolically rich Mariposa; he sees the present as shaping the past. Elliott, on the other hand, explores the reverberations of myth and ritual within those same maple-shaded streets; the past, here, shapes the present. Elliott reveals his affinity to the concerns of the modern primitivists with his book's epigraph from T.S. Eliot's *Notes towards the Definition of Culture*: "But when I speak of the family, I have in mind a bond which embraces ... a piety towards the dead, however obscure, and a solicitude for the unborn, however remote." This epigraph immediately places the book within a lineage that is less concerned with exploring the echoes of the past of place than it is in examining the mythic echoes of a fluid, "universal" heritage that carries on within the unconscious of the collective. Elliott's work is not so much an exploration of small-town Ontario as it is a belated work of modern primitivism that explores the rhythms of ritual that exist, according to those who adhere to such theories, within all cultural forms. Elliott does not necessarily see small-town Ontario as a "home place"; rather, he sees within small-town Ontario the cultural echoes extending from the mists of time. Return, in this case, is not something necessarily physical or geographical: it is an unconscious movement towards the ingrained patterns that are hardwired in cultural expressions (or so the thinking goes).

Robertson Davies's Deptford Trilogy also explores the same thematic ground covered by Leacock. Davies's *Fifth Business* (1970), the first of the trilogy, is a return story that follows a former small-town resident who, like Richard Milne but unlike Leacock's club men, is able to revisit his place of origins.[2] Rather than depicting a small-town exile either

---

2 Writing in the guise of Samuel Marchbanks, Davies comments on his own return to his hometown, Thamesville: "I found this Sentimental Journey quite exhausting, and returned to London in the shaky condition of a man who has had a good long look at his past" (*Marchbanks' Almanack* 39 qtd. in Peterman 2).

longing for or chastising his place of birth, Davies explores the subtle process whereby these polarized responses take shape. He does more than invert Leacock's themes, as Knister does; Davies seeks a type of balance between the idyll and the anti-idyll through a mode of perception that declares its own awareness of small-town conventions and its insistence on its own descriptive and memorial accuracy. His novel reveals a process of rejecting not only Mariposa's influence but also that mode of memory that produces Mariposa's golden glow or perceives its opposite: the idyll and the anti-idyll. Through his distinctly ambivalent memories of Deptford, Dunstan Ramsay, Davies's narrator, explores the nostalgic small-town archetype for which Mariposa serves as a template, and his final departure from the small town constitutes an allegorical exodus from Mariposa's aesthetic and cultural influence, something that reverberated, and reverberates still, through much of small-town Ontario literature.[3] If Davies has stated that *Sunshine Sketches* is "one of the finest, if not the finest, book ever written about Canadian life" (*Papers* 65), this chapter examines what Mariposa's influence might be in Davies's own stories of small-town Ontario.

Deptford, meet Mariposa

Second only to Mariposa in terms of its significance to small-town Ontario's literary reputation is Davies's Deptford, a town that appears in his Deptford Trilogy. Davies was a Leacock scholar who produced a short biography and study of his works in *Feast of Stephen*.[4] The cover of that volume more than hints at an affinity between these prominent men of letters, giving equal standing to both names. The illustration

---

3 It should be clear that this chapter will not consider Mariposa as a Jungian or Frygean "archetype." In *A Smaller Infinity: The Jungian Self in the Novels of Robertson Davies*, Patricia Monk offers a thorough exploration of Davies's work in the context of Jung's influence. If Mariposa is a manifestation of an unconscious pattern or deep cultural symbol, it is not my goal to discuss it as such. Rather, Mariposa is an archetype in a culturally conscious (or for the Canadian context, a culturally self-conscious) sense, in that it constitutes a prototype for subsequent literary renditions of small-town Ontario; some suggest that Mariposa has a permanent status as intertext, intended or not (see Lynch's discussion of Alice Munro's *Who Do You Think You Are?* in *The One and the Many* 182–5).

4 Its long introduction was previously published as simply *Stephen Leacock*, part of McClelland and Stewart's New Canadian Library series.

by Graham Pilsworth is an ink drawing of both men shaking hands, with Davies staring out at the reader as if the current comic laureate is re-introducing us to the previous one.

Fifth Business, the first novel of the Deptford Trilogy, appeared in 1970, fifty-eight years after *Sunshine Sketches*. At that point, Davies was considered to be past his prime: his previous series of novels had been written in the 1950s, and he had, during the 1960s, settled into a busy life as master of Massey College at the University of Toronto. *Fifth Business* re-launched his writing career. This phase, which begins with *Fifth Business* and includes the remaining Deptford novels, also includes the Blairlogie trilogy, a series of novels set partly in a town based on Renfrew, Ontario. This phase culminated in both Booker and Nobel award buzz in 1986. Both Leacock and Davies were, in their own times, sought after literary and cultural authorities, and, importantly, their most significant works are not only set in small-town Ontario, but have helped establish that setting as a type of Canadian literary trope.

The Deptford Trilogy is not the first series of books Davies wrote that is set in an Ontario community. While the Deptford Trilogy appeared in the 1970s, his Salterton Trilogy appeared roughly twenty years before. In the latter, Davies is content to present amusing stories of the foibles of the citizens of Salterton, a university town closely modelled on Kingston, Ontario, a place where Davies spent a good part of his youth and early adulthood. Popular targets of his satire include pompous academics, overbearing mothers, and indecisive, bookish young men. Salterton is a large, urbane community set in the present in which it was written and home to a diverse cast of international, cosmopolitan characters. It seems, unlike Mariposa, to be very much caught up in the events of the larger outside world.

A resemblance to Mariposa is far more apparent in Deptford. The narrative premise of *Fifth Business* is, not surprisingly, similar to *Sunshine Sketches*. As the bases for their works, both Leacock and Davies were recalling past small-town experience from the very centres of elite urban academies: McGill University in Montreal and Massey College at the University of Toronto, respectively. Yet rather than nostalgically romanticize past experience, both authors draw attention to the process of memory, and how that process can embellish and idealize the distant long-ago.

At least a superficial link between the towns can be found in their similar temporal settings. While our first view of Deptford is prior to the First World War, Davies also depicts the town after the war. In the process, he reveals changes relating to postwar modernization, influences that do not affect Mariposa. Thus, unlike Mariposa, Deptford is not a static ideal, as the town is subject to external forces and influences. Nonetheless, Clara Thomas points out further similarities: "it [*Fifth Business*] is set in Southern Ontario and its total tone and makeup is specific to the past of this country, at a time when such towns played a keystone part in the country's development" ("The Town" 221). What Thomas means by the "total tone and makeup" of the novel may be clarified by W.J. Keith's comments on the "detached perspective" of Leacock's and Davies's narrators: "They have widened their own horizons and look *back* at the town in question with affection or amused irony or occasionally with disgust, but certainly from outside" (167). However, we must not confuse *looking back* with *looking at*, as the two modes of perception have very different consequences.

As the melancholic last chapter of *Sunshine Sketches* implies, the text's tone is influenced by, and also alludes to, the diminishing importance of the small town in early twentieth-century Ontario; as the final image of Mariposa fades, the club men and reader come to realize that the town may have been no more than a mirage of reminiscence. The early part of the twentieth century in Ontario was a period of general emigration from the small towns to the increasingly industrialized cities; with the decline of the countryside came the clearer definition and increased appeal of "rural values," a trend on which Leacock both capitalizes and comments. Thomas appears to commit the same error as other critics of Leacock's work: that is, to confuse the light-hearted, ironic, jovial tone of the book with an accurate distillation of the spirit of the age, one thought to be defined by the vitality of organic communities as opposed to their decline and desertion. It is a further error to read Deptford as an homage to the popular conception of that age and to its literary predecessor, as profound tension exists between Deptford and Davies's protagonists, all of whom experience acute anxiety as a result of the identity and moral confines the village erects around individuals.

The willingness to read similarities between *Sunshine Sketches* and *Fifth Business* glosses over some important differences. The most prominent features of Leacock's text are his sensitive character portrayals and the unanimity and collectivity of those characters, all of which contribute to a tone that oscillates between hilarity and sentimentality. Early critiques of Davies's *Fifth Business*, on the other hand, concentrate on the characters' "moral imperatives" (Reid 179) and Deptford's "practical common sense and … solid reliance on material, down-to-earth reality" (Bjerring qtd. in Lennox 24). Deptfordian sobriety provides a sharp contrast to the well-oiled exuberance of the Mariposans.

A more fruitful avenue of comparison is through one of the books' other similarities: their shared narrative premise. While the final chapter of *Sunshine Sketches* reveals that Mariposa exists only in the collective memories of melancholic urbanites, each of the Deptford novels consists of the reminiscences of successful men who spend their formative years in small-town Ontario: the narrative of *Fifth Business* consists of a letter Dunstan Ramsay has written to his former headmaster at Colborne College; *The Manticore* is made up largely of the writings and reminiscences of David Staunton while undergoing Jungian psychoanalysis; finally, *World of Wonders*, while narrated by Dunstan, is dominated by the voice of Magnus Eisengrim (Paul Dempster), a childhood resident of Deptford who was kidnapped by carnies. Mariposa and Deptford are products of memory, but a far more complicated relationship between retrospect and longing runs throughout Davies's novels. If nostalgia is largely responsible for Mariposa's allure, its alternating absence/presence in the Deptford novels marks an important difference between the two towns: the varying renditions of Deptford reveal more about the development of the reminiscing subjects and that development's influence on their "process of perception" as opposed to the reminisced object.

Patricia Monk states that a central concern of Davies's "*telos*" is "an understanding of the nature of human identity" (*Smaller Infinity* 17). She later states that one of Dunstan Ramsay's central struggles is "towards self-knowledge and individuation" (83). This process is often situated in terms of escape from the physical and moral restrictions of Deptford. Monk identifies the Jungian process of "individuation," or the development of the autonomous self, as a recurring theme in Davies's novels, and argues in *The Smaller Infinity* that this process in *Fifth Business* occurs largely through Dunstan's evolving "religious belief" (79). In this chapter, I read the effect of that process of individuation on the evolving nature of his childhood memories of Deptford. While an analysis of Mariposa reveals that town to be an inaccessible, retrospective ideal, an analysis of Dunstan's relationship to Deptford reveals the town to be the product of a developing, reminiscing subject. In *Sunshine Sketches*, the general trend is towards a return; Mariposa offers both the reader and the club men of the final chapter a passive, static, and contained small-town ideal situated in a generalized recent past. Deptford's influence, however, proves far more persistent, as it has an active role in the psyches of its residents.

While Deptford represents only a limited place along his trajectory of esoteric achievement in the field of hagiography, Dunstan's psychic escape from that village is never quite successful, and he must synthesize his current individuated self with the undesired, collective values of Deptford, what are really presented as the physical, spiritual, and moral confines placed on the individual and enforced by the village collective. Dunstan's struggle to negotiate the residue of his childhood results in shifting retrospective visions of the town, which, in effect, serve as alternating foils to best highlight the present state of his psychic individuation. As these versions construct a process of small-town escape, they can be read as Davies's own symbolic attempt at escaping from the cultural archetype epitomized by Mariposa. If Leacock's town is read as a "home place" of Canadian fiction and cultural identity, then *Fifth Business* draws attention to the mode of memory responsible for that type of exegesis and can be read as an allegorical leave-taking of Mariposa's cultural and literary hegemony. If Mariposa is the past perfect, Deptford is the past progressive.

Dunstan Ramsay's Deptford

The overarching concern of the narrator of *Fifth Business*, Dunstan Ramsay, is to represent both himself and his hometown accurately. In the opening section of the novel, Dunstan addresses a central problem of autobiographical writing: "Can I write truly of my boyhood? Or will that disgusting self-love which so often attaches itself to a man's idea of his youth creep in and falsify the story? I can but try. And to begin I must give you some notion of the village in which Percy Boyd Staunton and Paul Dempster and I were born" (15). With this attempt at disregarding childhood nostalgia, Dunstan declares that happy childhood memories often emerge during the intervening years between youth and adulthood, a temporal span that can allow the past to become, in one's imagination, both benevolent and stable. While the final train journey back through time and space in *Sunshine Sketches* suggests that this interim is responsible for the nature of Mariposa's representation, Dunstan wants to avoid the trap of idealization; his narrative may be a retrospective, but he wants it to be one unfiltered through this common method of stylization.

By further prefacing his description of Deptford with the following remark, Dunstan reveals his awareness of small-town life as a popular theme already thoroughly explored in literature and other cultural media:

> Once it was the fashion to represent villages as places inhabited by laughable, lovable simpletons, unspotted by the worldliness of city life, though occasionally shrewd in rural concerns. Later it was the popular thing to show villages as rotten with vice, and especially such sexual vice as Krafft-Ebing might have been surprised to uncover in Vienna; incest, sodomy, bestiality, sadism, and masochism ... Our village never seemed to me to be like that. It was more varied in what it offered to the observer than people from bigger and more sophisticated places generally think, and if it had sins and follies and roughnesses, it also had much to show of virtue, dignity, and even of nobility. (15–16)

While this passage contains Dunstan's thoughts on small-town conventions, thoughts that indirectly reference Leacock's dominance of the sunnier of the two conventions, it echoes Davies's own thoughts on small-town writing, which he expresses in *Feast of Stephen*, a book on Leacock and his writings. There Davies writes:

> Descriptions of small-town life have become commonplace, especially in the literature of this continent. In Leacock's day they tended, with a handful of notable exceptions, to look on the sunny side of village and rural life and to accept the widely-held view that small-town people were kindlier, less corrupt, and more chaste than dwellers in great cities. Since then, of course, a school has arisen which portrays small towns, very profitably, as microcosms of Sodom and Gomorrah in which everybody but a handful of just men and women are deep in corruption, especially of the sexual order. (14–15)

In *Fifth Business*, Dunstan's thoughts directly mirror those expressed by Davies himself. An obvious overlap between author and protagonist exists, at least in their shared awareness of a popular literary trope. Dunstan acknowledges the existence of small-town representational conventions, and thus attempts to situate his own portrayal beyond them by writing of the small town in a way that transcends the conventions. He is aware of the idyllic convention dominated by Leacock and the subsequent anti-idyll that arose after Leacock's time. In this chapter, I suggest that this idyllic/anti-idyllic frame has been formulated by Davies through Dunstan in order to transcend that frame in his small-town narrative; in the process, however, Dunstan reveals how alluring that idyllic mode can be when crafting a rural, small-town retrospective.

Dunstan Ramsay asserts a narrative voice that purports to provide an unconventional – in that it claims not to rely on convention – look at the past of small-town life by first identifying and then disregarding trends and fashions. Through Dunstan, Davies acknowledges the existence of small-town representational types, and thus attempts to situate his own portrayal beyond them. He speaks of small-town life with one eye on what has been said before. Furthermore, if the small-town type is popularly associated with this country's cultural foundations,[5] then particular versions sketch an author's nostalgic, critical, or condemnatory cultural perspective. Dunstan suggests that his narrative possesses no ulterior agenda other than to represent accurately his small-town childhood.

Dunstan's and Davies's discussions of small-town representational conventions also sketch a "problem of perspective"[6] that perhaps rests at the core of familiar small-town portrayals. The small-town convention that makes use of "laughable and lovable simpletons" is a veiled reference to Mariposa, and as the final chapter of Leacock's text reveals, the creative source for Mariposa is the urban club. Stylized versions are the creations of, and products for, those from "bigger and more sophisticated places." Dunstan maintains that these literary conventions are really generalizations produced by those with insufficient knowledge of small-town life, or by those whose distant perspective, across time and space, allows them to think they see what they want to see. This

---

5 This notion is particularly apparent in discussions of both *Sunshine Sketches* and *Fifth Business*. For Leacock's text, see Douglas Mantz and Gerald Lynch (*Stephen Leacock; The One*). For Davies's text, see Patricia Monk (*Mud*) and Barbara Godard ("World").

6 Raymond Williams uses this phrase to refer to the common practice of associating a receding rural past with disappearing traditions and the "timeless rhythms" of an agricultural past: "Is it anything more than a well-known habit of using the past, the 'good old days,' as a stick to beat the present? It is clearly something of that, but there are still difficulties. The apparent resting places, the successive Old Englands to which we are confidently referred but which then start to move and recede, have some actual significance, when they are looked at in their own terms" (12).

problem of spatio-temporal distance is also something Dunstan ironically draws attention to when he discusses the smaller village located near Deptford: "We did … look with pitying amusement on Bowles Corners, four miles distant and with a population of one hundred and fifty. To live in Bowles Corners, we felt, was to be rustic beyond redemption" (18). By ironically drawing an analogy to Deptford's own tendency to patronize smaller, distant locales, Dunstan claims to be aware of, and to have transcended, distance's simplifying effect, a claim supporting his own representational and rhetorical reliability. His initial claim is that Deptford is a village depicted by a village voice, one that provides a contrast to Mariposa's consolatory or "fashionable" social aesthetics. However, Dunstan's initial proposed mimesis of Deptford life is one he cannot maintain, as Deptford's representational in/stability relies on his self-identification with the village; that "problem of perspective" responsible for the creation of conventional representation comes to influence Dunstan's descriptions of town life as he begins to identify with those "bigger and more sophisticated places." This phenomenon is particularly striking during Dunstan's return to Deptford after the war.

The novel opens with an early-winter scene involving two boys sledding in the late afternoon in the days immediately following Christmas. Despite initial appearances, which resemble a type of Krieghoff-ian idealization, Dunstan refuses to infuse the scene with a warm retrospective glow; he is recounting not a happy memory, but an incident that comes to define the remainder of his life:

> My lifelong involvement with Mrs. Dempster began at 5:58 o'clock p.m. on the 27th of December, 1908, at which time I was ten years and seven months old.
>
> I am able to date the occasion with complete certainty because that afternoon I had been sledding with my lifelong friend and enemy Percy Boyd Staunton, and we had quarreled, because his fine new Christmas sled would not go as fast as my old one. (9)

The details of time and place reveal the magnitude the event takes in Dunstan's later consciousness, but these details, applied to what might otherwise be an idyllic memory, lend the scene an atmosphere of parodic gravity; how could such an apparently innocent scene be subject to this type of narrative treatment? The minutiae imply that this is no nostalgic memory: its precision reveals that Dunstan's grasp on his own past is as vivid as his present perception. The exact detail of time and place negates any sense of temporal distance separating the narrator from the events, a marked difference from the generalized nature of *Sunshine Sketches'* opening. Leacock's opening constructs a sense of ambiguity around the town's placement in time, and that ambiguity accommodates Mariposa's broad appeal, as particular regional or temporal details can be glossed over. The specificity of Dunstan's narrative, as he recounts particular events from over sixty years previous, focuses on the individualized nature of his experiences, highlighting their singularity in both time and place. Readers are not invited to identify with this initial description of village life in the same way they are encouraged to see their own past in Mariposa.

Dunstan intends to capture the distinctiveness of life in Deptford; this is a story about individuals, he makes us believe, not about character types. Davies seems to want to right a wrong by providing a view of village life based on verisimilitude, a view that is both interesting and mundane, as opposed to one based on an agenda. Dunstan sketches town life through unadorned details: one private banker, two doctors, a dentist with an unhappy domestic life, and a veterinarian "who drank" (16). The private life of the village is a little more colourful. For instance, Dunstan's story of the old Athelstan woman, "who used from time to time to escape from her nurse-housekeeper and rush into the road, where she threw herself down, raising a cloud of dust like a hen having a dirt-bath, shouting loudly, 'Christian men, come and help me!'" (16), is both pathetic and absurdly funny.[7] These details allude to a darker side of village life, a side that reveals (even revels in) unmentionable psychological aberrations tinged with prohibited erotic desire; here, Davies refuses to mitigate private eccentricities that Leacock either excludes or turns into an element of his comedy or sentimentality (e.g., Judge Pepperleigh's brusque approach to his wife, in Chapter 7). The Athelstan woman's behaviour and the exclusion of the First Nation soldier from the town's war commemoration (88) seem to be part of Davies's agenda in *Fifth Business*, which incorporates the bad and the ugly with the good. What is more important than the contents of Dunstan's narrative is how he conceives of and constructs it – the impression of it as "record" as opposed to memory.

---

7 Judith Skelton Grant tells us this story is based on events from Davies's own boyhood experiences in Thamesville, Ontario (11).

Deptford's Dunstan Ramsay

Although Dunstan's narrative initially claims Deptford's inimitability, the town itself does not accommodate individuality. Dunstan attributes Deptford's often narrow and intolerant perspective to the influence of the village's settlers: "[W]e were all too much the descendants of hard-bitten pioneers" (23–4). This offering explains Deptford's lack of an aesthetic sensibility, but it also helps explain the town's pious exclusion of those not involved in the same dominant improving-by-cultivation philosophy of which practicality, self-denial, and moral orthodoxy are inherited traits. The perceived strength of character derived from this pioneer lineage constitutes one side of a Janus-faced philosophical heritage, the other reflecting a restrictive morality and literal mindedness. Dunstan diagnoses this lineage long after he has both felt and escaped its imperatives, yet his narrative reveals to what extent the village's moral heritage played a chafing but determining role in the making of his identity prior to his initial departure.

This small-town moral norm marks the core difference between the nature of Mariposa's ethos and that of Deptford. Mariposa's moral lenience reflects the source of the town's construction, the urban sphere. The retrospective image of the town seems to offer leisure opportunities to the wealthy urban dweller, much like the fishing and hunting camps of the north or a steamship voyage to Europe. Mariposa is the fantasy of childhood, perhaps conjured to sooth temporarily some metaphysical ache or feeling of urban alienation, but it also contributes to the diversity of experience available to the urban plutocrat, although this experience is accessed not through money but a nostalgic memory. The small-town fantasy in *Sunshine Sketches* is an experience not of any specific past, but of an agglomerated cultural childhood, and it is the product of the collective memories of the wealthy deep in the heart of the city. As it is the product of leisure time, those idle hours spent at the club, it offers other possible existences in which complex moral confrontations and alienation cannot exist. Mariposa offers a fantasy in which identity exists in perfect harmony with place, a fantasy that is projected onto the past and subsequently becomes an exuberant and glossy, but finally impossible, historical model for the present. The indeterminacy of Mariposa's eventual melancholic dissolution into ephemeral fantasy can be interpreted as Leacock's refusal to allow the leisure class its desired simulation of a childhood idyll. This may be read as a manifestation of Leacock's well-known dislike for that class's profligacy, a dislike on fuller display in his subsequent *Arcadian Adventures with the Idle Rich.*

While Deptford is similarly reconstructed through memory, its main ontological thrust is towards the closing off of experiential possibility. It is a product of neither recreation nor yearning; instead, the source of the village's ethos is a circumscribing past, an overbearing moral heritage. The past weighs heavily on Deptford. Dunstan's lack of nostalgia for his childhood is partly the result of his ability to place the village into an historical trajectory, a sequence of events that contains a before (pioneer ancestry) and an after (post–First World War Deptford), unlike Mariposa's static and temporally contained ideal.

Tension between the rural past and urban present, therefore, exists entirely within Dunstan's psyche; the dichotomy's polarities are represented by the moral imperatives of the village's forebears and the more cosmopolitan life Dunstan reads about in his books and yearns for. His mother subscribes to the historically sanctioned proscription of unconventional intellectual activity and is a practical embodiment of the town's pioneer morality, wholly disapproving of Dunstan's increasing idiosyncratic intellectualism; the result is a fearsome domestic tension in the Ramsay household. This tension suggests that Deptfordian identity is modelled on a convention different from that found in *Sunshine Sketches*; it is wholly opposed to Mariposa's welcoming bonhomie. The controlling impetus for these constrictions is ostensibly the past. Unlike the experiential freedom the urban present projects onto the Mariposa past, Deptford projects onto itself experiential limitations ascribed to its revered ancestry; in Deptford the absent, imagined moral past determines the moral present.

Deptford's deference to its forebears presents the major obstacle to Dunstan's personal, social, and intellectual individuation. This struggle mainly involves Mrs Ramsay's disapproval of her son's wholly conscious attempt at becoming a "polymath," which includes his interest in saints and his fumbling cracks at mastering some simple examples of sleight-of-hand; for Dunstan, these actions exemplify the larger world outside of Deptford, particularly cosmopolitan Europe. Mrs Ramsay's anxiety about her son's divergence from a modest historical norm is liberated in a flood of resentment after an incident of Dunstan's cheek: "She cried too, hysterically, and beat me harder, storming about my impudence, my want of respect for her, of my increasing oddity and intellectual arrogance – not that she used these words, but I do not intend to put down what she actually said – until at last her fury was spent" (33). Mrs Ramsay's anger is enflamed by Dunstan's developing personality, his lack of "respect," and his refusal to acquiesce to the dictates of the previous generation. His behaviour is aberrant only according to the behavioural norms of Deptford's practicality, the internal sweep of the village's history.

Mary Dempster's transgression with Joel Surgeoner reveals Mrs Ramsay's full adherence to the collective values of the community, and it also reveals Dunstan's inability to subscribe to the town's moral code, which neglects the mystery of the spirit in favour of the demonstrability of the flesh. Patricia Monk sees Mrs Dempster's experience with the behavioural codes of the town as prefiguring Dunstan's own increasing moral independence from his home place (*Mud* 69). Like all Deptford women, Mrs Ramsay feels she had "standards of decency to defend" (*Fifth* 45); this phrase encapsulates the generalized female opinion that ostracizes the Dempsters. Mrs Ramsay's intolerance clashes with the earlier impression that Dunstan creates about his family as the "literary leaders of the community" (17), a description alluding to their independence of mind. Yet their literary distinction amounts to very little against the sway of moral orthodoxy.

Because she conflates her religious beliefs with the dictates of Deptford's limiting moralism, Mrs Ramsay, like the majority of Deptfordians, does not appreciate the nature of what she opposes. Dunstan, however, is developing a nascent understanding of the metaphorical in reality, what Monk refers to as the "numinosum" (*Smaller Infinity* 80). His initial sympathy for Mary later develops into his belief that her act was a Christian miracle resulting in the saving of a lost soul, and although he struggles against Deptford's religious understanding during the length of his adult career, he must first extract himself from the consequential grasp of this blinkered comprehension. During this process, he is aware that the Dempsters' expulsion from the town serves as a warning to those who would transgress Deptford's conception of normality. The initial stages of Dunstan's movement towards something "bigger and more sophisticated," really a spiritual understanding whose basis lies outside of Deptford, is further fraught with difficulty since he is still very much a part of the town and experiences acute emotional anguish as a result of this tension.

Through her eventual ultimatum, Mrs Ramsay demands that Dunstan clarify his loyalty, something he conceives of as a type of identity proscription: "she was so anxious to root out of my mind any fragment of belief in what I had seen, and to exact from me promises that I would

never see Mrs. Dempster again and furthermore would accept the village's opinion of her" (57–58). To resign himself to the town's opinion
would compromise Dunstan's growth: "She did not know how much
I loved her, and how miserable it made me to defy her, but what was I
to do? Deep inside myself I knew that to yield, and promise what she
wanted, would be the end of anything that was any good in me" (58).
Yet to his mother, such a promise would symbolize his final acquies-
cence to the collective morality of the village, or a normative standard
derived from custom.

A fatalistic streak underlies Mrs Ramsay's ultimatum: she is really
demanding that her son comply with the moral outlook conveyed
by his received station in life. His refusal would cast off the yoke of
historical and cultural determinism; by resisting the influence of the
synchronic collective, Deptford in the present, he would also resist the
diachronic demands of Deptford's collective historical voice. He opts
for a third choice: "the next day I skipped school, went to the county
town, and enlisted" (58). His military service allows Dunstan at least
to delay his mother's demand to accept his place in Deptford's moral
fold. This third choice initiates his European education, which only succeeds in protracting the existing intellectual/cultural distance between
the increasingly cosmopolitan Dunstan and the parochial Deptford.
Yet upon his return, this distance results in his temporary utilization
of the imagined rural-urban conventions as typified by the rural-urban
dichotomy in *Sunshine Sketches*; however briefly, Dunstan flirts with
those small-town conventions he initially claims to transcend.

Dunstan's Second Education: Something "Bigger and More Sophisticated"

While Dunstan is fairly reticent about his combat experience, he is
rather effusive about his recuperation from the war. This period takes
place mainly at the home of the Marfleets, an upper-middle-class English family: "How my spirit expanded in the home of the Marfleets!"
says Dunstan. "To a man who had been where I had been it was glori-
ous" (76). This last line, of course, refers to the trenches of France, but
"where [Dunstan] had been" also includes small-town Ontario. The
permissive atmosphere of the Marfleets' home helps heal Dunstan's
physical wounds acquired in France and also those invisible wounds
acquired in Deptford. His first taste of cosmopolitanism comes in the
form of a genteel, frivolous, even sensual intellectualism that provides

a direct experiential contrast to his first sixteen years in Deptford. During his stay with the Marfleets, Dunstan experiences his "sexual initiation" alongside his first notable cultural event, and he comments on their likeness: "I see that I have been so muddle-headed as to put my sexual initiation in direct conjunction with a visit to a musical show ... [T]he two, though very different, are not so unlike in psychological weight as you might suppose. Both were wonders, strange lands revealed to me in circumstances of great excitement" (77–8). The two events appear similar in "psychological weight" to Dunstan because their symbolic content – what really amounts to their emphasis on sensual and aesthetic pleasure – is antithetical to Deptford's ethos, what Monk describes as its corporeal notions of good and evil: "Deptford's ideas of good ... manifest an old-fashioned Puritanism whose cardinal virtues are prudery, prudence, and hard work ... Deptford 'good' ... is life-denying ... [I]t is essentially the world of thanatos, or anti-life" (*Smaller Infinity* 92). Dunstan's cultural initiation is a fitting counterpart to his transgression of Deptford's moral barriers because, just as intellectual paucity and chastity are his lot at home, experiential and epistemological possibility within this new place helps reveal the spiritual pleasures existing within and beyond the carnal encounter.

Mrs Marfleet, the Honourable, embodies the oppositional ethos of this new physical and conceptual space and is a binaristic counterpart to Mrs Ramsay: "The Honourable was a wonder, not like a mother at all. She was a witty, frivolous woman of a beauty congruous with her age ... and talked as if she hadn't a brain in her head. But I was not deceived" (76). She is the perfect contrast to Dunstan's existing icon of motherhood. His experiences with the Marfleets revise the previous dichotomy between Dunstan's "conjuring" – really just his naive conception of the sophisticated life – and Deptford's corporeal practicality. Now Dunstan's psyche negotiates the gaiety and frivolity of the Marfleets' home (middle-class English life) and the lingering asceticism of Deptford. The home of the Marfleets and the village of Deptford rest at opposite ends of a cultural spectrum, situating the Marfleets as representatives of an urban polarity analogous to the one in *Sunshine Sketches* that provides a productive contrast to Mariposa; the Marfleets give Dunstan a taste of the larger world, and, much like the Mariposans are drawn towards the supposedly more expansive world of the urbanites, Dunstan is attracted to the permissive luxuriousness of the British upper middle class.

While much of *Sunshine Sketches'* appeal stems from the humorous and ironic contrasts of urban and rural life, Daniel Coleman finds an analogous phenomenon occurring between two nodes on the imagined cultural continuum of empire. His model would suggest that the rural-urban dichotomy apparent within *Sunshine Sketches* really involves the past and the present of the same conceptual line of socio-cultural development. The relationship between imperial centre and colony, says Coleman, produces anxiety within the "settler-colonist" who has internalized his colonial subjectivity. This anxiety involves a feeling of "belatedness" resulting from the colonist's inability to adapt adequately to the imperial centre's model of "civility" (16), which itself stems from a belief in civilization's mono-linear trajectory. This conceptual timeline both produces and justifies the instructive posture adopted by the cultural and administrative centre, as it invariably conceives of its colonial possessions as following behind in its cultural-temporal wake. What I would like to take away from Coleman's text is his suggestion of a cultural chronology inherent to the physical and philosophical space resting between colonial outpost and imperial centre, a phenomenon similar to that within the rural past–urban present dichotomy.[8] Dunstan is a descendant of those "hard-bitten pioneers" who finds himself in the centre of the empire, and the Marfleets personify the "British model of civility," or normative standard for Anglo-Canadian cultural identity (Coleman 5). If we follow the logic of Coleman's reflections, Dunstan's sexual and cultural initiation represents the "updating" of his cultural temporality, as these firsts are part of the experience of place. What has previously been expressed as a cultural dichotomy between the urban present and rural past, or centre and margin, Coleman suggests, can also be expressed as two ends of a cultural continuum that only appear to be antithetical.

Therefore, Dunstan's implied engagement to Diana Marfleet offers him a hybrid identity that synthesizes divergent elements of the cultural continuum/polarity. The potential marriage between the daughter of old-world petits bourgeois and the descendant of new-world pioneers reveals Diana's romantic hopes for their future life, which will

---

8 In the rural past–urban present dichotomy, the former is associated with cultural origins. In Coleman's model, the site of origins has been reversed, as the cultural influence flows from the imperial centre. However, if one reads Mariposa's defining ethos as really the product of the urban sphere, the two cultural models are similar.

combine elements of both worlds: agrarianism and gentility. Dunstan, however, harbours no misconceptions about agricultural life:

> [A] life with Diana was simply not for me. As girls do, she assumed that we were drifting toward an engagement and marriage ... [I]t was clear she thought that when I was strong enough we would go to Canada, and if I did not mistake her utterly, she had in her mind's eye a fine big wheat farm in the West, for she had the English delusion that farming was a great way to live. I knew enough about farming to be sure it was not a life for amateurs or wounded men. (80)

Diana's "delusion" springs from the deliberately romantic tales of the Canadian West used to lure settlers in the late nineteenth and early twentieth centuries, but this idealized rural existence is one that Dunstan's childhood experience could never allow him either to internalize or to perform. What Dunstan characterizes as a particularly "English delusion" is really a misconception more representative of the Marfleets' class, as it is shared by a number of wealthy urbanites in *Sunshine Sketches*. For instance, as we have seen, Pupkin Sr, a particularly ensconced member of the urban elite, longs for the "simple, simple life ... some place that would remind him of the little old farm up the Aroostook where he was brought up" (102). Similarly, the club men stare longingly through the train window at the passing farm seen in the fading twilight during the final trip to Mariposa, while the narrator intones, "it must be comfortable there" (143). Rural nostalgia in both *Sunshine Sketches* and *Fifth Business* relates to the experiential distance between the classes, a distance that Diana longs to cross but one that Dunstan knows accommodates embellishment and projection. As Dunstan has emerged from the "belated" rural periphery, he knows something of farming's hardships and restrictions, while, for Diana, the occupation remains quaint and romantic, safely resting across the experiential divide.

His "escapes" from Deptford and Diana are crucial to Dunstan's process of individuation, yet these also represent departures from the roles each mother figure has devised for him: "I know how clear it is that what was wrong between Diana and me was that she was too much a mother to me, and as I had had one mother, and lost her, I was not in a hurry to acquire another ... If I could manage it, I had no intention of being anybody's own dear laddie, ever again" (80). "Dear Laddie" is Mrs Ramsay's pet name for Dunstan, and it suggests how her expectations, based largely on her own cultural past, inhibited Dunstan's internal process of self-development. He fears that Diana will similarly project onto him identity prescripts that clash with his process of individuation, a fear of hemming-in made explicit when he says about Diana, "I was not blind to the fact that she regarded me as her own creation" (79–80). Evading a marriage to Diana continues the process by which Dunstan circumnavigates the boundaries of a cultural narrative as opposed to developing within its parameters, suggesting Dunstan strives to be entirely of his own making.

His journey has an iconoclastic aura, as it involves his successful negotiation of the conventional cultural identities of a British colonial mentality; although Dunstan escapes maternal figures, he is symbolically eluding the sway of a cultural lineage. By first escaping the role small-town Ontario holds for him, and subsequently escaping a partnership to one of his own culture's elites, he navigates and seemingly rejects a rural-urban dichotomy that mirrors the provincial-cosmopolitan dichotomy inherent to colonization. He has experienced both the "old values" and "sophistication" that the rural and urban spaces offer, and his departure from both displays a desire for total self-fashioning. The symbolism of such a journey aligns with the Promethean vision of Canada during the Pierre Trudeau era, perhaps reflecting the cultural context out of which Davies was writing.

Dunstan recognizes that socio-cultural roles, much like small-town conventions, are products of "bigger and more sophisticated" places or, more appropriately, that both are products of those whose representational authority out-shouts any intrinsic identity possessed by the thing itself. However, one role Dunstan appears satisfied with is his designation as war hero. The Victoria Cross, given to him by the king, the powerful hub of the imperial centre, represents the completion of his second apprenticeship, this time in a place much "bigger and more sophisticated" than Deptford. The medal symbolizes a new experiential divide established between Dunstan and Deptford, one that temporarily affects his portrayal of the village upon his hero's return. Dunstan's "second education" hampers his ability to describe Deptford as an insider, as one whose propinquity to the village affords a precise appraisal.

Dunstan's Return and Deptford's Distance

Dunstan survives the war only to discover that both of his parents have died during the flu pandemic, and his rather callous response to their deaths suggests that he feels relief that he will no longer have to negotiate the moral norms of Deptford according to his mother's wishes. His attachment to the town is now severely limited, and his physical and psychical escape from Deptford now appears to be a matter of Dunstan's choice alone. His cultural distance from the village is revealed through the town's altered, conventional representation, and his return demonstrates his increasing cosmopolitanism through the narrative's temporary resemblance to Mariposa's narrative tone and description. This later description of village life marks Dunstan's emphasis on the distance – intellectual, emotional, and cultural – between himself and Deptford. Monk interprets Deptford as a "background of conventional Canadian attitudes and behaviour" that clashes with "Ramsay's new attitudes and behaviour" (*Mud* 14); yet only after his return from the imperial centre do his "new attitudes and behaviour" clash with what might be called "convention." This tension results in a temporarily benign and comic Deptford whose nature seems characteristic of the idyllic Mariposa, as Dunstan now sees and describes the village as someone who is more familiar with small-town types than with the idiosyncrasy of a particular settlement.

Dunstan first describes his grand tour of the village immediately upon his arrival as "the strangest procession I have ever seen, but it was in my honour and I will not laugh at it. It was Deptford's version of a Roman Triumph, and I tried to be worthy of it" (86). His designation as war hero by the fulcrum of empire, King George V, is a role Dunstan has accepted, but is also a role about which he remains self-aware, and this split subjectivity accounts for his tendency to condescend to the village's rituals and simultaneously resist that impulse. The procession appears odd to Dunstan because he now sees it as a provincial anachronism, as only a simulation of the imperial centre's grand rituals: this may exemplify Deptford's "belatedness," but it also reveals Dunstan's new sense of distance from the town.

The town has changed during the war years, a change reflected in the village's new interest in international affairs. Dunstan regards this new internationalism as one possible reason for his latest estrangement from the town: "I had little idea of what four years of war had done in creating a new atmosphere in Deptford, for it had shown little interest in world affairs in my schooldays. But here was our village shoe-repair man, Moses Langirand, in what was meant to be a French uniform, personating Marshal Foch" (85). What has changed more than the village itself is Dunstan's perspective, enhanced by his own vast experience in the larger world and revealed by an altered narrative tone that has acquired an element absent from his earlier descriptions of Deptford. He sees the town now with that fond kindliness of the sort present in *Sunshine Sketches*: "There were two John Bulls, owing to some misunderstanding that could not be resolved without hurt feelings. There were Red Cross nurses in plenty – six or seven of them. A girl celebrated in my day for having big feet, named Katie Orchard, was swathed in bunting and had a bandage over one eye; she was Gallant Little Belgium" (*Fifth Business* 85).

As Dunstan's experiences have increased his sense of distance – social, cultural, or otherwise – from Deptford, his reliance on literary convention similarly increases. Gone is the town's small and quiet dignity, best displayed in the dead-serious search for the missing Mrs Dempster: "But if Mrs. Dempster was lost at night, all daylight considerations must be set aside. There was a good deal of the pioneer left in people in those days, and they knew what was serious ... I was surprised to see Mr. Mahaffey, our magistrate, among them. He and the policeman were our law, and his presence meant grave public concern" (41–42). Dunstan's involvement in this search marks his official recognition by his mother "as a man, fit to go on serious business" (41). The lack of irony in his recollection mirrors the pride he feels that this event, with its great significance to the whole community, marks his coming of age, a good indication of his previous cultural propinquity to Deptford's rituals and markers of maturity.

W.J. Keith claims that both Leacock and Davies write of the small town "from a detached perspective. [Their narrators] have widened their own horizons and look *back* at the town in question with affection or amused irony" (167). In *Fifth Business*, however, it is Dunstan's description of his triumphant return to Deptford after the war that marks the beginning of his bemused irony and detached observation of the village's spectacles, celebrations, and rituals. This is best displayed by his ironic appreciation of the (very) local talent performing at the ceremony held in honour of the returning soldiers. It may be genuine, but his condescending affection is directed more towards the performers than their talent. Muriel Parkinson's singing voice is affecting, but Dunstan considers her songs "shrieked (for her voice was powerful rather than sweet)" (88). The humour of Murray Tiffin is perhaps funnier for its intractable parochialism and good nature than for the wit of the actual jokes: "Then Murray got off several other good ones, about how much cheaper it was to buy groceries in Bowles Corners than it was even to steal them from the merchants of Deptford, and similar local wit of the sort that age cannot wither nor custom stale" (88). Prior to his departure for war, Dunstan describes Bowles Corners as "rustic beyond redemption," yet, after his return, Deptford appears that way as well, as Dunstan's new frame of reference extends to the stages of London's West End and the habits of the British upper middle class.

. Dunstan's narrative becomes most like Leacock's in his treatment of Deptford's gifts for its veterans; the railway watches are valued for their practicality and they further reveal Deptford's inability to condone luxury. This pragmatism becomes an element of fun, as it no longer represents an effective opposition to Dunstan's developing personality: "These were no ordinary watches but railway watches, warranted to tell time accurately under the most trying conditions, and probably for all eternity. We understood the merit of these watches because, as we all knew, his [the reeve's] son Jack was a railwayman, a brakeman on the Grand Trunk, and Jack swore that these were the best watches to be had anywhere" (89). This passage contains a slip into free indirect discourse, a common characteristic of Leacock's narrative, through a subtle break from Dunstan's elevated diction in the latter half of the quote; the break is made up of elements of the reeve's presentation speech. But the irony of the preceding passage rests in the insinuation that Deptford's luminaries most likely got the "'family discount" when procuring these keepsakes, a situation that does not necessarily diminish their authentic gratitude for the veterans' efforts but comically re-emphasizes the village's thrift. A similar duplicity occurs in Dunstan's review of the member of Parliament's attitude towards the allied nations of the First World War: "Then the Member of Parliament was let loose upon us, and he talked for three minutes more than one hour ... hinting pretty strongly that although Lloyd George, Clemenceau, and Wilson were unquestionably good men, Sir Robert Borden had really pushed the war to a successful conclusion" (89). The MP's speech contains those types of inflated cosmopolitan comparisons that are ubiquitous in *Sunshine Sketches*: the real nation of consequence is not those grand industrial and military powers, but the relatively diminutive Canada, a boast perhaps suitable for the mouth of a Mariposan comparing the wide streets of the town to the grand boulevards of Paris.

Through this irony, Dunstan reveals his increased emotional and cultural remove from Deptford. Deptford now appears as a provincial village of diminished significance to the hero/narrator, and as a refuge from the horrors of modern warfare. Mariposa's bucolic character is the product of the urban sphere, its representational source. The distance between the retrospective gaze of the narrator and Mariposa consists of a spatial-temporal gap that accommodates idealization, and the description of the town can only be that of a non-, or perhaps one-time, resident. This same process now occurs in Dunstan's review of his hometown; he is simultaneously looking *back* at Deptford while he is looking *at* Deptford. As Dunstan's psyche is no longer fully subject to Deptford's restrictions, his version of the town displays a corresponding shift towards the innocent, and despite his stated awareness of small-town conventions, the town now appears to be a place "inhabited by laughable, lovable simpletons, unspotted by the worldliness of city life" (15), a characterization suggesting Dunstan is no longer a fully integrated member of the community.

This narrative shift implies that the dominant tone of *Sunshine Sketches*, that which helps construct the idyllic small-town archetype, is possible only for those narrators who can put that home place into a context that also includes life after the small town. When the small-town influence is impotent or exists only in memory, a narrator is then free to project onto that influence associations with bucolic or provincial naivety, or what Davies terms elsewhere Canada's "myth of innocence" (*One Half* 275) – that is, the popular belief in the country's inherent benevolence and simplicity. In the initial chapters of *Fifth Business*, however, Dunstan recounts his experiences in the town with the real, imposing, and even menacing influence of naivety's ugly cousins: ignorance and intolerance. During his return to Deptford, a time when he is free to escape the village's influence, the town temporarily appears backwards, charming, harmless, and colourful. Dunstan's situation now mirrors that of the club men in *Sunshine Sketches*' "L'Envoi," as his material independence offers him freedom of mind, values, and opinion. As the phrase "home place" entails subsequent experience, Mariposa as "cultural archetype" is suitable only for a "culture of experience"; its rural simplicity is an urban projection of an imaginary loss. Dunstan's unsettled narrative tone offers a type of meta-critique on a conventional rendering of small-town childhoods: his journey outlines the process of psychical, cultural, and temporal detachment from his origins, and their subsequent, idealized retrospective.

However, Dunstan's utilization of this "fashion" amounts only to a brief foray into convention. After the comical proceedings of the official welcome-home ceremony, Dunstan provides an inversion or "anti-masque" of the dominant archetype of small-town Ontario, a portrayal that steps out of the sunshine and into torchlight. Immediately after the official proceedings at the courthouse, the members of the village gather outside, and ·the atmosphere acquires a palpable difference: "here the crowd was lively and expectant; children dodged to and fro, and there was a lot of laughter about nothing in particular" (91–2). That is until "down our main street came a procession, lit by the flame of brooms dipped in oil – a ruddy, smoky light – accompanying Marshal Foch, the two John Bulls, Uncle Sam, Gallant Little Belgium, the whole gang dragging at a rope's end Deptford's own conception of the German Emperor, fat Myron Papple" (92). Ultimately, the town burns and hangs the Kaiser in effigy. This scene displays an inversion of the earlier moral imperatives that the village received from its pioneer forebears. While the village may still demand moral conformity, that unanimity now more clearly revolves around a muscular and rancorous political identity.

Dunstan's description of these unofficial events lacks the "amused irony" of his earlier description of the ceremony. During the anti-masque, Dunstan "watches them with dismay that mounted toward horror" as he realizes this "symbolic act of cruelty and hatred" is perpetrated by "my own people" (92). The symbolic act is an inverted manifestation of the same impulse that ostracizes the Dempsters, which precipitates the first of Dunstan's crises. While the exclusion of the Dempsters is ostensibly based on collective Christian norms, the hanging of the kaiser is a grotesque parody of those norms; both involve an individual punished by a collective as the result of that individual's moral or military transgression. Each retributive act has the same effect on Dunstan, disgust and horror, as both reflect the dark side of the imperatives of unanimity, whether it is moral or political: the majority revels in both its dominance and its opponent's defeat. What before was portrayed as Dunstan's moral unorthodoxy as a result of his refusal to acquiesce to "Deptford morality" is, during the anti-masque, fully articulated as direct opposition to the collective and unconcealed cruelty that is another part of such unexamined conformism. At this moment, Dunstan would most like to distance himself from the actions of his fellow townsfolk, yet this moment marks the reaffirmation of his shared identity with the town, when he calls the Deptfordians "my own people." Dunstan thus rejects the special role into which he has been thrust, that of hero, as he can no longer be a representative icon of what he is witness to. By rejecting this role, Dunstan negates the heroic status that both distinguishes him from the rest of Deptford and renders him beholden to it through that role's attendant obligations. This rejection also dissolves the narrative's slip into Mariposan convention, as Dunstan can no longer maintain the newly minted distance resting between his imperial identity and the peripheral village; Dunstan's and Deptford's colonial roles dissolve.

The instability of Dunstan's temporary "amused" distance from the town points to the instability of the very archetypes it helps construct. The village before Dunstan's eyes is composed of complexities, some noble and some sinister. His earlier desire to escape the clutches of "Deptford morality" first turns into a simplistic re-view of village life and characters, which then translates into his more mature realization that, as his own origins rest within Deptford, to render it with anything less than an understanding of its complexity is doing the village and himself a disservice. The archetype represented by *Sunshine Sketches* emerges from a colonial mentality that perceives out-of-the-way places as the antidote to modernity; Dunstan discovers differently, and the dissolution of that archetype in his own narrative signals his transcendence of an immature flirtation with a colonial mentality that condescends to the imagined periphery. To write of small-town Ontario with a kindliness created by one's cultural, temporal, or spatial distance from it is to write of it falsely, and, at least for Dunstan, this narrative technique cannot maintain itself in the presence of its literary subject.

Dunstan's mature individuation can thus account for his Deptfordian past and his place within its historical lineage. This individuation does not reject origins by seeking a solitary place outside of a heritage, but rather incorporates them into his current subject position, a realization Dunstan later confirms when speaking to Joel Surgeoner, the formerly homeless man with whom Mary Dempster had sex: "What Surgeoner told me made it clear that any new life must include Deptford. There was to be no release by muffling up the past" (122). The small-town archetype is a type of "muffling up" of the past, as it conceals or resists historical complexity and can be used to justify a belief in one's current moral infallibility through a nostalgic approach to the past. (For example, see Pupkin Sr from *Sunshine Sketches*: if this rich industrialist is schooled in the old-fashioned virtues of farm life, how could he possibly do harm in the present?) Dunstan's complex realization allows him to resist locating a small-town idyll in Deptford, and it suggests the capacity for evil is inherent in human nature as opposed to a specific time, place, or culture.

The instability of Dunstan's retrospective also hints at the increasingly difficult distinction between the provincial and the cosmopolitan in the modernizing postwar world. Dunstan's description makes special mention of Deptford's new interest in global affairs (85), a result, perhaps, of the ongoing technological dissolution of the divide between the rural and urban spheres in an age of rapid communication. Particularly revealing of this nascent modern homogeneity is the behaviour Dunstan witnesses in both cultural centre and outpost. Immediately after the war, Dunstan watches a disturbing spectacle in London: "I saw some of the excitement and a few things that shocked me; people, having been delivered from destruction, became horribly destructive themselves; people, having been delivered from license and riot, pawed and mauled and shouted dirty phrases in the streets" (77). These depictions of postwar rampage indicate that both imperial centre and periphery are affected by, and respond to, the same global events, news of which is transmitted instantaneously along transatlantic cables. Deptfordians and Londoners fight in the same war and celebrate its conclusion in similarly degraded fashions. Deptford's insular identity has been replaced by its own self-identification with a type of "imagined community," a community whose centre of influence is situated beyond the borders of not only the town, but also the nation; the town's moral imperatives are now determined not by the village elders or its own particular past, but by the demands of the larger international community into which it now imagines itself. The increasingly globalized experience reflected in postwar Deptford resists the tangibility of rural difference, as modernity collapses the spatial relation upon which imagined rural and urban values are ostensibly based; the distance between the rural and urban spheres can no longer maintain the mirage of difference, as modernity degrades the effects of that distance. This process, though, does nothing to eliminate the rural nostalgia of those seeking a more innocent antitype to modern, urban experience; it is a nostalgic impulse, however, that Dunstan has overcome. The divide between the rural and urban spheres, however productive in *Sunshine Sketches*, is shown to be increasingly tenuous in *Fifth Business*.

Leacock was, of course, self-aware in his depiction of the "good old days" of the small town, and his narrator's incessant irony continually draws attention to and undercuts the more idyllic aspects of his depictions. The danger, however, is in simply disregarding the irony and viewing Mariposa as a veritable representation of Canada's golden age of the small town, as various critics have nostalgically done. Nostalgia, says Jonathan Steinwand, relies on distance, either temporal or spatial, to help "fashion a more aesthetically complete and satisfying recollection of what is longed for" (9). In order to read Mariposa, we must first acknowledge the source of its depiction deep within a melancholic, urban club for wealthy businessmen. Mariposa is a nostalgic consolation projected onto a distant past in order to help soothe the effects of urban anomie. At the margins of Leacock's text rests the reality that Mariposa's community idyll is not a memory, but a fabrication prompted by the dominance of an urban sphere and its attendant features: anonymity, industrialism, and impersonal commerce, all things conspicuously missing from Mariposa. Dunstan's resistance to, in the words of Eli Mandel, the "process of perception" (115) that allows the small town to be viewed as an innocent or bucolic urban antitype is effected by his continued spatial and cultural propinquity to his hometown; in other words, his physical return dispels any small-town illusions distance may protract.

Life in Mariposa offers an imagined escape for urban titans of capitalism. Mariposa is remembered from a distance in both time and space, allowing life in the town to be re-imagined as that of the idyllic, organic community. Because its purpose is to provide imagined escape and consolation, Mariposa exists as the direct polarized counterpart to the urban sphere, a town wholly separate from the economic and cultural systems of modernity (apart from those it chooses to involve itself in), as that is exactly what its creators in the urban club desire; they want to remember other, better selves, and this imagined past accommodates that fantasy. Dunstan's similar illusions of Deptford as a parochial complement or antitype to urban modernity rapidly dissolve upon his return to the town. Deptford, Dunstan's reminiscences suggest, is fully implicated in the economic, cultural, and martial forces that shape the globe.

Deptford's postwar international concerns reflect its movement from what Benedict Anderson may define as a "primordial village," a community defined by "face-to-face contact" (6), to a larger imagined community in which the townsfolk see themselves as full participants in global affairs. For their part, the residents would not be incorrect in discerning a place for themselves and their village within the fabric of a global modernity; Dunstan's experiences in both the war and London are testament to those dissolving spatial boundaries. However, just as important as Deptford's changes is Dunstan's response to them. Rather than remembering his rural childhood hometown as the antitype to the forces of modernity, as the safe space of childhood embedded in the surety of the past, Dunstan perceives the ease with which its traditional moralism transmutes into modern martial nationalism; the latter, Dunstan suggests, does not corrupt the former, but rather both are expressions of a similar impulse.[9]

Yet as boundaries appear to dissolve, the effect on cultural and place-based identities can be paradoxical: "The more global our interrelations becomes ... and the more spatial barriers disintegrate, so more rather than less of the world's population clings to place and neighborhood or to nation, region, ethnic grouping, or religious belief as specific marks of identity" (Harvey "Between" 427). David Harvey's statement proclaims that cultural identification becomes firmer as spatial, and thus cultural, boundaries become increasingly fluid; it might also suggest that Mariposa as home place, or any home place recalled fondly, is, in some measure, a nostalgic response to broader cultural exposure. Mariposa is not a vision of a past, either cultural or individual, but a study in how the past is reshaped as an alternative to the culturally dislocating present. In *Fifth Business*, however, this process is far less benign. Dunstan's observations suggest that the town's pioneer morality has been shaped by an influence whose stress on the collective is perhaps even stronger and whose reach extends to any who have access to modern forms of communication – that is, modern nationalism. In that shift, the town's process of cultural identification has become intransigent, muscular, not only exclusionary but also vindictive. Deptford is no home place; it merely refracts its dominant influence, whether that stems from a pioneer past or a transnational modernity.

Dunstan's new "horror" is the expression of an individual against the calcification of a political-cultural identity, and not simply against Deptford's collective moral voice. His sentiment may be based on a culturally elitist impulse, but it is a message of critical and independent

---

9 The alteration of Deptford's traditional moralism into a force reflecting broader political-cultural concerns is on full display during the evening celebrations in honour of its war vets. This type of shift, suggests poet/critic Jeff Derksen, should not be seen as the triumph of the global over the local. Rather, Derksen speculates that the "discourses" of the local and global are not contradictory, but that the "discourse" of globalization can utilize "aspect[s] of place" (110) in order to conceal the constitutive effects of the global on the local. The night-time parade of nations in Deptford, while conducted by the exceedingly local cast of Deptfordians, enacts a type of transnational narrative that incorporates the idiosyncrasies of the village, both past and present, with the fluid cultural exchange of a transnational modernity. This event is a conflation of its exclusionary moral past and the synchronous events occurring on the other side of the ocean.

thought that will be crucial to that dark age of political polarities about to begin, an age of extremes that is replacing Deptford's moral conformism with a seemingly more potent message of postwar nationalism; and this new force similarly relies on cultural myths to support its manufactured sense of inherent righteousness. Dunstan's inability to gaze lovingly upon that small village from which he emerged is the type of sober historical consciousness needed to think clearly about the "biggest outburst of mass lunacy" (171) the first war precipitates and to resist the pull of ideologies that will soon plunge the globe into an even larger conflagration than the one Dunstan was fortunate enough to have survived.

Postscript: Deptford's Other Sons

The Deptford Trilogy includes two other novels, *The Manticore* and *World of Wonders*, which were released in 1972 and 1975, respectively. Like in *Fifth Business*, Deptford plays an important role in the early life of each book's protagonist; unlike in *Fifth Business*, however, the representations of the town in these later novels approach the polarized convention of small-town writing that Dunstan Ramsay is both aware of and transcends in the trilogy's first entry. While in *Fifth Business*, Dunstan denies the small-town nostalgia and retrospective condemnation that help craft these conventions, the latter two novels explore how both idyllic and anti-idyllic small-town representations emerge in the minds of remembering subjects. The trilogy as a whole offers a type of "meta-" critique of the conventions of rural writing, conventions that the major figure of the trilogy, Dunstan Ramsay, mentions at the trilogy's outset, as if his thoughts present a loose thematic frame for the entire series.

The Manticore is a novel narrated in large part by Boy Staunton's son, David. Traumatized by the sudden death of his father, an event that occupies the final sections of *Fifth Business*, David flees to Zurich at the outset of the second novel in order to undergo Jungian psychoanalysis. What develops is a talky narrative in which David's psychoanalyst examines the Jungian archetypes that populate David's autobiographical ramblings. Deptford plays a minor but important role in his story. Unhappy with his early life in Toronto, David spends his summers in Deptford with his rich grandparents. His parents have roundly rejected Deptford, a place they refer to as "that hole" (80), yet it is a place David longs for, indeed, a place that inhabits his happiest memories of childhood. It offers an escape not only from life in the city, but also from the simmering domestic difficulties darkening the Staunton household: "I suppose unless you are unlucky, anywhere you spend your summers as a child is an Arcadia forever" (80–1). For David, Deptford is a traditional Arcadia, a conventional pastoral landscape; his summer visits generate memories of a perpetually sunny rural landscape in which he enjoys a relative amount of autonomy.

Generations of critics view traditional pastorals as forming a literature of "retreat," in which protagonists flee from the confines of a restrictive society into the relative freedom of a controlled nature. The pastoral landscape is not untouched or pristine wilderness, but a gentle "middle landscape," as Leo Marx calls it, located between civilization and wilderness; the "middle landscape" is the "garden" that combines elements of the "half-wild, half civilized" (104–5). This literature can offer merely an escapist fantasy, what Marx labels a "sentimental pastoral," or it can offer a sophisticated commentary on the nature of modern experience, what Marx terms a "complex pastoral." The former is a simple nostalgic mode of writing that figures the countryside as the innocent antidote to the corruption, vice, and restrictions of the urban centre; the latter, however, "do[es] not finally permit us to come away with anything like the simple, affirmative attitude we adopt toward pleasing rural scenery" (25). Complex pastorals urge us to reflect on the contrasting and often illusory experiential differences between rural landscapes and urban centres, a process of reflection that ultimately "enrich[es] and clarif[ies] our experience" (11). Both complex and sentimental pastorals are the literature of retreat, but they have different outcomes: one confirms the sentimental understanding of the healing properties of nature, while the other, rather than denying complexity, engenders a deeper understanding of the self within modernity.

David's middle landscape is not necessarily Deptford proper but, rather, his grandfather's massive sugar beet plantation. His visit to Deptford may be his first proper retreat from the city, but it is a compromised one, in part because he fails to achieve the freedom that such a move should entail. That is because he is hounded at all hours by his nanny – his grandmother's domestic servant, Netty Quelch. Netty is a personification of rural Ontario, an embodiment of place and of the values it ostensibly represents. David explains:

Her parents, Abel and Hannah Quelch, had been farmers, and were wiped out by one of those fires caused by an overheated stove which were such

a common disaster in rural Ontario ... Netty regards work as the natural
state of man. Not to be doing something is, to her, to be either seriously
unwell or bone idle, which ranks well below crime. I do not suppose it
ever occurred to her when she took on the job of being my nurse that she
was to have any time to herself or let me out of her sight, and that was
how she functioned. I ate, prayed, defecated, and even slept in the closest
proximity with her. (81–2)

David enjoys life in Deptford, and, as he explains to his psychoanalyst,
his memories of it are "happy" (80). Yet, unlike in other simple pastorals, David is not fully autonomous within this rural landscape but is
under the control of Netty, a literal and figurative shepherd. The appeal
of the pastoral rests largely on the absence of restriction placed on the
retreating figure. Shepherds, those who inhabit the pastoral landscape,
are generally picturesque background figures, distant objects that contribute to the beauty of the rural scene. This distance maintains the
illusion that the life of the shepherd is enviable, one of relative ease
and freedom; they should have no power over the experiences of the
retreating figure. Yet, because David's summers are spent in close proximity to Netty, she limits the potential of his pastoral experience. She
denies David's stature, which in pastoral literature is something Terry
Gifford calls a "privileged observer." Netty's coarse common sense
erodes David's "privileged" status, and only by escaping or retreating
from Netty can young David flee his real position as a ward and enjoy
his autonomy within the rural landscape.

His grandfather's massive sugar beet plantation offers to David an
escape within an escape, a doubling of pastoral retreats that serves a
distinct purpose. His time on the farm provides David with his only
opportunity to escape Netty and thus to gain the status of privileged
observer. His grandfather, sensing David needs a break, sends him
out into the fields on a miniature train designed to pick up loads of
beets: "Whether Grandfather wanted to give me a rest, or whether he
simply thought women had no place near engines, I don't know, but
he never allowed Netty to go with me, and she sat at the mill, fret-
ting" (90). David's train journey represents a successful pastoral retreat
within a retreat that has been compromised, as his experiences are
no longer dependent on the whims of his shepherd-guardian. David
and the train's driver, Elmo, "chuffed and rattled through the fields,
flat as Holland, which seemed to be filled with dwarves, for most
of the workers were Belgian immigrants who worked on their knees

with sawed-off hoes" (90). Elmo is the "laughable, lovable simpleton" found in the more benign variety of rural writing, as his ignorance of ethnic nationalities (he thinks the Belgians working in the field are "Eye-talians") is not malicious but, rather, comical to the more urbane folks who know better. David's miniature train journey is analogous to the train journey at the conclusion of *Sunshine Sketches,* as both allow the traveller to view the rural landscape from a comfortable distance with no obligation to interact with or respond to the landscape's inhabitants; furthermore, the distance between the privileged observer and the landscape maintains the scene's picturesqueness, and it is this distance that accommodates the feeling of being within the rural landscape without being a part of it. From David's perspective, the Belgians are not itinerant workers toiling on their knees in the full heat of the sun, as they might view themselves, but rather obliging dwarves cheerfully earning their day's pay. This moment yields David's happiest memories of Deptford, yet it is also the moment that re-establishes the distance between the one retreating and the rural landscape, distance that allows him to be a privileged observer who mentally sculpts the scene according to his own wishes. This moment most closely resembles a sentimental pastoral and is the source of David's most acute nostalgia.

In contrast, for the central figure of *World of Wonders,* Paul Dempster, Deptford is a village that is "rotten with vice ... [the site of] incest, sodomy, bestiality, sadism, and masochism" (*Fifth* 15–16). Paul's upbringing is of the gothic variety; his fiercely religious father, a misguided Baptist minister, possesses a narrow understanding of religious values, which consigns Paul to a life of bible verses and strict, ascetic morality. Paul grew up in a home in which his mother was tied to a wall with a rope in order to keep her confined to the house. As bleak and gothic as Paul's domestic life is, being outside among the Deptfordians offers no solace, as the town is cruel and mocking. In his discussion of the special cruelty of the town's children, Paul, as the illusionist Magnus Eisengrim, his adult persona, states:

> They really enjoy giving pain. This is described by sentimentalists as innocence. I was tormented by the children of our village from the earliest days I can remember. My mother had done something – I never found out what it was – that made most of the village hate her ... They said my mother was a hoor ... When I cried, somebody might say, "Aw, let the kid alone; he can't help it his mother's a hoor." I suppose the philosopher-kings who struggled up to that level have since become the rulers of the place. (23)

To ease the oppression, Paul surreptitiously visits the annual agricultural fair: "O what a delicious release it was!" (24) he says of the experience. However, after being enchanted by a travelling carnival troupe, he
is raped and subsequently kidnapped by its magician, a heroin addict
by the name of Willard the Wizard. Paul's life after this traumatic event
only gets worse: he may have been taken out of the frying pan, but has
been forced into the fire.

Paul becomes the "gaff" in Willard's act, a card-playing automaton,
Abdullah. This device is, of course, not an automaton at all but rather
inhabited by the diminutive Paul who is controlling things from the
inside. As the carnival travels from small town to small town, year after
year, Paul observes the people for whom Abdullah represents a sort
of wonder. The portrait of Deptfordians, indeed of all of small-town
Ontario inhabitants, painted by Paul's later stage persona, Magnus
Eisengrim, is decidedly negative. His intimate knowledge has been
acquired not strictly through his own experiences with those unkind
acquaintances of his childhood, but by his unimpeded observation of
the audience, which largely comprises small-town folk:

> As I sat inside Abdullah, I saw them without being seen, while they gaped
> at the curiosities of the World of Wonders. What I saw in most of those
> faces was contempt and patronage for the show folks ... They wanted
> us; they needed us to mix a little leaven in their doughy lives, but they
> did not like us ... But how much they revealed as they stared! When the
> Pharisees saw us they marveled, but it seemed to me that their inward
> parts were full of ravening and wickedness ... Day after day, year after
> year, I defeated them, and scorned them because they could not grasp the
> very simple fact that if Abdullah could be defeated, Abdullah would cease
> to be. (119–20)

Inside Abdullah, Paul is a "nobody," the unseen hinge of a cheap carnival trick, and in this role he develops an intimate knowledge of audiences. What Paul discovers of the audience, all audiences, is that they
willingly participate in the illusion to which they are witness.

Paul's subsequent apprenticeships teach him how to craft not just
illusions, but illusions in which the audience is complicit. As an actor
with Sir John Tresize's theatre troupe, Paul understands that the
romance of the theatre is an exquisitely crafted illusion that requires
the audience to want to believe in what they are watching: not merely
a suspension of disbelief, but a desire to believe. And it is in this troupe

that Paul must be "born again" into the image of Sir John, an image that is, just like Abdullah, a patina of exterior detail. A stage play's illusion is a series of carefully crafted detail, and, as Sir John's stunt double, Paul must craft his stage time to maximize the illusion's effect. Davies suggests that both the magician's show and a theatrical production possess parallel functions; both are designed to entertain, but they can do so only through the careful management of what remains visible and invisible to the audience.

In his discussion of his final apprenticeship, as a clockmaker, Paul explores this idea of the seen and unseen components of illusion through an extended metaphor of the mechanical toys. In his story of fixing the toy contraption of a monkey's head at the end of a cane, Paul relates in some detail the inner workings and gears that allow the monkey to stick out his tongue at the press of a button. The monkey's animation is the illusion, and Paul's expertise rests with orchestrating the mechanisms that rest beneath the façade but that are crucial for the illusion to occur. Paul's entire life, indeed his very survival, has depended upon his ability to craft illusions by orchestrating detail.[10]

If Paul as Magnus is renowned for crafting illusion, and if his entire professional career has been spent mastering the choreography of control, there was a time during which he was utterly powerless: his boyhood in Deptford. In order for Paul to gain some level of autonomy in his life, he has to become someone else: first he inhabits Abdullah, then he becomes Sir John's doppelgänger, and finally he becomes Magnus Eisengrim. Paul is never able to develop from his boyhood self and mature into an older version of Paul Dempster, but rather he continually thrusts himself into the identity of something or someone else: while inhabiting Abdullah, he is reborn as a "nobody," and during his time as an actor in England, he had "to get inside Sir John," which required him to be "born again physically" (202). His life is spent mastering the external details that are required to adopt the visible markings of a different identity, yet this does not necessitate intellectual or spiritual growth; underneath the accumulated layers of artifice, Magnus Eisengrim is still Paul Dempster, a fact that he reveals in his solitary return to Deptford.

---

10 The profuse detail of his autobiographical narrative suggests that his life story is, just like his stage illusions, an exquisitely crafted misdirection. There remains the possibility that his entire narrative is another of his hoodwinkings – that it is a carefully managed ploy to distract and enchant.

Deptford was the one place in which Paul did not control how others saw him, and it is in Deptford that Magnus refers to and thinks of himself in his original incarnation: Paul Dempster. Much like in other small-town novels, *World of Wonders* contains a homecoming scene that is very similar to those in *Fifth Business* and *Sunshine Sketches*. It occurs while Paul is on tour in Canada with Sir John's company. As the train stops at the Deptford station, Paul steps down and views the town, which has changed very little in the intervening years.

> I recognized a few buildings and saw the spires of the five churches … among the leafless trees. Solemnly, I spat … Spitting is not a ceremonious action, but I crowded it with loathing, and when I climbed back on the train I felt immeasurably better. I had not settled any scores, or altered my feelings, but I had done something of importance. Nobody knew it, but Paul Dempster had visited his childhood home. I have never returned. (293–4)

Deptford is the one place in which Paul cannot see himself as anybody other than Paul. That is the identity he has attempted to bury beneath years of alternative, surface identities, which were merely stage illusions. When he states that he has "never returned" after this visit, he is referring not only to Deptford but also to his identity as Paul Dempster, whom he refers to in the third person in the passage.

Deptford, though, will always be his home, not in the comforting aspect of that word, but rather as the place from which he emerged. His Deptfordian identity is the one he did not craft as an illusion, and it is one he can no longer abide. The distance between Paul's former and current selves is very short indeed; his current self, Magnus Eisengrim, is merely a series of carefully crafted details, a stage artifice that is the cumulative effect of Paul's training. However, small-town Ontario is Paul's earliest influential environment, and the only place in which Paul had no ability to craft his identity. It is something from which he is thrust, and therefore, something he did not grow apart from organically, under his own power, into an older version of Paul. Dunstan has an epiphany in *Fifth Business* when he realizes that to bury his past would give it unparalleled power over his current life, a realization that sheds light on Paul's situation: "I had tried to get Deptford out of my head; I wanted a new life. What Surgeoner told me made it clear that any new life must include Deptford. There was to be no release by muffling up the past" (*Fifth* 122). In order to grow – psychologically, intellectually, and spiritually – Dunstan must remain conscious of the impact his experiences in Deptford have on his identity. In contrast, by burying his past self, Paul "muffles up" the past, which then remains in stasis underneath the layers of his subsequent identities. For Paul, that past is his small-town Ontario upbringing, something with which he remains intimately familiar and, therefore, something that he acutely despises.

The degree of distance between perceiving subject and perceived object determines the nature of how Deptford will be remembered. All three novels of the Deptford Trilogy adopt a different mode of small-town writing, modes that Dunstan Ramsay explicates at the beginning of *Fifth Business*, almost as if his identification of small-town conventions should alert the reader to the nature of subsequent representations of Deptford. While Dunstan's experiences lead him to transcend these conventions, the protagonists of the other two novels illustrate just how the small-town idyll and the anti-idyll are manufactured. David Staunton's momentary autonomy, his freedom from restraint in the beet fields, is what allows him to form a happy memory of his trip through his grandfather's acreage. For David, Deptford is an Arcadia because his freedom from labour and his return to Toronto are always assured. Paul Dempster, though, has concealed his original identity underneath layers of artifice, yet underneath those manufactured details rests the frightened, abused boy for whom small-town life was a nightmare. Upon his brief return to Deptford, he still despises the town: during that moment, the layers of artifice slip away and he thinks of himself again, perhaps for the last time, as Paul. Those early experiences are the impetus for his continued burying or "muffling" of his past. Yet, because he merely muffles his past, it remains at the very core of his continued and elaborate attempts to distance himself from it; despite his marvellous stage persona, or perhaps because of it, Magnus Eisengrim will forever remain Paul Dempster.

The Deptford Trilogy, in both name and function, explores how different modes of perception form and which determine how very different people will establish very different understandings of one place. While memorial representations of the small town may be as numerous as its inhabitants, the nature of those memories depends not simply on what happened in the past. The memories under our control, those that can be remembered as what we need them to be, are the ones most distant and inconsequential to our present identities; those memories that control us, however, those that motivate us in the here and now,

are the ones that rest at the very core of our identities. For David, Deptford is a pleasant diversion from the real life he led in Toronto, and his
happy memories of the place reflect that. For Paul, however, his time
in Deptford is what consistently motivates him to transcend the place,
yet, paradoxically, it is for this reason that Paul will never achieve that
desired escape from his hometown.

Chapter Three

Memory and Departure

PART ONE: SYNTHESIZING MEMORY – THE ARTIST AS COMMUNITY

In her story "Home," collected in *The View from Castle Rock*, Alice Munro re-imagines the crepuscular journey from city centre to small-town home, a journey that occupies the final chapter of Leacock's *Sunshine Sketches* and that echoes throughout much of the subsequent literature of Ontario's small towns. Unlike Leacock's characters, who travel by train, Munro's narrator travels by bus; it is a long, largely inconvenient, sometimes uncomfortable ride. Like Leacock's journey, though, this bus trip carries Munro's narrator into the place of her childhood, a place she enters to measure the changes time has wrought. Her childhood home has been updated by her father and step-mother: old furnishings have been stored or sold at a discount, and comfortable, modern conveniences rest in their stead. While her father feels obliged to apologize for these changes to her childhood home, Munro's narrator thinks, "I don't tell him that I am not sure now whether I love any place, and that it seems to me it was myself that I loved here – some self that I have finished with, and none too soon" (231). This is the home place for the narrator, yet as soon as she encounters it, she feels no more pull towards it, no more attachment to it.

The narrator does not simply revisit her childhood home; she revisits the site of her first lucid memory. As she is completing chores in the barn (feeding sheep, in a nice pastoral twist), she enters a corner where she remembers watching her father milking cows. It could be a peaceful, comfortable scene in which the narrator feels a sense of calm while remembering the pleasant rusticity, security, and simplicity of her earlier life. However, what washes over her is not a sense of safety or peace, but rather a growing sense of panic: "the very corner of the stable where I was standing, to spread the hay, and where the beginning of panic came on me, is the scene of the first clear memory of my life" (250). What this place holds for her is neither an antidote to an adult malaise nor a restorative balm achieved through invigorating manual labour; rather this site dashes the illusion of secure place and time projected by nostalgia.

While she stands in this place, the memory cannot stand on its own, freed from context as a type of pneumonic crystal untethered from a timeline. This scene fits into a definite time and place for the narrator, the late fall of 1934 or early winter of 1935, and the harsh events that occur shortly after this scene come to shade her memory of it: the subsequent brutal winter that ravaged the area's trees and orchards and led to the deaths of livestock and loved pets. The sense of panic the narrator feels is the result of remembering, actually recalling, the conditions she felt while growing into her remembered childhood: the sense of menace in the barn resulting from the "cobwebbed windows, the large brutal tools – scythes and axes and rakes – hanging out of my reach. Outside of that, the dark of the country nights when few cars came down our road and there were no outdoor lights" (250). Her childhood, like all childhoods, is coloured by confusion caused by the unknown and fear resulting from the glimpses into the adult world children are periodically afforded. Childhood, or rather the feeling this memory of childhood provides her, is not a safe harbour offering solace through memory, but a time just as dislocating, frightening, and threatening as anything that follows. The escape one gets through childhood memories is the result of shaping those memories into something needed in the present. Eliminating that distance between past and present through a return, or, rather, inhabiting that physical space of her past, thrusts her back into that psychological state: the uncertainty, fear, and confusion caused by the half-understood brutality that surrounds her. The memory of watching her father milk the cow, an animal soon dead from pneumonia, may be a peaceful scene when left on its own, but it cannot be recalled without embedding it into a timeline of events.

Whereas distance in time and space can render childhood memories safe, secure, charming, and harmless – and, indeed, this is the type of representation that shapes the towns of Mariposa and, at times, Deptford – Munro's works offer a different understanding of memory. What "Home," in particular, demonstrates is a negotiation of memory that can no longer be held at a distance and that must be negotiated with the present self. Memory is powerful, and the echoes of past experience reverberate throughout the lives of Munro's characters; in Munro's work, the present self must navigate the psychological and physiological effects of memories, and not simply memories of childhood, but memories of childhood in a specific place. Munro's representation of small-town place is intricately attached to the power and inescapability of memory. Place is indelible for Munro's characters, and memory is the main vehicle through which place is understood.

Munro does not simply chronicle the history of Ontario's Huron County through thinly disguised fictionalizations. She constructs narratives not of people's history in place, but of the relationship between people and place. In attempting to understand the status of small-town place and the role of memory in Munro's fiction, this chapter focuses on two key Munro texts: *Lives of Girls and Women* and *Who Do You Think You Are?* The chapter first focuses on the perspective of the narrator in *Lives*, specifically on the role of temporal and spatial distance resting between Del Jordan's narrative's vantage point and her narrative's subject, and how this distance affects the nature of her small-town depiction. In the previous two chapters, this distance was shown to shape the nature of small-town retrospective according to a convention. In Munro's text, however, there is no clear distinction between then and now, there and here. Del's narration is a shifting mixture of past and present, and her voice seemingly disregards time and space. Del's narrative technique is composed of different historical perspectives that she garners from her artistic and epistemological models. These influences are distinguished by their vastly different historical consciousnesses, and, while they coalesce to form Del's voice, they are the very same forces that shape the topography of Wawanash County, Huron County's fictional stand-in. The first part of this chapter discusses the intricate attachment and formal influence existing among the obscured boundaries of landscape, history, and artist within the text itself. Del's exploration of her personal past reflects her present artistic technique, or, rather, the form of her narrative technique determines how she tells her own story, how she renders her experience in small-town place. The second part of this chapter focuses on the development of Munro's representation of small-town place and a gradual distrust of memory in her latter volume *Who Do You Think You Are?* I argue that the representation of the small town contained in that book reveals that the nostalgic return to one's small-town origins, as portrayed in *Sunshine Sketches* and *Fifth Business*, is a privileged act that requires a sense of, or actual distance between, remembering subject and remembered object. Revisiting the place of the past reveals memory's misdirection, its falsity, and subsequently spurs a continued search for identity in the present.

In 1971, one year after the publication of Robertson Davies's *Fifth Business*, Alice Munro's *Lives of Girls and Women* was released. The initial sales were disappointing (Metcalf 62) and might suggest that Munro's vision of a small-town childhood, even though ostensibly patterned on an established genre of Ontarian fiction, did not suit a public's palate more accommodated to either Stephen Leacock's populist mixture of humour and pathos or Davies's affectionate censure. Leacock's and Davies's critics often read Mariposa and Deptford as symbolic portraits of a small-town past that forms a current of national identity; their small towns appear to readers as images of a kinder, simpler Canadian self-portrait, one that is compelling in its wistful fictionalization of a national type. These national parallels are absent from Munro's criticism; no one reads her towns as representative of anything beyond the specific region of southern Ontario in which her stories are set. This is because of the specificity with which she documents place. Munro's use of quotidian detail, of landscapes and townscapes, of country manners, of work, recreation, and even diet, is matched by no other Ontario writer, except, perhaps, James Reaney.[1] By reading Munro's work, the reader understands the place in which it is set: its limits of economy and convention, its perverse sense of modesty, and its class system that underpins all interaction.

Even though a distinct sense of place develops in her stories, Munro resists the primacy of region in her writing, as she considers the regionalist content secondary, even unintentional: "I never think I'm writing a story about Wingham or I'm writing a story about a Southwestern Ontario small town. Ever. I just use that stuff because it is familiar to me ...

---

1 Reaney focuses intently on elements of the hyper local – for instance, the names of local plants. In "The Wild Flora of Elgin County," his persona advocates for knowledge of the local foliage, positing that understanding your region will make you "more serene & thoughtful / In doing so." In the essay "Ontario Culture and – What?" he states, "I happen to believe that if you don't know the weed that grows at your doorstep – knotweed – or the grass that grows in cemeteries – orchard or poverty grass – or the name of the tree outside your window, then you're not rooted in your environment" (253).

I'm not concerned with any kind of comprehensive picture" (Struthers "Real" 33). Yet a comprehensive picture develops nonetheless, specifically of how the unique qualities of place and character depend one on the other.

In order to construct her characters, Munro must establish the land to which they are attached. Her style of realism may accurately depict the region's society and topography, but this realism also complicates a rural trope that in the work of Leacock and Davies provides a background for the physical and psychological journeys of the characters. The proximity of Munro's narrators to the places they describe helps them resist the influence of an existing rural-urban associative value binary in their narratives. Her narrators see the small town for what it is, not what a small-town convention may dictate; there is no conventional way of remembering a small-town childhood in Munro's work, since place does more than simply act as a parochial starting point for nationally symbolic characters who then imaginatively shape those origins through recall. The relationship between Munro's characters and place is subtle, active, shifting, and symbiotic, and, despite her suggestion that regionalism is an unintended by-product of her stories, she does acknowledge that place is an important component of her texts: "I am certainly a regional writer in that whatever I do I seem only able to make things work ... if I use this ... this plot of land that is mine ... I should be able to write a novel about somebody living in Don Mills ... but I'm not" (Metcalf 56). Place is imperative for Munro's writing, and it operates as the mortar for the pieces of her plots and identities of her characters; any study of her work must address its role and function. This first section explores the exceedingly complex influence between the narrator in *Lives of Girls and Women*, Del Jordan, and the place she inhabits, Wawanash County. Del remembers her childhood in this specific place, but, more than that, this place has influenced the very form of her narrative, how she remembers and tells her story.

Del Jordan(s): Narrator(s)

Critics have long discussed a sense of doubleness in Del's narration: that there are two Dels of the text, one experiencing and one narrating. Both are difficult to distinguish from one another: where does one begin and the other end? This section begins by sketching the arguments of other critics who comment on the style of Del's narration. I do this in order to establish a critical framework for what follows. This section focuses primarily on those theories that either locate a split in the temporal fabric of Del's narrative or identify a dialectic in the composition of her retrospective; identifying these features helps distinguish some formal elements of Munro's novel from those of Leacock and Davies. In *Sunshine Sketches,* a definitive time and place materialize from which the narrator constructs the town, and by the end of the book Mariposa is revealed to be a product of the collective nostalgic, melancholic memories of the successful businessmen who recollect what turns out to be the text's past, Mariposa, deep in the heart of the text's present, the city. The narrator is a companion to these men, and he instructs them in appropriate methods of retrospect, methods that utilize the temporal gap to idealize generic memories: they see things from a distance. In *Fifth Business*, Dunstan Ramsay reveals his temporal location, his text's present, from the outset of the novel; he is an elderly man of cosmopolitan experience recalling significant events for the benefit of his former headmaster: the story of his past is interpreted by his present self.

The past and the present in both texts remain distinct, and, as in all retrospectives, the present holds a hegemonic interpretive position. Laurajane Smith contends that the influence of the past shifts according to the needs of the present: "it [the past] can never be understood solely within its own terms; the present continually rewrites the meaning of the past" (*Uses* 58); its influence, therefore, is always reinterpreted "through the dominant discourses of the present day" (58–9), often to address the "needs of the present" (58). Mariposa is a necessary counterpart to the strained and harried nature of urban life, providing the solace of an imagined stable past to the actual present; it is safe to assume that Mariposa would appear much different had it been recollected under different circumstances. Similarly, Deptford's narrow parochialism provides Dunstan with the retrospective justification he needs when reviewing his life of solitary, idiosyncratic, intellectual pursuits, a life deemed unacceptable by Deptfordian standards. In these two texts, the present shapes the past according to the desires of those looking back across time and space. The relationship of the past and present in Del's narration, however, is far more complex, as neither element exists as a stable narrative pole between which rests the distance between the narrated and the narrator.

W.J. Keith claims that, while Leacock and Davies write of the small town from an outsider perspective, Munro writes from a rural perspective with "total immediacy" (167). If this "total immediacy" stretches the bounds of retrospective plausibility, many critics resolve Del's uncanny ability to remember by identifying "doubleness" in her narrative voice: that is, doubleness of perspective and time involved in Del's autobiographical persona. Some (John Orange, John Moss, Robert Thacker, Ildikó de Papp Carrington) suggest that there are two Dels simultaneously narrating her past experience. These critics posit two intertwined narrative voices: a younger Del who experiences and an older Del who can contextualize and reflect on that experience. These voices exist simultaneously and unmediated from one another – "memory" would not be the best word to characterize Del's narration.

This hybrid of voices would suggest Del's transcendence of the effect of a spatio-temporal gap on memory, as there is little distance between narrator (narrating subject, or present self) and narrated (narrative object, or past self). As already discussed, the effect of this distance is central to the appeal of Mariposa, and, as the final train journey navigates the distance between present and past, the process of the town's aesthetic shaping is revealed; Leacock draws attention to the malleability of memory, the distortion of objects when viewed from a temporal distance. This distortion appeals to Dunstan when he revisits his own hometown after extending his circle of reference to the grand locales of the wider world, but is something he ultimately rejects. In all three texts, it is possible to approximate the years in which the stories take place, but apparent only in Leacock's and Davies's is the duration of time that separates the narrators from their pasts. The temporal synthesis in *Lives* conceals the narrator's present position, thus obscuring the growth of the child into the adult, a Bildungsroman-type growth that is commonly rendered as the journey from rural beginnings to urban achievement. Del's past remains unenclosed by the "dominant discourses of the present day" (Smith *Uses* 59); her past, it would seem, is unfiltered by her present, and, because it remains unshaped by the directed retrospect of longing, it offers no solace or balm or justification to the remembering subject.

A contrastive reading helps put Del's narrative style in relief. Consider this passage from *Fifth Business* in which Dunstan weighs his guilt immediately after describing the circumstances around the throwing of the central snowball: "Ah, if dying were all there was to it! Hell and torment at once ... the more time that passed, the less I was able to accuse Percy Boyd Staunton of having thrown the snowball that sent Mrs. Dempster simple. His brazen-faced refusal to accept responsibility seemed to deepen my own guilt, which had now become the guilt of concealment as well as action" (55). The ironically elevated diction of Dunstan the narrator comically exaggerates and thus limits the guilt experienced during his childhood; the narrator patronizes his earlier self, mitigating his earlier shame through the context of his vast later experience. Dunstan pats Dunny on the head and clucks "there there."

In recounting a similar instance of juvenile misbehaviour, Del does not comically exaggerate her sensations in her description of biting her cousin Mary Agnes during Craig's funeral; rather, she renders those physical feelings through a comprehensive immediacy that accounts for momentary, shifting, and fleeting sensations:

> Being forgiven creates a peculiar shame. I felt hot, and not just from the blanket. I felt held close, stifled, as if it was not air I had to move and talk through in this world but something thick as cotton wool. This shame was physical, but went far beyond sexual shame, my former shame of nakedness; now it was as if not the naked body but all the organs inside it – stomach, heart, lungs, liver – were laid bare and helpless. The nearest thing to this that I had ever known before was the feeling I got when I was tickled beyond endurance – horrible, voluptuous feeling of exposure, of impotence, self-betrayal. (57)

Del relates the intensity of the emotion through detailed simile and understanding, but there is no questioning of the depth and legitimacy of this feeling through the diminishing effects of the intervening years, those resting between event and remembrance. Instead, Del characterizes the exact nature of emotion, an understanding that could result only from contemplative distance; this retrospect does not necessarily *recount* but *relates* by translating the emotional intensity of a child into the understanding of an adult. As Thacker states, Del simultaneously "experiences and understands" ("Clear" 58).

This narrative technique complicates the idea of innocence and simplicity commonly identified with both childhood and countryside; the rural past can be simple only when looking back from a distance, which Del is not doing. While Del's countryside accommodates complex childhood experience in which the child understands both significance and consequence through a purposeful mélange of past and present, it would be difficult to characterize that child as more innocent than an adult. Because Munro elides the stable temporal vantage points of past and present in this narrative, there is a resulting effect on her representation of landscape and small town. Jubilee and Wawanash County are not products of retrospection in the traditional sense, but they are landscapes described through Del's ostensible transcendence of temporal and physical distance. The subject-object relationship of the city and country seen in previous texts, and an integral part of the pastoral design, is stretched beyond the point of recognition in *Lives*; while the book shares features with pastoral writing, the breakdown of the pastoral design within its pages makes it difficult to classify the work as such.

Del's experience of time obfuscates the operation of an urban and rural polarity within the text, a significant break from the general trend in small-town fiction. There is little beyond the "covert" indications of Del's adult life to suggest the presence of an urban alternative to which the rural inhabitant has gradually made her way, in terms of both geography and culture.[2] With the entirety of her artistic vision comes an extra-textual tension with her literary predecessors, since Jubilee is a site that accommodates experience atypical of the small-town convention or archetype represented by Mariposa and toyed with in *Fifth Business*; Jubilee is not simply reconstructed through memory to address some present need. Del's voice does not locate a divide between the rural past and urban present, as her narration obscures the line upon which those types of relations are built.

Place and Historical Perspective

The small-town idyll is constructed through the falsifying lens of retrospect. Dunstan's "problem of perspective" is a reflection of this view, as it detracts from his ability to establish a stable and accurate version of Deptford, to resolve the Mariposan ideal with the Deptfordian reality. The associative complement that the small town of the past provides to the urban centre of the present is absent in *Lives* because of the distinctive perspective of the narrator. Locating the geographical and temporal source of Del's narration is difficult, and, as her present "time and place" is concealed, a rural-urban dichotomy cannot develop through her small-town retrospective. Thus, Jubilee is constructed not

---

2   That is, except for the university entrance exam for which Del is seen studying. At the end of the book, her attendance at university remains in question, but, while the book ends with Del's subsequent movements remaining indeterminable, she does resolve to live a life of independence. The end of the "Epilogue" alludes to the direction of her artistic life more so than it does her thoughts on the location that can accommodate that life.

as a ready contrast to urban life but as a complex place that remains uninfluenced by the enclosing conventions of those influential rural associative values.

Munro generally writes of a period after the heyday of the small town and of an area that, having experienced a flurry of activity in the late nineteenth century, had subsequently "entered its present slow decline" (*Lives* 31). The inhabitants of Jubilee have been left behind a generation ago by their more ambitious cousins (those perhaps likely to recall Jubilee fondly) and are more likely to hang around, mouldering in a sense of "perverse pride," much like Del's cousin Ruth McQueen. Leacock and Davies both write of a period before urbanization established its cultural dominance over the stagnating small towns, but also, and more importantly, they write of characters yearning for larger fortunes in the booming cities. By contrast, Jubilee is that stagnated small town, complacent, proud, slightly masochistic. It is, in fact, an unwelcome reminder of the degree to which the nation's business is located in the urban centres. Munro offers a vision of a more recent small-town Ontario past, one set after that period in which critics locate a communal image of national import.

The specificity of place involved in Munro's writing is another factor that resists parallels to a national past. While critics such as Coral Ann Howells and John Weaver laud Munro's accurate vision of the local, they also offer accounts of readers within her depicted regions who feel her stories are not really so accurate after all, but rather "scandalous gossip" (Howells *Alice Munro* 3) or skewed versions of the past (Thacker "Connection" 215). Other critics argue that Munro's writing possesses universal appeal, since its documentation of rural-Ontario townscapes transcends regional and national concerns: "Fairgrounds, grandstands, racetrack oval, mills, hostelries, floods, house plots – all are timeless features of human communal life; there are no garages, drive-ins, or strip malls to suggest organic discontinuity" (Martin and Ober 139). These features are hardly "timeless," nor do they suggest "organic" features of the civilized society, and Martin and Ober seem to mistake the townscapes of yesteryear for innate manifestations of human civilization itself.

The significance of Munro's accurate depiction of place fully develops when viewed in relation to Del's artistic technique, since an organic continuity exists between the landscapes of Wawanash County and her narrative style – the same influences shape both artistic technique and topography. The landscapes of Wawanash have been inscribed with a language of settlement, and Del's characteristic fusion of past and present is really a synthesis of the different historical consciousnesses that have shaped that landscape. Struthers has called the text a "portrait of the girl as a young artist" ("Real" 25), a comment signifying that this story documents the development of a life as well as of an artistic approach: a *Künstlerroman*. I argue that Del's artistry emerges from her encounters with those historical perspectives that dominate the psychological and physical landscape of both Jubilee and Wawanash County.

Del's first artistic model is her Uncle Craig, an amateur historian documenting the history of Wawanash County. His perspective on history is authoritative, and his reverence for, and solemn attitude towards, the region's past outlines a respectful approach that he then prescribes for Del's own relationship with familial forebears. That respect demands an accurate sense of chronology, as a precise knowledge of the linearity of events is an important component of his reverence for the past. When a young Del asks a question that betrays her ignorance of sequential time, Craig becomes irritated: "He was displeased with me not on account of any vanity about his age, but because of my inaccurate notions of time and history" (29). Craig's written history of the region is a dry, comprehensive document that excludes nothing. The facts in his historical work tick by like seconds on a clock, with no sense of an overarching or unifying frame. When Del comes into possession of this document, she abandons it in her basement and it is ruined in a flood some years later; the document itself is washed away by one of the minor events that Craig had so diligently recorded, almost as if it was overwhelmed by the current of time it had painstakingly tried to plot.

Not only does Craig's acute sense of chronology inform his written history, but it also overwhelms it. Craig's methods involve simply the recording of detail, and he embodies a negative artistic example for Del. As Del describes it, Craig's history is "a great accumulation of the most ordinary facts, which it was his business to get in order. Everything had to go into his history, to make it the whole history of Wawanash County. He could not leave anything out" (31). While Craig may not fictionalize or reconstruct the past according to his own purposes, he also fails to interpret it, and, as a result, his history lacks coherence, a sense of regional definition that his diligent recording should, at the very least, outline. His reverence for the past is rooted simply in images of precedence and does not stem from any significance or meaning within those images, as he can decipher no unifying message within his pathological recording. Craig betrays his anxiety that the potential for regional meaning and order in the past exists, but his compulsive recording has been unsuccessful in uncovering it.

John Weaver suggests that a dichotomy of "historical inquiry" exists within the text, a dichotomy composed of Craig's and Del's methods of understanding the past (381). Yet Del's method does not form a total rejection of Craig's artistic example. Rather, a constructive influence exists between uncle and niece: Del explicitly relates her attraction to Craig's compulsive historical recording in the "Epilogue." The covert voice of the adult Del dominates in her outline of the difference between her adolescent artistic method and that of her later life:

> It did not occur to me then that one day I would be so greedy for Jubilee. Voracious and misguided as Uncle Craig out at Jenkin's Bend, writing his History, I would want to write things down.
>
> I would try to make lists. A list of all the stores and businesses going up and down the main street and who owned them, a list of family names, names on the tombstones in the cemetery … The hope of accuracy we bring to such tasks is crazy, heartbreaking.
>
> And no list could hold what I wanted, for what I wanted was every last thing, every layer of speech and thought, stroke of light on bark or walls … held still and held together – radiant, everlasting. (253)

Beyond ordering the minutiae of her past life, Del wants to preserve those momentary flashes in which she perceives the order of fleeting experiences, and also to synthesize these moments to provide her past life with a sense of coherence. But this passage also marks both Del's acceptance in principle of Craig's project of documenting the region, and her decision to supplement his methods.

Del's eventual artistic method contrasts sharply with the one she employs in the outline for her adolescent novel, sketched in the final chapter. This novel, while based on life in Jubilee, finds its form through Del's thorough familiarity with genres of fiction rather than through her truthful observations of the town. The adolescent novel, constructed according to the precepts of genre, is ostensibly about the town's noteworthy, yet collapsed, family the Sherriffs. Del, however, realizes the mimetic shortcomings of her tale: "I did not pay much attention to the real Sherriffs, once I had transformed them for fictional purposes" (248). In an instance in which her adult contemplation merges with her youthful experience, Del's suggestion that her ultimate artistic vision will aim for an impossible accuracy comes only after a meeting with one of the real Sherriffs, Bobby, who has spent much time in a mental hospital. This meeting is an artistic revelation for Del, as she comes to reject the dishonest prerequisites of imported generic forms that direct the artistic eye and circumscribe observation (Smythe 127–8). Del's subsequent attraction to Craig's compulsive accuracy, his voracious veracity, is balanced by her recognition of the Sisyphean futility of simple documentation.

Craig's approach to the past is laboured, and its drudgery registers on his body. In describing Craig's office, Del takes special notice of a photograph on his wall, and imparts the parallels that exist between these photographic figures and Craig himself: "Several men in shirtsleeves, with droopy moustaches, and fierce but somehow helpless expressions, stood around a horse and wagon" (28). The physical exhaustion of these men's lives is symbolized by the "droop" of their mustaches; the "helpless expressions" on their faces betray otherwise stoic countenances as only so much posturing. That physical depletion is echoed in Del's description of Craig: "One of his eyes was blind, and had been operated on but remained dark and clouded; that eyelid had a menacing droop. His face was square and sagging, his body stout" (29). Much like his ancestors now tacked to his wall, Craig is weighed down by his task. The unselective recording of historical fact produces a weighty, voluminous manuscript constructed through the same blind work ethic required to clear land; each recorded fact is analogous to another felled tree, yet Craig fails to realize that his purpose is not to establish a field of facts. His effort exhausts and counteracts whatever artistic invigoration is required to shape his tome. Similarly, the family tree he compiles may be an "intricate structure of lives supporting us from the past" (31), but through Craig's comprehensive methods of "historical inquiry," it becomes a cumbersome edifice bearing down on the survivors, demanding tribute, Craig imagines, through precision.

Craig is unselfconscious enough to continue the plodding labours of his forebears, and he fails to recognize a cautionary significance in his documented litany of tragedies; emulation of the past, a past marked by failure and disappointment, is the only purpose Craig takes from his work. When Del finally provides a selection of Craig's history at the end of "Heirs of the Living Body," she reveals a record of futility, death, and defeat (61). Craig's own death comes long before he completes his labour, and thus he fails at his task of ordering "a great accumulation of the most ordinary facts" (31). This pattern of failure speaks to the real lineage of the region, as the settlers' and Craig's task is nothing less than to establish a full external model of their comprehensive ideal of order. Craig, then, carries on a tradition in which the realization of the futility of one's efforts is avoided only through death. Del's ultimate refusal to continue Craig's project is a refusal to carry out an enumerative surveying of the past. Her artistic decision at the end of the book reveals her ambivalence towards a cultural heritage for which Craig serves as a model, and this decision displays her desire to be both part of a historical tradition and also outside of it by serving as its artist. By keeping one foot along the community's historical trajectory (or historical rut) and one foot outside of it, Del feels a part of this lineage but can also observe it from across an established distance.

"Heirs of the Living Body" is a key to understanding the origins of Del's artistic technique. In a lecture to her daughter, Addie Jordan constructs a different understanding of our relationship with time and our surroundings: a symbolic cyclical alternative to Craig's staunch linearity. In discussing Craig's death, Addie states "'[s]o we say, Uncle Craig is dead. The person is dead. But that's just our way of looking at it. That's just our human way. If we weren't thinking all the time in terms of persons, if we were thinking of Nature, all Nature going on and on, parts of it dying – well not dying, changing, *changing* is the word I want, changing into something else'" (47). Addie's musings propose a transcendence of death by seeing individuals not as autonomous and temporary selves, but as part of a natural world; by connecting the human to a natural cycle, she revises Craig's linear understanding of time through which he plots human progress. While Craig remembers and reveres the dead, Addie suggests that the living embody the dead. Addie presents an alternative structure of family as an organic continuity that flourishes despite the demise of individual parts; the organic whole merges individuals through time, a notion that echoes in Del's later decision to continue with but alter Craig's history, to accept his project but revise his artistic methods. This image of the family as an organic whole stands in stark contradistinction to that of Craig and of Del's aunts, as Del's father makes clear: "they do have a different set of notions, and they might easy be upset" (49). They revere the primacy and integrity of the individual who, after death, survives in memory but also in the emulation of his or her life's work by the living. This is something encouraged by Del's aunts when they bequeath to her Craig's manuscript: "'Maybe you could learn to copy his way,'" they tell Del (62), lines that, in fact, caution Del against continuing Craig's plodding deference to both history and family.

Craig, Elspeth, and Grace see both history and family as a linear narrative; their historical perspective has, at its core, an assumption that the trajectory of familial and regional "progress" will experience an eventual culmination, an apex that will retroactively provide meaning to all previous events and experience. This perspective is distinctly opposed to the cycles of the family body charted by Addie. The guiding principle of Craig's history mirrors Sylviane Agacinski's distillation of a western conception of time; epochs form only in retrospect, and it is the belief in the end of time, the millenarian design that rests at the heart of understandings of progress, that provides all preceding history with a sense of purpose (4). Historical order can form only in retrospect, and, despite Craig's best efforts at accounting for the smallest of details, providing his regional history with a sense of meaning eludes him, since that history is ongoing; no matter how comprehensive it may be, its underlying pattern incorporates an endlessly deferred signified, only an expectation of meaning at some point in the future.

In an apparent acknowledgment of her mother's musings on natural metamorphosis, Del is able to incorporate Craig's method of "historical inquiry," the "crazy, heartbreaking" "hope of accuracy" (253), into her own distinct, synthetic narrative style. Del comes to document her own life not as a linear narrative seen from a present vantage point, but as a shifting organic whole whose composite parts she can simultaneously experience and understand. Del inherits Craig's overt concern with detail, but, to understand the entirety of her experience, its final, formal meaning, she must complement her inheritance with an alternative method of historical understanding, one that denies the primacy of linearity and allows her to perceive order within a life in progression. While Addie's theory initially raises the spectre of a possible alternative relationship with family, temporality, and a type of genetic memory, it is only through Del's relationship to Garnet French that she accesses that alternate understanding of time, family, and the individual.

Primitivism, Simultaneity, and Continuity

Discussions on the meaning of landscape and its connection to primitivism in Munro's work focus largely on the divide between town and country, between "primitive" and civilized spaces (see, e.g., Rasporich, *Dance*; Robson). These readings tend to see the town and country in contrast to one another, as offering a counterpoint to one another's symbolic associations: the town as civilized, ordered site; the country representing disorder, the uncivilized, and the wild. The tension within Munro's regions occurs between this dichotomy. However, *Lives of Girls and Women* displays a far more nuanced influence of primitivism. Dichotomies of urban-rural, civilized-primitive, and ordered-chaotic only *appear* to frame Munro's representation of landscape and town, since, on a closer look, the rural landscape surrounding Jubilee offers no symbolic counterpoint to the town itself; rural and urban associations are not bound by geography or topography.

In one sense, this complication of a spatial binary echoes what Thacker calls Munro's narrative "dialectic" of past and present. Del's narrative technique treats her life as a continuum that she experiences as a simultaneous whole, whereas in *Sunshine Sketches* a past-present dichotomy is maintained largely because of the inaccessibility of an imagined small-town past to a present urban reality. Just as Del's narrative transcends the past-present structure of retrospective narratives, so too does she disregard the complementary spatial associations of Leacock and Davies; Munro renders experience exclusive to neither urban nor rural areas, nor to adult or childhood consciousness. And I would point out a further destabilization of the binary in Munro's text, particularly through her depiction of Garnet French and family. This family has a greater significance in the text than to simply provide an associative counterpoint to the townsfolk of Jubilee, and, when we examine this significance in relation to that of Craig, we see emerging the influence both have on Del's narrative technique.

What occurs beyond the boundaries of Jubilee proper, I suggest, only *seems* shaped by Del's primitivism. On the Flats Road one evening during the height of her relationship with Garnet, Del notices her misshapen shadow as the sun sets behind her: "I watched this strange elongated figure with the faraway, small round head ... and it seemed to me the shadow of a stately, unfamiliar African girl" (231). The shadow, or in other words the outline or shape of her body, allows for Del's self-observation at strictly the level of form. Here, beyond the borders of the town, Del finds that form unfamiliar. This recognition alludes to her current situation with Garnet; she has temporarily abandoned a life of the mind with her friend Jerry Storey for a life of the body with Garnet, and this moment of crepuscular reflection intimates Del's awareness of not only this migration, but also her lack of familiarity with a life ruled by physical sensation.

The shadow spread out before her offers Del an image in the abstract of the nature of the life she could expect with Garnet, in which sensation may trump thought but would constitute a type of performance for Del. Del's primitivist use of the connotative content of "Africa" to elaborate on the primacy of the body speaks of the state of ethnographic paradigms in rural Ontario in the late 1940s. If indeed Munro locates "primal energy and sexuality" and "chaos and disorder" beyond the borders of Jubilee, as Rasporich claims (*Dance* 138), then she betrays her attraction to the idea of the "primitive" as a representative of the unconscious mind and the hazards of, and attraction to, human impulse. Here, Munro may be self-consciously playing with the types of primitivist notions expressed in many modernist works of the early twentieth century, notably those of T.S. Eliot and D.H. Lawrence. In *T.S. Eliot and the Cultural Divide*, David Chinitz suggests that, for modern primitivists, Africans were thought to be connected to those original rhythmical rituals upon which all culture and religion is based, but from which modern societies have strayed. While this fallacious expression is based on discredited notions of cultural evolution, the modernists felt that their project involved a sort of cultural triage. Del, a well-read teenager in rural Ontario in the 1940s, someone who reveals her familiarity with modernist literature (175), projects onto her shadow an image of an "African girl," a result, perhaps, of her familiarity with modern primitivist theories and her precocious willingness to use them to self-dramatize her life. But as Del projects the "primitive" associations merely onto her shadow, onto a distorted image of herself, she is, in fact, self-consciously playing with literary self-perception, with the tendency to aggrandize personal situation and identity, which, in this case, is heavily influenced by her love affair with Garnet. She is not simply writing of her experience; she is writing about perceiving herself in the process of experiencing. Neither is it her physical location, the Flats Road, that entices these types of associations; rather, they emerge from Del's tendency to view her life through genre precepts and literary convention. This passage begins to reveal the source of the associative qualities of the various corners of Wawanash County, as these possess only the associative connotations that have been projected on to them by their inhabitants.

Locating a primitive/modern split along Jubilee's town line is an easy generalization of Munro's topographies. Munro is too complex a writer to simply follow in a primitivist vein that in the 1960s and '70s, when she was writing this book, would have been out of fashion and, more likely, challenged due to its overt racism. Beyond the "ordered" pattern of Jubilee's streets, which in the Manichean constructs put forward by Rasporich and Robson denote order and control, rests the chaos of the French household, yet Uncle Craig also lives outside of Jubliee's perimeter, at Jenkin's Bend; and, if anything, Craig is a stalwart of order, control, reason, and precise (Western) chronology. Unlike the pattern apparent in the fiction of Leacock and Davies, landscape does not inform character in Munro's text, as there are no characteristics naturalized by the discursive categories of the rural and urban; parochialism and urbanity are traits belonging to individuals, not landscape. The inhabitants of Wawanash County provide whatever associations the land and town may possess, and thus, in *Lives*, it is the people who shape the physical and connotative makeup of the land, not vice versa.[3]

This reading contrasts with those of others, such as Rasporich's claim that a "landscape of gothic mind" related to Frye's theory of the "deep terror in confronting the frontier and a northern land" (*Dance* 136) exists within the landscape of Wawanash County. However, all land in *Lives* has been inhabited and, in many cases, abandoned by humans, thus sketching onto the landscape the faint outlines of failed human intentions: "It was the same with the history of the county, which had been opened up, settled, and had grown, and entered its present slow decline" (31). This is no frontier, and confrontation occurs not between cowering settlers and a fearsome, inanimate landscape, but between the remaining inhabitants and the failures of their forebears; the land's illuminating spirit emerges from its deep texture of dashed hopes. In reading Munro's stories, we enter a landscape in which the late-Victorian optimism of *Sunshine Sketches* has stagnated long ago, as exuberance and hope have decayed into the melancholy of a waning stability; Munro's Wawanash County is an old landscape, a landscape darkened by a long history of declining settlement. Here, the rural areas provide no corrective counterpoint to the fluidity, anomie, and vagaries of city life, as the rural areas themselves are shifting entities replete with their own malaise; there is no hint of Jubilee, despite its name, presenting an ideal, pastoral or otherwise.

---

3 Further evidence of the lack of a town-country, order-chaos binary comes from Aunt Moira's depiction of Porterfield: "not a dry town like Jubilee, it had two beer parlours facing each other across the main street, one in each of the hotels ... From behind her darkened front windows she had watched men hooting like savages" (40).

The primitivist inflection of Munro's characters is unconnected to topographic boundaries in the landscape. For instance, Del first encounters Garnet at a Baptist revival at the town hall, the centre of the community. The ceremony itself is characterized by its collective impulses in which the body is to be moved by the Holy Spirit and merge with the sensations of others. The rhythms of the preacher's sermon are more important than his actual words in establishing a bodily continuity among the crowd: "'And some of your ropes can't take much more! Some of your ropes are almost past the point of no return. They are frayed out with sin, they are eaten away with sin, they are nothing left but a thread! Nothing but a thread is holding you out of Hell!'" (212). The sermon pulsates, and it is during this very sensual and even sexually cathartic ritual that Del is attracted to Garnet entirely through physical impressions: "I smelled the thin hot cotton shirt, sunburnt skin, soap and machine oil … He put his hand on the back of the chair about two inches from mine. Then it seemed as if all sensation in my body, all hope, life, potential, flowed down into that one hand" (211–12). Garnet's presence takes Del out of her usual conscious activity, which would have been to analyse the words of the preacher: "Ordinarily I would have been interested in listening to this and in seeing how people were taking it … But my attention was taken up with our two hands on the back of the chair … I felt angelic with gratitude, truly as if I had come out on another level of existence" (213). These furtive movements towards romance produce physical euphoria in Del, a sensation that resists the conscious mind's examination and limitation of its affect. Garnet's actions constitute a surrogate proselytizing, as his body has produced in Del a feeling of spiritual transcendence that the rhythms and words of the sermon were powerless to produce. This euphoria transcends the individual and results from entering a type of "primitive cultural totality" (Chinitz 73), which the Baptist revival both represents and produces; Garnet's touch initiates Del into this bodily collective. As they hold hands, Del may refuse the sheet music with the printed words, but her participation in the ritual is no longer subject to her conscious decision: "I remembered the words and sang. I would have sung anything" (214). Despite the appearance of initiating a romantic intrigue, Garnet's attentions have "caught, bound borne away" (214) Del into the massed collectivity of the gathering: "Singing, people swayed together" (213).[4]

---

4 The mention of the word "revival" suggests a return according to a cyclical rhythm and associates Garnet with something other than the linearity of Del's relatives.

This first contact does not produce a verbal exchange but ends with Garnet leaving and "joining a crowd of people who were all going down to the front of the hall, responding to an invitation to make a decision for Jesus" (214). Del is left alone, but left desiring a conduit into a type of sensation that will, again, submerge the primacy of her conscious mind. This has been one of her baptisms, as the title of the chapter suggests: it is her first experience of the non-individuating passions of the collective human body, where she has felt the pull of the rhythms of ritual for which the proximity of Garnet serves as a surrogate.

What Del craves through her relationship with Garnet are the imperatives of the body, which are first presented as part of a religious ritual. Later, during their first "approaches to sex" (218), Del experiences a feeling similar to that felt during the Baptist ceremony, a "floating feeling, feeling of being languid and protected and at the same time possessing unlimited power" (218). The pleasures of the body provide this feeling of protection, as they allow Del to experience something akin to the transcendence of linear time and the individual self. While Addie stresses the importance of individual distinction and accomplishment, Del's relationship with Garnet involves something more akin to the biological; she no longer feels the threat of remaining undifferentiated, as simply part of Jubilee. By submerging her conscious mind into the warm ocean of a gratification that can come only from the merging of one body with another, she temporarily retreats from her conscious identity; Del's mother Addie may characterize this as a "'softening of the brain'" (220), but Del's relationship with Garnet also limits the demands, perhaps even tyranny, of individual consciousness, experience, and distinction.

Soon Del is attending Garnet's "Baptist Young People's Society," and her observations of those in attendance focus almost exclusively on the physical. Those associated with Garnet are defined by their physicality and provided with only a limited individuality. Caddie McQuaig is "hefty and jovial," Ivan and Orrin Walpole are a pair of "monkey-faced brothers ... who do gymnastic tricks," "Holy Betty" is a "big-busted, raw faced girl," and a number of unremarkable girls from the Chainway store remain indistinguishable, except for one, Del "could not remember which," who is identifiable only for her apparent past pregnancy (216). Overtones of class taint Del's depictions: "I smiled at everybody but was jealous, appalled, waiting only for all this to end" (217). The real difference between Del and the Baptists is that the physicality of the latter relegates them to a barely individuated and debased

horde. These figures are clear examples of the "backwardness, ignorance, [and] limitation" (R. Williams 1) of the anti-idyllic rural associative values, yet their physical anomalies are equal parts town and
country, not simply inbred farmers as Davies might insinuate; this
"other side" of Wawanash County cannot be located geographically.

Wawanash County has been shaped by its generations of inhabitants,
and the land itself does not readily reflect a complementary urban-rural
binary. Even though the fringes of the county seem sheltered from the
main current of modernity, the landscape simply mirrors the historical epistemology of its inhabitants. During her trip with Garnet into
the depths of the Jericho Valley, Del remembers an earlier trip that she
took with her mother into this isolated part of the county: "Wild roses
brushed the cab. We drove for miles through thick bush. There was a
field full of stumps. I remembered that, remembered my mother saying, 'One time it was all like that, all this country. They haven't pro-
gressed here much beyond the pioneer stage. Maybe they're too lazy.
Or the land isn't worth it. Or a combination of both'" (221). The road
to Jericho Valley is not a trip back to an earlier period of the county's
development, but a corridor offering an exit from those other parts of
the county that reflect a chronological sense of progress, such as the
ordered, cultivated land documented in Craig's text; Jericho Valley has
become detached from a linear sense of order and time. The field of
stumps is the only indication of settlement, but even that was abandoned before it became tenable for agriculture. Apart from these echoes
of a possibility, the land has, as a result of human neglect, slipped back
into a pre-modern, even atemporal existence outside the dominant
chronology of the surrounding land.

Members of Garnet's family, aside from the matriarch, remain loosely
differentiated. Names as markers of individual identity are unimportant to Garnet and his family. James Carscallen comments on Del's
perception of Garnet's reality as a "'world without names'" (45) and
contrasts Garnet with Jerry Storey, who lives in a "world with names ...
but without things" (45).[5] Del's introduction to Garnet's family does not

---

5 Carscallen's comments on Garnet's "world" are reminiscent of Michael Bell's
   description of the primitive sensibility as an inability to make a distinction "between
   the inner world of feeling and the external order of existence" (8). Garnet's
   impulsiveness, his history of violence, and his sensuality define his character,
   suggesting his inner world of feeling transcribes itself, with little filtering, into his
   external surroundings.

involve the nominal markers needed to distinguish one member from another: "He did not introduce me to anybody. Members of his family would appear – I was not sure which were members of his immediate family and which were uncles, aunts, cousins – and would start talking to him, looking sideways at me" (222). The precision with which Craig renders his family tree is absent among the Frenches, who are numerable ("[t]here were twelve people around the table" (226)), but whose hierarchical family structure remains hazy, almost unimportant. For Craig, "it was not the individual names that were important, but the whole solid, intricate structure of lives supporting us from the past" (31). While the names plotted along Craig's family tree are secondary, its structure pinpoints the individual's relationship to linear history, a chronology absent from Del's impressions of the French family. Craig's tree possesses an intricate syntax in which an individual's position accrues meaning through its relational antecedents, and that meaning, while ostensibly precise, lacks satisfactory signification because the narrative of the family is incomplete. The lines drawn from one individual to another configure his family tree much like a linguistic analysis of grammatical structure. Indeed, the family is much like a sentence in which coherent meaning is constituted of individual parts progressing linearly from left to right, from the past into the present, a fitting symbol for Craig's understanding of the past, which exists in language and unfolds as narrative. With the Frenches, however, no such possibility of precise meaning exists.

In Garnet's family, structure and individuals are subordinate to a collectivized, non-hierarchical mass. In much the same way that Del's narrative voice disregards a division between past and present, the Frenches appear unconcerned with a hierarchy of temporally bound familial sequence, of keeping precedence and subsequence separate, a situation extending into their near-primordial living arrangement. They live in a house "down in a hollow, with big trees around so close you could not get a look at it as a whole house" (221). The lack of a clear perspective renders impossible a complete survey of their physical situation. Any fields or fences, markers of historical progression that construct a temporal linearity of the land, are hidden, and the house in which the Frenches live is literally merged with the surrounding landscape; the lack of these milestones obfuscates the past, dissolving a sense of chronological progress. I am not trying to suggest that the Frenches are "one" with the natural surroundings, but rather that their relationship with both history and landscape remains undefined or, at the very least, under-defined, because they have not clearly expressed it through the articulation of the present onto the surrounding landscape. The Frenches have an unstructured, and thus an unarticulated, relationship with history and landscape in language; by language, I mean written and oral, but also the various signifiers that inscribe evidence of a presence onto the land. These inscriptions allow one to see the landscape as a text, and to read it as an unfolding narrative from the past into the present, and they also imply a future trajectory.[6]

As a result of their inability to maintain the temporal signifiers of inhabitation, the Frenches appear to inhabit decay: "[s]keletons of a burned-out house and barn"; the house "painted yellow so long ago the paint was just streaks now on the splintered wood"; the linoleum "black and bumpy, just islands of the old pattern left, under the table, by the windows where it didn't get so much wear" (221–4). This is disorder only according to a historical perspective that demands the reiteration of a human presence through material growth according and in deference to historically established norms. This disorder conflates past and present by failing to maintain the rigid structures of interaction with a landscape, which establish historical texture through the chronological sediments of activity. The vitality and fluidity of the Frenches' alternative generational interaction, reflected in the irreverent pranks of the unnamed children and the gruff self-satisfaction and competence of the matriarch, attract Del: "There is no denying I was happy in that house" (226). Her happiness results from the absence of forms that would dictate the nature of familial relationships.

Decay results from a lack of maintenance. Maintenance is the reassertion of the present moment and denies the ravages and accumulation of time; it is also an expression of deference to one's ancestors by tending to an established order, both in terms of culture and practices of labour. Fences, orchards, and cultivated fields constitute the syntax of a community's expression on the surrounding landscape, and thus establish the signifiers of a region's history: a chronology of human activity on the land. Maintaining these signifiers becomes as important

---

6 The patriarch of the Frenches is a symbol for their uncontemplated, unvocalized, and even unconscious relationship with history and landscape: "In the corner of the verandah sat a man in overalls, vast and yellow as a Buddha, but with no such peaceful expression. He kept raising his eyebrows and showing his teeth in an immediately fading grin … [L]ater I realized it was a facial tic" (223).

in revealing one's place in a linear structure as the establishment and maintenance of a clear family tree. The lack of these expressions on the land surrounding the Frenches' farm denotes their lack of concern for expanding or even maintaining the temporal and physical boundaries of growth. By not reasserting the present moment onto the landscape, the Frenches allow the signifiers of a Western, linear temporality to decay, and they and their belongings blend into the atemporality of a non-chronology; a trip to the Frenches is a trip out of time as it is represented by, and as it dictates the life of, Uncle Craig.[7]

Wawanash County: The Orchard and the Hollow

The landscape is inscribed with physical manifestations of, at the very least, two historical perspectives, two manifestly different understandings of the past and its relationship to the present. Del's narrative is both influenced by and synthesizes the same influences, which can be termed the "orchard" and the "hollow." The orchard behind Uncle Craig's house at Jenkin's Bend is a physical correlative of his consciousness of the past, a metaphor for his conception of time and history as mediated by language. While it possesses conscious synchronic order that has been grafted onto the landscape, it also exudes a Western sense of progressive chronology through its suggestion of historical texture. The orchard possesses clear boundaries and requires regular maintenance; this maintenance will, over time, increase fruition, which can also be read as increased signification potential through an accrual of facts, a defining feature of Craig's plodding history. This symbol finds fuller expression in Craig's and Del's compulsion to make lists, to pile up ordinary details of which the ultimate significance can be evident only within a unifying frame, which is absent. This absence constitutes the major difference between Del's retrospective narrative and those of Leacock's narrator and Dunstan, as Del's absent, under-articulated vantage point does not allow her to provide a definitive interpretation of the significance of her past for the present.

An orchard may comprise simply fruit and trees, but the formal symbol of the "orchard" is needed to unify these individual objects. It is an

---

7 There is much to suggest that the rest of the county is struggling to maintain the expressions of a western chronology on the land, and particularly significant is Del's characterization of the region in a "slow decline" (31).

ideal symbol for Craig's compulsive documentation, as it is impossible for him to actuate a framing device. He needs that symbolic purpose, that sense of anticipated culmination, to project a sense of order onto the past, yet in doing so any evident past meaning is nullified by the assertion of present intentions. Thus, there rests in an orchard a dia-chronic signification in which the past is layered underneath a series of successive presents, the current one holding interpretive dominance. The formal significance of the orchard, the framing symbol for Craig's historical consciousness, can materialize only through recognition of its limitations, its boundaries, which Craig cannot or will not perceive. Del alone can do this, while her uncle, to paraphrase an old adage, cannot see the orchard through the trees: Craig cannot discern a meaning in the past despite its multitude of signifiers.

Craig's influence on Del is reflected in her compulsion to make lists. Here is her inventory of the Frenches' dinner: "For supper we had stewed chicken, not too tough, and good gravy to soften it, light dumplings, potatoes ... flat, round, floury biscuits, home-canned beans and tomatoes, several kinds of pickles, and bowls of green onions and radishes and leaf lettuce, in vinegar, a heavy molasses-flavoured cake, black-berry preserves" (225–6). She and Owen feel compelled to list the objects in Uncle Benny's house: "Owen and I, going home, would sometimes try to name off the things he had in his house, or just in his kitchen" (4). And then there is Del's description of the Anglican Church: "They had no furnace, evidently, just a space heater by the door, making its steady domestic noise. A strip of the same brown mat-ting went across the back and up the aisle; otherwise there was just a wooden floor, not varnished or painted, rather wide boards occasion-ally springy underfoot. Seven or eight pews on either side, no more" (97). Del's catalogues reveal the influence of Craig, who attempts to clarify the past through compulsive list making. He believes that an understanding of the past is possible through a collection of names, a strictly linguistic understanding of the past; the signification of that accumulating plethora of words, however, remains unknown, end-lessly deferred.

Del acquires a different understanding of time, heritage, and tem-poral relation, allowing her to form an alternative relationship with her own past, suggesting that she has escaped both from her family's historically determined psychological ethos and from the repetition of time-honoured but inadequate customs. This other relationship is represented by the contrasting symbol of the "hollow." The hollow in which the French homestead is built is an external metaphor for their historical consciousness; it is an unmaintained plot of land upon which any chronology that may have been sketched has been allowed to dissolve. It possesses no definite boundaries and no defined historical texture sculpted by human hands, which continuously reassert a dominant ideology of progress; it, therefore, connotes an indistinct linearity, a disorder of past and present. One's place in the hollow is not decided by the order established by one's ancestry, as that line from the past to the present is obfuscated; individual identity is subordinated not by the "intricate lives supporting [one] from the past" (31), but by an atemporal human collective in which relation remains undefined.

Del's refusal to be submerged fully into this collective is literally enacted in the baptism scene involving Garnet and Del. While this violent encounter marks the end of their relationship, it also marks the culmination of Del's artistic apprenticeship. On her subsequent walk back into Jubilee, Del reclaims the individuating intellectualism that previously characterized her personality before she "descended" into an unindividuating physicality with Garnet: "I felt my old self – my old devious, ironic, isolated self – beginning to breathe again and stretch and settle, though all around it my body clung cracked and bewildered, in the stupid pain of loss" (240). Del has been permanently altered, as her old self is newly conscious of the indelible influence of Garnet. Furthermore, the end of this affair has resulted in a new self-consciousness, one that allows her to observe herself while in the process of experiencing: "I was amazed to think that the person suffering was me, for it was not me at all; I was watching. I was watching, I was suffering" (241). While this is a fuller literary self-perception than was evident in Del's projection of an image of an "African girl" onto her shadow, it also reveals that Del's experiences have allowed her to enter into a life of the "self-created self," a life that remains aware of the effect, both on the self and others, of "gesture [and] image" (184). The simultaneity of experience and understanding is the culmination of her artistic journey, as her life, now clearly the subject of her study, is rendered from a perspective that acknowledges the distance between the thinking and feeling selves but also recognizes the inherent connection between the two. The mirror scene marks her new awareness of this distance, yet also displays how one affects the other; Del's ironic recitation of Tennyson's "silly" poem "Mariana," an attempt to disavow her deep sense of hurt, only makes her "tears flow harder" (242). This scene may mark a division between her thinking and feeling selves, yet, in a much more fundamental sense, they remain wholly integrated, fully symbiotic.

In recognizing the impossibility of creating the order she desires by simply making lists, Del has merged her uncle's pedantic method of "historical inquiry" with the simultaneity of experience suggested by the disintegration of boundaries implicit in the Frenches' familial structure and associated landscape; Del's fluid perspective is a personal literalization of the latter's historical consciousness. By crossing temporal boundaries to revisit earlier incarnations of her self, Del simultaneously "experiences and understands" in a type of first-person "primitivism"; she has become a collective through time, rendering all personal experience through an unmediated, organic relationship with her selves, testing the limits of the past and transcending the representational biases of the present. The formal significance of these episodes does not emerge from an anticipated but endlessly deferred culmination, as the episodic nature of Del's autobiography lacks a conventional climax that can retrospectively integrate preceding experience. The lack of a clear, temporally stable narrative vantage point reveals little about her current, remembering self, which then prevents an interpretive projection that renders past experience contingent on present understanding. Instead, the formal significance of these episodes comes strictly from the juxtaposition of one against the other, experienced in a type of primitive simultaneity, with the significance of each event immediately understood.

If there is a climax to the story, it is in the artistic and aesthetic decisions that Del sketches in the epilogue, a point implicitly supported by Struthers when he states, "I feel that the emphasis is on a portrait of the girl *as a young artist*, rather than a portrait of the artist *as a young girl*" ("Real" 25). Del's is not a narrative that reconstructs the past through retrospect, but one that obscures the distance between the past and the present. Her methods are fully informed by those inhabitants that shape the landscape, and thus her artistic method reflects or, more appropriately, approaches an organic continuity between the artist, her history, and the landscape upon which members of her community have sketched their lives; the artist's technique is a manifestation of place and its people and has made the past of the artist fully available to the artist of the present.

In *Lives of Girls and Women*, memory does not operate across a polarized divide; rather, past and present inhabit the narrator at the same moment in a type of simultaneous experience, just as the landscape of Wawanash County exists as a reflection of both present and past influences. All time itself is reflected in the county's landscape, and when Del looks at this landscape, she is looking both at the present and into the past. Del does not look back across time and space to render place and her experiences within it. Rather, that place has formed her artistic method, and, in that sense, place is inescapable. She will present Jubilee and Wawanash County in not simply what she creates but in how she creates it: artistic technique as an extended metaphor of landscape. In one sense, this is Munro's attempt to transcend the problems associated with stories based on memory – that the past can never be seen in its own terms – but it is a position she comes to revise in a later collection of short stories, *Who Do You Think You Are?*

PART TWO: DEPARTURE, RETURN, DEPARTURE

Alice Munro has commented on the conditions under which she wrote *Lives of Girls and Women*. She was, at the time, living in Victoria, British Columbia; roughly twenty years had elapsed since she had first left Ontario, and thousands of kilometres separated her from this home place. She has suggested that the temporal and spatial distance that lay between her and Huron County was responsible for any nostalgia that may have influenced her depiction of the landscape. Nostalgic memories may indeed tint Munro's depiction of her home place in her text, as she suggests in a quote from Thacker's biography of her: "The home she wrote about from British Columbia, she recalled, 'was just like an enchanted land of your childhood'" (*Alice Munro: Writing* 328). Del's description of the landscape of Wawanash County is, no doubt, affectionate, yet it would be a stretch to suggest that the landscape is part of a nostalgic look back at a rural childhood. Segments of the landscape's description in *Lives* are certainly lovingly rendered: Del's summer evening walk back to Jubilee after her final and traumatic confrontation with Garnet at the swimming bridge and her car trips into the country with her encyclopedia-selling mother are prime examples of the narrator's love for her surroundings. However, it would be difficult to classify these landscapes as idealized. In this text, the landscapes are not the silent screen upon which the protagonist projects her wish image. For Del, the landscapes and the people who inhabit them are intertwined, and, as argued above, the topography itself is a type of figurative pattern shaped by the same forces that have moulded Del's artistic method.

Lives ends just as Del is on the cusp of departing from Jubilee into the wider world. If Del ever returns to Jubilee, the text never reveals that homecoming. A return is, however, a central part of a later text. In 1978, Munro published *Who Do You Think You Are?*[8] This book follows another single, small-town protagonist, in this case Rose, and possesses a plot arc very similar to that in *Lives*. One of the central differences between the two texts, though, rests in Rose's return to her small town after experiencing and succeeding in the urban world beyond her home place. The scope and theme of each text are very similar. Therefore, this section treats the later book as, in some measure, a continuation and even revision of *Lives*; Rose returns to the town of her youth and, in doing so, gauges the changes to both herself and her home place. This section also suggests that, whereas *Lives* is not a book of conventional small-town memory, as if conventional memory cannot recapture the entirety of one's childhood experiences, *Who* similarly casts doubt on memory's ability to understand the past, and Rose, at seemingly every juncture, distrusts the impressions fed to her by her own memory. Finally, this section argues that it is when one stops distrusting memory that one is enticed back to the home place, a return that subsequently allows the small town to escape the safe confines of memory and reassert control over its one-time inhabitant. *Who* suggests that memory should not be trusted to guide one in the present, a realization that reflects Munro's own homecoming in the mid-1970s.

Formally and thematically, these two books are very similar, but the differences are, of course, in the details. One striking difference is in the roles the small towns play in the lives of their inhabitants. Whereas *Lives* ends while Del is contemplating her departure from Jubilee, *Who* follows Rose from Hanratty to university in the city, adulthood on the west coast, and finally back to Hanratty. She returns "home" in middle age. More importantly, Rose's return results in an altered vision of the role the small town and rural community can play in an individual's life. In *Lives*, the influence of the community may not be without tension but it is essentially productive, whereas its influence in *Who* is rendered as restrictive, limiting, virtually inescapable.

Significantly, these divergent representations seem influenced by Munro's own proximity to her home place. As mentioned previously, *Lives* was written at a debatably affectionate distance, in both time and space, from Wingham and western Ontario. In *Who*, Rose's literary return mirrors Munro's actual homecoming to Huron County from the west coast in the mid-1970s after her marriage, much like Rose's, fell

---

8 Published as *The Beggar Maid: Stories of Flo and Rose* in the United States and Britain.

apart. Thacker argues that Munro's vision in the later book has darkened largely because she was writing about the place she inhabited as opposed to the place she remembered:

> [T]he Huron County she had returned to and began seeing anew in 1975 was harsher and a place she saw in a more sociological way. With Huron's people, Huron's culture, Huron's life staring her full in the face – no longer being remembered over time and distance – Munro saw social differences even more clearly, resulting in greater complexity from *Who* on. That book felt in some ways like *Lives*, but its longer perspective and its much more complex composition suggest a writer finding a new relation to her material. (*Alice Munro: Writing* 328)

Who involves a much longer temporal span. Whereas *Lives* is a story about a young woman and artist coming of age in a place that is in equal measure hostile to, and generative of, her aspirations, *Who* is a story of a woman who escapes that hostility, only to return and both see it anew and understand its real influence. Her return may engender deeper understanding of her home place, but that understanding is more knowing and, as a result, much more complex and even pessimistic than it is in *Lives*. Susan Warwick comments that the "bleaker and harsher vision" of the later book is because its protagonist, Rose, reaches adulthood and can thus see the community with a more holistic understanding (209). While both Warwick and Thacker observe a darker vision in Munro's *Who*, Warwick sees the age of the protagonist as the root of this new pessimism, while Thacker suggests that Munro's proximity to her subject results in this new shadow in her writing.

This darkness is reflected in what Rose recalls of the Hanratty of her youth: the violent deaths, the beatings, the terminal illness, the molestation, the poverty and want, the intractable class system, it's all prominent in a way that it was not in *Lives*. Yet these are not simply present in the text as a result of memory, as memory is not the sole access that Rose has to the small town; she physically revisits the community of her birth at certain points in the text. Similarly, Munro did not write *Who* with the sole assistance of memory, unlike *Lives*, but rather she returned to the place that she was fictionalizing. What these returns, both fictional and literal, have produced is a collection of short stories in *Who* that casts doubt upon the ability of memory to capture the past, as those memories of the home place often clash with the reality. While *Lives* utilizes transcendent memory in an attempt to convey a stable and complete comprehension of place, *Who* questions memory's ability to reliably reconstruct those episodes that form a vision and understanding of place; we can never understand something, the book implies, when the only way we have access to it is through our memories.

The ongoing distrust of memory in *Who* can relate to one of the major formal differences between the two texts: *Who* is written in the third person, whereas *Lives* is written in the first. Because *Lives* is very much concerned with the personal and artistic formation of Del, her first-person narration reveals those sudden flashes of insight, such as her encounter with Bobby Sherriff, or those long periods of artistic apprenticeship, such as her initial rejection and ultimate acceptance of Craig's project of local documentation. Del's narration offers an unmediated glimpse into this development, and the book ends just as she finds her artistic method, a method that reaffirms, indeed solidifies, the community's place in her creative future. *Who*'s third-person narration implies distance between the protagonist and narrator. No longer are those two personages one and the same, and, therefore, no longer is the text subject to the limitations and aporias of the memory of a first-person narrator. The earlier book depicts the search for genuine methods of artistic expression, or rather how best to represent the community from which one emerges, but the later book examines an individual's attempt to understand the self, as well as to come to terms with the often ambivalent role the home place has in the development of that self. By writing in the third person, Munro both sidesteps and draws attention to the practical difficulties associated with a narrative of reminiscence.[9]

Memory: A False Companion

Beyond merely attempting to understand the past, *Who* concerns, according to Coral Ann Howells, the process of "how the past is

---

9 For instance, Del is the omniscient narrator of her prior selves, which stretches the bounds of plausible memory and sidesteps the question of what is and is not recoverable through memory. In *Lives*, the answer to that question is, seemingly, that everything is recoverable. In response to this memorial omniscience, critics have devised a "two-Del solution" to the narrative involving the Del who experiences and the Del who understands. By keeping the narrator of *Who* unnamed, however, Munro has allowed critics of the work to avoid establishing complex theories to explain the narrative structure, even though the narrator's perspective rarely deviates from that of Rose. The narrator remains close to Rose, and Ajay Heble suggests that the narrative is a "limited third-person point of view" that rarely offers a perspective other than Rose's (102–3).

remembered and reconstructed" (*Alice Munro* 51). Munro's formal method of examining this past, the third-person narrator, differs from the narrative structure of *Lives*, and it is a method that was made consistent throughout the book only during last-minute edits. Both Helen Hoy and Robert Thacker have detailed the hurried, dramatic revision process that came about through Munro's insistence (for Hoy's account, see "Rose and Janet"; for Thacker's, see *Alice Munro: Writing* 344–52). The book originally consisted of stories focused not only on Rose, but also on an additional protagonist, Janet, whose stories occupied the latter portion of the collection and were written in the first person. At one point during the collection's construction, Munro portrayed Janet as the author of the Rose stories, which are those set in Hanratty. However, Munro grew exceedingly uneasy with this structure as the book neared its printing date and subsequently edited the book so that all of the stories were written in third person and all about a single protagonist, Rose. Those Janet stories that were not rewritten as Rose stories for inclusion in *Who* subsequently wound up in Munro's next collection, *Moons of Jupiter*.

The resulting collection in *Who* is formally consistent throughout. Had the Janet device been maintained, it would have further distanced Rose's memories of Hanratty, as they would have been two steps removed from the reader: a fiction within a fiction, as if it were that structure that was needed to soften the hard realities of Rose's rural upbringing for the reader, an escape clause for squeamish, doubtful readers. Without the Janet device, though, Rose's memories, while still conveyed by a third-person narrator, are no longer mediated through an additional voice within the text's form. Rather, the narrator can now highlight Rose's struggle with the nature of memory, her ambivalence and creeping doubt about what it tells her of her own past. The Janet device presented an overly complicated method to draw attention to the fictionality of memory; in abandoning this device, Munro's narrator acknowledges the ambiguity of memory and its imperfection in capturing the truth of a past and depicts a remembering subject in conflict with her past.

Of particular concern to the idea that memory and its nature is a central focus of the narrative is Ajay Heble's characterization of the text as indicative of Munro's "involvement with a poetics of uncertainty and a rhetoric of mistrust" (96). Heble's broader argument is that Munro's fiction "reveals itself to be maintaining and undoing reality at one and the same time, operating as both an instance and a criticism of fictional representation" (4). In much the same way, her characters rely on memory but distrust it at the same time. Throughout the text, the narrator draws attention to the failures of memory, and she shows the past that it manifests as a fickle chimera that, when used as a crutch, leaves the remembering subject without a stable ground to experience and understand the present. If memory serves as the basis for identity, then the question "who do you think you are" is a fitting title for a work that examines the glosses and misrepresentations of memory.

The first example of how memory fails to offer a stable representation of the past occurs in the story "Royal Beatings." Towards the end of the story, modern-day Rose is listening to a radio program on which an old man from Hanratty, Hat Nettleton, is being interviewed on the occasion of his 102nd birthday. Munro's narrator has earlier introduced Hat as part of a group that killed a man in Hanratty many years earlier. This group, assembled by some of the town's leading citizens and spurred by whiskey, horsewhipped its victim until he was a staggering pulp, a beating that results in his death a few agonizing days later. This anecdote of viciousness would never be included within the history sanctioned by the radio program. The radio announcer, rather, celebrates the age and status of Hat by calling him "a living link with our past" (22). Rose has reservations about the manner in which the announcer uses this phrase, as expressed through the questioning repetition of the phrase in her own thoughts. By repeating the phrase "living link with our past," Rose begins to ironize the phrase's intention, an ironization that calls into question the nature of the past to which Hat supposedly offers a connection. The link he offers through his venerable age and his memories of the "good old days," or at least those few carefully edited anecdotes that he shares, is one that links Rose's present to a past constructed of half truths and distractions; yet this past becomes the accepted version, the one that has become sanctioned by public institutions.

The announcer, Rose's thoughts suggest, has no idea about the nature of the past to which Hat supposedly links the present; the view that the announcer propagates in his program would prettify hardships, turning tough experience into a repository for charming, harmless stories. The interviewer may appreciate this comical, ornery old man's admission to eating groundhog meat during lean times, but that appreciation is possible only because he and his listeners are so far removed from any similar experience that this distance has made Hat's experience completely non-threatening; it is not the act of eating groundhog meat that is approved, but rather the idea of something so far removed from the comfort of modern experience. But this type of historical softening in no way lessens the severity of the experience itself, as the acute misery and pain of hunger really did drive Hat to eat groundhog meat one winter, just as he and two other men drunkenly beat another until he was a paste of raw, bloody flesh.

Furthermore, Hat himself uncomplainingly adopts the role that he is supposed to play so that the majority of his experiences relayed through the program are filtered through the announcer himself:

> "You didn't have so many strikes then, I don't suppose? You didn't have so many unions?"
>
> *Everybody taking it easy nowadays. We worked and we was glad to get it. Worked and was glad to get it.*
>
> "You didn't have television."
>
> *Didn't have no T.V. Didn't have no radio. No picture show.*
>
> "You made your own entertainment."
>
> *That's the way we did.*
>
> "You had a lot of experiences young men growing up today will never have."
>
> *Experiences.* (22)

What begins as a series of questions from the announcer turns into declarations, and Hat's role in the interview devolves into merely confirming the announcer's historical impressions. This version of the past is the folksy and benevolent one that is ostensibly based on Hat's own memories, yet, in reality, it is concocted through the complicity between the announcer and Hat. More accurately, this past is a product of the present, and Hat's memories, or at least those he shares, are channelled by the suggestions of the announcer; Hat is not simply recalling his own past but is also confirming a past that many in the present would like to imagine. As a "living link with *our* past," (emphasis mine), Hat is not necessarily included in the possessive adjective "our," but he is required to validate what is essentially a projection, a wish-image regarding how those in the present want to understand the past; the bargain struck here is that he remembers what he is required to remember and is celebrated for it. Yet what is suggested by Rose's historical counter-narrative, a sort of underground history in the apocryphal story of Hat's horsewhipping, is that memory often conceals and

circumscribes, particularly when it is working in collaboration with the
public record of authorized history, becoming sanctioned nostalgia.[10]

The announcer may see Hat as a "living link to our past," but he
is a link to something so distant that his recalled experiences become
almost pleasant diversions fully emptied of consequence. They have
become merely stories, dissociated from the corporeal reality in which
we experience either pain or pleasure. Munro's narrator reminds us,
though, that that type of historical consciousness denies the reality, the
actual physicality of the past, the past of blood and bone. Warwick suggests in her essay "Growing Up: The Novels of Alice Munro" that *Who*
contains juxtaposed levels of time, a type of hierarchy of reminiscence
within the book, and she points to the different time levels in "Royal
Beatings" as an example. I suggest that this technique further reminds
readers that there exists equivalence between past and present: the past
is not merely stories relegated to the temporal distance. For example,
while "Royal Beatings" ends in the text's present, it also contains a time
level of the more recent past in which the child Rose is beaten by her
father. This horrendous beating becomes a type of objective correlative to the distant past of Hat, specifically the terrible beating death in
which he participated and which is absent from the official historical
record; the raw mental and physical impact of Rose's beating indirectly
animates those events that are fading or have disappeared from living memory, events so distant that their connection to lived reality has
nearly been severed. This technique of juxtaposition reminds readers
that, to understand the quotidian past of the everyday, as opposed to
the lists of events in the annals of history, one needs no further knowledge than one's own experience. What was the experience of the past
like? Much like we experience the present. While the radio announcer

---

10 This interview with Hat is reminiscent of a symposium held at the University of
Guelph in 1981 called "The Country Town in Ontario's Rural Past." The purpose
of the symposium was to understand the nature of the small town around the turn
of the century. As part of the proceedings, three "old timers" were brought onstage
to discuss their experiences of going to town in their childhood. This oral history
component was conducted through a sincere desire of the organizers to understand
the differences between how people lived in the past and in the present. The three
participants readily adopted the role they were to play, and they convey personas
very similar to Hat's: eager to contradict, witty, and critical of how soft society has
become (80–90).

and Hat may suggest that there exists a qualitative gap between the nature of past and present experiences, Munro's narrator implies that "experiences" in the past and the present are effectively the same: a beating is still a beating today as it was one hundred years ago, just as victims then, as now, bleed and cry out in terror: to forget this equivalence equates to a failure of historical consciousness.

Munro's use of memory operates in contrast to Leacock's. In *Sunshine Sketches*, Leacock explores how the passage of time allows us to cast the benign light of memory onto even troubling events, yet those events are always seen from a harmless distance. In *Lives*, there is not a stable present, or rather an anchoring present time from which the narrator speaks; past and present become fluid temporal categories in which the first-person narrator feels and understands past events as acutely as she does events in the present. In *Who*, however, Munro's use of a third-person narrator distances the text from a narrative of retrospective; Rose, in fact, cannot tell her own story, as then her narrative would be subject to the aporias and misdirections she begins to suspect are an inseparable part of memory itself.

For instance, when discussing the ignominies of her rural schoolyard with her companions in the present, Rose has to assure them that she is not relaying fabrications: "When Rose told people these things, in later years, they had considerable effect. She had to swear they were true, she was not exaggerating. And they were true, but the effect was off-balance. Her schooling seemed deplorable. It seemed she must have been miserable, and that was not so. She was learning" (28). Here memory serves as the basis for oral storytelling, just as it does during the radio interview with Hat Nettleton, yet her auditors approach her memory sceptically, thinking that it is somehow disingenuous. And Rose seems to agree with their approach to the tall tales of memory, as she doubts the impression that her own memory creates, that it is somehow "off-balance," not capable of capturing and conveying the whole experience of the past situation; she does not trust what her own memory tells her. Just as time can have a softening effect on deeds past, or conceal those deeds altogether, it can also exaggerate the gothic malignance of difficult memories; neither method, Rose feels, adequately captures the often banal truth of an everyday, casual detail, whether it be comforting or disturbing. Rose continually questions the impressions memory creates. With this in mind, we see that the interrogative of the title can encompass this notion. If memory informs identity, how can that memory be trusted to understand one's self? The central interrogative of the title is one that Rose asks herself, but what is suggested is that memory is incapable of revealing the answer to that question. Much like Rose's acting profession, memory offers only a version, a re-creation, of the truth both of one's past and of one's self.

Are These Small-Town Memories?

Memory is particularly distrusted in the text when it functions as one of the spurs that prompt former residents back to a small town with the promise of a quiet, comfortable, known life. Throughout her career, Munro has consistently worked against any romanticized or simplified version of Ontario's rural past or, rather, a version akin to Leacock's popular idyll. An idealized rural childhood or rural past, Munro's writing emphasizes, can only ever be one version of the past as opposed to a true rendering. For instance, in *Lives*, the stories of the rural childhood of Del's mother, Ada, seem lifted from the pages of a gothic novel, and they clash fiercely with the insistence of Ada's brother (who has moved to the city, it must be noted) on the healthful, moral advantages of their farm upbringing. From Munro's later writing, "Wilderness Station" stands out as a particularly frank depiction of homesteaders' experiences in the region of western Ontario that subsequently became known as "Munro Country," yet the epistolary nature of that story constantly throws that harsh depiction into doubt. Her story "Chaddeleys and Flemings 2: The Stone in the Field" from *The Moons of Jupiter* contains a line that is a pithy synopsis of Munro's approach to depicting the rural past of Huron County through which she consistently questions the commemorative yearning of other rural and small-town stories: "the life buried here is one you have to think twice about regretting" (35). As this passage suggests, objective knowledge of the past is hard to acquire, and those who regret the passing of the rural past may know only too little of its hardships. Memory too often circumscribes or misrepresents a rural past. After returning to small-town Ontario from her many years in Vancouver, Rose learns this truth about memory, particularly how it can function as a lure coaxing her back to her childhood home place.

Upon first arriving back in Ontario, Rose lives in a small crossroads village north of Kingston in a landscape very different from that of western Ontario. What draws her here is a preconceived notion of small-town life, which leads her to believe that she will be living among retired farmers and members of the "respectable" Protestant sects (170). The reality is far different:

"Country life," she said. "I came here with some ideas about how I would live. I thought I would go for long walks on the deserted country roads. And the first time I did, I heard a car coming tearing along the gravel behind me. I got well off. Then I heard shots. I was terrified. I hid in the bushes and a car came roaring past, weaving all over the road – and they were shooting out of the windows. I cut back through the fields and told the woman at the store I thought we should call the police. She said oh, yes, weekends the boys get a case of beer in the car and they go out shooting groundhogs. Then she said, what were you doing up that road anyway? I could see she thought going for walks by yourself was a lot more suspicious than shooting groundhogs. There were lots of things like that. I don't think I'd stay, but the job's here and the rent's cheap." (166)

The question arises: have Rose's memories of life in a small town failed her and subsequently led her into thinking that this life can be bucolic and peaceful, offering salve to her wounded soul, or is her surprise at the situation the result of regional differences, as eastern Ontario is a far more hard-scrabble place than is western Ontario?[11] Have Rose's twenty years away on the west coast caused her to forget or perhaps misremember the hard reality of life in West Hanratty, the reality with which she is all-too familiar at other points in the text? This single walk down the country road succeeds in dispelling the illusions that Rose has somehow acquired about rural life.

Rose tells this story to her companion, Simon, and he, in return, shares with her a similar experience. As a young boy in France, he was on the run from the Nazis. He found sanctuary in the south of France in a mountain village that was something of an isolated enclave that had changed little in hundreds of years; it remained literally untouched by

---

11 Rose has entered the landscape that has been fictionalized by Matt Cohen: a rougher, harsher landscape in which people's lives are even more precarious than they are in Huron County. Matt Cohen made a career out of writing about eastern Ontario small towns, and particularly about the lives of the type of men Rose sees in the car speeding down the country road. His Salem Pentalogy, a collection of novels centred on one small town in eastern Ontario, documents the often grim hardships of people in the towns and farms north of Kingston. The rural life depicted in the Salem novels is unrelentingly rough; in seemingly every paragraph, poor, struggling farmers or jacks-of-all-trades are either lighting yet another cigarette, resisting the urge to pour themselves another drink, or wallowing in the detritus and castaway bric-a-brac of their perilous lives.

the outside world. Rather than thinking that he had stumbled upon a pristine, bucolic idyll undisturbed by the raging war that had consumed the rest of the continent, Simon immediately noticed the deprivations from which these people suffered. For instance, while a veterinarian visited the community once a year to look after the farm animals, no doctor performed similar services for humans. After Simon punctures his foot with a pitchfork, he had to convince his caretakers to fetch the vet, who at that time was in a neighbouring village, in order to save his life. Simon comments: "The household was bewildered and amused to see such measures taken on behalf of human life" (167). Rose's sardonic response, simply "Country life," to Simon's tale summarizes their sceptical approach to false notions of the rural idyll. Taken together, both Rose and Simon's stories interrogate the notion of "country life" as a retreat, in reality or in memory, to escape the troubles of the contemporary world.

That phrase, "Country life," begins and ends Rose's and Simon's anecdotes; the phrase functions, essentially, as bookends to their tales. While pithy, her response to Simon's story emerges from Rose's own buried knowledge of what country life is or, rather, what life in the country can be. Furthermore, the ironic tone of her response suggests a bitter tinge to that newly rediscovered knowledge, and it recalls for both Rose and the reader those tales of West Hanratty she relays to her companions in "Privilege": the rape of a mentally handicapped sister by her brother in the schoolyard outhouse; the vicious, sectarian schoolyard violence to which there is no claiming neutrality; and the exhausted teacher who is powerless to prevent the older boys from their mayhem: all examples, Rose would suggest, of "country life." Her response to Simon's story is not simply one of recognition, but also one that reminds herself that preconceptions of the country idyll are most likely misconceptions: the often rough nature of rural life, the deprivations and haphazard lifestyle of the inhabitants are all familiar to Rose, all very much aspects of life in West Hanratty, but all things that surprise her when she makes her return to the country. It is as if her memory has excised these aspects of country life as a result of years of a very different style of life on the west coast. Both Rose's and Simon's anecdotes depict recklessness and disregard towards human life that, seen from a different, perhaps more distant perspective, could very easily become comical stories of blundering, ignorant rural bumpkins; when directly threatened by that recklessness, Rose and Simon both view these actions as signs of abject neglect and menacing carelessness.

Rose's temporary residence in this eastern Ontario town serves as a type of prelude for her real homecoming to Hanratty, which is the central element of the final two stories of the collection. Gerald Lynch calls the entire collection a story cycle largely because of these return stories. Their function, says Lynch, is much like that of "L'Envoi" in *Sunshine Sketches*, and similar to a long line of Canadian literature stretching from Charles G.D. Roberts and D.C. Scott, in that they reacquaint the protagonist with elements of her original identity, which cause the protagonist to reflect on her growth and change that has occurred over the years ("No Honey" 90–1). Lynch also suggests that these stories "priorize" the importance of place within that identity (90–1); place is integral to the formation of the protagonist, a formation that is inescapable and irreversible. The early experience of place is central to Rose's identity, just as it is for the club men of Leacock's collection. Lynch has noted the similarities between Leacock's and Munro's texts, particularly the centrality of the small town to characters' identities. But because Leacock's club men never re-enter their hometown, that home place will remain largely a shifting spectre whose influence is more imagined than realized. To answer the central interrogative of Munro's text – "Who do you think you are?" – Rose does "go home again," but this return provides her with newfound understanding of the constricting, unforgiving role that Hanratty plays, and has always played, in the lives of its current and former inhabitants.

In commenting on the importance of her return home, Lynch states that it is "remarkable … that a contemporary short story cycle … concludes by suggesting an answer to the riddle of self-identity that priorizes the definitive power of place-as-home" ("No Honey" 91). Rose discovers the answer to this riddle only indirectly, however, through an epiphany she has regarding her friend Ralph Gillespie and his relationship with Hanratty. Ralph, a friend of Rose since high school, is another figure who has left Hanratty to pursue larger ambitions, but, unlike Rose, Ralph has permanently returned home. While still at the Hanratty high school, he was known in the town primarily as an impersonator of Milton Homer, an intellectually handicapped man who appears unsolicited at all town events. To the understanding of an outsider, Milton may be called the "town idiot," as he is labelled by Rose's sister-in-law (197). But Rose resists that term, as she sees Milton as much more than simply the town oddity. He is the heir to a once-influential family in Hanratty, a sort of scion of the town's forefathers.

Ralph is not known for much beyond his uncanny impression of Milton; yet, like all jesters, Ralph's imitative acts possess social, critical potency. Milton was a symbol of the town's fading power structures during Rose's teenage years, and Ralph's impression, therefore, is at once a callous impersonation that mocks an intellectual handicap and a derisive, irreverent act that distinguishes him from the rest of Rose's classmates: "He was so successful that Rose was amazed, and so was everybody else ... She wanted to do the same ... She wanted to fill up in that magical releasing way, transform herself; she wanted the courage and the power" (204). Not long after Ralph starts his imitations, he drops out of school and leaves town, as if this act of irreverence were merely the necessary precursor to his eventual rejection of the community and his enlistment in the navy. Mocking Milton is that necessary act of both defiance and rejection.

Ralph's act is analogous to Rose's ability to memorize poetry. In response to Rose's ability to memorize and recite poems, her English teacher, the one who should be most encouraging of this talent, states "'You can't go thinking you are better than other people just because you can learn poems. Who do you think you are?'" (200). Their transgressive acts afford Rose and Ralph a certain amount of distinction, and both share the same desire to stand out from the background of the town's blandness, to discard the reflexive modesty that becomes second nature to those who inhabit Hanratty for any length of time. Rose leaves town for university immediately after high school; both Rose and Ralph depart to pursue what exists only beyond Hanratty's boundaries.

While Rose goes to the west coast to assume a life of marriage and motherhood, Ralph goes to the east coast to take up a post in the navy; their paths mirror one another. Both of their lives beyond Hanratty, however, end in trauma: Ralph's in crippling injury and Rose's in divorce. Ralph's traumatic accident required that he spend three years in a military hospital and, essentially, be "rebuil[t] from scratch" (205). In response to her split from her husband, Rose becomes an actor, and with each new role she assumes a new identity. Ralph's injury and Rose's divorce leave them bereft, without the identity that they had cultivated beyond the confines of Hanratty; the temptation, resisted by Rose but not by Ralph, is to fall back to the identities cultivated prior to their departures, those in which Hanratty is central. If the riddle of the text, that regarding identity, is reflected in the text's title, Lynch argues that the solution to that riddle rests in the home place. Rose does eventually go home again, and there she finds that Ralph has already made that return. Their similar trajectories suggest that the titular question encompasses not only Rose's experience, but also Ralph's, yet the answer that Ralph has found to that question serves as a warning to Rose not to follow the same path.

When Rose does meet Ralph again, her first impression of him is of a man who, even in his mode of dress, is attempting to reacquire the status of his former self. Ralph's sweater "seemed to Rose to speak of aging jauntiness, a kind of petrified adolescence" (208). She finds that he has largely taken up the role he had prior to his departure from Hanratty many years ago; rather than doing impressions in the classroom, he now does them in the bar of the Royal Canadian Legion. Ralph has returned to his home place because he found himself with few other options, and he is attempting to revive his previous role in Hanratty through his memories of his time in that home place. However, whereas the impressions Ralph performed as a teenager were irreverent, affording him special status, they always intimated his impending departure because they always represented his rejection of the town: they were potent mockeries of Hanratty and its inhabitants before he took his leave of them. Ralph now has nowhere else to go, and the impressions thus grow stale; so too does his status at the legion. As Rose's stepmother Flo says, "he carries on just the same, imitating, and half the time he's imitating somebody that the newer people that's come to town, they don't know even who the person was ... How do they know it's supposed to be Milton Homer and what was Milton Homer like? They don't know. Ralph don't know when to stop" (206). No longer do these impressions afford Ralph special status, largely because no longer do these impressions contain any notion of a transgression; rather, people are confused by them and confounded by Ralph. Try as he might, Ralph cannot regain that "power" he once acquired by mocking the town's more colourful inhabitants. He may have returned to his home place, yet he cannot regain the identity he cultivated while a child, not only because his home place will not accept that identity, but also because his home place has changed.

In the closing lines of the final story, Rose comes to understand the parallel lives she and Ralph have led: "What could she say about herself and Ralph Gillespie, except that she felt his life, close, closer than the lives of men she's loved, one slot over from her own?" (210). Whatever epiphany she may have about Ralph's life can then offer clues to her own self-knowledge, and the realizations that Rose does have about the role of Hanratty in Ralph's life, and thus her own, are not particularly positive. Ralph, essentially stuck in Hanratty, has ceased his impressions, and he has come to an uncomfortable balance in the town, a way of accepting as opposed to living life there: he is "self-sufficient, resigned to living in bafflement, perhaps proud. She wished that he would speak to her from that level, and she thought he wished it, too, but they were prevented" (209). As she talks to Ralph, she feels the conversation could be from a level she both knows that they are capable of, a level that assumes difference and distinction from Hanratty and its norms; however, this level would now further compromise Ralph's precarious position in the town. He now needs Hanratty because there are no more departures in his future, and, by speaking to Ralph in their old manner, that which prefigured their departure from Hanratty, Rose puts at risk the identity at which Ralph grasps after his return.

This, then, begins to answer the riddle of identity that is reflected in the titular question, Who do you think you are? Hanratty has an answer to that question for its returned inhabitants, yet the answer is one that neither Rose nor Ralph want to accept. Rose's continued mobility allows for her future departure and thus her ability to extricate herself from the restrictions of Hanratty's answer to the question, but Ralph has no similar latitude. While Rose's life and search for identity continues beyond the confines of Hanratty (indeed, her acting profession is, essentially, a continuous exploration of identity), Ralph, led by memory and necessity, has retreated back to Hanratty, his home place. As Lynch states, this contemporary short-story cycle concludes by "suggesting an answer to the riddle of self-identity" rests in the home place; for Ralph, at least, he sadly, if not reluctantly, resigns himself to that answer.

Hanratty is a limiting, constricting place, unaccommodating of difference, accomplishment, or idiosyncrasy. Those within its physical confines must also remain within its behavioural confines. Rose feels this prescription more strongly when in Hanratty: "she had to control what she recognized in herself as an absurd impulse to apologize. Here in Hanratty the impulse was stronger than usual. She was aware of having done things that must seem high-handed. She remembered her days as a television interviewer, her beguiling confidence and charm; here as nowhere else they must understand how that was a sham" (207). Rose experiences this revelation while sitting in the bar of the Legion with Flo's neighbours; the whole evening affords Rose a glimpse into her possible life in Hanratty had she stayed or returned for good. While in Hanratty, though, she feels compelled to apologize for all that she has accomplished beyond the confines of her home place, what she refers to as part of the "sham" as those in the town must see it. The "sham" is Rose's behaviour, that which has brought her a considerable degree of success in the urban sphere; the sham originates in the notion that no one in Hanratty acts in that manner, and thus by acting in this way, Rose is denying the proffered identity of her home place. While residents of Hanratty, and indeed Rose herself, feel that her "beguiling confidence and charm" is an act, this act is also a critical repudiation of the town's limitations, limitations she feels more acutely after she has returned to Hanratty. Rose once saw Ralph as full of similar "courage and power" to do the same, but, upon her return, he is a dim shadow of his former self.

The story and, therefore, the collection end with Rose reading of Ralph's death in the Hanratty paper: "Mr. Ralph Gillespie, Naval Petty Officer, retired, sustained fatal head injuries at the Legion Hall on Saturday night last … It is thought that he mistook the basement door for the exit door and lost his balance, which was precarious due to an old injury suffered in his naval career which left him partly disabled" (210). After she reads this news, Rose has the revelation of how close she feels to Ralph, that his life has been lived "one slot over from her own" (210). Rose understands how easily a similar fate of permanently returning to Hanratty could befall her, and, to avoid such a return, which would be a relinquishing of her precarious grip on the control over her identity, she must keep asking herself the titular question. Rose may have no answer to that question, but, unlike Ralph, she will not accept the answer that is waiting for her within the confines of her home place.

In both *Who* and in Davies's *Fifth Business*, the protagonists make a return to their home towns, yet neither remains; in fact, both measure the small town negatively against the growth they have experienced in the larger world, a reversal of the relationship between small town and city in Leacock's book. The small towns in these texts represent the anti-idyll, what Linda Hutcheon characterizes as a "limited and limiting society from which protagonists yearned to escape," what she suggests is a phenomenon most particular to Canadian small-town literature in the 1970s (*Canadian* 197). In *Sunshine Sketches*, the final return journey to Mariposa is imaginary, spectral, and the town retains its aura of benignity and innocence; no actual return occurs, and so the town's status as the idyll and the nostalgia the club men feel for it remain intact. As Ralph demonstrates, though, to make an actual return, to flee to the comforting embrace of the town itself, to re-acquire one's status as a full-fledged member of the community, one must relinquish the status, power, and identity gained beyond the confines of the town. This is the bind in which Leacock's club men find themselves; while lamenting the passing of so-called better days and simpler lives in places like Mariposa, they are also reluctant to relinquish all they have gained deep in the heart of the city in order to pursue what is bygone. Ralph's actual return, therefore, is a reflection of his powerlessness, and he resigns himself to the life that Hanratty has waiting for him.

Small-town nostalgia, it would seem, can be a sensation of privilege. Acting on that impulse to return is not necessarily a reflection of powerlessness; what is a reflection of powerlessness, however, is the inability to come back to one's current, other life, urban or otherwise. The nostalgic re-creation in *Sunshine Sketches* is a method of escaping into the past, but it is a safe escape, as the return to the urban present is always assured. Nostalgia requires distance, distance that remains a part of *Sunshine Sketches'* entire narrative structure, but, when that distance is traversed, one discovers that the control over this wish image has dissipated; no longer is the small town a passive product of memory but an active entity with the ability to shape itself and those within its boundaries. In *Who*, Rose's temporary nostalgia quickly evaporates upon her return to the country. With the limited, provisional power she does have, she decides not to imaginatively reshape her home place through memory. Because she fears that the answer to the titular question rests in Hanratty, Rose continues to trust that the solution to that riddle rests not in her known past but at some point or place in her unknown future.

Chapter Four

Past Dependencies and Consolatory Histories

Jane Urquhart's fiction is set largely in what Margaret Atwood characterizes as the "long past." It utilizes a temporal distance far more expansive than that found in Leacock's, Davies's, or Munro's texts; this distance is greater than that of living memory. This distance assists Urquhart's protagonists in locating consolatory images of stability and tradition in the rural past for which they then subsequently yearn. While the symbolic relationship between past and present in Urquhart's work mirrors that of Leacock's, the wider temporal gap between the narrative's past and present suggests that Urquhart's rural communities are severed from any anchor of reminiscence, devoid of the influence of living memory; neither are her depictions accompanied by the type of self-conscious, undermining irony of Leacock's narrator. The temporal distances involved in Urquhart's narrative structures allow her characters to imagine the small-town and rural Ontario of the distant past as the imaginative solace needed to counter a degraded modernity in which they bewilderingly find themselves. However, a study of two of Urquhart's works largely set in the "long past," *The Stone Carvers* (2001) and *A Map of Glass* (2005), reveals that, while she ostensibly crafts comprehensible, nostalgic rural pasts, these histories serve as only temporary consolation; indeed, in her characters' desire for something known and stable, their protracted longing for the past can result in a pathological projection of the self.

"Remembering the past," says David Lowenthal, "is crucial for our sense of identity ... [T]o know what we were confirms that we are" (*The Past* 197). In that sense, the distant long past seems to offer an alluring cache of stories that, once illuminated, can both destabilize and enrich individual and collective identity in the present; with no history, as it is with no memory, there is no identity. Anna Branach-Kallas identifies this theme in Urquhart's fiction: Urquhart "suggests that memory is constitutive of our sense of personal identity; our awareness of ourselves as individuals requires continuous recollection of our past experience" (*In the Whirlpool* 65). The past that figures most prominently in Urquhart's work is not the "personal past" that preoccupied writers in the 1960s and 1970s, but rather the "long past," which Atwood defines as "anything before the time at which the novel-writer came to consciousness" (*In Search* 21). Urquhart's texts, unlike those of Davies and Munro, disregard the durational limits of personal memory to explore the relationship between individuals in the present with a rural "long past." And it is the long past of Ontario that Urquhart typically explores.

In reflecting on her own work in interviews, Urquhart recognizes its reliance on the history of the province, and she believes that her readers have come to expect her to "open up another chapter of Ontario history" (Bonner 79) with each successive book. The province's rural landscape is her foremost influence, as she reveals in an interview with Herb Wyile: "my fiction will likely continue to be Ontario-based because Ontario is the landscape that I know best, the landscape that provides me with some sense of reality … [M]y visual memory bank is stocked with images of rural Ontario" (Wyile "Jane Urquhart" 82). While this statement echoes Munro's reflections on her own work, that she can only "make things work … if I use this … plot of land that is mine" (Metcalf 56), Urquhart's inspiration is far less dependent on specific place. Where Munro's writing employs distinct "plots of *land*" to which she feels an immutable attachment, Urquhart's writing employs *landscape*; the latter term implies a broad view or distant vista in which a viewer perceives recognizable order. Urquhart does not bring to her writing the same felt physical and experiential proximity to her rural subject as Munro, a fact that becomes more evident through a comparative contrast of their writing. Part of this chapter's argument is that spatial and temporal distance act as analogous framing devices in Urquhart's writing; where spatial distance facilitates the appearance of a unified landscape, temporal distance allows one to perceive the rural past as the unified, comprehensible cradle of conventional rural associations. Urquhart explores these two parallel processes of perception in *The Stone Carvers*.

Urquhart writes with a very particular understanding of the past, an understanding that she acknowledges has been influenced by personal conversations with Munro: "I remember once Alice Munro said something to me that I found intriguing: she said we write about the past because we can see it whole. We may not see it accurately, but we know what transpired, how events unfolded, whereas in the present you're in the middle of it, you're experiencing it; there's no sense of completion, there's no sense of ..." While Urquhart searches for her words, interviewer Herb Wyile offers "[d]istance" to suggest how a retrospective gap allows one to perceive the past as both stable and complete ("Jane Urquhart" 60). Urquhart's comments echo Jonathan Steinwand's statement on the process of nostalgia: "Because nostalgia necessarily relies on a distance – temporal and/or spatial – separating the subject from the object of its longing, the imagination is encouraged to gloss over forgetfulness in order to fashion a more aesthetically complete and satisfying recollection of what is longed for" (9). While Munro may understand "wholeness" to imply social and cultural comprehensiveness or complexity – that is, the whole of the community in all of its contradictoriness – the wholeness of Urquhart's past is characterized more by cultural unity and social idealization, an original cultural unity that modernity has fragmented. In parallel fashion, the distance between club dweller and Mariposa in *Sunshine Sketches* facilitates a depiction of the town as a place free from all of the hardship experienced in the urban sphere; the longer temporal distance involved in Urquhart's fiction, one stretching to a past prior to her own living memory, results in a sober deference to, and solemnization of, the culturally holistic past for many residents of *The Stone Carvers*'s central small-town setting, Shoneval. Whereas Mariposa's distance in time and space allows the careworn club dwellers to project onto it the spirit of a carefree world, the Shoneval of the distant past offers to an increasingly fragmented community a memory of a time and place bounded by tradition and ethnic memory.

Memory in Urquhart's novels is often physically contained within the rural landscape itself. As she states, "The agricultural landscape, where you can see evidence of the past, interests me ... I probably should have been a historical geographer ... [I]t's a person who pays attention to marks made by previous human activity on the landscape" (Wyile, "Jane Urquhart" 80). Urquhart both views and depicts rural Ontario's landscape as a form of legible collective memory that can be reconstructed by reading human inscriptions: rail fences, barns, stone cairns, and fields. These legible texts, however, are perpetually threatened with erasure by the physical and spatial effects of an encroaching urban modernity. Urquhart's thoughts on the relationship between the rural and urban essentially temporalize space. A rural past–urban present dichotomy forms in her work, a dichotomy similar to the one traversed by the Mariposa Express in the final chapter of *Sunshine Sketches*: a journey out of the city is a journey into the past. Whereas the journey is one by rail in Leacock's work, in Urquhart's, the journey occurs by highway, which "connects everything: the countryside and the city, the known and the unknown ..." (*Changing Heaven* 44). While Leacock sketches this temporal geography in his last chapter, he ultimately undermines it through the final dissolution of the train trip, revealing that that particular version of the small town not only is irrevocably lost to urban nostalgics but also originates within an urban memory in the first place. Urquhart, on the other hand, maintains the dichotomy, and her statements on the matter suggest that it comes from personal conviction, since she has suggested in an interview that her one-time residence in a small town in rural Ontario is partially responsible for feeling "cut off from what's going on today ... [from] contemporary life as it seems to exist" (Naves 9).

The past, for Urquhart, is accessible through its artefacts, its inscribed memory, as she explains: "the past as I knew it survived in a physical sort of way. It existed in barns and rail fences and Ontario gothic farmhouses, old woodstoves, and various other phenomena, all of which I'd had complete access to on my uncles' farms and at my grandmother's house in the village of Castleton" (Wyile "Jane Urquhart" 63). Farms, villages, and small towns exist on the fringes of Urquhart's socio-cultural present, and they offer a physical refuge from the main current of modernity.

Urquhart's third novel, *Away*, contains perhaps the most explicit example of the rural past–urban present dichotomy in her work, mainly through the framing image of a limestone quarry situated on the north shore of Lake Ontario. The image is based on her own experience; her one-time summer residence was situated close to a cement factory whose quarry she watched consume "another few farms and fields and apple orchards" each year; the landscape of the past is devoured in order to expand modern cityscapes (Wyile "Jane Urquhart" 72). Wyile interprets this image as "the urban eating the rural" ("Jane Urquhart" 72), an interpretation Urquhart substantiates by acknowledging it as a "metaphor in terms of disappearing history" (72). Wyile also aligns *Away* with the increased "speculative" dimension of contemporary Canadian historical fiction, a genre that departs from historical realism and displays "skepticism" about historical knowledge, but whose depictions of the past are "extrapolat[ed] from present circumstances" (*Speculative Fictions* xii). And much as in Leacock's text, *Away*'s rendering of the rural past is formed in the context of, and in contrast to, an increasingly accumulative modern rationality.

The past in Urquhart's fiction is an enclosed, stable site of consolation for a present that is both alienating and dislocating, and her characters often find solace in its physical or imagistic remnants: "the three-pronged ladders leaning against trees in autumn orchards, the arrival at barn doors of wagons filled with hay, the winter sleighs, the suppers held on draped tables outdoors in summer" (Urquhart *Map* 37). Branach-Kallas would suggest that these objects reflect both a way of life rooted to natural cycles and a more "holistic vision of the world" in Urquhart's fiction, one that equates the natural and authentic with the past (*In the Whirlpool* 66). Yet, on further reflection, they can also be interpreted as simply aestheticized, disconnected images of past rural life upon which her characters project their desire for stability and wholeness. For instance, as the narrator of *The Underpainter*, Austin Fraser, recalls his teenage summers on the north shore of Lake Ontario, he recalls this impression of Ontario's rural landscape: "the rail and stump fences, the cairns of boulders assembled a century before were charged, radiant, their awkwardness a shining memorial to the labour of the men who had built them ... I felt the scene before me to be one of perfect harmony. I had never before suspected it was possible that landscape – this impression – might be a compensation for misery, for loss" (60). The landscape does not exist outside the "impression" of this observer, as he is the one who projects unity and meaning onto disparate elements and, subsequently, draws from it a sense of recompense.

The import Urquhart assigns to the material remnants of the past recalls what Laurajane Smith identifies as "authorized heritage discourse," which "focuses attention on aesthetically pleasing material objects, sites, places and/or landscapes that current generations 'must' care for, protect and revere so that they may be passed to nebulous future generations for their 'education,' and to forge a sense of common identity based on that past" (*Uses* 29). For Urquhart, rural artefacts can be instructive remnants that contain and confer an authentic and holistic life. Yet her aesthetically pleasing rural pasts yield narratives that are stitched together by, or projected through the filter of, vague notions of tradition, heritage, and community; her novels appear related to Smith's definition of authorized heritage discourse by implying that an instructive, moral imperative inhabits the material remnants of the past; that is, the inanimate bric-a-brac of history speaks, if only we could listen closely enough.[1]

For this reason, it might be more appropriate to call Urquhart's works heritage as opposed to historical novels, since, while her works focus on how a past reverberates in the present, they also manufacture pasts appealing to contemporary sensibilities. A number of scholars who study heritage movements propose that heritage is in opposition to history. History, says David Lowenthal, is an academic study of the past that "explores and explains pasts grown ever more opaque over time" (*Heritage Crusade* xv). Heritage, on the other hand, "clarifies pasts so as to infuse them with present purposes" (xv). Particularly, says Lowenthal, it is the heritage of rural landscapes that are valued: "The heritage of rural life is exalted because everywhere at risk, if not already lost ... Landscape-as-heritage stresses time-honored verities at risk" (6). Acts of heritage, while ostensibly concerned with conserving the past, project onto that past the zeitgeist of the present. Different epochs have different approaches to, and uses for, the past. For instance, whereas in one era, a municipality may have torn down a block of mouldering row houses to make room for modern housing, forty years later, that act is looked on as one of historical desecration: what was, at the time, thought of as a progressive, practical action to improve the housing stock of a region is subsequently condemned in moral terms as a violation of a collective legacy, a transgression of heritage. Such valued artefacts, it would seem, are revered just as much for their alignment with a contemporary or fashionable aesthetic as they are from a concern

---

1   Her treatment of the past is the reason many critics dissociate Urquhart's fiction from Linda Hutcheon's definition of "historiographic metafiction" or, rather, fiction that consciously interrogates the problems and processes of historical knowledge and historical writing. Gordon Bölling notes that *The Stone Carvers* examines the "interrelatedness of present and past" (298), but also that, while it "hints at the epistemological questions associated with historical representation, [it] is clearly to be distinguished from metafictional Canadian historical novels ... which extensively examine the problematic nature of historical knowledge" (298). Neta Gordon acknowledges history as Urquhart's "inspiration," but Urquhart does not "transform historical data into mere fodder for endless undertakings in skepticism [as she] employ[s] a realistic mode that eschews the playful use of the historical document in favour of a more generalized historical setting" ("Artist" 61). Finally, Wyile notices that *Away* lacks the "discursive heterogeneity and interrogativeness typical of the historiographical metafiction so prevalent in recent English-Canadian literature" ("Opposite" 43).

for historical solicitude. What we value about the past has so much to do with present-day concerns, and the way in which Urquhart writes about the past, as well as what she values about it, reflects this tendency. The remnants of the past are silent, which allows her to create a context within which she can place them.

Furthermore, Urquhart's fiction presents a definite historical divide between the pre-modern and modern eras, a discernible historical rupture after which a traditional society became a modern one. From its onset, the First World War killed off entire "chain[s] of inheritance" that had existed in families for thousands of years, essentially fragmenting the present from a contiguous history:

> It really was the end of innocence in the sense that we moved into mechanized warfare, we moved into mass destruction in ways that no one had ever imagined. When I look at the history of the Western world, I really think the true industrial revolution began then, in the sense that suddenly it was possible to use machines in this way, in this horrible mass killing ... I don't think it was going to be possible to look at the world in the same way after the First World War ... [T]he line was broken, the chain of inheritance was broken. The father who would have taught the son how to apply the gold leaf to a painted ceiling was killed in the First World War. (Wyile "Jane Urquhart" 73–4)

Much as Virginia Woolf conceived of the First World War as the "line down the centre of the picture," segmenting Britain's cultural past from its present (Beer 53), Urquhart views the war as the end point for an age-old cultural lineage, since those who should have passed on the artisanal legacy had fallen on the battlefields of Europe. This discontinuity of physical heritage then prevents the transmission of the non-material links of heritage, those aspects that link the past to the present, "things such as memories, names, associations, stories, privileges, family traditions, memberships, and so on" (Graburn 69). There is, as a result, a sense of decay and disintegration in her novels' presents.

Urquhart is not alone among contemporary Ontario novelists who write of the small town through this conception of a historical rift that divides the order of the past from the disorder of a chaotic modernity. John Bemrose's *The Island Walkers* depicts a labour struggle between management and a fledgling union within the confines of small-town Ontario. The central setting here is Attawan in the early 1960s, a town inspired by the atypical topography of Paris, Ontario, its rivers, hills, and valleys. For decades, the Bannerman textile mill has been the town's main employer, and because this factory is owned and operated by townsfolk, the mill, and the town by extension, constitutes an organic human community. Previous attempts at unionization have failed, and the union itself has been considered by most in the town as a rabble of usurpers. Yet, after the mill has been sold to a conglomerate from Montreal, the town's sense of timeless organic order is disrupted, and the union drive experiences renewed momentum; the modern union is figured as the only check to a global capitalism. This new managerial order, however, erodes traditional power hierarchies within the town itself, a process mirrored in the dissolution of the paternal order within the novel's central family, the Walkers. The nostalgia here is not necessarily for a pre-modern past but for an industrial past that offers a more traditional alternative to the iniquity of an impersonal, cosmopolitan modernity. The ability to reacquire that organic order is gone forever when the mill, the focal point of the town's communal life, is lost to fire. This fire not only permanently separates the town's known past from its unknown future, but it destroys the familial order of the Walkers when it kills the central family's father. *The Island Walkers* portrays the anti-traditionalist vagaries of modern peripatetic capital, certainly, and this modern economic system produces the historical rift that leaves the town's modern residents forever yearning for the lost sense of order they believe that their forebears once enjoyed.

Like Bemrose's novel, Urquhart's work often hinges on this historical rift that separates the past and present. While Urquhart's novels *Away* and *The Underpainter*, argues Branach-Kallas, advocate for "a conservative return to the past" and express a "profound nostalgia for pre-modern times, [and] a feeling of loss in the modern world" (*In the Whirlpool* 173), this chapter suggests that her later works, *The Stone Carvers* and *A Map of Glass*, problematize their ostensible "nostalgia" for the holistic past. The main protagonist of *The Stone Carvers*, Klara Becker, may long for a time prior to the First World War when tradition presided over her isolated small town, but her longing constitutes only a temporary solution for a particularly modern alienation. By symbolically solidifying her increasingly distant memories in physical form, she transcends an isolating melancholy and enters into a new modern community that is both defined and united by loss; through Klara's final transcendence, Urquhart portrays the ubiquity of personal and cultural loss in the postwar era as the catalyzing force that ultimately coalesces the rural and urban polarities into a modern, mournful nation. *A Map of Glass*, however, presents a far more ambivalent, unresolved view on rural nostalgia. This text suggests that, in a modern world irreversibly separated from a culturally holistic tradition, rural nostalgia can only project fragments of the self onto an unknowable past; the pre-modern rural past that Urquhart's characters think they know is really one they have compiled from its silent, voiceless remnants.

Communal Pasts, Multiple Narrators

The Stone Carvers opens with an allusive description of the Vimy memorial's construction in the summer of 1934. This preliminary narrative framing passage alludes to a time and place in a specific past that will take a more prominent role in the latter third of the novel. Ostensibly like Munro's *Lives*, the deictics pointing to the narrator's time and place remain only hinted at. The narrator of *The Stone Carvers* initially recounts this past from an unrevealed narrative vantage point sometime after the described events; unlike Del, however, Urquhart's narrator is omniscient. Whereas Del's narration is limited to her own sensory and intellectual past, Urquhart's narrator moves seamlessly through time and space to recount the experiences of a broad range of figures, both real and fictional. Urquhart's narrator focuses mainly on one particular Ontario community, Shoneval, and does not claim to be a participant in the events of that community, unlike Leacock's small-town persona within *Sunshine Sketches*. Rather, the narrator recounts this "long past" from a temporal position only faintly sketched by her description of the lingering effects of the battle for Vimy Ridge: "Almost a century later there would still be territorial restrictions on this land as active mines and grenades would occasionally ignite" (268). This is not a solitary incidence of prolepsis, since the narrator laments the later obscurity of both the monument and its creator, Walter Allward (381). The text's present is the twenty-first century, and its primary past is the 1930s; as the story develops, though, multiple personae implicate multiple pasts.

The narrator's gaze subsequently moves to the Depression-era town of Shoneval in the first of the text's three sections, "The Needle and the Chisel." This Ontario town, like many others during the time, is "in a state of decay usually associated with the decline of a complete civilization" (5). This description recalls Del's thoughts on the Wawanash County of the 1940s, "which had been opened up, settled, and had grown, and entered its present slow decline" (31). Both texts offer imaginative renditions of Leacock's statements on somnolent small-town

Ontario, which seems to have expended its energy during a brief and productive flurry: "the little Ontario town grew till the maples planted in its streets overtopped it and it fell asleep and grew no more. It is strange this, and peculiar to our country, the aspect of a town grown from infancy to old age within a human lifetime" (*Boy* 109). In *The Stone Carvers*, Shoneval is introduced only after its settlement, growth, and decline, and a sense of loss is central to its Depression-era ethos, just as the memory of more hopeful times haunts the streets of Jubilee, and saddens Leacock's club men in the urban centre.

The Shoneval first introduced is "tattered ... and sagging," and its buildings are only mementoes of a happier time. With the degradation of the town's physicality, its "culture [has also broken] down under the weight of economic failure" (6); the ruins of the village, its historic architecture and the "seldom-visited cemetery [where Shoneval's] fore-bears slept" (6), may be fading into the irretrievability of a forgotten past, but so are those non-material things they represent: tradition, memory, and heritage. As most of Shoneval's residents struggle in their present, preserving the collective past is an unnecessary chore, a super-fluous extra for which economic and emotional resources are unavail-able: "not many villagers had the energy for the present, never mind the past" (5). The failure of Shoneval's shared memory would suggest that its identity in the present is similarly fading. Indeed, the "sloppy, half-finished attempts at twentieth-century industry" (5–6) indicate an increasing economic and architectural standardization with the outside world; in Urquhart's texts, these modern forms of industry are part of a destructive modernity that erases the heterogeneous signs of a local past. Disconnected from its ancestry, Shoneval has been set adrift in the world of modern economies.

Some do preserve the town's past, such as Klara Becker, a "thirty-eight-year-old spinster who lived half a mile away from the village" (6), and the nuns of a nearby convent; all carry with them the story of Shoneval's founding. This act of preservation is also an act of unifica-tion that constructs a diachronic community between Shoneval's past and present: "these women believed the story connected them, through ancestry, through work and worship, and through vocation to the vil-lage's inception ... The nuns and the one spinster clung to the story, as if by telling the tale they became witnesses, perhaps even partici-pants in the awkward fabrication of matter, the difficult architecture of a new world" (6). Preservation and piety share allegiances here, and implicit in these descriptions is the sense of memory as an obligation, an act of piety towards the past. The communal act of narration links participants both to each other and to a past that they reconstruct. Klara and the nuns may not have experienced the founding of Shoneval, and therefore cannot possess individual memories of the period, but the stories have come into their possession by virtue of their status as full members of the community. The oral narrative of Shoneval's past, increasingly all that remains of it, is entrusted to their stewardship, yet even these fragments of continuity are fading and must be continuously reiterated by their stewards to retain their influence.

After a brief introduction of the text's primary past, the oral narrative of Shoneval's origins begins; set between 1866 and the First World War, it constitutes the text's secondary past. At this point, rather than ceding full narrative control to Klara, the narrator merges her voice with those of Klara and the nuns in a collaboration that reflects the communal nature of this collective memory. Gordon Bölling argues that the story of the secondary past "borders on the edge of nostalgia" (297) because it readily blurs "fact and fiction." A nostalgic past, argues Steinwand, offers "consolation" for a lost sense of "wholeness only vaguely recollected" (9), and, indeed, the function of this secondary past is to console Klara, as she acutely feels Shoneval's cultural degradation as well as the loss of her lover in the war, two interconnected events. Her need for stories of Shoneval's earliest days is pronounced, and, during the Depression, she frequently visits the nuns at the nearby convent "where her desire to tell, or be told, stories concerning Shoneval's early days was indulged" (222). The embedded narrative's story of cultural unity temporarily distracts Klara from her mournful, fragmented present.

The combination of fact and fiction in Shoneval's secondary past resembles Urquhart's own creative process, as she readily utilizes a similar amalgam: "the facts are points of embarkation for me," she says, "rather than a final destination" (Wyile "Jane Urquhart" 62). *The Stone Carvers*'s opening line, "There was a story, a true if slightly embellished story" (5), offers a pithy, extra-textual overview for Urquhart's own approach to writing about the past. Her utilization of the actual history of Formosa, Ontario, offered her, in Urquhart's own words, "a very large space for the imagination to roam around in. That is where the fiction comes in, of course, to create a structure within which one can place the facts" (Bonner 81). The "slightly embellished story" of Shoneval's past may be part of the text's embedded narrative, but it also refers to Urquhart's own creative process, a process that parallels nostalgia's tendency to blur fact and fiction, and to create a past more easily narrated, understood, and mourned.

The tale of Klara and the nuns gives shape to the past, as all narratives do, but theirs does so with a profound intention: to imbue the past with a meaning that is absent, or thought to be absent, from the present. Geoffrey Cubitt writes that malleable, communal pasts provide the majority of people with a sense of meaning in the present:

> Collective pasts are fluid imaginative constructions. Only a small proportion of the texts, images or performances that we may speak of as offering representations of, for example, the past of a nation make any pretence of mapping that past as a coherent and detailed whole. For most people and for most purposes, having a sense of such a past is a vaguer and more impressionistic experience, at once elusive and allusive – less a matter of having the past precisely plotted than of possessing a few relatively central symbolic references ... around which broader associations of meaning can be flexibly organized. (203)

These "symbolic references" are the plot markers allowing one to narrativize a past, to construct a coherent framework by linking disparate references into a fluid whole. Shoneval's secondary past becomes a network of a few central events through which a narrative of personal and collective meaning is sketched. By extension, Klara's journey to Vimy in the text's primary past, the 1930s, provides the "symbolic references" for the twenty-first-century narrator in the larger frame narrative. The symbolic importance of Shoneval's distant past alludes to the parallels that exist in the text's larger frame narrative, which is solely the product of the twenty-first-century narrator.

Arrivals, Departures, and the Bookends of the Past

The embedded narrative of Shoneval's distant past alternates between town-founder Father Gstir's arrival in the 1860s and Klara's childhood and adolescence prior to the First World War. The stories about Gstir come to Klara from her grandfather, Joseph, who also bequeaths to Klara the family trade: wood carving. These tales suggest that Shoneval has changed little between the time of its settlement and the war: its way of life appears remarkably consistent between the town's "long past" and the personal past of Klara's adolescence. As the embedded narrative progresses, these two points begin to demarcate the beginning and end of the period for which Klara longs, the apogee of Shoneval's established and unbroken way of life. During this period, Shoneval remained isolated from modern, urban influences, and maintained its fidelity to traditions imported from the old country, or at least this is how Klara conceives of this era from the 1930s.

Gstir's arrival in Shoneval marks the point at which the nameless settlement becomes a community, since Gstir's influence catalyses a common purpose and identity. As he comes across the clearing situated in a picturesque valley, Gstir has a moment of prescience as he gazes down upon the community-in-progress: "he also saw how it would be later, with crops and orchards growing in the cleared areas, and with painted houses and barns, and with gardens sprouting flowers. He beheld all that was there in front of him, and all that he believed would be there in the future, and he knew he was home" (14). Through this projection, Gstir imagines a thriving community in the future, a future in which he takes a pivotal role.

Father Gstir is the focal point for Klara's tales, as he enables the collective (and collectivizing) effort required to construct a massive stone church, what becomes "the community's place of worship" (136). The holy building is the product of the community's first communal act: it had earlier been characterized by internal segregation and external isolation. Urquhart is careful here to avoid the type of depictions that characterize "folk" culture,[2] as, although the settlers remain a faceless, huddled mass for which Gstir soon becomes leader, their lives are not yet linked to each other and to place by common tradition. Rather, their separate lives are characterized by labour and deprivation, by "shanties and huts that barely kept out the cold, greasy fireplaces, animals too sick to travel, buried babies, mud, and a bone-chilling fear of the dispirited native peoples" (104). They are an enfeebled lot, hardly the hearty conduits of a thriving culture.

Gstir's first priority for Shoneval is to gather the parishioners for a Corpus Christi procession, which effectively produces the congregation needed for the massive church he hopes to raise. The settlers of the area are only too willing to participate in the "pageantry" of this "collective experience" (23) in order to temporarily escape the "labour that never ceased" (24) waiting for them at their homesteads. The

---

2 Ian McKay argues that "urban cultural producers" have constructed the idea of "Folk" culture as the "antithesis to everything they disliked about modern urban and industrial life" (4). The "Folk" become the "cultural core" who constitute the *"essential and unchanging solidarity* of traditional society" (12).

procession establishes more than a congregation; it forges a fragmented local population into a community for the first time: "None of them had ever been to a fair, or a dance, or a strawberry social. Few had even spent time at their neighbours' houses" (104). The procession is a pivotal moment in Shoneval's history, and its description is replete with the "embellishment" that pushes this embedded narrative into the realm of nostalgia. Temporal distance gives Leacock's sketches their characteristic embellished tone, and in Urquhart's text this same distance helps shape a past, one in which the Catholic Church has become oddly permissive: one horse involved in the Corpus Christi procession ultimately mounts another; the procession includes models for not only a brewery but also a brothel; and, in a passage reminiscent of the continual and inclusive parading of Mariposa, the Orangemen who travel to Shoneval to halt this demonstration of papistry inevitably become full participants, and, stuffed with "fellowship and food [announce] before leaving that they would return each June at the feast of Corpus Christi" (108). The oblivious Gstir, "who had never seen an 'orange man,' naturally enough believed that, if and when one appeared in his life, he would be dressed in pumpkin-coloured clothing" (107), blesses the Orangemen as they take their more-than-amicable leave. Shoneval's secondary past resembles Mariposa's in that religious observance is emptied of its serious import and is simply an extension of the town's bonhomie. Furthermore, potentially dangerous situations are defused of consequence, and an atmosphere of fellowship pervades.

The town's founding myth continues in the story of the area's young men who slowly begin to assemble the stone church; what is assembled alongside the church is also a contiguous community, since the growing community is unified by "work and worship." When the day's labour is complete, these men bathe in the local creek: "Everyone in the village could hear the sound of their laughter through open summer windows" (135). Even when not physically participating in the church's construction, the entire settlement is aurally implicated in the process, reminded through sound of the edifice's significance to the present and future life of Shoneval. The construction of the church occurs only because of Gstir's efforts, and its solidity comes to symbolize the integrity of Shoneval's sentimental coalescence. Even after the death of this "spiritual leader," his memory casts a long shadow over subsequent generations. Klara thinks to herself: "How beautiful the day was! Shoneval, finally at the peak of what Father Gstir had envisaged as its destiny" (89). Her thoughts may denote the full flourishing of Shoneval's heyday, but they also suggest that this period has been the work of generations inspired by the original vision of Gstir. Prior to the First World War, Shoneval's identity and way of life appear established, rooted, and continuous, yet this ostensible security only prefigures the imminent fragmentation of the community in the postwar era.

The story of Shoneval's earliest days represents, says Bölling, a type of "social memory" (299), and the narrative connects the village in the 1930s with an identity rooted in the past, but does so only as long as this story is sustained in living memory. During the Depression, Shoneval has largely discarded this past, and thus the town has become loosened from its history, dislodged from both the narrative and materiality of tradition. Laura Ferri argues that one of *The Stone Carvers*'s main themes involves "fragmentation in the present" ("Introduction" 11), and the enfeeblement of Shoneval's tradition in the text's primary past indicates that a process of cultural fragmentation has occurred at some point in the interim between the war and the Depression. The first crack in the community's cultural narrative occurs during the build-up to the First World War. Until then, those who grew up in Shoneval stayed in Shoneval, and children apprenticed in the occupations and trades of their forebears. The war presents the first opportunity for Shoneval's young men to leave the town, but it is an opportunity all but one decline. This solitary departure is all that is needed for the town to forge a link with the outside, modernizing world, which may contribute to the discontinuity of the town's way of life, but ultimately provides the town with a connection to a larger national community; the outside world may be Shoneval's serpent, but it is also ultimately its salvation.

While only one of the town's young men departs for war, Klara's older brother, Tilman Becker, leaves Shoneval long before the war in order to wander Ontario's rural roads. Tilman has been diagnosed with "wanderlust" by his grandfather, and his condition ostensibly threatens the chain of familial tradition, since his grandfather has plans for making Tilman the heir to the family trade. Tilman shows little interest (93). His condition is "almost common among boys in Bavaria" (95), his ancestral "homeland," and thus his wanderlust establishes a different type of continuity between the past and present. Although he may threaten a chain of continuity within the family, Tilman's wanderlust is presented as a manifestation of a type of ethnic memory whose source rests in the old country, an unconscious expression of a mythological past. In Ontario, certain natural barriers constrict his travels: the Great Lakes to the south and west, and the country north of Lakefield, where "the roads petered out in a tangle of bush" (62). Tilman's wanderings, then, not only re-animate the folklore of the old country but also trace onto the landscape of rural Ontario the echoes of a cultural myth. Klara eventually sees Tilman's departure as "the part of us that is learning the world" (167), a characterization that conceives of the family as a unit, and Tilman as the appendage apprenticing outside of that unit. "Us," however, also includes Shoneval, and his experience will ultimately benefit both Klara and the town, as only his knowledge of "the road" allows Klara to make the pivotal journey to Vimy.

While Tilman's departure from the community reflects a connection to the old country's past, it also facilitates Shoneval's entrance into a modern, national community. On the other hand, the departure of Klara's lover, Eamon O'Sullivan, for war in 1914 is the direct result of modern technology's siren song. During the summer of that year, Klara and Eamon carry out an innocent love affair. They rendezvous at a creek that is hidden from the rest of the village by "fallen logs ... [and] branches of aspen and poplar that grew near the bank" (121). This near-prelapsarian garden is unsullied by any self-conscious lust. Rather, the pond is the site of Eamon and Klara's innocent "communion ... Though they couldn't see each other or touch, they were connected by the pool and by laughter" (121). This brief utilization of idyllic imagery is subsequently shattered by the appearance of an airplane that has run out of fuel and is forced to land in a nearby field. The descent of this plane references the original fall of the rebel angels: "The racket might have been made by a bellowing Lucifer angrily approaching earth after being thrown out of heaven ... This was the first time in Klara's life that anything other than familiar, comforting sounds had entered her afternoons" (123). Klara's life up to this point resembles that of previous generations, and her character emphasizes Urquhart's conception of prewar rural society as the last manifestation of a continuous chain of cultural tradition. The pilot, sheathed entirely in leather, the skin of an animal not his own, is the agent of temptation that will eventually lead Eamon away from both Klara and Shoneval, a departure that reflects the imminent experiential shifts brought about by the war. As Klara regards the pilot as "one of the demons her grandfather had carved in a *Last Judgment*" (126), Urquhart establishes a correlation between the introduction of a technological modernity and the end of a way of life she equates to a near-prelapsarian innocence.[3]

The airplane seems completely foreign in a place that continues the life of the town's earliest settlers, a town in which the existence of the telegraph, railroad, automobiles, and even electricity remains in doubt. Its three telephones appear as the only practical connection to an outside modern world, and even these "everyone distrusted" (119). There is no significant difference between the Shoneval of 1914 and that of the late nineteenth century; the mill, the brewery, and farming are the main sources of employment in 1914 as they were in 1867. Through Shoneval's traditional past, Urquhart offers an image of a pre-industrial society in its last days before the Great War, a time that Urquhart imagines as more holistic, and subsequently a time for which she acknowledges her particular longing (see Wyile "Jane Urquhart" 73–4; Ferri "Conversations" 29). The airplane introduces a form of progress to a place that remains, *prima facie*, timeless, in the sense that it lacks indicators of a technical progression, and whose contact with the outside world is extremely limited. Although prewar Shoneval is the product of Klara's and the nuns' consolatory stories, it is also the product of a broader nostalgia for the very idea of tradition that some see as characteristic of Urquhart's texts.

The town's isolation makes it exceptional; it is a type of holdout against the tide of a technical modernity and also a political identity. Shoneval is relatively immune to the war rhetoric that has captivated the rest of the province:

All over Ontario boys were being worshipped and wept over as they covered themselves in khaki and marched toward a collection of similar brick train stations, part of a massive reverse migration ... In the small, unimportant village of Shoneval there was an experience of a slightly different nature as only one young man, dressed in a red waistcoat far too heavy for the perfect weather, walked out of town without fanfare. (152–3)

---

3 This scene nicely illustrates Leo Marx's discussion of the effects of the pastoral counterforce – that is, the introduction of the machine in the garden – which often comes across as "a sudden, shocking intruder upon a fantasy of idyllic satisfaction. It invariably is associated with crude, masculine aggressiveness in contrast with the tender, feminine, and submissive attitudes traditionally attached to the landscape" (29).

In Shoneval, the influence of the community's older generations is stronger than that of the larger political community: "nobody wanted to enlist because they had spent the Sunday afternoons of their child-hoods listening to grandparents count their blessings – the most impor-tant of which was freedom from armed conflict" (136). Shoneval is an exception, a town not reluctant to perform its duty, but rather one that recognizes the primacy of "tribal" and cultural affiliations over political identities. It remains only on the fringes of a modern nation that com-pels its citizens through a collectivizing rhetoric: "for the first time they [the soldiers] felt themselves to be larger than life, a force so sweep-ing and elemental they were on the verge of forgetting their individual names. The word 'we' sprang so easily and so joyfully to their lips that the word 'them' would not be long to follow" (153). In Shoneval, the word "we" has held sway since the time of Father Gstir, and incorpo-rates a collective far more unified than that modern national identity, which functions more as an expedient necessitated by a geo-political crisis.

For Eamon, his ride in the airplane is a novel lark, but the experience leaves its mark, as, for the first time, he is taken outside and above the physical and cultural confines of the village. The airplane allows him to gaze down upon Shoneval from a height, an incident that mirrors Father Gstir's elevated view of the valley settlement upon his arrival. Yet, unlike Gstir, Eamon sees the town from an unnaturally high dis-tance, which confounds his view of it and its people: "Klara had not waved, she didn't tell Eamon this, but she had not waved. He had mis-taken someone else for her. She had become interchangeable. He could not see her. This adventure had nothing to do with her" (127). While Eamon's falsely empowering perspective allows him to see the town in its entirety, Shoneval has diminished in importance for this young man: "He told her that everything looked so small from that height he could have held Shoneval in the palm of his hand" (127). This novel perspec-tive reduces the town's place in the world of technological marvels, of which Eamon has had a small taste, and the lens through which he now gazes at Shoneval only magnifies the town's faults: "He could see that shingles were missing from the roofs of most houses ... Old Ham-macher's rows of corn weren't straight" (127). Eamon's new perspec-tive is the product of modernity's exacting heuristic, which critiques the seemingly archaic disorganization of traditional societies, with their derivation from right angles and plumb lines. Both incidents of height-ened perspective, Gstir's and Eamon's, allow for a comprehensive vision of Shoneval's expanse (for Gstir, in both time and space), and each marks a type of bookend between which is cradled a characteristically unified, continuous way of life, or so Klara's narrative suggests. While, upon his arrival, Gstir looks into the future at the earliest point of Shoneval's existence, Eamon, on the cusp of his departure, symbolically gazes into a past that will soon be further disrupted by the long arm of a homogenizing modernity.

Klara synaesthetically witnesses the airplane's real impact: "The noise shook the leaves of all the trees around her and seemed to leave visible fissures in the atmosphere, lesions that affected Klara's vision in a disturbing way, making her believe that she would never see anything whole again" (127). While Eamon is enthralled by the intoxicating sense of power as he looks down upon Shoneval, Klara, looking up at the airplane, sees only fragmentation in its wake. Both lovers are altered: Eamon's distant view, both symbolically and literally, results from his extraction from the fold of tradition on the ground; Klara, who remains "anchored to their own village landscape" (125), perceives the plane for what it really represents, the fragmentation of a unified and traditional way of life. Shoneval's physical and temporal frame has been pierced, and Eamon's subsequent departure for war suggests that a degradation of the town's insular and continuous traditions is imminent. Klara seems to recognize the disruption to the circularity of traditional time through her increasing awareness, during those dark days of the war, of time as linear: "She listened to the slow beat of the pendulum clock, the stupid progression of time" (163). The stability of tradition precludes nostalgic longing (Chase and Shaw 2), but with the supplanting of Shoneval's traditional ways by the introjection of linear temporality, by what is really an epistemological paradigm that sees each passing moment as an irrecoverable loss, Klara begins to see the past receding and longs for a remembered time of stability.

The mixture of communal and personal histories in the text's embedded narrative is constructed from two distinct points in the future, and by those who recognize some logical structure in the narrative of the community's past. Lowenthal contends: "The past we reconstruct is more coherent than the past was when it happened ... To make history intelligible, the historian must reveal a retrospectively immanent structure in past events" (*The Past* 234). The war marks the split between the secondary and primary pasts, a coherent partition of eras, a disjunction only emphasized by the anomie of Shoneval in the 1930s: besides neglecting the town's past, its residents have a new preoccupation with turning a profit, something fully absent from the less mercenary economy of its primary past (224). By linking disparate events into a narrative whole – that is, the arrival of Gstir with the departure of Eamon – Klara and the present-day narrator construct a framework for the past that explicates Shoneval's present ruin. The past, as she reconstructs it, is all that has meaning for Klara in her solitary present: "Her own connections continually slipped downstream, against the current, toward the swiftly disappearing past. What, beyond the most cursory, practical knowledge of fashion, had the present to do with her?" (169).

Klara is a respected but peripheral member of the Depression-era community; she has "roots deep in the town's pioneer past and therefore commanded the respect such things still engendered at this time in these communities, though, beyond that, being the end of [her] line in a society mostly tribal, [she has] no real social life" (221–2). Because she has few prospects for her life or love in the present, the town's past is the only defining aspect in Klara's life, and yet her need for these historical narratives is really a sublimated desire for a present identity; at one point she conveys this fear to her grandfather: "'I seem to be disappearing, even when I am present in a room'" (167). Shoneval's secondary past, a past that is part truth, part myth, a past in which Catholics and Orangemen can overcome their differences through innocent, good-humoured misunderstandings, provides solace for a life that holds little hope for personal distinction or even happiness. However, her journey to Vimy Ridge, as the next section argues, allows Klara to overcome her dependence on the past. Much like Shoneval's cathedral symbolizes the establishment of a once-cohesive rural community, Urquhart suggests a parallel function for the Vimy monument: it is a symbol of a nascent and mournful, but also unified, national community.

From Distance to Detail: Transcending Nostalgia's Frame

Klara's ability to structure the past through a retrospective narrative frame finds a spatial analogue in Tilman's landscape carving. He is "a genius of distant views, a kind of miniaturist when it came to detail but concerned with phenomena so far away their specificities dissolved into texture when looked upon by an unpractised eye" (97). Within his work's frame rests an image of landscape, an illusion of unified texture comprising disparate details, a spatial pattern possible only when seen from a distance. As Tilman physically approaches the distant landscape, it necessarily dissolves into its composite detail, a situation not unlike the dissolution of Mariposa as the Mariposa Express pulls into the station in *Sunshine Sketches'* final lines; distance is needed to maintain the illusion. Tilman fabricates spatial coherence from spatial disorder only through the distance between his vantage point and his subject; this results in a type of spatial longing, a desire for but inability to access the distant landscape. If Klara arranges an intelligible history, a coherent temporal narrative, from isolated past events, Tilman constructs a type of narrative of the land; both are possible only at a remove from their subjects across which detail simply becomes texture.

The consolidating influence of temporal/spatial distance on perspective is a recurring theme in Urquhart's text, and in certain cases constitutes a privileged mode of viewing. For instance, while Gstir acknowledges the ugliness of detail, the tree stumps, mud, and precarious buildings, on first entering Shoneval's valley, he is roused by their combined effect, which constitutes the area's landscape. This mode of perception glosses faults and imperfections in favour of a unified panorama in both time and space: "He beheld all that was there in front of him, and all that he believed would be there in the future" (14). Eamon, on the other hand, surveys a distant Shoneval after he literally and figuratively departs from his safe, grounded past and enters an intoxicating but dangerous modernity. His modern, distant vantage point fragments Shoneval into its composite parts, and he refuses to gloss over the town's imperfections. Eamon's gaze constitutes a degraded retrospect, since, while on the cusp of his doomed future, he sees only the faults, as opposed to the value, of his ancestral past.

Gstir and Eamon provide the introduction and climax for Klara's narrative of Shoneval's past, and the continual reiteration of this narrative is her trauma's symptom and solace. Upon first hearing the news of Eamon's disappearance, she gives up her carving, the family craft, in a gesture suggesting that the endless detail of a three-dimensional human figure parallels the frameless detail of the present, a time increasingly irrelevant to her. The sensual details of carving require propinquity as opposed to distance, but, after the loss of Eamon, Klara requires the consolation afforded by distance and the illusion of "wholeness" it facilitates. Tilman shares a similar aversion to sensuous detail. As a boy, he recoils from "the facial expressions and gestures in his grandfather's carving as if embarrassed by them" (98). Although Klara and Tilman employ different media, both incorporate distance between artist and subject that signifies a lack of integration with the family, the community, and the present. Klara's desire for personal and communal memories comes at the expense of physical and emotional proximity in her here and now. Tilman's landscape carving is a sublimated expression of his desire to escape into the alluring distance. Klara's temporal nostalgia finds a companion in her brother's spatial nostalgia.

According to Neta Gordon, Urquhart distrusts a rendered distance between artist and subject, a point she formulates by examining two of Urquhart's novels in relation to metafictional texts that "foreground narrative reconstruction" ("The Artist" 63) and that always threaten to dissolve into "mere fodder for endless undertakings in skepticism" (61). Gordon argues that, in metafictional texts about the Great War, particularly Timothy Findley's *The Wars*, the artist is given priority over the witness in the attempt to avoid "complicity" with any political agenda. This self-conscious writing

> both signals authorial hesitancy and invites readerly skepticism regarding the stability of the historical record ... In highlighting the control he or she has over historical material, however, the postmodern writer will simultaneously announce that such an exercise of control is essentially meaningless because of the pains taken to make the procedure highly visible and therefore unfixed. ("The Artist" 61)

I suggest that Urquhart utilizes "experiential distance" (60) in temporal and spatial forms not to undermine her "historical material" but to allow her characters to recognize or, more appropriately, project an underlying, remedial structure across that distance. This projection, however, also signifies a character's unfulfilled longing and suggests that, while retrospective distance offers a temporary refuge, a truly therapeutic movement will be one that bridges the temporal/spatial distance between artist and subject, a movement that both Klara and Tilman eventually undertake.

Accompanied by her recently returned brother, himself a veteran of the battle at Vimy, Klara embarks on her first journey outside of Shoneval, and only Tilman's knowledge of the road makes this journey possible. By travelling with her brother "into the world that had so often lured him away" (261), Klara hopes to transcend her melancholic stasis of perpetual mourning. If Klara continues to live her spartan, solitary life in Shoneval, "it would be not only as if Eamon had never put his foot on the grass that surrounded Shoneval, had never gone off to the war believing that he was stepping into harmless ether, but also as if his skin had never touched hers, as if her own passion had never existed" (262).

Klara's memories are fading, and, if we assent to Branach-Kallas' statement that in Urquhart's fiction "memory is constitutive of identity" (*In the Whirlpool* 65), the failure of Klara's memory erodes her identity in the present; indeed, memory is all that remains relevant for Klara at this point, and she risks becoming a phantom drifting through Shoneval's streets, connected only to a past that is increasingly uncertain, unreal. This pilgrimage offers her a way to solidify her memory of Eamon and, in so doing, transcend her nostalgic melancholy to reaffirm a distinct and distinguishing present identity.

Klara and Tilman arrive at Vimy in the autumn of 1934 during the height of the monument's construction. The monument's designer, Walter Allward, closely watches all aspects of construction, ensuring that no worker carves anything outside his original designs. Despite his surveillance, and twenty years after she last saw Eamon, Klara resumes her carving by secretly chiselling her lover's face onto the figure of the torchbearer. Allward has designed the faces to be allegorical, as opposed to manifestations of individual memory, and says to Klara: "'You must understand. He was meant to be everyone, all of them ... You've changed that'" (338). By inscribing her memory into three-dimensional space, Klara's increasingly distant memory of Eamon is now an object unbounded by a frame and cast in stone for perpetuity. Klara's carving recalls Urquhart's thoughts regarding the inscriptions on the landscape as evidence of the past; the inscriptions made by chisel and hammer become confirmations of Klara's personal past and, by extension, reconfirm Klara's existence in the present. Consequentially, Klara's carving signals her readiness to turn her gaze away from the nostalgic distance and re-engage with the untotalizable, frameless detail of her present surroundings; her movement from the distant, framed past to present detail is here depicted as therapeutic.

A similar transcendence of the nostalgic frame occurs for Tilman while at Vimy. Notoriously hesitant to engage in any type of intimacy, Tilman falls in love with Recouvrir, a French chef in nearby Arras. Tilman overcomes his desire for distance through Recouvrir: "Tilman was amazed to find beauty in his friend's enormous body ... amazed too by the map of scars that made Recouvrir's skin appear to have been ceremonially patterned ... The white marks left by the entrance and the exit of hundreds of bits of shrapnel covered his arms and chest" (329). Tilman, "having avoided proximity of any kind" (330), now delights in the close details of intimacy as opposed to the satisfying texture of distance, suggesting he has undergone an equally healing movement towards present detail.

The embedded narrative of Shoneval is Klara's distant, consolatory past, and her description of Shoneval's cathedral becomes a symbol of the community's past unification; this object finds its double in the image of the Vimy monument in the main narrative. Both are the physical manifestations of a response to loss, whether it is the loss of a homeland, of tradition, or of loved ones, and thus both become symbols of new unifications, new communities. Unlike Klara's and the nuns' oral memory, the Vimy monument is a form of textual history, since the name of each missing soldier is carved onto its surface. Textual history attempts to assemble a knowable, solid record, in contrast to the fluid, embellished collective past that operates within Klara's narrative. Klara's longing for Shoneval's collective past signals its deterioration from its former integrity – or, rather, the coherence that is projected onto it – but the Vimy monument refers to the virtual evisceration of that continuity. Geoffrey Cubitt explains by paraphrasing Halbwachs: "Memory is 'a current of continuous thought,' persisting so long as the group which sustains it persists ... [H]istory is an intellectual system premised on discontinuity ... [It] produces narratives of change that emphasize ... discontinuities in human experience, dividing the past into periods as well as distancing it from the present" (43). The Vimy monument is not a manifestation of memory but a memorial to what has been lost as a result of the war's disruption, the change that it has wrought. By solidifying her memory through carving, Klara acknowledges and accepts the disruption to Shoneval's group consciousness that Eamon's departure and disappearance portended. Yet by Klara's engaging in a form of textual history, her memory becomes a memorial, a type of recall that only confirms that the "current of continuous thought" defining traditional group consciousness has terminated; a textual history, as opposed to collective memory, is the only viable method of recall in the fragmented modern era, a method that compensates for a perceived discontinuity with the past by attempting to solidify that past.

Yet the loss of tradition does not go uncompensated. David Staines suggests that *The Stone Carvers* marks the end of a "sectarian" exploration of Canada's past ("The Stone Carvers"), and this statement particularly resonates in Urquhart's depiction of the coalescence of ethnic identities (Bavarian, Italian, English, Alsatian etc.) into a nascent national identity. This new identity is possible only through the disruption to the continuity of collective memory within traditional groups and the subsequent synthesis of those multifarious identities; if the war is this disruption, then the Vimy monument at once memorializes the loss and symbolizes, much like the church in the wilderness, the forging of new links among formerly enclosed ethnic communities. Urquhart depicts Canada's consolidation through the discontinuity of collective memories; it becomes a nation defined by common loss just as Shoneval was once a community defined by the loss of ancestral homelands. Like many of Leacock's critics, Urquhart locates the sites of national origins perhaps not exclusively in small-town Ontario but in enclosed, organic communities of which the ideal of small-town Ontario is one example. For the twenty-first-century narrator, the Vimy monument becomes an emblem of the modern nation-as-consolation, a political-cultural identity substituting for collective "traditional" identities lost to the ravages of a far-reaching technological and economic modernity.

This symbolic status is made explicit through the realizations of Giorgio Vigamonti. Giorgio, Klara's redemptive lover at Vimy and also a carver, searches for the identity of Klara's unknown past lover by scanning the rolls of the hometowns of those whose names will be carved onto the monument: "By the time he came to the final name, every crossroad, every city, every rural township, each Indian reserve, and almost all the concession roads in Canada had been present in his mind" (369). Every community in Canada has lost one of its own, and, when Klara eventually carves Eamon's name onto the monument in one final textual memorial, she integrates Shoneval into a modern patchwork defined not by collective memory but by a collectively felt absence. Had it not been for Eamon stepping out of the past and into the modern world, Shoneval would have remained isolated from this emergent, although abstract, collective.

The Stone Carvers suggests that Canada was not forged through the national self-expression of valour on the battlefields of Vimy. Instead, Canada's entrance into the postwar modern era comes as the result of a massive and multivalent loss, of husbands, sons, and lovers, but also of the continuity of tradition and collective memory, dissolved by the same technological modernity that makes possible such wholesale slaughter. Absence and remembrance constitute the nascent national fabric of which Shoneval is now a part. The wedding of Klara and Giorgio makes the new cohesion explicit. Giorgio is from an Italian society in Hamilton, Ontario, as insular as Shoneval, and their union signals that what were once hermetic communities have now opened their boundaries. The war has disrupted previously continuous lines of collective memory and identity, and it is up to the survivors to begin new chains of inheritance.

Urquhart's vision of urban modernity does not parrot the conventional cityscape that honks and roars in Leacock's final chapter. She may see the rural sphere as a palimpsest of the past and repository for ethnic traditions, but so is her cityscape. The influence of modernity dissolves the continuity of tradition but, in so doing, establishes new emotive interchanges between previously segregated societies in both the rural and urban centres; these sentimental links also extend out from the nascent nation through a modern universal mourning, as reflected in Tilman's relationship with Recouvrir. Paradoxically, all of this presents a much more hopeful vision of the urban present than does Leacock's text. While both situate the vibrant and organic small town in the past, Leacock's club men cannot recover from the primary loss of Mariposa, and the text concludes with their "talking of the little Town in the Sunshine that once we knew" (145). The urban club is an inadequate replacement for Mariposa's loss, and, therefore, the club men's final thoughts are melancholic in the Freudian sense of the term; their discourse continually re-emphasizes that loss. Urquhart suggests that something is gained from the dissolution of the enclosed community for which Shoneval is a model: a modern nation that is distanced from ethnic and religious exclusivity. Small-town Ontario is not irrevocably lost to the past; it may no longer function as a separate and self-sufficient entity, but it has become part of a much larger political-cultural body whose independence has been assured through the collective suffering of its constituents. Small-town Ontario, just like all small towns, villages, and enclosed communities, has entered into a national narrative of loss; yet that loss catalyses a national synthesis. Canada, then, is a community of mourners, and only through loss does the nation become whole. Like Shoneval's cathedral, the Vimy monument symbolizes the beginning of a national narrative for which the ending has not yet been written: only through the monument does the slaughter, or rather *can* the slaughter, make sense.

A Map of Glass: The Past as Mirror of the Self

Apart from a few instances of narrative prolepsis in *The Stone Carvers*, the text rarely alludes to the expansive gap between the present narrator and the primary past. Yet, just as the temporal-spatial distance between urban present and rural past in *Sketches* helps stylize Mariposa as an idyllic townscape of the past, so too does Depression-era Shoneval accommodate anachronistically modern, even cosmopolitan, social perspectives. This is a reflection of the "dehistoricized" nature of historical representation that Wyile identifies as part of contemporary speculative historical fictions (*Speculative Fictions* xiii). Klara, a devout Catholic in early twentieth-century rural Ontario, unhesitatingly accepts her brother's homosexuality. Moreover, while she is sexually active outside the permitting boundaries of wedlock, tension with her religious identification is absent; this, of course, can be attributed to the prerogative of the individual, but the total absence of religious tension is conspicuous. More importantly, the temporal gap affects the way Urquhart revises the hegemonic historical narrative of Vimy Ridge; national self-consciousness did not necessarily emerge on the battlefield but rather during those subsequent mournful years when the country gradually came to comprehend the collectivizing nature of the massive loss, which *The Stone Carvers* also suggests resulted in a deceptively harmonious ethnic diversity. This national narrative, much like the tale of Shoneval's origins, is still a malleable collective past that has been "organized" around a few "symbolic references" and provides only a "vague" and "impressionistic" (Cubitt) understanding, and this vagueness allows for easy explication of the present. No such clear dichotomous relationship between past and present exists in Urquhart's subsequent book, *A Map of Glass*. This novel is set largely in the present long after the traditional pasts of *The Stone Carvers* have faded away; glimpses of this past are suggested through the physical remnants that imbue the landscape. One woman, Sylvia Bradley, comes to depend psychologically on the visions of the past she derives from these remnants, yet the consoling images of peace, wholeness, and comprehensibility offered by this holistic past are ultimately revealed as the product of unsubstantiated projections of rural difference.

As mentioned earlier, memory significantly impacts identity in Urquhart's work. Place also has an important role. For Sylvia, place is valued for its temporal depth, which is revealed through its marks of longevity. This appearance of temporal depth has a determining influence on her identity and also on her psychological equilibrium in what sometimes appears as an obsessive relationship with the physical sense of place. However, the nature of Sylvia's reliance on these traces of the rural past, traces that Urquhart herself claims constitute the landscape's "embedded physicalized memory" (Wyile "Jane Urquhart" 81), suggests that these inscriptions constitute not so much a collective memory that informs identity in the present as an unstable text that accommodates innumerable interpretations. Through Sylvia, Urquhart proposes that modern rural landscapes offer not a stable set of signi-fiers, but an unstructured syntax, an inscrutable palimpsest through which a number of interpretations of the past can only be imagina-tively construed. Reading the rural landscape, then, does not reveal a stable past, one comprising the "peace, innocence, and simple virtue" (R. Williams 1) for which Urquhart's characters often long; rather, it is, as the text's title suggests, a subjective process that reveals only the self. Landscape becomes a looking-glass that reflects back the unacknowl-edged desires of the gazer.

Sylvia has resided in a small town in rural Prince Edward County for her entire life and has developed a particularly knowledgeable relationship with the local past, a relationship she refers to as a sense of "emplacement," or, in other words, an emotive attachment to the physical and temporal texture of the land. This sense of "emplacement" often draws Sylvia's attention to signifiers of the local past: "She loved the trees, their reliability, the fact that they had always been there on the boundaries of fields or along the edges of roads. She loved certain boul-ders for the same reason. And there were cairns left behind as a visual reminder of the past" (*Map* 37). The practical function of the cairns has been forgotten, and they are now part of a patina of "pastness," an aes-thetic rural landscape to which Sylvia is expressing an attraction; the cairns were not left as a "reminder of the past," and Sylvia's interpre-tation of the landscape effectively imposes her own misreading on to it. Particularly revealing of her monologic relationship with the rural past is how she regards features of the landscape as objects that "had always been there." This assumption of permanence displays a type of solipsistic historical consciousness and reflects Atwood's definition of the "long past" as "anything before the time at which the novel-writer came to consciousness" (*In Search* 21). These rural artefacts constitute a façade of permanence that allow Sylvia to imagine her own connection to a long past; this sense of "emplacement," as she calls it, provides her with a feeling of stability, a psychological comfort that is easily upset by any movement away from this home place, particularly by a trip to that centre of urban alienation, Toronto.

Sylvia's rural life initially seems one of solitude, peace, and simplic-ity, and, at the outset, she appears a tranquil figure reluctant to depart for the city even for a few days: "The word *city* had hissed in her mind all week long, first as an idea, then as a possibility, and, finally, now as a certain destination" (33). She expands this initial contrast between her valued rural life and her dread of urban space during her trip to Belleville's train station, a contrast protracted by her sense of spatial and temporal "emplacement":

> The road that was taking her out of the County was lined by the homes of some of the earliest settlers in the province ... [M]uch of this old architecture was sad, neglected; some of the properties were completely abandoned. A few houses in the County had been restored by city people seeking charm, however, and always seemed to her to be unnaturally fresh and clean, as if the past had been scrubbed out of their interiors, then thrown carelessly out the door like a bucketful of soiled water. (36–7)

The urban retreat to the county, Sylvia feels, conceals rural authenticity by aestheticizing the physical inscriptions of the past. While Sylvia laments the urban retreat, she is affected by a similar impulse, a similar attraction to the connotations of the rural sphere; like those critiqued urban migrants, she too feels that this rural space still contains fragments of the "old values ..., peace, and stability" (New *Land Sliding* 156) that distinguish the common associations of rural space from the urban, yet she sees her own connection to them as more authentic than those of the urban migrants seeking rural charm.

Sylvia's reluctance to travel appears at first to be a manifestation of her fear of the unfamiliar and incomprehensible urban sphere. For instance, she displays an antipathy to certain modern fixtures, such as fluorescent lights, that abound in the city: "She had always believed she could hear the sound of artificial light and, as a result, had only once ventured into a department store, where the dissonant, rasping sound of the light had proved to be too much for her" (45). Sylvia's "emplacement" in her rural small town appears to account for her aversion to all things urban, or at least modern. When Sylvia says to herself while standing on a busy street corner in Toronto, "'I am now in the world'" (41), her sentiments simply reiterate the ancient conflict between the modern urban experience and the illusory shelter from modernity that rural life provides. "Where was she before, if not in the world?" one might respond to Sylvia's assertion.

On further reflection, however, Sylvia's connection to the rural past consists largely of an attraction to surface aesthetics. As the text progresses, she emerges as a virtual embodiment of Laurajane Smith's "authorized heritage discourse," the reverential rhetoric advocating for the conservation of the "material" remnants of the past; this rhetoric seeks to maintain continuity between the modern era and the past through artefacts. Sylvia uses her familiarity with the physical makeup of the country to construct a near-idyllic vision of the local past:

> She knew the histories of the old settlers as well as she knew her own body. Better, in some ways. She knew the three-pronged ladders leaning against trees in autumn orchards, the arrival at barn doors of wagons filled with hay, the winter sleighs, the suppers held on draped tables outdoors in summer, the feuds over boundary lines, politics, family property, the arrival of the first motor car, the first telephone, the departure of young men for wars, the funeral processions departing from front parlours. She knew these things as well, as if they bore some weighty significance in her own life lived behind the brick walls of a house situated in the town. (37)

These "histories" are composed primarily of imagistic fragments that provide, at best, only a glimpse into a past life. As Northrop Frye contends, a "pastoral social ideal" is often associated "with some earlier social condition – pioneer life, the small town, the *habitant* rooted to his land" ("Conclusion" 238–9). Sylvia constructs from disparate physical remnants and scenes from the local "long past" a collage-like version of, if not a pastoral ideal, at least an esteemed period of rural life. Yet she imagines her attitude to be about reverence and preservation, as opposed to what Leo Marx calls a "sentimental pastoral" characterized by "[a]n inchoate longing for a more 'natural' environment ... [and a] contemptuous attitude ... towards urban life" (5). Sylvia's longing is directed not merely towards an idealized rural "way of life" but also towards the ontological comprehensibility she finds therein. Her knowledge of the county's history, she feels, is a reflection of a particularly acute historical consciousness, yet her understanding of the past seems to arise from her relation to its inanimate material remnants. Malcolm Chase and Christopher Shaw draw attention to the pitfalls of an understanding of the past derived from its artefacts: "our dialogue with them is one-sided; the deep sense of connection with the past one might feel can be simply a unilateral projection of our present anxieties and fantasies" (4). And as the text progresses, Sylvia increasingly acknowledges that this comprehensive knowledge of the local past is, in fact, a reflection of her own anxious desires.

Like other Urquhart texts, *Map* contains a frame narrative set in the present, yet, unlike the others, this frame narrative constitutes the majority of the text. An extended section, the book's middle third, takes place in the "long past," and, despite initial appearances, the author of this embedded narrative is Sylvia. She travels to Toronto to seek out Jerome McNaughton, a young artist who discovered the body of Sylvia's lover, Andrew Woodman, encased in ice the previous spring. Andrew, who had deep family roots in the county, was a historical geographer who treated landscape as a type of "Braille." Sylvia is compelled to talk about Andrew, to reveal the intricate and intimate details of their affair, but she has also travelled to Toronto to provide Jerome with Andrew's notebooks, which ostensibly contain Andrew's family history in nineteenth- and early twentieth-century Ontario. The content of these notebooks is the middle third, or "long past," of the novel, and it traces the rise and fall of the Woodmans at the mouth of the St Lawrence River and along the shores of Lake Ontario. The novel's conclusion reveals that the "long past" contained within the notebooks has been penned not by Andrew but, in fact, by Sylvia. The conclusion also discloses that their relationship is only a figment of her imagination, a product of her unnamed "condition" alluded to in flashbacks. The revelations of the notebook's authorship cast Sylvia as an artist figure, yet they also raise questions regarding the impetus behind her relationship to her county's landscape and the past she imagines therein. These revelations suggest that the process of her *anamnesis*, as opposed to its product, is the real subject of interest in this book.

Anne Compton's look at the elements of Frygean romance in Urquhart's first three novels presents an intriguing summary of the relationship between landscape and character:

The landscape makes excessive (even absolute) claims upon the lives of those living it and, then, reabsorbs into itself the stories of those lives. As a repository of those stories, it becomes mythhoard, a wordpool. The well-being of those living that landscape in the present depends upon the telling of those stories. There is an ecologic dimension to Urquhart's fiction. Passing on the story is crucial to the balance of relations between human organism and environment. (119)

Sylvia is compelled to "pass on" both her personal story and the story of her county's past to Jerome, yet her motivation emerges not from the landscape but from herself. To treat the "relations between human organism and environment" as a "balance" is to see the organism as distinct from the environment, even though Urquhart conceives of rural landscapes as reflections of their inhabiting societies; these physical impressions shape landscape, a process that composes a type of textual history for future generations. Urquhart understands landscape as intricately bound to its inhabiting "organisms." However, *Map*, like *The Stone Carvers*, is set in what constitutes a fragmented present, one in which the longed-for organic relationship between past and present sought by Sylvia has dissolved. Missing from Sylvia's understanding of her local history is temporal-cultural contiguity between the present and past, suggesting that Sylvia's interpretations of the landscape's past is not limited by any exegetical precept. The "repository" of stories contained within the landscape's inscribed memory, therefore, is a babel that requires not merely an interpreter but also an artist figure without whom the text of the landscape remains unintelligible.

Both Klara and Sylvia depend on their connections to the past to maintain psychological equilibrium in the present, but, whereas Klara's reliance on stories provides only temporary consolation, Sylvia's desire for solidity can result only in a perpetual melancholic longing. Klara's self-imposed seclusion culminates in her perpetual nostalgic attachment to Shoneval's prewar socio-cultural apex. Sylvia's longing, however, reflects a particularly modern melancholy in which her perpetual desire for something permanent, something that transcends the continual flux of modern experience, results in an obsessive fixation on remnants of the past, remnants that allow her to construct a mirage of stability retreating into the past. Lowenthal explains how the past garners this image: "The past is appreciated because it is over; what happened in it has ended. Termination gives it a sense of completion, of stability, of permanence lacking in the ongoing present" (*The Past* 62). While her lifelong propinquity to the static remnants of the local past, the trees, fields, cairns, and barns, allows her to feel that a connection to her imagined past is possible, even probable, Sylvia's desire for a full and unambiguous union with its "solidity" will always be deferred because the historicity of the landscape is silent, except for the voice provided to it by Sylvia herself. She alludes to her own anxiety regarding the possible flux of this self-composed narrative of the county's past: "Was it Andrew's reconstruction that had filled in the gaps, or had his memory already grown so thin that imaginary events began to appear on the page? It had been impossible for Sylvia to find the solidity she sought" (74). Sylvia remains aware of the instability of historical interpretation, an instability she continually attempts to overcome but ultimately acknowledges.

The concluding image of Sylvia's embedded narrative reveals that she is conscious of her monologic relationship with the past. She may claim that the embedded narrative emerges from her intimate knowledge of her community's landscape, yet its true source lies in a mind incapable of knowing anything else, as she reveals to Jerome directly:

> *All the while I have been talking to you I have been listening for the sound of Andrew's voice, because they are his stories, really, these things he told me. But now I have to admit that I have been listening in the way I listened to a stethoscope that belonged to my father ... I loved the little silver bell at the end of the double hose, a bell I could place against my chest in order to listen to the drum, to the pounding music of my own complicated, fascinating heart.* (369; italics in original)

Sylvia's narrative has revealed nothing more than the inner workings of her own anomalous preoccupations. If, as Branach-Kallas argues, Urquhart's earlier works display a conservative nostalgia for a pre-modern past, here she both develops and complicates that theme, since Sylvia's pre-modern rural past is an endlessly fading product of her own imagination. Sylvia's construction of the rural past is not filtered through individual memory, and thus there is no continuity, no discernible personal line connecting the past she imagines and the present she inhabits; rather, in Sylvia's narrative, the associative values contained by Ontario's rural landscape are part of a vague and distant construct that emerges from an intense identification with place. This identification, however, is much like recognizing one's self in a looking glass.

The final revelation of Sylvia's authorship of the embedded narrative, something that she had attributed to Andrew, unsettles an otherwise straightforward story about a family's "long past" and the related romance in the present. Urquhart's construction of an elaborate historical narrative, as well as an intricate attachment to that past in the frame narrative, only to fully undermine both in the denouement by drawing attention to their fictionality, might suggest Urquhart's creeping reservation regarding her historical material. More importantly, Urquhart's presentation of Sylvia's relationship to Andrew as only a manifestation of the character's mind, and her attribution of the historical narrative to a woman living with autism, suggests an underlying tension that adds a new element of doubt to Urquhart's historical fiction: not doubt regarding hegemonic historical narratives, such as that posited by historiographic metafiction, but rather doubt surrounding our ability to know and write about the quotidian past. This reservation finds fuller expression in the concealing sand dunes, one of the embedded narrative's most fecund pieces of landscape imagery, which present an intractable challenge to the landscape as historical text. The ultimate triumph of the dunes is a fundamental image of time's shroud thrown over the distant past, a shroud that can be repelled only through regular and insistent maintenance.

The embedded narrative of the "long past" contains a description of the Ballagh Oisin hotel run by Andrew's great-grandfather, Branwell. Due to miscalculations in the farming practices in the area, as well as the destabilization of the fragile dune ecology, the dunes begin to engulf the hotel itself, relentlessly creeping through its cracks to blend in with the objects in the building. To the historical geographer, the encroaching sands obscure the past, covering the landscape with a featureless patina and obfuscating its inscribed historical record. While, on one level, the dunes symbolize the ruin that results from ignoring time-honoured, balanced agricultural practices, they also symbolize the inevitable decay that occurs to all human landscapes that are unmaintained; the fields fill in, the rail fences rot, and even the stone cairns collapse. By defying the imperative of temporal decay, maintenance attempts to preserve the legibility of the human landscape, without which all traces of activity will be veiled. Branwell has a similar realization after his failure to repel the dunes: "Maintenance ... is so central to human life, it's a wonder the very enormity of it didn't cause hopeless exhaustion in those who thought about it" (289). Maintenance is exactly what is required to clarify the landscape-as-text for the historical geographer, to keep the past legible; but this is essentially impossible against the onslaught of the dunes, the literal "sands of time" that inevitably obscure the history of all human endeavour. Much as maintenance defies the dunes, Sylvia's continual process of fictionalizing the landscape attempts to animate and solidify the embedded memory through narrative.

Here develops a paradox in Urquhart's text, as it suggests that the only human landscape that gives the impression of permanence is that which is maintained, yet maintenance is the continual re-assertion of the present moment onto that landscape, and not simply, or necessarily, the preservation of a pristine past. Herein lies the difference between the type of maintenance performed by Uncle Craig from Munro's *Lives* and the type Sylvia requires: Craig actively defers to the order established by his forebears; Sylvia, on the other hand, requires aged but still legible remnants within the landscape in order to construct the consolatory narrative of the past. As collective memory no longer animates the landscape, the physical inscriptions become the morphemes from which imagined pasts are assembled and which subsequently allow them to create something "other" than the present. Sylvia can imagine the past as a stable precursor to the fluctuating, degraded present only because of the conspicuous, legible, "stable" signifiers within the landscape. The same fixation explains her stated attraction to old pictures. "'These are safe'" Sylvia says, "'because everything that was going to happen to them, in them, has already happened. There will be no more changes'" (88). She is drawn to their static silence, their voicelessness masked as fixed meaning. Yet the vacant silence of old pictures defines their very malleability, what Susan Sontag describes as their tendency to "change according to the context in which [they are] seen" (106). The landscape's inscribed past, much like old pictures, is composed of empty signifiers that accrue meaning only through the projecting gaze of a subject in the present. The past does not speak to the present; rather, the past is spoken by the present.

The image of the sand dunes becomes a symbol of Sylvia's anxiety about the lack of fixity in both the collective memory "embedded" in the landscape and individual memory: "'Memories are fixed, aren't they?'" Sylvia asks Jerome. "'They might diminish, they might fade, but they don't change, become something else'" (75). When Jerome expresses his doubt, Sylvia only intensifies her insistence on the veritable access memory provides to the past: "Perhaps it [memory] only becomes stronger, purer" (76). While the conclusion of the book suggests that memory, both individual and collective, is anything but fixed, it continually attempts to link the self with a past whose traditional values can only be imagined in the present.

Sylvia's overarching concern for "stability" in her longing for the past is hardly a concern for Leacock's club men, whose memories of a happier small-town past quite consciously move between the humorously and sentimentally nostalgic. What remains for Leacock's club men is an incomplete existence, one that, while materially complete, is melancholic, existentially lacking. Sylvia Bradley's knowledge of the local past lacks the benefit of memory, yet her fictionalization of the landscape seeks knowledge of a past that is accurate and unambiguous, one within which she can find both surety and safety. Yet, compared to the other protagonists I have discussed, Sylvia rests at the greatest remove from the object of her longing. The past that she constructs is like that of Leacock's club men in that it is a manifestation of present malaise, yet Sylvia's is not an aesthetic redesign of actual memories, but a wholly original narrative compiled through interpretation of the silent landscape.

The Stone Carvers suggests that the effects of a homogenizing modernity threaten place-bound collective memories, and it is during this contemporary period in which collective memory has all but faded from the landscape that A Map of Glass opens. In the absence of a heuristic limit, the potential signification of a rural past is thrown open. While it is beyond my goal to guess at Urquhart's intentions in portraying the rural landscape as an interpretable text, by doing so she is only emphasizing the discontinuity between the past and the present, since all that remains within the landscape are manifestations of textual history as opposed to collective memory. The rural past of Ontario is silent. This inarticulacy allows Sylvia to imagine it as a time of holistic stability and comprehensibility, but its disconnected and incoherent textual signifiers allow her to construct the past as whatever she needs it to be.

Reflecting on Nostalgia's Restoration

Baden, Ontario,[1] and its larger counterpart, New Hamburg, are the two most prominent settlements in Wilmot Township. Recently, change has come not only to these towns but also to the township at large; its built environment has certainly been altered by Baden's new housing tracts and by other alterations to the physicality of the region. While the marketing for those new subdivisions has drawn in residents with a proffered promise of a peaceful small-town life, a marketing campaign reliant on popular tropes, other dramatic and sudden changes to the township's built environment have elicited a response from the township's residents. These changes are integrated into a narrative of the community through appeals to the past, and the responses reconceive the past in order to situate the community in the present.

While the housing tracts have accrued on the edges of Baden, perhaps the more dramatic change to the township's built environment occurred one night in early January 2007, when New Hamburg's heritage grandstand burned to the ground. The resulting coverage in local media celebrated the structure as a locus of identity, as a centre of community life, and as a place ensuring the connection to, and continuity of, local traditions. With the loss of that significant structure, many in the township felt untethered from the local past, a feeling of alienation only compounded by the expansion of the township's communities; people came to feel alienated within their home place.

---

1 In Jane Urquhart's *A Map of Glass*, Baden has a minor role, as its tavern is where the character Branwell stops to wait out a winter storm.

After the fire, the township immediately committed to rebuilding the grandstand, which, it should be noted, was used only for three or four events during the year. For the rest of the time, it served largely as a place for the township's youth to congregate away from prying eyes. The previous grandstand was wooden, but the rebuilt grandstand is constructed out of concrete and steel, otherwise a precise replica of its predecessor. Rather than objectively examining the practical need for a structure of such size (it was originally built to accommodate the large crowds at horse racing events in the 1940s and 1950s), the township inscribed onto its built environment a more permanent version of a past ideal, largely as a reaction to sudden change; the current grandstand functions both as a practical structure, and as a type of monument, an embodiment of a celebrated vision of the local past. The township is self-consciously shaping its built environment to reflect an impression of a past, and it is doing so largely as a reaction to the recent sudden shifts in the physicality of the community. The ability of residents to situate their sense of local identity within a continuum that bridges the past and present has been interrupted as a result of the shifting built environment. As the area around them changes, local residents can no longer see a clear connection between the community of the past and that of the present.

To ensure the sense of connection to a past remains vivid, the township initiated projects to shape its built environment, and the resurrection of the grandstand is a recent reflection of an ongoing trend. As a sense of distance from a valued past has only grown for local residents over the recent decades, the township erected monuments distilling and highlighting certain aspects of the region's history. For instance, a heritage waterwheel was erected along the banks of the Nith River in New Hamburg, a structure that celebrates the centrality of water power to the region's early days by inflating and displaying its most recognizable apparatus. The township also devoted millions of dollars to the restoration and preservation of Baden's Castle Kilbride, the township's most prominent residence, which was built by the flax and linseed oil magnate James Livingston in the late nineteenth century. Prior to this restoration work, the house had fallen into disrepair, and it dominated Baden's streets as an imposing, somewhat bleak structure of a faded, half-forgotten past.

The township has selected various features from its past and has determined that it is those things, those recognizable structures, that should be resurrected and scrubbed clean in order to revivify the historicity of the region. In choosing what to remember, the township has selected a few structures – the grandstand and the prominent residences – which become metonyms of the past, dots in an implied pattern that are strung together and made comprehensible through a projected sense of historical understanding. This is the past that the township has constructed for itself during a time of rapid change to its communities' built environments. It is a past invoked to address a present need. The township has shaped its past through a type of physical narrativization of the land and townscapes, which shapes a story to tell itself during times of change.

The narrative of the past then becomes a type of consolation, a soothing story used to bridge times of flux. Yet, in the process, the narrative of the past becomes a focused story contingent not on the broad sweep of living memory but on those aspects of the past that those in the present value. So often, past values are vague projections from the present focusing on ill-defined notions of community and identity. This narrative becomes a type of veneration conceived of as a bulwark against decline: the valued past or at least its remnants are disappearing, and only through narrativizing that past can we slow the movement away from the cultural touchstone that, it should be said, is really a construction of the process of remembrance. Alongside this narrative of change emerges a narrative of loss; each development that does not emulate the past becomes a loss of that past. But what is really lost is the ability to connect the community's narrative of itself to the past on which the story itself relies. The physical objects, the monuments and reconstructions, allow the community to continue to tell the story about itself, a story that relies on an understanding of the past as harbouring a kinder, more authentic version of the town and its residents.

What has occurred in Wilmot is one example of how an idea or ideal of a small town is employed for any number of purposes: "small-town Ontario" is an expression commonly used in literature and popular culture to denote a sense of loss; an image of a knowable, familiar community; a gothic sense of perverse provincialism; or a holistic cultural touchstone that has since degraded as a result of a dislocating modernity. What this study has argued is that small-town, rural Ontario is, or can be, whatever is needed by the one who invokes it, an invocation so often masked as memory. In the case of Wilmot Township, the revival of the past occurs because of an unfamiliar present in which many township residents find themselves. To re-imagine the familiar, or rather to make more familiar that which was taken for granted until it was gone, is a method of situating oneself in the present by reconceiving the past.

In the literature of small-town Ontario, the idea of the small-town past is so often a projection. This is made explicit in Richard Wright's *Clara Callan*, set in both small-town Ontario and Manhattan in the 1930s. The novel contains a radio serial called *The House on Chestnut Street*, which offers to its audience a vision of the sunny, feel-good town of Meadowvale, a place designed to accord with most sentimental and conventional notions of the small-town idyll. This program is produced and performed by actors deep in the heart of Manhattan, who broadcast the most obvious stereotypes of bucolic small-town life, a version that proves exceedingly popular. Meadowvale is a world in which plot complications are resolved through daily denouements catalysed by small-town good will and common sense. This urban fictionalization of the small-town world provides a ready contrast to the complexity, melancholy, and final hard-won happiness of protagonist Clara's real small-town life in Whitfield, Ontario. The space between those two experiential, economic, cultural places – the small town and the big city – has proven a vast gulf for Ontario writers to explore, and it has yielded a dichotomous tension at the heart of small-town fiction from Ontario. Yet this binary always breaks down on the margins of the texts. The productive opposition between the two temporal-spatial poles is often a sublimation of tension within the characters themselves, tension that plays out within this imaginary temporal-spatial dichotomy between the familiar and the unfamiliar, the past and the present, the small town and the city. Small-town memory may offer an alternative to the present, but the content of that memory is distrusted, doubted, or perpetually inaccessible.

In Elizabeth Hay's *Alone in the Classroom*, the narrator comments on the gap between past and present and how it is both navigated and used in works of fiction. In this novel, which is set partially in Argyle, Ontario, a small town based on Renfrew, the conclusion contains a twinned image that proposes that the gaps in our knowledge of the past can be filled only by imagination. Hay's narrator, Anne, is attempting to write a story of her family's history, part of which is based in Argyle and part in the town of Jewel, Saskatchewan. The novel ends with a description of the narrator scraping some lichen off of the grave of Parley Burns, a central figure and the enigma around which the action of the novel revolves: the question of the novel is, what role did he play in the deaths of two girls in each of the novel's central small-town settings?

What becomes more important than the answer to that question is suggested by the final image of the lichen sitting in a box on the narrator's desk, an image that echoes that of stones that rested in a similar box on her mother's table; these stones were taken from an arctic creek bed only one week prior to a glacial slide that buried the creek for untold millennia. The stones are a symbol of the buried past, something now inaccessible, covered by the movement of time and change. The lichen, similarly, is a symbol of a past about which Anne's questions will never be answered; the problem of Burns' role in the deaths will never be resolved because he himself, the only one who could provide satisfactory answers, is now buried. The lichen is a reminder to Anne about the futility of total historical access and knowledge; we will only ever have small fragments of the past, and yet it is from these fragments that we spin complete, complex narratives. This is an act of weaving together, an act of connecting events into a narrative. In order to understand the past, we have to fill it out, provide a context for the wisps and scraps that we do have.

James Reaney addresses this question of historical knowledge head on in his poem "Prose for the Past." It begins conventionally enough with the persona visiting the archives at the local library to inquire "What was it like in the past?" He then seeks answers to that question by reviewing stacks of faded newspapers, that "shaky fading paper rope into the darkness of the past" (13). The conventional catalogue of items and events of the local past, the contrasting price of cordwood in the winter and summer, the frustrations of local poets, and the arrival of the railway to town, soon becomes a catalogue of more personal images, perhaps scenes or stories from his own past: "There were the old ladies who stopped the church bells from ringing after midnight because it disturbed their slumbers / An Indian crossing the Market Square in the November twilight with a long feather in his hat" (15). This final image spurs the persona's memory further, and he introduces the figure of Granny Crack, a mythical character from local lore, a wanderer of country roads. "She speaks from the past," the persona confirms, as if to leave her out of the town record is to miss something central to any account of the region. The poem ends with an image of the twin mythical figures of the town, Granny Crack and the Winter Janitor:

> The old woman of the country, Summer Wanderer,
> The old man of the town, Winter Janitor,

Old Women, Granny Crack
Old man, old woman
Revolving back to back
Looking down
Granny Janitor Angel
On my town.

This twinned figure comprises marginal, even dreaded figures in official town life, inhabitants of country roads and back closets, and yet this
twinned figure is an essential answer to that initial interrogative, "What
was it like in the past?" What begins with a look into the official record
of the town, in order to know what it was like "back then," subsequently
merges into a mythical and yet personal alternative or addendum to the
town's history: the answers to the question can only be manifold, as
numerous as those who remember the past, since the official chronicler
of town life, the newspaper, can supply only one type of answer.

One distinguishing feature of the literary Ontario small town originates with Leacock's portrayal, according to Gerald Lynch, who says
that small-town Ontario embodies the idea of the "home place," as it
relates to "individual, communal, and national identity" (*The One* 182) –
that is, the small town as common past. However, as I have argued,
Leacock's work is more about the loss of the home place and its failed
recuperation through memory. Furthermore, Leacock's work reveals a
process of thinking about and remembering home as largely a response
to change. This influence reverberates throughout the work of Ontario
writers, writers who never simply parrot Leacock but do negotiate his
influence. What Leacock's work firmly establishes, and what echoes
throughout the subsequent literature, is that literary small-town
Ontario may be a home place, but as a home place it can exist only in
memory. When a physical return does occur, that place is no longer
recognized as home: home, now, is in the cities located at the far end of
the train tracks running through town.

What this study has argued is that the nature of these small-town
memories does not simply depend on the experiences of the past, but
rather they depend on the needs of the present, needs that invariably
shape the past. If Laurajane Smith argues that the past we conceive is
always a product of the present we inhabit, literary small-town Ontario
offers examples of how this projected past becomes an object of ambivalence for the very source that projects it. For instance, Mariposa is
not situated in the past, but rather it exists as an idea of the past that

has been formed by experience in the urban present. Mariposa as the quintessential Ontarian small town is, paradoxically, the result of the increasing urbanization of the province and the attendant perceived ills of the modern city; the town is both the response to and antidote for those ills but can only ever exist in collective memory. When Robertson Davies's protagonist Dunstan Ramsay revisits Deptford after returning from a "bigger and more sophisticated" place and acquiring a supposedly broader perspective, his initial Mariposan or conventional perspective of the town as the parochial counterpoint to urban sophistication disintegrates when he can no longer see the small town as separate from the homogenizing forces of a global modernity; what affects the city also affects the country. Alice Munro's works suggest that the influence of the small town is inescapable or, more accurately, that the past one experiences, whether it be rural or urban, is formative at the deepest levels. The past in Munro's *Lives of Girls and Women* offers a full-immersion sensory repository that is always available to the artist in the present; the individual's past becomes as vivid as the present, as that is what the remembering artist requires according to her narrative technique. This vision of the past is revised in Munro's *Who Do You Think You Are?* as Rose understands that the past recalled through memory always serves the purpose of storytelling. Rose begins to doubt the impressions that her memory feeds to her; it can never escape the shaping principles of narrative, since memory abides by the requirements of storytelling – it attempts to make sense of a past, to give it shape and meaning. Furthermore, when these memorial narratives influence one's actions in the present, they lead to dead ends, traps, or pitfalls, as Rose discovers of her friend Ralph, whose return to Hanratty has preceded her own. To revisit the town one remembers is, in fact, a necessary journey to re-engage subsequently with an unfamiliar or dislocating present. Jane Urquhart shows how an understanding or conception of a past home place is not reliant on having experienced that particular place and time. The present in Urquhart's novels is always fallen from a projected past ideal, but the rural past, the idyllic touchstone against which the present is weighed, can only ever be imagined, never experienced. Her pasts are invariably consolatory, essentially solace for a vague but perpetual sense of loss in a dislocating, inescapable present; the past is a palimpsest written and rewritten through the lens of the present, and the persistent storytelling about that past, its framing through narrative, offers Urquhart's characters their only recompense for perceived loss in the present.

And yet even this imperfect consolation of the past that is indirectly displayed in *A Map of Glass* only anticipates a further movement in Urquhart's subsequent novel and most recent work set in rural Ontario, *Sanctuary Line*. For the past to have comprehensible meaning for the present, it has to be framed, narrativized, but by doing these things, one is limiting its possible meanings and interpretations. In Urquhart's novels, this framing allows characters to understand the significance of the past, and yet this understanding is really only of a circumscribed past, one shaped for the benefit of those in the present. The frame narratives of Urquhart's earlier work, which become more complex in *A Map of Glass*, virtually disappear in *Sanctuary Line*. The latter novel, which takes place on the north shore of Lake Erie, focuses on the dissolution of a farming family who had inhabited this land for generations, so many generations, in fact, that the stories their descendants tell about their ancestors cannot be distinguished one from the other. They are referred to vaguely as "the great greats," and the various threads of their stories cannot be untangled; their meaning, therefore, cannot be clarified for the benefit of those in the present. The distant past is almost absent from the dominant narrative, or at least is muddled, appearing here or there in the form of a near-mythical story of some great or dramatic occurrence. This past, rendered not by a framing narrator but indirectly, second-hand, and at a further remove, through a central character and offered only in jumbled fragments and scraps, is more distant than in Urquhart's other texts. This is the result of a disappearing family who can no longer recount family lore but also of a modernizing landscape in which inscriptions of the past, those signs that allow Urquhart's characters to string together narratives, have disappeared.

Urquhart's novels contain people in the present imagining a historical world in which they feel more *at home*, as they seem uncertain of, or disconnected from, contemporary life. Small, rural Ontario communities occupy a central role in this imagined world. But this world remains intact only in the imagination. Urquhart and Leacock present places that foster a sense of being at home, yet this feeling of belonging can be sustained only as long as one remains distant from that home place. Davies and Munro show that actual returns to the home place dispel the feeling of belonging. Small-town Ontario, it would seem, is far more evocative as a remembered or imagined home place as opposed to an inhabited one. These works also reveal two very different approaches to the past: one approach views the past as a locus for both meaning and value that is absent in the present; the other critically examines the past to understand the home place as opposed to the role it is assigned from the present. The latter approach gazes towards the possible culmination of identity in the future, while the former laments the loss of the possibility of authentic identity in the past.

Throughout this study, I have rarely used the word "nostalgia," which literally means a pain or longing for home. I have been far more concerned with the labyrinthine meanderings of memory, of which nostalgia can be only one manifestation, and how the role and function of the small town emerges from these memories. Only two of the studied authors' works may be called nostalgic, in that their characters yearn for a lost home, and even these differ in the nature of their longing. While Leacock and Urquhart bookend this study, their texts posit very different assumptions about the present significance of the rural past. The distance between the nostalgic projections of Leacock's and Urquhart's characters might best be explained by Svetlana Boym's different types of nostalgia. "Reflective nostalgia," says Boym, "dwells in *algia* [pain], in longing and loss, the imperfect process of remembrance" (41), and it is through this type of longing that Leacock's remembering subjects shape Mariposa. Boym develops reflective nostalgia's characteristics:

> [It is] more concerned with historical and individual time, with the irrevocability of the past and human finitude. *Re-flection* suggests new flexibility, not the reestablishment of stasis. The focus here is not on recovery of what is perceived to be an absolute truth but on the meditation on history and passage of time ... [T]hese kind of nostalgics ... take sensual delight in the texture of time not measurable by clocks and calendars ... Reflective nostalgia can be ironic and humorous. (49)

Leacock's narrator, while at times melancholic, also delights in the flexibility temporal distance bestows on memories. He leads his fellow club men in remembering "correct" versions of Mariposa, versions that never claim to recapture the "truth" of an original but are relayed by a narrator who quite consciously acknowledges the enhancing effect of temporal-spatial distance. The narrative voice is both "ironic and humorous," in part because the Mariposa reflected in his narration can exist only in memory. The whimsical concluding train journey is itself a "meditation on history and passage of time," for it reveals the irrevocable effects of time passing without encouraging the club men to attempt a further recovery of the past, to overcome those differences between now and then in some ill-conceived attempt at heritage revival. The final chapter retroactively casts the previous eleven chapters as products of memory, certainly, but memories that provide some compensatory pleasure for their central, absent signified. Not only does *Sunshine Sketches* end by affirming the "irrevocability" of temporal change, but it also proposes that a type of consolation can emerge from the very suppleness of memory itself.

Boym's "restorative nostalgia" is a far more conservative impulse, which

> puts emphasis on *nostos* [home] and proposes to rebuild the lost home and patch up the memory gaps ... [Restorative nostalgics] do not think of themselves as nostalgic; they believe that their project is about truth. This kind of nostalgia characterizes national and nationalist revivals all over the world, which engage in the antimodern myth-making of history by means of a return to national symbols and myths and, occasionally, through swapping conspiracy theories. Restorative nostalgia manifests itself in total reconstructions of monuments of the past. (41)

It is a stretch to suggest that Urquhart's fiction is thoroughly and unambiguously "restorative" in its nostalgic longing, but, and as Boym points out, these categories of nostalgia reflect "tendencies" rather than "types" (41), and the unambiguous cultural value Urquhart continually relegates to the past reflects a restorative tendency. Where Leacock's narrator recognizes the effects of distance on memory with little concern regarding the "truth" of his past, Urquhart's characters lament what has been lost and seek to solidify the remembered past through its memorialization. The impulse in Urquhart's texts is not simply to remember but to use those memories as the impetus to restore, to carry the past into the present. However, by revealing Sylvia's active fictionalizations of the past in *A Map of Glass*, Urquhart herself may be recognizing the sheer folly of the assumption of total historical knowledge: restoration can only ever be imperfect, incomplete, as the past is a changeable construction.

Because of Urquhart's ongoing concern over the ephemeral nature of memory and her characters' attempts to find a stable cultural value in the rural past, we must reiterate what Boym sees as the problematic associations of restorative nostalgia: "This kind of nostalgia characterizes national and nationalist revivals all over the world, which engage in the antimodern myth-making of history by means of a return to national symbols and myths" (41). While Urquhart may be accused of conservative nostalgia, her works simultaneously display unease with the types of revivals they ostensibly advocate. David Harvey also identifies a more recent revival of cultural identities that, he suggests, is the result of individuals within a world that is increasingly "placeless":

> The more global our interrelations become ... and the more spatial barriers disintegrate, so more rather than less of the world's population clings to place and neighborhood or to nation, region, ethnic grouping, or religious belief as specific marks of identity ... [T]here is still an insistent urge to look for roots in a world where image streams accelerate and become more and more placeless ... Who are we and to what space/place do we belong? ... [T]he diminution of spatial barriers has provoked an increasing sense of nationalism and localism, and excessive geopolitical rivalries and tensions, precisely because of the reduction in the power of spatial barriers to separate and defend against others. ("Between" 427)

The search for identity rooted in place is, of course, an active concern for Leacock, but the temporal-spatial location of Mariposa is vague, more a concept than a locale, somewhere out there and back then, and it remains as such at the text's conclusion. This search is far more intense in Urquhart's writing, as her characters participate in a drama through which the loss, lamentation, and subsequent search for an identity rooted to the past of specific place becomes the recurrent plot. Together, the two texts by Urquhart examined in this study contain anxious interrogations of the "roots" of identity precipitated by the cultural flux and disorientation of an urban or cosmopolitan modernity. Urquhart's fiction harnesses various memorial processes in order to restore an originary ideal that the small-town and rural Ontario of the past represents for her characters (not to mention for Urquhart herself, as is evident in her interviews). Where Leacock's reflective nostalgia harnesses distance to provide an alternative form of consolation through the process of memory, Urquhart's restorative tendency disavows distance, even while it remains dependent on that distance for the manufacture of its longed-for, authentic rural past.[2]

Urquhart's works are the most recent studied in this book, and they also point to another possibility that contemporary Ontarians face: the inability to distinguish rural and urban modes of life, since, as her works suggest, an all-encompassing modernity blankets both city and country alike. The only possibility of difference between these two spaces exists

---

2 Again, the ambiguity of the ending of *A Map of Glass* complicates this conclusion, as, through the image of the sand dunes, Urquhart's narrator symbolically alludes to time's continual shroud thrown over the physical signs of the past.

through the malleability of retrospect and the subsequent shaping of the past according to present desires. This suggestion raises the questions: what does it even mean to live a rural, small-town life? Is it simply one that is located beyond the city's boundaries, or is life qualitatively different in rural space? That is, is a rural life determined by location in space or by the adoption of certain rural markers or lifestyles? If, as Glenn Willmott has argued in *Unreal Country*, the rural in the Canadian modern novel represents an invisible city, that it is always already dominated by modern forms of commerce and thus can offer only an "uncanny double" of urban experience, what value can there be in maintaining a rural-urban binary in that literature, and will that binary, then, always reflect an inauthentic reality, an illusion of difference based on a faulty type of retrospect? Why are these boundaries demarcating the rural from the urban – spatial, psychological, economic, even temporal – necessary to maintain? Can Urquhart's "conservative nostalgia for premodern times," and the value her characters locate in the land and townscapes of the past, be a tactical negotiation of modernity itself rather than the blinkered misapprehension of the past that the phrase "conservative nostalgia" might otherwise suggest? What is clear from this study is that the small-town past in Ontario's literature is not unambiguously positive; rather, it is formed largely from the present and is used as a tool to help characters negotiate the present, to make the unknown present more familiar, to help a protagonist re-engage with contemporary difficulties, or to carry some sense of known value into the present. The danger, however, is in defining that value as unambiguous. That definition always occurs in retrospect: to use, then, that definition as a template to critique the present, whether for its inauthenticity, its disparateness, or its sense of disorienting change, is to misunderstand the process of how popular notions of the past form. It is a tool used by tyrants and authoritarians the world over to promote a historically naive form of nativism.[3]

---

3 It must be said here that Donald Trump's 2016 election victory in the United States had much to do with his slogan, "Make America Great Again," the effectiveness of which, I think, can be explained by the remarkably prescient quote from David Harvey included above. The slogan at once assumes that the present is degraded and that the nation's apogee rests within an indefinite past. When was it great, how was it great, how did it become great, for whom was it great (and, therefore, for whom was it not great), why do we imagine it as such … seeking answers to these questions is discouraged by the sheer blunt pithiness of this indirect appeal to vague notions of a past. The vagueness is intentional, as many different retrospective visions can then be projected onto the indeterminate period and status evoked by the slogan. This is a bullying restorative nostalgia that, it goes without saying, is unaware of itself as nostalgia.

In the concluding remarks in his book on pastoral literature, Terry Gifford writes:

> If our lives now lack a separation between urban and rural existence, we need a post-pastoral literature that will help us understand that dialectical experience and how we can take responsibility for it. Against necessary notions of roots, neighbourhood and community there is another necessary impulse towards retreat, renewal and return. This is the circle of postmodern mobility. The paradox with which the post-pastoral engages is the fact that retreat informs our sense of community, and at a time when we are conscious of the need to improve our relationship with our neighbours on this planet, no literature could be more important to our imaging our very survival. (174)

Gifford stresses that the retreat away from our modern world that is part of pastoral literature will in fact help us engage more productively with it; through the renewal we experience by visiting the rural sphere, we can return to the modern, urban world better able to steer ourselves towards a future in which we have not been obliterated. Yet the problem remains: what value exists in a rural or small-town setting that we can then transfer into the urban sphere? Can we actually engage in productive retreats to the rural sphere if no qualitative difference exists between these two dichotomous poles? Can nostalgia result in anything other than a type of irresolvable melancholy for an imagined past that shades the ending of Leacock's *Sunshine Sketches*, or the wistful hyperbole that a new strain of political populists use to bulldoze any semblance of liberal pluralism? Can the imagined past be used for anything other than to reinforce existing preferences and biases?

Perhaps the answers to these questions begin not with dismissing the imagined difference between the rural and urban spheres as the projections of the disgruntled, alienated, and dissatisfied, or by theorizing away the imagined economic and cultural separation of the country and city, but in studying how notions of difference actually create tangible manifestations.[4] The rural past is invoked for innumerable political and cultural purposes, and we must pay more attention to *how* and *why* it is invoked, either as a "stick to beat the present" (R. Williams

---

4 One manifestation, for instance, is that location seems an indicator of political preference, as increasingly there is a divide between political persuasions among rural and urban voters.

12) or as a repository that allows us to "take what is good and pass it on" (Elliott, *The Kissing Man* 20) – that is, as reactionary or productive impulses. The associations related to the rural past–urban present divide may exist simply in a cultural imagination, but rather than suggesting these reflect a naive nostalgia or blinkered historical consciousness, we should try to understand how different imagined pasts have vastly different implications in and for the present.

Regardless of political or cultural assumptions, imagining a world alternative to the present one, somewhere out there and back then, is practically a reflex. We can see the manifestations of this conception of the past all around us: organic farmers' markets in the middle of the city staffed by people whose garb is reminiscent of old-order Mennonites; urban farming and the farm-to-table and locavore movements influenced by vague notions of how people in the past fed themselves; the popularity of rural heritage and small-town tourism, which are marketed as trips into the past; even in popular bands like Nathaniel Rateliff and the Night Sweats, Mumford and Sons and the Lumineers, or Ontario's own Elliot Brood and the Gertrudes, bands that wear waistcoats, woollen slacks, shaggy beards, suspenders, and fedoras: heritage hipsters. Rather than reflecting a naive understanding of the value of the rural past, these trends utilize a mish-mash of signifiers, a pastiche of pastness, to provide cultural manifestations, pop or otherwise, with a sense of greater authenticity, timelessness, and meaning than their seemingly vacuous, more contemporary contemporaries may possess. These quintessentially modern activities are masked as a rejection of modernity, a retreat away from the cacophony of current life, all the while being part of one of its dominant expressions. The value acquired simply through the performance of an idea of the past is self-evident, it would seem, because, for many, the past has an unqualified association with all that we have lost, all that we have sacrificed, to the temptations of modernity. And yet, these manifestations are merely the integration of an idea of a past into very contemporary trends, not an outright rejection of the heterogeneity of contemporary modes of existence. These manifestations reflect not simply aesthetic preferences but earnest desires to improve a world seen as deficient.

In Ontario's small-town literature, two types of return to the rural past occur. Whether the return occurs through the meanderings of memory or imagination, or is an actual return, the rural past is used to help structure or encourage a more livable present. Because the rendered rural pasts in small-town Ontario fiction are irretrievably lost to temporal distance, or left behind by a striving protagonist, these literary figures are left with only a present whose shape is, in the words of Raymond Williams, "undefined" (297). All of these works engage with the rural past to find, as Williams states, "a world in which one is not necessarily a stranger and an agent, but can be a member, a discoverer, in a shared source of life" (298). The understanding of the rural past formed in these works is used to help shape, or at least come to terms with, the "undefined" or incomprehensible present.

As Ontario and Canada become even more urbanized, and as small communities continue to lose their economic autonomy, the tangible influence of this rural space decreases; paradoxically, as has been seen in the last century, while the rural sphere's influence diminishes, its imagined significance, its place in our understanding of the past and, thus, our present, becomes stronger. If we view modernity as, essentially, a homogenizing force, then we must acknowledge that its influence has a reactive consequence; the same force that disintegrates differences – cultural, lifestyle, regional – also ensures the availability of alternatives, antidotes, and antitypes. For urban Ontario, the rural past is the site distant enough to maintain these necessary notions of difference.

Works Cited and Consulted

Activa Group. "Baden Country Estates." 2016. http://www.activagroup.ca/ what-we-do/neighbourhoods/baden-country-estates. Accessed 16 June 2016.

Agacinski, Sylviane. *Time Passing: Modernity and Nostalgia.* New York: Columbia UP, 2003.

Alpers, Paul. *What Is Pastoral?* Chicago: U of Chicago P, 1996.

AlSayyad, Nezar. "Global Norms and Urban Forms in the Age of Tourism: Manufacturing Heritage, Consuming Tradition." *Consuming Tradition, Manufacturing Heritage.* Edited by Nezar AlSayyad. New York: Routledge, 2001, 1–33.

Anderson, Benedict. *Imagined Communities: Reflections on the Origin and Spread of Nationalism.* 1983. London: Verso, 2006.

Anderson, Sherwood. *Winesburg, Ohio.* 1919. New York: W.W. Norton, 1996.

Atwood, Margaret. "Alice Munro: An Appreciation." *The Guardian,* 11 Oct. 2008. https://www.theguardian.com/books/2008/oct/11/alice-munro.

– *In Search of* Alias Grace*: On Writing Canadian Historical Fiction.* Ottawa: U of Ottawa P, 1997.

– "*Lives of Girls and Women*: A Portrait of the Artist as a Young Woman." Staines, *Cambridge,* 96–115.

– "Reaney Connected." *Canadian Literature* 57 (1973): 113–17.

Bailey, Nancy. "The Role of Dunstan Ramsay, the 'Almost' Saint of Robertson Davies's Deptford Trilogy." *Journal of Commonwealth Literature* 19.1 (1984): 27–43.

Bal, Mieke, Jonathan Crewe, and Leo Spitzer, eds. *Acts of Memory: Cultural Recall in the Present.* Hanover, NH: UP of New England, 1999.

Balestra, Gianfranca. "Alice Munro as Historian and Geographer: A Reading of 'Meneseteung.'" *Intersections: La narrativa canadese tra storia e geografia.* Edited by Liana Nissim and Carlo Pagetti. Milan: Cisalpino, 1999, 119–36.

Baskerville, Peter A. *Ontario: Image, Identity, Power.* Don Mills, ON: Oxford UP, 2002.

Baudrillard, Jean. *Simulacra and Simulation.* Translated by Shelia Faria Glaser. Ann Arbor: U of Michigan P, 1994.

Beer, Gillian. *Virginia Woolf: The Common Ground.* Edinburgh: Edinburgh UP, 1996.

Bell, Michael. *Primitivism.* London: Methuen, 1972.

Bemrose, John. *The Island Walkers.* Toronto: McClelland and Steward, 2003.

Bentley, D.M.R. "Boxing the Compass: Ontario's Geopoetics." *Canadian Poetry* 18 (1986): v–xiii.

– *The Gay]Grey Moose: Essays on the Ecologies and Mythologies of Canadian Poetry, 1690–1990.* Ottawa: U of Ottawa P, 1997.

– "Parading Past." *Mnemographia Canadensis: Essays on Memory, Community, and Environment in Canada with Particular Reference to London, ON.* Edited by D.M.R. Bentley. 2 vols. London: Canadian Poetry P, 1999, 379–402.

Bentley, D.M.R., ed. *Sunshine Sketches of a Little Town: Norton Critical Edition.* New York: W.W. Norton, 2006.

Birbalsingh, Frank. "Stephen Leacock and the Canadian Literary Sensibility." Bentley, *Sunshine*, 194–201.

Bligh, John. "The Spiritual Climacteric of Dunstan Ramsay." *World Literature Written in English* 21.3 (1982): 575–93.

Bölling, Gordon. "Acts of (Re-)Construction: Traces of Germany in Jane Urquhart's Novel *The Stone Carvers.*" *Refractions of Germany in Canadian Literature and Culture.* Edited by Heinz Antor, Sylvia Brown, John Considine, and Klaus Stierstorfer. Berlin: Walter de Gruyter, 2003, 295–317.

Bonner, Margaret O'Shea. "Finding Your Place in the Story: A Conversation with Jane Urquhart." *New Quarterly: New Directions in Canadian Writing* 88 (2003): 71–90.

Boym, Svetlana. *The Future of Nostalgia.* New York: Basic Books, 2000.

Branach-Kallas, Anna. *In the Whirlpool of the Past: Memory, Intertextuality and History in the Fiction of Jane Urquhart.* Torun, PL: Wydawnictwo Uniwersytetu Mikolaja Kopernika, 2003.

– "Old Environment or New Environment? Place and Self in Jane Urquhart's *Changing Heaven.*" *Literary Environments: Canada and the Old World.* Edited by Britta Olinder. Brussels: Peter Lang, 2006, 219–25.

Brookes, Alan A. "Introduction." *The Country Town in Rural Ontario's Past: Proceedings of the Sixth Annual Agricultural History of Ontario Seminar.* Edited by Alan A. Brookes. U of Guelph, 1981. iii–v.

Bryant, Christopher R., Philip M. Coppack, and Clare J.A. Mitchell. "The City's Countryside." *Canadian Cities in Transition: The Twenty-First Century.* Edited by Trudi Bunting and Pierre Filion. Toronto: Oxford UP, 2000, 333–54.

Bunce, Michael. *The Countryside Ideal.* London: Routledge, 1994.

Bush, Douglas. "Stephen Leacock." *The Canadian Imagination: Dimensions of a Literary Culture.* Edited by David Staines. Cambridge: Harvard UP, 1977, 123–51.

Cameron, Silver Donald. "Ironist." Bentley, *Sunshine,* 163–70.

Carrington, Ildikó de Papp. *Controlling the Uncontrollable: The Fiction of Alice Munro.* Dekalb: Northern Illinois UP, 1989.

Carscallen, James. *The Other Country: Patterns in the Writing of Alice Munro.* Toronto: ECW P, 1993.

Charman, Cailtin. "'Secretly Devoted to Nature': Place Sense in Alice Munro's *The View from Castle Rock.*" May, 259–75.

Chase, Malcolm, and Christopher Shaw. "The Dimensions of Nostalgia." *The Imagined Past: History and Nostalgia.* Edited by Malcolm Chase and Christopher Shaw. Manchester: Manchester UP, 1989, 1–17.

Chinitz, David. *T.S. Eliot and the Cultural Divide.* Chicago: Chicago UP, 2003.

Claval, Paul. "Changing Conceptions of Heritage and Landscape." *Heritage, Memory and the Politics of Identity: New Perspectives on the Cultural Landscape.* Edited by Niamh Moore and Yvonne Whelan. Aldershot, UK: Ashgate P, 2007, 85–91.

Cohen, Matt. *The Colours of War.* Toronto: McClelland and Stewart, 1977.

– *The Disinherited.* Toronto: McClelland and Stewart, 1974.

– *Elizabeth and After.* Toronto: Vintage Canada, 2000.

– *Flowers of Darkness.* Toronto: McClelland and Stewart, 1981.

– *The Sweet Second Summer of Kitty Malone.* Toronto: McClelland and Stewart, 1979.

Coleman, Daniel. *White Civility: The Literary Project of English Canada.* Toronto: U of Toronto P, 2006.

Compton, Anne. "Romancing the Landscape: Jane Urquhart's Fiction." Ferri, *Jane Urquhart,* 115–43.

Condé, Mary. "The Ambiguities of History in Alice Munro's *The Love of a Good Woman.*" *Etudes canadiennes/Canadian Studies: Revue interdisciplinaire des études canadiennes en France* 46 (1999): 123–30.

– "'True Lies': Photographs in the Short Stories of Alice Munro." *Etudes canadiennes/Canadian Studies: Revue interdisciplinaire des études canadiennes en France* 18.32 (1992): 97–110.

Cook, David, and Craig Swauger. "Preface." *The Small Town in American Literature.* Edited by David Cook and Craig Swauger. New York: Dodd, Mead, 1969.

Cook, Ramsay. "Stephen Leacock and the Age of Plutocracy, 1903–1921." *Character and Circumstance*. Edited by John S. Moir. Toronto: Macmillan, 1970, 163–81.

Coupland, Douglas. "What Is CanLit?" *New York Times*, 22 Aug. 2006. https://coupland.blogs.nytimes.com/tag/canlit/.

Cox, Alissa. *Alice Munro*. Tavistock: Northcote, 2004.

Cronon, William. "Introduction: In Search of Nature." *Uncommon Ground: Toward Reinventing Nature*. Edited by William Cronon. New York: W.W. Norton, 1995, 23–68.

– "The Trouble with Wilderness; or, Getting Back to the Wrong Nature." *Uncommon Ground: Toward Reinventing Nature*. Edited by William Cronon. New York: W.W. Norton, 1995, 69–90.

Cubitt, Geoffrey. *History and Memory*. Manchester: Manchester UP, 2007.

Cuder-Domínguez, Pilar. "A Biography of Stones: Mourning and Mutability in Jane Urquhart's *A Map of Glass* and Michael Redhill's *Consolation*." Daziron-Ventura and Dvořák, 201–14.

Curry, Ralph L. *Stephen Leacock: Humorist and Humanist*. Garden City, NY: Doubleday, 1959.

Dahms, F.A. "The Evolving Spatial Organization of Small Settlements." Dasgupta, *Community*, 200–11.

– "The Role of the Country Town in Ontario Yesterday and Today: The Case of Wellington and Huron Counties." *The Country Town in Ontario's Rural Past: Proceedings of the Sixth Annual Agricultural History of Ontario Seminar*. Edited by A.A. Brookes. U of Guelph, 1981.

Daniels, Cindy Lou. "Creating Fictionality: Re-living Reality in Alice Munro's Fiction." *Eureka Studies in Teaching Short Fiction* 6.2 (2006): 94–105.

Dasgupta, Satadal, ed. *The Community in Canada: Rural and Urban*. Lanham, MD: University Press of America, 1996.

– "Modernization and Rural Community Organization: Changing Community Structure on Prince Edward Island." Dasgupta, *Community*, 166–79.

– "The Rural Neighborhood." Dasgupta, *Community*, 93–6.

– "The Small Town as a Structural Type: Change and Persistence." Dasgupta, *Community*, 183–6.

Davey, Frank. "Towards the Ends of Regionalism." *Sense of Place: Re-Evaluating Regionalism in Canadian and American Writing*. Edited by Christian Riegel and Herb Wyile. Edmonton: U of Alberta P, 1998, 1–18.

Davies, Robertson. *Fifth Business*. New York: Signet, 1971.

– "From *Stephen Leacock*." Bentley, *Sunshine*, 219–25.

– "Introduction." *Feast of Stephen: A Cornucopia of Delights by Stephen Leacock*. Toronto: McClelland and Stewart, 1971, 1–49.

– *Leaven of Malice*. Toronto: Clarke Irwin, 1954.

– *The Manticore*. New York: Viking Press, 1972.

– *A Mixture of Frailties*. Toronto: Macmillan, 1958.

– *One Half of Robertson Davies: Provocative Pronouncements on a Wide Range of Topics*. Toronto: Macmillan, 1977.

– *The Papers of Samuel Marchbanks*. New York: Viking Press, 1985.

– *Tempest-Tost*. Toronto: Clarke Irwin, 1951.

– *World of Wonders*. Toronto: Macmillan, 1975.

Davis, Fred. *Yearning for Yesterday: A Sociology of Nostalgia*. London: Free Press, 1979.

Daziron, Heliane. "Alice Munro's 'The Flats Road'." *Canadian Woman Studies/ Les cahiers de la femme* 6.1 (1985): 103–4.

Daziron-Ventura, Héliane, and Marta Dvořák, eds. *Resurgence in Jane Urquhart's Oeuvre*. Brussels: Peter Lang, 2010.

de Bolla, Peter. "A Second Look at *The Country and the City*." *Cultural Materialism: On Raymond Williams*. Edited by Christopher Prendergast. Minnesota: U of Minnesota P, 1995, 173–87.

Derksen, Jeff. "'Text' and the Site of Writing." *Biting the Error: Writers Explore Narrative*. Edited by Mary Burger, Robert Glück, Camille Roy, and Gail Scott. Toronto: Coach House, 2004, 108–12.

Diemert, Brian. "Out of the Water: The Presence of Virginia Woolf in Alice Munro's *Lives of Girls and Women*." *Eureka Studies in Teaching Short Fiction* 6.2 (2006): 120–30.

Dragland, Stan, ed. *Approaches to the Work of James Reaney*. Downsview, ON: ECW P, 1983.

Duffy, Denis. "George Elliott: *The Kissing Man*." *Canadian Literature* 63 (1975): 52–63.

Duncan, Isla. *Alice Munro's Narrative Art*. New York: Palgrave/Macmillan, 2011.

Duncan, Sara Jeannette. *The Imperialist*. 1904. Toronto: McClelland and Stewart, 1971.

El-Hassan, Karla. "Reflections of the Special Unity of Stephen Leacock's *Sunshine Sketches of a Little Town*." *Gaining Ground: European Critics on Canadian Literature*. Edited by Robert Kroetsch and Reingard M. Nischik. Edmonton: NeWest P, 1985, 171–85.

Elliott, George. *God's Big Acre: Life in 401 Country*. Photography by John Reeves. Toronto: Methuen, 1986.

– *The Kissing Man*. Toronto: Macmillan, 1962.

Empson, William. *Some Versions of Pastoral*. 1935. London: Chatto and Windus, 1968.

Everitt, J.C., and A.M. Gill. "The Social Geography of Small Towns." *The Changing Social Geography of Canadian Cities*. Edited by Larry S. Bourne and David F. Ley. Montreal: McGill-Queen's UP, 1993, 252–64.

Ferri, Laura. "Conversations with Jane Urquhart." Ferri. *Jane Urquhart*, 15-41.

– "Introduction." Ferri, *Jane Urquhart*, 9–13.

Ferri, Laura, ed. *Jane Urquhart: Essays on Her Works*. Toronto: Guernica Editions, 2005.

Ferris, Ina. "The Face in the Window." *Studies in Canadian Literature* 3.2 (1978): 178–85.

Fiamengo, Janice. "Regionalism and Urbanism." *The Cambridge Companion to Canadian Literature*. Edited by Eva-Marie Kröller. Toronto: U of Cambridge P, 2004, 241–62.

Findley, Timothy. "Riding Off in All Directions: A Few Wild Words in Search of Stephen Leacock." Staines, *Stephen Leacock*, 5–9.

Finlayson, Carolyn. "Defining the Country: Memory and Nationhood in the Canadian Museum of Civilization." *Mnemographia Canadensis: Essays on Memory, Community, and Environment in Canada with Particular Reference to London, ON*. 2 vols. Edited by D.M.R. Bentley. London: Canadian Poetry P, 1999, 195–234.

Foran, Charles. "Alice in Borderland." *The Walrus*, Sept. 2009. https://thewalrus.ca/alice-in-borderland/.

Fowler, Rowena. "The Art of Alice Munro: *The Beggar Maid* and *Lives of Girls and Women*." *Critique: Studies in Contemporary Fiction* 25.4 (1984): 189–97.

Frye, Northrop. "Conclusion to a *Literary History of Canada*." *The Bush Garden: Essays on the Canadian Imagination*. Toronto: House of Anansi P, 1971, 213–51.

– "Culture and Society in Ontario, 1784–1984." *Mythologizing Canada: Essays on the Canadian Literary Imagination*. Toronto: Legas, 1997, 175–89.

Galante, Paul. "The 'Problematic' Fictions of Historical Narrative in Alice Munro's 'A Wilderness Station'." *Eureka Studies in Teaching Short Fiction* 6.2 (2006): 62–73.

Gerson, Carole. "Adeline Teskey." *The Encyclopedia of Canadian Literature*. Edited by W.H. New. Toronto: U of Toronto P, 2002, 1096.

Gifford, Terry. *Pastoral*. New York: Routledge, 1999.

Godard, Barbara. "'Heirs of the Living Body': Alice Munro and the Question of a Female Aesthetic." Miller, *Art*, 43–71.

– "Robertson Davies's Dialogic Imagination." *Essays on Canadian Writing* 34 (1987): 64–80.

– "World of Wonders: Robertson Davies's Carnival." *Essays on Canadian Writing* 30 (1984–85): 239–86.

Gold, Joseph. "Our Feeling Exactly: The Writing of Alice Munro." Miller, *Art*, 1–13.

Goldsmith, Oliver. "The Rising Village." *Canadian Poetry: From the Beginnings through the First World War*. Edited by Carole Gerson and Gwendolyn Davies. Toronto: McClelland and Stewart, 1994, 53–70.

Gordon, Neta. "The Artist and the Witness: Jane Urquhart's *The Underpainter* and *The Stone Carvers*." *Studies in Canadian Literature* 28.2 (2003): 59–73.

– "Intimate and Conditional: Artistic Gesture in Jane Urquhart's *False Shuffles, The Underpainter* and *A Map of Glass*," Daziron-Ventura and Dvořák, 159–74.

Graburn, Nelson H.H. "Learning to Consume: What Is Heritage and When Is It Traditional?" *Consuming Tradition, Manufacturing Heritage*. Edited by Nezar AlSayyad. New York: Routledge, 2001, 68–89.

Grant, Judith Skelton. *Robertson Davies: Man of Myth*. Toronto: Viking, 1994.

Hancu, Laura. "Escaping the Frame: Circumscribing the Narrative in *The Whirlpool*." *Studies in Canadian Literature* 20.1 (1995): 45–64.

Harris, Joseph. "The Idea of Community in the Study of Writing." *College Composition and Communication* 40.1 (1989): 11–22.

Harvey, David. "Between Space and Time: Reflections on the Geographical Imagination." *Annals of the Association of American Geographers* 80.3 (1990): 418–34.

– *The Condition of Postmodernity: An Enquiry into the Origins of Cultural Change*. Oxford: Blackwell, 1989.

Hay, Elizabeth. *Alone in the Classroom*. Leicester, UK: Thorpe, 2014.

Heble, Ajay. *The Tumble of Reason: Alice Munro's Discourse of Absence*. Toronto: U of Toronto P, 1994.

Hepburn, Allan. "Beautiful Mourning: *The Stone Carvers*." Ferri, *Jane Urquhart*, 45–50.

Hewison, Robert. *The Heritage Industry*. London: Methuen, 1987.

Higgins, John. "Raymond Williams and the Problem of Ideology." *Boundary 2: A Journal of Postmodern Literature and Culture* 11.1–2 (1982–83): 145–54.

Hilfer, Anthony. *The Revolt from the Village, 1915–1930*. Chapel Hill: U of North Carolina P, 1969.

Hobsbawm, Eric. "Introduction: Inventing Traditions." *The Invention of Tradition*. Edited by Eric Hobsbawm and Terence Ranger. Cambridge: Cambridge UP, 1983, 1–14.

Homel, David. "The Bittersweet Man." *Books in Canada* 23.6 (1994): 10–14.

Homer, Sean. "Narratives of History, Narratives of Time." *On Jameson: From Postmodernism to Globalization*. Edited by Caren Irr and Ian Buchanan. Albany: State U of New York P, 2006, 71–91.

Horwood, Harold. "Interview with Alice Munro." Miller, *Art*, 123–35.

Howells, Coral Ann. *Alice Munro*. Manchester: Manchester UP, 1998.

– "Alice Munro's Heritage Narratives." *Where Are the Voices Coming From?* Edited by Coral Ann Howells. Amsterdam: Rodopi P, 2004, 5–14.

– "A Question of Inheritance: Canadian Women's Short Stories." *Determined Women: Studies in the Construction of the Female Subject*. Edited by Jennifer Birkett and Elizabeth Harvey. London: Macmillan, 1991, 108–19.

Hoy, Helen. "Alice Munro: 'Unforgettable, Indigestible Messages'." *Journal of Canadian Studies* 26.1 (1991): 5–21.

– "'Rose and Janet': Alice Munro's Metafiction." *Canadian Literature* 121 (1989): 59–83.

Hutcheon, Linda. *The Canadian Postmodern*. Toronto: Oxford UP, 1988.

– "Irony, Nostalgia, and the Postmodern." *Methods for the Study of Literature as Cultural Memory*. Edited by Raymond Vervliet and Annemarie Estor. Amsterdam: Rodopi, 2000, 189–207.

Ivison, Douglas, and Justin D. Edwards. "Introduction: Writing Canadian Cities." *Downtown Canada: Writing Canadian Cities*. Edited by Justin D. Edwards and Douglas Ivison. Toronto: U of Toronto P, 2005, 3–13.

Jameson, Fredric. "Nostalgia for the Present." *Classical Hollywood Narrative*. Edited by Jane Gaines. Durham, NC: Duke UP, 1992, 253–74.

Jewinski, Ed. "Untestable Inferences: Post-Structuralism and Leacock's Achievement in Sunshine Sketches." Staines, *Stephen Leacock*, 107–20.

Johler, Reinhard. "The EU as Manufacturer of Tradition and Cultural Heritage." *Culture and Economy: Contemporary Perspectives*. Edited by Ullrich Kockel. Bristol: Ashgate, 2002, 221–30.

Jordan, David M. *New World Regionalism: Literature in the Americas*. Toronto: U of Toronto P, 1994.

Keith, W.J. *Literary Images of Ontario*. Toronto: U of Toronto P, 1992.

Knister, Raymond. *White Narcissus*. 1929. Toronto: McClelland and Stewart, 1990.

Kroetsch, Robert. "No Name Is My Name." *Lovely Treachery of Words*. Don Mills, ON: Oxford UP, 1989, 41–52.

Kushner, J. and R.D. Macdonald. "Leacock: Economist/Satirist in *Arcadian Adventures* and *Sunshine Sketches*." *Dalhousie Review* 56.3 (1976): 493–509.

Ladino, Jennifer. "Longing for Wonderland: Nostalgia for Nature in Post-Frontier America." *Iowa Journal of Cultural Studies* 5 (2004): 88–111.

Lasch, Christopher. "The Politics of Nostalgia: Losing History in the Mists of Ideology." *Harper's*, Nov. 1984, 65–70.

– *The True and Only Heaven: Progress and Its Critics*. New York: W.W. Norton, 1991.

Leacock, Stephen. *Arcadian Adventures with the Idle Rich*. 1914. Toronto: McClelland and Stewart, 1959.

– *The Boy I Left Behind Me.* New York: Doubleday, 1946.

– *Happy Stories Just to Laugh at.* New York: Dodd, 1943.

– *Short Circuits.* Toronto: McClelland and Stewart, 1928.

– *Sunshine Sketches of a Little Town.* Edited by Gerald Lynch. 1912. Ottawa: Tecumseh P, 1996.

Lecker, Robert. "Machines, Readers, Gardens: Alice Munro's 'Carried Away'." Thacker, *Rest*, 103–27.

Lennox, John Watt. "Manawaka and Deptford: Place and Voice." *Journal of Canadian Studies* 13.3 (1978): 23–30.

Lewis, Sinclair. *Main Street.* 1920. New York: Signet, 1961.

Lippard, Lucy. *The Lure of the Local.* New York: New Press, 1997.

Lorre, Christine. "Reconstructing the Past Through Objects in *A Map of Glass*." Daziron-Ventura and Dvořák, 185–99.

Lovejoy, Arthur O., and George Boas. *Primitivism and Related Ideas in Antiquity.* Baltimore, MD: Johns Hopkins UP, 1935.

Lowenthal, David. *The Heritage Crusade.* Cambridge: Cambridge UP, 1996.

– "Nostalgia Tells It Like It Wasn't." *The Imagined Past: History and Nostalgia.* Edited by Malcolm Chase and Christopher Shaw. Manchester: Manchester UP, 1989, 18–30.

– *The Past Is a Foreign Country.* Cambridge: Cambridge UP, 1985.

– "Past Time, Present Place: Landscape and Memory." *Geographical Review* 65.1 (1975): 1–36.

Lower, Arthur. "Ontario: Does It Exist?" *Ontario History* 60 (1969): 65–9.

Lucking, David. "A Will and Two Ways: The Ambivalence of Evil in Robertson Davies's *The Deptford Trilogy*." *Canadian Literature* 165 (2000): 44–56.

Lynch, Gerald. "No Honey, I'm Home: Place over Love in Alice Munro's Short Story Cycle *Who Do You Think You Are?*" *Canadian Literature* 160 (1999): 73–98.

– *The One and the Many: English-Canadian Short Story Cycles.* Toronto: U of Toronto P, 2001.

– *Stephen Leacock: Humour and Humanity.* Montreal and Kingston: McGill-Queen's UP, 1988.

Lynch, Gerald, ed. *Sunshine Sketches of a Little Town: Canadian Critical Edition.* Ottawa: Tecumseh P, 1996.

MacCannell, Dean. *Empty Meeting Grounds: The Tourist Papers.* London: Routledge, 1992.

– *The Tourist.* New York: Schocken Books, 1976.

MacDonald, R.D. "Measuring Leacock's Mariposa against Lewis's Gopher Prairie: A Question of Monuments." *Dalhousie Review* 71.1 (1991): 84–103.

– "Small-Town Ontario in Robertson Davies' *Fifth Business*: Mariposa Revised?" *Studies in Canadian Literature* 9.1 (1984): 61–77.

MacKendrick, Louis K., ed. *Probable Fictions: Alice Munro's Narrative Acts.* Downsview, ON: ECW Press, 1983.

MacLean, Gerald, Donna Landry, and Joseph P. Ward. "Introduction: The Country and the City Revisited." *The Country and the City Revisited: England and the Politics of Culture, 1550–1850.* Cambridge: Cambridge UP, 1999, 1–23.

MacLennan, Hugh. "If You Drop a Stone." *Thirty and Three.* Toronto: Macmillan, 1953, 175–81.

MacMillan, Margaret. *The Uses and Abuses of History.* Toronto: Viking Canada, 2008.

Magee, W.H. "Genial Humour in Stephen Leacock." *Dalhousie Review* 56 (1976): 268–82.

– "Stephen Leacock: Local Colourist." *Canadian Literature* 39 (1969): 34–42.

Mandel, Eli. "The City in Canadian Poetry." *Another Time.* Erin, ON: Press Porcépic, 1977, 114–23.

Mantz, Douglas. "The Preposterous and the Profound: A New Look at the Envoi of *Sunshine Sketches.*" *Journal of Canadian Fiction* 19 (1977): 95–105.

Marinelli, Peter V. *Pastoral.* London: Methuen, 1971.

Marshall, Tom. "False Pastoral: Stephen Leacock's Conflicting Worlds." *Journal of Canadian Fiction* 19 (1977): 86–94.

Martin, W.R., and Warren U. Ober. "Alice Munro as Small-Town Historian: 'Spaceships Have Landed.'" Thacker, *Rest,* 128–46.

Marx, Leo. *The Machine in the Garden: Technology and the Pastoral Ideal in America.* New York: Oxford UP, 1964.

Massey, Doreen. *Space, Place, and Gender.* Cambridge: Polity P, 1994.

May, Charles, ed. *Critical Insights: Alice Munro.* Ipswich, UK: Salem Press, 2013.

Mayberry, Katherine J. "'Every Last Thing … Everlasting': Alice Munro and the Limits of Narrative." *Alice Munro: Bloom's Modern Critical Views,* Edited by Harold Bloom. New York: Infobase Publishing, 2009, 29–39.

McClung, William Alexander. "The Mediating Structure of the Small Town." *Journal of Architectural Education* 38.3 (1985): 2–7.

McGill, Robert. "Somewhere I've Been Meaning to Tell You: Alice Munro's Fiction of Distance." *Journal of Commonwealth Literature* 37.1 (2002): 9–29.

McGranahan, David A. "Changes in the Social and Spatial Structure of the Rural Community." *Technology and Social Change in Rural Areas.* Edited by Gene F. Summers. Boulder, CO: Westview P, 1983. 163–78.

McIntyre, Timothy. "Doing Her Duty and Writing Her Life: Alice Munro's Cultural and Historical Context." May, 52–67.

McKay, Ian. *The Quest of the Folk: Antimodernism and Cultural Selection in Twentieth Century Nova Scotia.* Montreal and Kingston: McGill-Queen's UP, 1994.

McMullen, Lorraine. "'Shameless, Marvellous, Shattering Absurdity': The Humour of Paradox in Alice Munro." MacKendrick, 144–62.

McWilliams, Ellen. "Alice Munro's *Lives of Girls and Women*: A Case Study of Literary Influence." *Eureka Studies in Teaching Short Fiction* 6.2 (2006): 150–3.

Merchant, Carolyn. "Reinventing Eden: Western Culture as a Recovery Narrative." *Uncommon Ground: Toward Reinventing Nature.* Edited by William Cronon. New York: W.W. Norton, 1995, 91–113.

Metcalf, John. "A Conversation with Alice Munro." *Journal of Canadian Fiction* 1.4 (1972): 54–62.

Meyers, Leonard W. "Stephen Leacock, Canada's Mark Twain." *Antigonish Review* 98 (1994): 35–9.

Micros, Marianne. "*Et in Ontario Ego*: The Pastoral Ideal and the Blazon Tradition in Alice Munro's 'Lichen'." Thacker, *Rest,* 44–59.

Middleton, J.E. *The Romance of Ontario.* Toronto: W.J. Gage, 1931.

Miller, John E. "The Distance between Gopher Prairie and Lake Wobegon: Sinclair Lewis and Garrison Keillor on the Small-Town Experience." *Centennial Review* 31.4 (1987): 432–46.

Miller, Judith, ed. *The Art of Alice Munro: Saying the Unsayable. Papers from the Waterloo Conference.* Waterloo, ON: U of Waterloo P, 1984.

Milner, Andrew. "Cultural Materialism, Culturalism and Post-Culturalism: The Legacy of Raymond Williams." *Theory, Culture and Society* 11.1 (1994): 43–73.

Monk, Patricia. *Mud and Magic Shows: Robertson Davies's Fifth Business.* Toronto: ECW P, 1992.

– *The Smaller Infinity: The Jungian Self in the Novels of Robertson Davies.* Toronto: U of Toronto P, 1982.

Moodie, Susanna. *Life in the Clearings.* Edited by Robert L. McDougall. 1853. Toronto: Macmillan, 1959.

Moritz, Albert, and Theresa Moritz. *Stephen Leacock: His Remarkable Life.* Toronto: Stoddart, 1985.

Moss, John. *Sex and Violence in the Canadian Novel.* Toronto: McClelland and Stewart, 1977.

Munro, Alice. *Lives of Girls and Women.* Toronto: McGraw-Hill, 1971.

– *Moons of Jupiter.* Toronto: Macmillan, 1982.

– *Open Secrets.* Toronto: McClelland and Stewart, 1994.

– *The View from Castle Rock.* 2006. Toronto: Penguin, 2010.

– "Walker Brothers Cowboy." *Selected Stories.* Toronto: McClelland and Stewart, 1996, 3–15.

– *Who Do You Think You Are?* Toronto: Signet, 1978.

Murphy, Georgeann. "The Art of Alice Munro: Memory, Identity, and the Aesthetics of Connection." *Canadian Women Writing Fiction*. Edited by Mickey Pearlman. Jackson: UP of Mississippi, 1993, 12–27.

Natali, Marcos Piason. "History and the Politics of Nostalgia." *Iowa Journal of Cultural Studies* 5 (2004): 10–25.

Naves, Elaine Kalman. "Interview/ Jane Urquhart: Home from Away." *Books in Canada* 24.4 (1995): 7–13.

New, W.H. *A History of Canadian Literature*. Montreal and Kingston: McGill-Queen's UP, 2003.

– *Land Sliding: Imagining Space, Presence, and Power in Canadian Writing*. Toronto: U of Toronto P, 1997.

Nonini, Donald M. "Race, Land, Nation: A(t)-Tribute to Raymond Williams." *Cultural Critique* 41 (1999): 158–83.

Noonan, Gerald. "The Structure of Style in Alice Munro's Fiction." MacKendrick, 163–80.

Norris, Darrell. "Preserving Main Street: Some Lessons of Leacock's Mariposa." *Journal of Canadian Studies* 17.2 (1982): 128–36.

O'Keefe, Tadhg. "Landscape and Memory: Historiography, Theory, Methodology." *Heritage, Memory and the Politics of Identity: New Perspectives on the Cultural Landscape*. Edited by Niamh Moore and Yvonne Whelan. Aldershot, UK: Ashgate P, 2007, 3–13.

Orange, John. "Alice Munro and a Maze of Time." MacKendrick, 83–98.

Osachoff, Margaret Gail. "'Treacheries of the Heart': Memoir, Confession, and Meditation in the Stories of Alice Munro." MacKendrick, 61–82.

Pacey, Desmond. "The Eighteenth Century Tory." Lynch, *Sunshine*, 180–3.

Peck, David. "Who Does Rose Think She Is? Acting and Being in *The Beggar Maid: Stories of Flo and Rose*." May, 128–41.

Peterman, Michael. *Robertson Davies*. Boston: Twayne, 1986.

Porter, Ryan. "Pictures of the Past: The Small-Town Myth as Heritage, or Understanding and Articulating Community through Texts of the Past." *Topia: Canadian Journal of Cultural Studies* 22 (2009): 139–58.

Prince Edward County. "Welcome to the County." http://prince-edward-county.com/. Accessed 13 Sept. 2016.

Radford, F.L. "The Great Mother and the Boy: Jung, Davies, and *Fifth Business*." *Studies in Robertson Davies' Deptford Trilogy*. Edited by Robert G. Lawrence and Samuel L. Macey. Victoria, BC: U of Victoria P, 1980, 66–81.

Rasporich, Beverly. "Charles Dickens and Stephen Leacock: A Legacy of Sentimental Humour." Bentley, *Sunshine*, 179–83.

– *Dance of the Sexes: Art and Gender in the Fiction of Alice Munro*. Edmonton: U of Alberta P, 1990.

– "The Leacock Persona and the Canadian Character." *Mosaic: A Journal for the Interdisciplinary Study of Literature* 14.2 (1981): 77–92.

– "The New Eden Dream: The Source of Canadian Humour – McCulloch, Haliburton, and Leacock." *Studies in Canadian Literature* 7.2 (1982): 227–40.

Rayside, David M. *A Small Town in Modern Times.* Montreal and Kingston: McGill-Queen's UP, 1991.

Reaney, James. "Ontario Culture and – What?" *Canadian Literature* 100 (1984): 252–7.

– *Souwesto Home.* London, ON: Brick Books, 2005.

– *Twelve Letters to a Small Town.* Toronto: Ryerson P, 1962.

Reaney, James Stewart. "Author Robertson Davies Thinly Veiled the Village in His Celebrated Canadian Novel *Fifth Business.*" *London Free Press,* 31 July 2013. http://lfpress.com/2013/07/31/my-london-author-robertson-davis-thinly-veiled-the-village-in-his-celebrated-canadian-novel-fifth-business. Accessed 20 Dec. 2016.

Redekop, Magdalene. "Alice Munro and the Scottish Nostalgic Grotesque." Thacker, *Rest,* 21–41.

Reid, Verna. "The Small Town in Canadian Fiction." *English Quarterly* 6.2 (1973): 171–81.

Reimer, Bill. "Immigration in the New Rural Economy." *Our Diverse Cities: Rural Communities* 3 (2007): 3–8.

Richler, Mordecai. "Spend a Few Hours in Mariposa." *National Post,* 25 March 2000, B8.

Rifkin, Jeremy. *The Age of Access: How the Shift from Ownership to Access Is Transforming Capitalism.* London: Penguin Books, 2000.

Roberts, Charles G.D. *Selected Poems of Charles G.D. Roberts.* Edited by Desmond Pacey. Ottawa: Tecumseh P, 1980.

Robertson, Ian Ross. "The Historical Leacock." Staines, *Stephen Leacock,* 33–49.

Robson, Nora. "Sense of Place in Alice Munro's Fiction." *Literary Criterion* 19.3–4 (1984): 138–46.

Roche, Mazo de la. *Jalna.* Toronto: Macmillan, 1927.

Samuel, Raphael. *Theatres of Memory.* London: Verso, 1994.

Santesso, Aaron. *A Careful Longing: The Poetics and Problems of Nostalgia.* Newark: U of Delaware P, 2006.

Scott, Duncan Campbell. *In the Village of Viger.* Boston: Copeland and Day, 1896.

Sheldrick-Ross, Catherine. "'At Least Part Legend': The Fiction of Alice Munro." MacKendrick, 112–26.

Simonds, Marilyn. "Where Do You Think You Are? Place in the Short Stories of Alice Munro." Staines, *Cambridge,* 26–44.

Smith, Laurajane. "Introduction." *Cultural Heritage Reader*. Vol 1. Edited by
    Laurajane Smith. New York: Routledge, 2007, 1–23.
– *Uses of Heritage*. New York: Routledge, 2006.
Smith, Russell. "Dear [Non-] Reader, It Might Not Be Your Fault." *Globe and
    Mail*, 11 Dec. 2002, R1–R2.
– *Noise*. Erin, ON: Porcupine Quill P, 1998.
Smythe, Karen. *Figuring Grief: Gallant, Munro, and the Poetics of Elegy*. Montreal
    and Kingston: McGill-Queen's UP, 1992.
Sontag, Susan. *On Photography*. New York: Farrar, Straus and Giroux, 1977.
Spadoni, Carl. "Introduction." *Sunshine Sketches of a Little Town*. Edited by Carl
    Spadoni. Peterborough, ON: Broadview P, 2002, vii–lxxxi.
Staines, David. "From Wingham to Clinton: Alice Munro in Her Canadian
    Context." Staines, *Cambridge*, 7–25.
– "The Stone Carvers." Ferri, *Jane Urquhart*, 42–4.
Staines, David, ed. *Cambridge Companion to Alice Munro*. Cambridge:
    Cambridge UP, 2016.
––, ed. *The Letters of Stephen Leacock*. Toronto: Oxford UP, 2006.
– , ed. *Stephen Leacock: A Reappraisal*. Ottawa: U of Ottawa P, 1986.
Steele, James. "Imperial Cosmopolitanism, or the Partly Solved Riddle of
    Leacock's Multi-National Persona." Staines, *Stephen Leacock*, 59–68.
Steinwand, Jonathan. "The Future of Nostalgia in Friedrich Schlegel's Gender
    Theory: Casting German Aesthetics beyond Ancient Greece and Modern
    Europe." *Narratives of Nostalgia, Gender and Nationalism*. Basingstoke, UK:
    Macmillan, 1997, 9–29.
Stott, Siân. "The Iceman and the Frozen Women." *Telegraph* (UK), 18 Dec.
    2005. https://www.telegraph.co.uk/culture/books/3648851/The-iceman-
    and-the-frozen-woman.html.
Stovel, Nora Foster. "Temples and Tabernacles: Alternative Religions in the
    Fictional Microcosms of Robertson Davies, Margaret Laurence, and Alice
    Munro." *International Fiction Review* 31.1–2 (2004): 65–77.
Struthers, Tim. "Alice Munro's Fictive Imagination." Miller, *Art*, 103–12.
– "The Real Material: An Interview with Alice Munro." MacKendrick, 5–36.
Stubbs, Andrew. "Fictional Landscape: Mythology and Dialectic in the
    Fiction of Alice Munro." *World Literature Written in English* 23.1 (1984):
    53–62.
Su, John J. *Ethics and Nostalgia in the Contemporary Novel*. Cambridge:
    Cambridge UP, 2005.
Suttles, Gerald D. *The Social Construction of Communities*. Chicago: U of
    Chicago P, 1972.
Tener, Jean F. "The Invisible Iceberg." Miller, *Art*, 37–42.

Teskey, Adeline. *Where the Sugar Maple Grows: Idylls of a Canadian Village.* Toronto: Musson Book Co., 1901.

Thacker, Robert. *Alice Munro: Writing Her Lives.* Toronto: McClelland and Stewart, 2005.

– "Alice Munro's Ontario." *Tropes and Territories: Short Fiction, Postcolonial Readings, Canadian Writing in Context.* Edited by Marta Dvorak and W.H. New. Montreal and Kingston: McGill-Queen's UP, 2007, 103–18.

– "'Clear Jelly': Alice Munro's Narrative Dialectics." MacKendrick, 37–60.

– "Connection: Alice Munro and Ontario." *American Review of Canadian Studies* 14.2 (1984): 213–26.

– "Introduction: Alice Munro, Writing 'Home': 'Seeing This Trickle in Time.'" Thacker, *Rest*, 1–20.

– "'So Shocking a Verdict in Real Life': Autobiography in Alice Munro's Stories." *Reflections: Autobiography and Canadian Literature.* Edited by K.P. Stich. Ottawa: U of Ottawa P, 1988, 153–61.

Thacker, Robert, ed. *The Rest of the Story: Critical Essays on Alice Munro.* Toronto: ECW P, 1999.

Thomas, Clara. "Canadian Social Mythologies in Sara Jeannette Duncan's *The Imperialist.*" *Journal of Canadian Studies* 12.2 (1977): 38–49.

– "The Roads Back: *Sunshine Sketches of a Little Town* and George Elliott's *The Kissing Man.*" Staines, *Stephen Leacock*, 97–105.

– "The Town: Our Tribe." *Literary Half-Yearly* 13.2 (1972): 210–26.

Urquhart, Jane. "Afterword." *No Love Lost* by Alice Munro. Toronto: McClelland and Stewart, 2003.

– *Away.* 1993. Toronto: McClelland and Stewart, 1997.

– *Changing Heaven.* 1990. Toronto: McClelland and Stewart, 1994.

– *A Map of Glass.* Toronto: McClelland and Stewart, 2005.

– *Sanctuary Line.* Toronto: McClelland and Stewart, 2010.

– *The Stone Carvers.* Toronto: McClelland and Stewart, 2001.

– *The Underpainter.* Toronto: McClelland and Stewart, 1997.

Urry, John. "How Societies Remember the Past." *Cultural Heritage Reader.* Vol. 2. Edited by Laurajane Smith. New York: Routledge, 2007, 188–205.

Vanderhaeghe, Guy. "Leacock and Understanding Canada." Staines *Stephen Leacock*, 17–21.

Vidich, Arthur J., and Joseph Bensman. *Small Town in Mass Society: Class, Power and Religion in a Rural Community.* Garden City, NY: Anchor Books, 1960.

Wagamese, Richard. *Keeper'n Me.* Toronto: Doubleday Canada, 1994.

Wagner, Tamara S. *Longing: Narratives of Nostalgia in the British Novel, 1740– 1890.* Lewisburg, NY: Bucknell UP, 2004.

Walsh, Kevin. *The Representation of the Past: Museums and Heritage in the Post-Modern World*. London: Routledge, 1992.

Warwick, Susan. "Growing Up: The Novels of Alice Munro." *Essays on Canadian Writing* 29 (1984): 204–25.

Waterston, Elizabeth. "Regions and Eras in Ontario Poetry." *Canadian Poetry* 18 (1986): 1–10.

Weaver, John. "Society and Culture in Rural and Small-Town Ontario: Alice Munro's Testimony on the Last Forty Years." *Patterns of the Past: Interpreting Ontario's History*. Edited by Roger Hall, William Westfall, and Laurel Sefton MacDowell. Toronto: Dundurn P, 1988, 381–402.

"Welcome to the County." *Prince Edward County, Ontario, Canada*. http://prince-edward-county.com/. Accessed 20 Dec. 2016.

West, Nancy Martha. *Kodak and the Lens of Nostalgia*. Charlottesville: U of Virginia P, 2000.

Williams, David. "The Confessions of a Self-Made Man: Forms of Autobiography in *Fifth Business*." *Journal of Canadian Studies* 24.1 (1989): 81–102.

Williams, Raymond. *Country and the City*. London: Oxford UP, 1973.

Willmott, Glenn. "The Cost of a Drink in Mariposa." *Essays on Canadian Writing* 68 (1999): 46–77.

– *Unreal Country: Modernity in the Canadian Novel in English*. Montreal and Kingston: McGill-Queen's UP, 2002.

Wright, Richard. *Clara Callan*. Toronto: HarperCollins, 2001.

Wyile, Herb. "As for Me and Me Arse: Strategic Regionalism and the Home Place in Lynn Coady's *Strange Heaven*." *Canadian Literature* 189 (2006): 85–101.

– "Jane Urquhart: Confessions of a Historical Geographer." *Essays on Canadian Writing* 81 (2004): 58–83.

– "'The Opposite of History Is Forgetfulness': Myth, History and the New Dominion in Jane Urquhart's *Away*." *Studies in Canadian Literature* 24.1 (1999): 20–45.

– *Speculative Fictions: Contemporary Canadian Novelists and the Writing of History*. Montreal and Kingston: McGill-Queen's UP, 2002.

Yudice, George. *The Expediency of Culture*. Durham, NC: Duke UP, 2003.

Zezulka, J.M. "Passionate Provincials: Imperialism, Regionalism, and Point of View." *Journal of Canadian Fiction* 22 (1978): 80–92.

Zichy, Francis. "The Narrator, the Reader, and Mariposa: The Cost of Preserving the Status Quo in *Sunshine Sketches of a Little Town*." *Journal of Canadian Studies* 22.1 (1987): 51–65.

Index

Agacinski, Sylviane, 111
Anderson, Benedict, 86
Atwood, Margaret, 14, 143–4, 170

Baden, ON, 6–9, 179–82
Baskerville, Peter, 28, 31
Belleville, ON, 12
Bemrose, John, 23; *The Island Walkers*, 149–50
Bildungsroman, 39–40, 103
Boym, Svetlana, 187–8

Chase, Malcolm, 172
Cohen, Matt, 23; *The Disinherited*, 16–17; Salem Pentalogy, 134n11
Collingwood, ON, 12n1
Coleman, Daniel, 76

Davies, Robertson, 4, 6, 22, 24, 185; Kingston as Salterton, 63; at Massey College, 63; Renfrew as Blairlogie, 22; Thamesville, 22, 61n2, 70n7
Davies, Robertson, works of: Blairlogie trilogy, 63

Deptford trilogy, 6, 20, 24; as exploring the idyll/anti-idyll, 24, 62, 67–8, 79, 84, 88–96, 140
Feast of Stephen: A Cornucopia of Delights by Stephen Leacock, 62–3, 67
Fifth Business, 24, 61; accuracy of memory, 66–7, 70, 72; cosmopolitanism, influence on Dunstan of, 74–8; Dunstan's homecoming, effect on Deptford's representation, 78–88; the idyll and anti-idyll, as exploring, 62, 67–8; the past, influence on Deptford of, 71–3; small-town literary conventions, influence of, 67–9; and *Sunshine Sketches*, 62–7, 70–2, 76–7, 81–2, 85–6
The Manticore, 65, 88–91, 95–6
Marchbanks' Almanack, 61n2
One Half of Robertson Davies, 82
Salterton trilogy, 63
World of Wonders, 65, 88, 91–6
Duncan, Sara Jeannette, 23; *The Imperialist*, 33, 38–9

Elliott, George, 23; *The Kissing Man*, 61, 192

Formosa, ON, 23, 153
Frye, Northrop, 10, 12, 60, 172

Gifford, Terry, 90, 191

Harvey, David, 87, 188–9
Hay, Elizabeth, 23; *Alone in the Classroom*, 182–3
heritage: definition of, 5–6, 45; as depicted in *Sunshine Sketches of a Little Town*, 45–7; as depicted in Urquhart, 147–9, 172; problematic use of, 10
Hewison, Robert, 46n5
Hutcheon, Linda, 140, 148n1

idyll in small-town Ontario literature, 3, 4, 7, 9, 24. *See also* Leacock, Stephen, works of, *Sunshine Sketches*, Mariposa; Davies, Robertson, works of, *Fifth Business*, Deptford; and Urquhart, Jane

Keith, W.J., 15, 22, 36, 46, 64, 80, 102
Kitchener, ON, 6
Knister, Raymond, 23; *White Narcissus*, 59–62
Kroetsch, Robert, 26

Leacock, Stephen, 4, 6, 14, 17–18, 19, 22, 23, 27, 184; McGill University, 63; *Montreal Star*, 27; Orillia, ON, 22, 33
Leacock, Stephen, works of:
Arcadian Adventures of the Idle Rich, 57, 72

Boy I left Behind Me, The, 14, 18, 152
Happy Stories, Just to Laugh At: "Mariposa Moves On," 27n1
The Letters of Stephen Leacock, 29
Sunshine Sketches of a Little Town, 6, 14, 17, 23; as comment on memory, 33–4, 41–6; influence on *Fifth Business, see* Davies, Robertson, *Fifth Business*; Josiah Smith, role of, 47, 48, 49–57; as literary parody of rural idyll, 28–30; Mariposa, 6, 17, 19–20, 184; Mariposa as idyll, 19, 23, 30, 32, 34, 39, 44, 56, 60, 71, 82, 86, 169; Mariposa as "middle landscape," 23; narrator of, 32, 34–8; nostalgia, influence of, 29, 31, 34, 38; reflective nostalgia, relationship to, 187–8, 189; rural depopulation, influence of, 28, 28n2; temporal distance, 31
Lippard, Lucy, 12n1
Lowenthal, David, 41, 46n5, 49, 143, 148, 161, 174
Lynch, Gerald, 13, 32, 34, 36, 45, 47, 49, 50, 52n7, 59n1, 62n3, 68n5, 136–7, 139, 184

Mandel, Eli, 17–18, 86
Marx, Leo, 46, 89, 159n3, 172; complex pastoral, 19, 46–7, 89; middle landscape, 23, 48, 55, 89; pastoral design, 19, 105; pastoral counterforce, 159n3
Massey, Doreen, 46n5
Monk, Patricia, 62n3, 65, 68n5, 73, 75, 79
Moodie, Susanna, 12

Munro, Alice, 4, 14–15, 18, 19, 20, 22, 24, 185; Wingham, ON, 22, 100, 125
Munro, Alice, works of:
"Chaddeleys and Flemings 2: The Stone in the Field," 133
"Home," 97–9
Lives of Girls and Women, 20, 22, 24, 99, 185; Garnet French, influence on Del of, 111–13, 115–18, 122, 124; as *Künstlerroman*, 107; narrative style and landscape, relationship between, 120–4; narrator, 101–5; place, importance of, 100–1, 106; primitivism, influence of, 111–20; and *Sunshine Sketches* and *Fifth Business*, 100, 102–6; Uncle Craig, influence on Del of, 107–11, 112, 114, 120–1, 127; and *Who Do You Think You Are?*, 125–7, 132
Moons of Jupiter, 133
"Walker Brothers Cowboy," 18
Who Do You Think You Are? 22, 24–5, 99, 185; and *Lives of Girls and Women*, 125–7, 132; memory, distrust of, 127–33; memory, hazards of, 133–41; and *Sunshine Sketches*, 132, 136, 140–41; and *Fifth Business*, 140
"Wilderness Station," 133

New Hamburg, ON, 6, 179–82
New, W.H, 17, 171
nostalgia, 18–19, 85–6; reflective nostalgia, 187–88; restorative nostalgia, 188

Paris, ON, 149
pastoral, 3, 7, 9, 10, 89; complex pastoral, 19, 46–7, 89; pastoral counterforce, 159n3; pastoral design, 19, 105; simple pastoral, 3, 90
Picton, ON, 12n1
Prince Edward County, ON, 23, 170

Reaney, James, 15, 23, 100; "Instructions: How to Make a Model of the Town," 15; "Prose for the Past," 183–4; "Wild Flora of Elgin County," 100n1
regional/rural idyll, 9, 20, 23, 28–30
Renfrew, 22, 63, 182
Roberts, Charles G.D., 11
Roche, Mazo de la, 23, 30; *Jalna* as rural idyll, 30
rural vs small-town Ontario, 15

Samuel, Raphael, 46n5
Scott, D.C, 12–13
Shaw, Christopher, 172
Smith, Laurajane, 5, 45, 102–3, 147, 171–2, 184
small-town Ontario: definition of, 14–15; as idyll/anti-idyll, 7, 19, 20, 24, 105, 182; as representative of the past, 9; settlement patterns, 11; small-town myth/mythos, 7, 9, 16; small-town Ontario vs rural Ontario, 15; small-town and rural Ontario's literary associations, 8
Sontag, Susan, 178
Stratford, ON, 6

Teskey, Adeline, 14, 18, 23, 28, 29, 30; *Where the Sugar Maple Grows*, 28–30
Thacker, Robert, 4, 11, 103–4, 106, 112, 124, 128

Thamesville, 22, 61n2, 70n7
Thomas, Clara, 39, 64

Urquhart, Jane, 4, 22, 23, 25, 143,
    185; and heritage, 147–9; and
    the idyll, 172; Munro,
    influence of, 143–5, 177; and
    nostalgia, 145; and restorative
    nostalgia, 188–9; works
    compared to other Ontario
    fiction, 143–6, 149–50, 151,
    169, 177–8
Urquhart, Jane, works of
    Away, 146–7, 150
    Changing Heaven, 21, 146
    A Map of Glass, 23, 25, 143, 147,
        150–1, 169; doubts about
        knowledge of the past,
        175–8; embedded memory in
        landscape, 170; projection of the
        self onto rural past/landscape,
        172–5; representation of rural
        past vs urban present, 170–2
    Sanctuary Line, 186

The Stone Carvers, 23, 25, 143–4,
    150, 178; dehistoricized nature
    of historical representation, 169;
    narration of founding myths,
    154–7; narrator's identity, 151–4;
    transcending nostalgia, 162–8;
    traditional society, fragmentation
    of, 158–62; Vimy monument and
    collective mourning, 165–8
The Underpainter, 147, 150

Vanderhaeghe, Guy, 45n4

Waterloo, ON, 6
Welland, ON, 28
Welland Canal, 30
Williams, Raymond, 4, 16, 21, 68n6,
    117, 191–2, 193
Willmott, Glenn, 39, 49, 190
Wilmot Township, ON, 179–82
Wingham, ON, 22, 100, 125
Wright, Richard, 23; *Clara Callan*, 182
Wyile, Herb, 11, 144, 148n1, 149,
    153, 169